The
HAVENER
SISTERS

ARDEANA HAMLIN

Other Islandport Press books

Abbott's Reach
by Ardeana Hamlin

Windswept
Mary Ellen Chase

Mary Peters
Mary Ellen Chase

Silas Crockett
Mary Ellen Chase

Contentment Cover
Miriam Colwell

Shoutin' into the Fog:
Growing Up on Maine's Ragged Edge
Thomas Hanna

Nine Mile Bridge:
Three Years in the Maine Woods
Helen Hamlin

My Life in the Maine Woods:
A Game Warden's Wife in the Allagash Country
Annette Jackson

For Lois,
  with my best regards —

The HAVENER SISTERS

ARDEANA HAMLIN

Ardeana Hamlin

ISLANDPORT PRESS

THE HAVENER SISTERS
by Ardeana Hamlin

First Islandport Edition September 2015
All Rights Reserved.

Copyright © 2015 by Ardeana Hamlin

ISBN: 978-1-939017-85-7
Library of Congress Card Number: 2014959679

Islandport Press
P.O. Box 10
Yarmouth, ME 04096
www.islandportpress.com
books@islandportpress.com

Publisher: Dean L. Lunt
Book Jacket design: Karen Hoots/Hoots Design
Interior Book design: Teresa Lagrange
Cover photo courtesy of iStock, by wbritten

Printed in the USA

For Nancy Tancredi, my friend of 60 years,
and for my friends of many years,
Cathryn Marquez and Janet Danforth.
Full circle.

1.

China Havener had spent much of the morning going over the household accounts. Ordinarily it was a task she enjoyed. She and her sisters, India and Persia, were good at managing their income, adept at living within their means. They were sensible and thrifty, so it wasn't as if they didn't know the ins and outs of their financial status. Indeed, their current dilemma had nothing to do with extravagance. In fact, the sisters had noted a need to buy a little less tea, to mend their stockings rather than purchase a new pair, and to forego the purchase of a pretty silk flower for a hat. They did not resent making such small economies, and had done so for several years, but now things had taken a definite turn for the worse.

China and her sisters were triplets, an oddity they never thought much about except when they stood together before a mirror and gazed at their fifty-five-year-old selves, their faces identical.

China checked a column of figures in the ledger a second time. She thumbed through a pile of invoices, statements, and bills to recheck her figures. Well, there it was, plain and simple: The *Empress*, the ship they had been born on in 1826 and had lived on most of their lives, was bringing in much less money than it had in the past year. That came as no surprise. For years, steamships had encroached on the revenue of sailing ships. She had known it would catch up with them eventually. And now it had.

That was the thing about life; it was a long series of compromises requiring periodic adjustment to new realities. But even though she well understood that aspect of the human condition, it was quite another matter to embrace it. She also knew that embracing change in its early phases was never easy and rarely ran smoothly. She expected resistance from India and Persia, but she knew she could rely on them to discuss the matter sensibly. She went to the kitchen to find them.

"I must speak with you," China said. "Come to the front room with me."

"Oh, dear," said India as she and Persia seated themselves near China's desk. "You don't look at all happy, China. Trouble with the accounts again, I presume."

"More than trouble, I'm afraid," China said.

"Better spit it out quickly then," said Persia, the more direct and practical of the three.

"We can't afford to keep this house," China said. She ran her long index finger down the column of figures in the leather-bound ledger. "As you know, since Father died, we have no secure means of income apart from the cargoes carried in the *Empress*, which are few and far between these days. We must begin to economize drastically." Though she spoke calmly, China knew her words came as a blow to India and Persia.

China wore a brown dress, sprigged with tiny white flowers, not new, the hem a bit frayed, perfectly good enough to wear around the house. Her hair was pulled back into a loose knot at the nape of her neck and secured with a pair of silver combs she had purchased at an outdoor market in Cadiz, Spain, many years ago. She regarded India and Persia, carbon copies of herself, trying to gauge the depth of their worry.

India and Persia glanced at one another. They trusted China's judgment and knew she wasn't making a fuss about something that didn't need fussing about. China was not a rattle-head. She thought carefully about things and was not prone to overdramatizing any bad situation.

A long, heavy silence dropped into the room. China's thoughts drifted to the problem at hand.

She, India, and Persia had been raised to consider themselves something of a miracle, though they never dwelled on the fact they were triplets, nor had they given themselves airs because of it. It was simply a fact of life, despite how unusual it was to everyone else.

They had spent a good part of their lives aboard the *Empress*, in the company of their mother, who had treated them as individuals and encouraged them to think of themselves as separate entities rather than as a trinity sharing the same looks, the same interests, ideas, and opinions.

No, thought China, as she gazed at India and Persia, look alike though they did, they had very different ideas about who they were as individuals, what interested them, how they felt about things. That, however, had not caused them to be at odds with one another. True, they had their disagreements from time to time, but their disputes were resolved fairly and equitably.

For the past eight years, since their father, Jonas Havener, had died in 1873, they had lived alongshore, his death making it impossible for them to go to sea any longer. Despite the fact they were skilled at navigation and knew the running of a ship and its business intimately, as women, they could not acquire the papers necessary to captain a ship, even though that was precisely what they had been born to do, and had done for much of their lives. After their father's burial at sea, when they were obliged to leave the *Empress*, they did so with good grace, using their knowledge to hire a skilled captain for the ship. As landlubbers, they looked for profitable cargoes for the *Empress* to haul up and down the Atlantic coast and, sometimes, around the world.

They took up residence in the commodious house in Castine, Maine, that their father had built for their mother in 1850. They divided up the tasks of keeping house. China kept the household accounts, India did the housekeeping, and Persia saw to the cooking, though there was much overlap in those duties, with all three helping with the cooking and cleaning.

They attended the Congregational church and helped with church suppers and bazaars. They joined the Ladies' Aid and sewed baby clothes for families in need. They wrote many letters in the course of a week, staying in touch with friends they had met in far parts of the world. Sometimes, when those seafarers were in port, they came to call. Village people stopped for tea. It was a good life, if somewhat more sedate than what they had been accustomed to, or indeed preferred.

Certainly, it was a pale life compared to the one they had lived at sea. They could boast—though they did not—of being among the first white women certain islanders in the Indian Ocean had ever seen. They had been set adrift in a lifeboat when the cargo of their vessel, the one before the *Empress*, had caught fire and all hands were obliged to abandon ship. They had endured two weeks of privation before they were spotted by another vessel and rescued. As terrifying as that had been, it did not terrify their mother, Ruth, enough to stay alongshore, though there came a time when she asked Jonas to build the house in Castine, on a high point of ground with a sweeping view of Penobscot Bay. At that point in her life, she had told her husband, she needed to know she had a home built firmly upon solid earth where she could retreat from time to time to reclaim her land legs.

The house had been built when Jonas still made ample amounts of money carrying cargoes to and from ports around the world. The house boasted a fireplace in every one of its ten rooms. It was filled with light from well-placed windows, and each room reflected the family's seafaring past, containing dishes from China, textiles from India, rugs from Persia, furniture from Spain, and accoutrements from every part of the world. They came home to the house every few years when Ruth wanted to stay alongshore to visit relatives in Searsport, Maine, or when she felt her daughters needed to socialize with cousins and other young people of their own age. She had loved the house, but more than anything, she had loved going to sea with Jonas. She thoroughly enjoyed the adventures she had as the wife of a sea captain.

Just before she died at sea in 1855, when China, India, and Persia were nearly thirty, Ruth had charged them to take care of their father. And they had done so, even as he had receded in his grief into an eternal fog of rum, leaving the running of the ship and its business to them. They rarely went back to the house in those years, left it in the hands of caretakers, making certain it was kept in repair against the day when they knew their father, too, would give up the ghost, obliging them to give up the sea.

China glanced at the small painting of herself and her sisters occupying a place of honor on the wall by the pretty mahogany table that served as her desk as she waited for India and Persia to react to the news she had just given them.

The little painting had been done in London in 1845, when they still believed they would marry one day. The artist had grouped them in a pretty way around a table draped with a paisley cloth, in front of a backdrop depicting an imaginary harbor. In the painting, they wore identical white lawn dresses, though they did not often dress in an identical way. Their mother did not encourage that. China held a sextant, India held a model of the *Empress*, and Persia held a spyglass. Their hair almost glowed, it was that fair, and the artist had accurately caught the color of their eyes—the bluest of blue. Certainly, much had changed since then. Now, instead of being white-blonde, their hair was white. But their eyes hadn't changed, nor their tall, proud bearing. China had only to look at India and Persia to know what she looked like—no matter how old they were.

She remembered the fine, silky texture of that white cotton dress, the tight-fitting sleeves, not at all the fashion of the time, but which suited her—their—long, willowy arms and statuesque height. She could almost feel the fall of the material and her ruffled petticoats cascading to the tops of her white kid-leather slippers. India's voice brought her thoughts abruptly back to the present.

"But this was Mother's house. Father built it for her—for us," said India, who tended to feel things very deeply. "Why, Mother would roll over in her grave if she knew we had sold this house. You know how she worried . . . us never marrying. She wanted to be sure we would always have a home of our own."

India wore a simple blue cotton dress, her hair pulled back into a snood Persia had crocheted of fine thread. Her sleeves were rolled up, and she toyed with the feather duster that had been in her hand when China had asked her and Persia to come to the front room. She had been about to clean a spare room that rarely saw the light of day, located as it was upstairs on the north side of the house, and where the sisters tended to store things they didn't often use, but thought might come in handy someday.

Persia, always practical and less inclined to see drama in anything, replied, "Hardly, India, considering she was buried at sea."

She, too, wore a simple cotton dress, in yellow. Her hair was done in braids wrapped around her head and fastened with hand-carved tortoiseshell hairpins one of their crew had fashioned for her when she was still a young girl. She had a straightforward view of things and barely a romantic bone in her body.

"You know what I mean, Persia! It's the principle of the thing."

"We can't eat principles," China said.

Of the three sisters, she was the eldest by several minutes—followed by India, then Persia. Their father had been their mother's only birth attendant. He had used a handheld scale to weigh them. They had weighed a little less than five pounds each. Many years later, he told them he did not think they would all survive—one or two, perhaps—but not all. But their mother had no such thoughts, and had devoted every ounce of her energy toward making certain they did thrive. The ship's cook and the mates had volunteered to watch the babies when she needed a breath of air or a change of scene for a few precious minutes as the *Empress* plowed the waters of the Atlantic, headed for Portland, where a midwife pronounced the triplets in good health.

China was the sister who had a head for figures. At sea, she had charted their course, taken readings on the sextant, and done the ciphering needed for accurate navigation. It was only natural when they stopped going to sea for her to take on the responsibility of the household accounts. She tended to be a bit more reserved than India and Persia, keeping her feelings to herself, slow to reveal what was in her heart. India wore her heart on her sleeve, and Persia was not one to mince words.

They had managed fairly well, all things considered, China thought. They had put money away in the bank. They did not need much beyond food, some of which they grew, wood for winter, and a few decent clothes and shoes. But during the last year their income had decreased significantly. Ships of four masts and more than a thousand tons, capable of carrying vast loads of cargo, were now the norm, far surpassing the carrying power of the *Empress*, which had been built for speed, along the lines of the old clipper ships. Steamships, too, were common in the waters now, replacing the old ships powered solely by the wind; they carried more cargo more quickly to destinations around the world. This was why their income would continue to decline.

China explained all of this to India and Persia, even though she knew they understood it perfectly well, for it was often a topic of conversation among them. But somehow, saying it aloud again, hearing herself speak the words, made it real, made it easier to make the awful suggestion to sell the house.

"Even so," China summed up, "we can't make so dire a decision as selling the house at this very moment. I'm not suggesting we should. I propose we consult our friends at Abbott's Reach. I know Sam Webber will have good advice. And we can always count on Madras Mitchell and his father, Isaiah, to steer us safely through this financial typhoon."

"And Fanny and Maude. They will have sound thoughts on the situation, too," Persia said. She was particularly fond of Fanny Abbott Harding and Maude Webber.

"Very well, then," said India. "I'll write to Fanny and ask her to set a day that suits everyone on that side of Penobscot Bay."

The sisters had made the acquaintance of Mercy Maude Giddings Mitchell—known as M—Fanny's granddaughter, in 1872, the year of M's honeymoon voyage. When they learned from mutual acquaintances that M was to be a mother, Persia had knit a blanket as a gift for the new baby.

During those years they did not often socialize at sea or in the harbors of the world, though their ship's mates often brought them news of Maine families who were in port. China hated to admit even to herself that in those days, they had kept up the illusion that it was their father who was in command of the *Empress*, even though the world, quite literally, knew differently.

After their father died and they went to live in Castine, they had paid a call when they heard that M's daughter, Blythe, had been born. Thus, they had made the acquaintance of Fanny and her husband, Ellis Harding, Sam and Maude Webber, and many of the Mitchell family connections. Soon, they had all become friends. Those friendships were very dear to them. China knew that whatever advice they received from the Abbott's Reach people would be sound and worth heeding.

2.

"Come in, come in," Fanny urged when China, India, and Persia arrived at Abbott's Reach, Fanny's boardinghouse at Fort Point on Penobscot Bay.

The sisters wore lightweight woolen dresses of similar cut, but in different colors—dove gray for China, wine for India, and rust for Persia. China had arranged her hair in a coil around her head, India wore hers caught in a loose knot at the nape of her neck, and Persia's hair was, as always, in braids fastened to the top of head.

Fanny was in her early sixties and still a handsome woman. Ellis had convinced her not to use henna rinses on her hair anymore, and now her naturally red hair was streaked liberally with silver. It was quite becoming, bringing out the blue of her eyes. She was still trim of figure and spry of step. She wore a pretty cotton dress of royal blue with pin tucks down the front.

China, India, and Persia knew of Fanny's irregular past—how it was linked to the notorious house known as Pink Chimneys, knew that Fanny had changed her ways many years ago to live an upright life. Although they did not know the specific details of Fanny's past, they knew it was colorful. The life she had led all those years ago, when she was very young, was long past, and even though it had shaped her life in a jagged way at the time, she had risen above it and proved her worth. Fanny's past was not a subject the Havener sisters ever discussed, even privately, though Fanny sometimes referred to those days.

"Everyone is here," Fanny said. "But let me warn you, the house is swarming with children. And M is about ready to have her fourth, give or take a few weeks. The other three are running through the house like banshees."

M and Madras Mitchell lived in a big house on the Searsport road, but often were at Abbott's Reach.

Fanny greeted the sisters with a kiss on the cheek, took their wraps, and led them to her favorite room overlooking Penobscot Bay, where a wall of windows let in the light and afforded a grand view. It was a comfortable room filled with furniture that coddled the body and held much for the eye to rest on and delight in. It was a room soothing to the spirit.

China, India, and Persia glanced at one another, each reading the others' thoughts, noting how Fanny wore her status as Mrs. Ellis Harding well. There was a lightness in her step, a contentment and happiness that had blossomed in her demeanor since her marriage to Ellis in 1873. They had been guests at the wedding. Indeed, they had cried during the ceremony—out of happiness for Fanny, of course, but also because it underscored for them how they had never found love, though secretly China sometimes still dreamed of it. She was quite sure India and Persia entertained a similar longing, though it was a subject they had stopped discussing long ago. Sometimes, China found herself watching Fanny and Ellis, and the other married couples in the family, feeling somehow inadequate, as if she lacked the qualities that made falling in love and marriage possible.

People filled the room with talk and motion. Maude and Sam Webber, white hair bright in the sunlight flowing through the window, occupied chairs by the fireplace where a small blaze had been kindled to take off April's morning chill.

"Forgive us for not getting up," Sam said. "We're setting pretty comfortable. Maude's knee is giving her a devil of a time, and I've got a kink in my back today." He winked at China so she would know he was not complaining, merely giving a much abbreviated diagnosis of what prevented him and Maude from rising to greet the three sisters.

Maude wore a voluminous white apron tied around her waist, as if, bad knee or not, she intended to be useful at some point during the day. Sam was in his shirtsleeves, a black vest buttoned across his spare middle, his shirt buttoned up to his chin.

"As for me," M said, laughing, "I couldn't get out of this chair if I wanted to. The only way I can get to my feet these days is if Madras hauls me up. He's very fond of telling me he may need a crane for the job soon. And to think I have six weeks to go."

M's happiness was, as always, evident in her face, her eyes moving often to rest in her husband's gaze, or to fix lovingly upon one of her children or on Sam and Maude Webber, on her parents or her grandmother. She was comfortably dressed in what was commonly called a Mother Hubbard, a garment fitted to the upper part of the torso, but with an inverted pleat down the front to accommodate an expanding middle.

M had had her adventure at sea on her honeymoon and had come home to stay because of an injury Madras had suffered during that voyage. He was fit now, but it had taken quite some time before he was fully well, and he had the scars to prove it. He counted his blessings every day, and M was always at the top of his list.

Laughter ensued at M's remark. Laughter was always in the air when Fanny and her clan gathered.

"That young one will be born sooner than that, M—you mark my words," Maude said. In her younger days, Maude had been a midwife, well known up and down the Penobscot River. Indeed, she had delivered M, and M's children, and would be present when the new baby was born.

M, China noted, bloomed with health, her skin clear and bright, her eyes full of life and laughter.

The sisters nodded greetings to the others in the room—Ellis Harding, Madras Mitchell and his parents, Isaiah and Zulema Mitchell, and M's parents, Abner and Elizabeth Giddings.

"As you can see," Fanny said, "it's as good as a town meeting. I've asked Sam to preside."

A girl and two small boys burst into the room. "Miss China, Miss India, Miss Persia," they shouted, running to the sisters.

"Stop, you mutinous creatures!" Madras commanded his daughter, Blythe, and sons, Lex and Samuel. "Where are your manners?" The children slowed their headlong flight and moved with greater decorum. Blythe dipped a small curtsy, and the boys made quick bows to the company in the room.

"Nicely done," M said to her children. Madras grinned at them so they would know he was not cross with them for forgetting their manners.

"Will you tell us a story, Miss India?" Blythe asked. Lex and Samuel nodded in agreement.

"Yes, of course I will, but first we have important grown-up things to talk about," India said, giving each child a hug.

"Indeed we do, my dears. Please go back to the kitchen and tell Aunt Honoria to find you some cookies," Fanny said.

Blythe gave an impatient sigh and disappointment showed in the faces of the little boys, but they did as they were told.

"Very well, that's settled," Sam said. "Now let's examine the situation at hand. Dear ladies, as we understand it, you are confronted with a decline in financial health and wish to consult us as to a cure." A ripple of laughter filled the room, for in his younger days, Sam had been a physician, serving mainly aboard various sailing vessels that had taken him to many ports up and down the eastern seaboard, and several times around the world. When he had given up the sea, he had set up a medical practice in Bangor and assisted Maude in her business as a midwife. But that was many years ago.

"Yes," China said. "The cost of taxes, upkeep on our house, and general cost of living will overtake us soon. Revenue from the *Empress* keeps the ship afloat but brings little income these days. We know we must alter our course. Therefore, we've come to seek your advice as to what we must do. Mr. Mitchell, I brought a copy of our accounts, if you would be so good as to look them over."

She handed the papers to Isaiah, who also had been a sea captain, but now was in the shipping business, and knew a great deal about financial matters.

"China has raised the idea of selling our house," India said, "but we are not in complete agreement about setting that course."

Just the mere mention of the idea of selling the house brought tears to her eyes, compromising her ability to listen carefully to the very advice she and her sisters had come to obtain. Fanny, with quiet tact and infinite sympathy, handed India a handkerchief edged in tatted lace.

Persia reached into her bag and drew out a mitten she was knitting on a set of four double-point bone needles.

"I have already decided what I am going to do to alleviate the situation. I am going to knit," she said firmly. She held up one hand to quell comment. "Yes, I know it's merely a drop in the vast ocean of finance, but it's something immediate I can do. There's a store in Castine that pays people for nicely knitted mittens, which will be in much demand come fall. And then there are my hooked rugs . . ." Everyone in the room had at one time or another been the recipient of Persia's mittens, knit beautifully with cables, bobbles, seed stitches, and designs of more than one color. One of her hooked rugs, depicting Fanny's coon cat, Tennyson, had a place of honor by the hearth, serving as a memorial to that much beloved feline, long since gone to its rest.

"Though I must say, I can make many more mittens in a month than I can rugs, so I believe I will stick with mittens."

"That is very clever of you, Miss Havener," Madras said, "and certainly a good way to trade for groceries or lengths of fabric, but unlikely to bring in enough to cover other expenses."

As usual, Madras, his dark hair falling across his brow, cut a handsome figure. Everyone counted on him for his practical approach to things.

"I'm quite aware of that," Persia said. "But I will do it, no matter what." Persia had a mind of her own, and once she had charted her course, she was unlikely to alter it for any reason.

Sam cleared his throat and the room became quiet again.

"We have good minds in this room, so perhaps each one of you would put in your two cents' worth on the situation, and then we'll try to make some sense of all this. Maude, my dear, why don't you begin."

"The fact is, my dears, you won't be young forever," said Maude, who wasn't one to shy away from the truth. This brought smiles, because by common standards the sisters were long past the day when they might have been called young.

"It's not wise to grow old far from friends . . . or family, blood ties or no. Your situation is about more than just the serious question of finances. It's about what will become of you if you do not take into account the fact that as you grow older, you will need others you can depend upon."

She spoke from experience. She and Sam had no children, but their friendship with Fanny, whom they regarded as a daughter, had evolved in such a way that they now lived at Abbott's Reach, helping out as they were able and being cared for in return by Fanny, Ellis, M, Madras, and other members of the family clan.

"As I see it," Fanny said, "Persia's idea is not a bad one. You must find a way to earn something. I believe it's a matter of reinvention. For example, Maude began compounding and selling herbal remedies when she was in her sixties. I opened Abbott's Reach after my disastrous years in Bangor at Pink Chimneys . . . Yes, I still blush to speak of it, but it is a fact of my life, and I don't wish to pretend it's not. Over the years, with help from Ellis, we have turned Abbott's Reach into a successful summer boardinghouse. I don't propose you do the same with your house, for I was much younger then than you are now when I began this business. However, many women take up teaching or keep shops—look at the Misses Merrithew and their dressmaking shop."

The Misses Merrithew, who lived in Stockton Springs village, also had been born and lived at sea, and when they came to live alongshore, they put their sewing skills to good use by taking in sewing. Though they were quite old now, they still managed to adjust hems and do simple mending.

"But we are not dressmakers, and I don't believe any of us have any inclination or aptitude toward teaching," India said, hastily. She did not like the turn the conversation was taking. It wasn't that she objected to work. Certainly not. It was simply that she and her sisters had neither the education nor the training to fit them for any job except that of ship's captain, a job not open to women, no matter how experienced or good at it they might be.

Isaiah Mitchell, his fine blue eyes scanning the ledger pages China had given him, turned another page.

"As I see it, you must divest yourself of something, given the circumstances," he said. "You could sell the *Empress* . . . indeed, I highly advise that. She's eating up nearly as much income as she produces. Trouble is, you won't get much for her, so I don't think that would solve your problem, long-term. But she must go. Your best asset is your house and the property it sits on . . . And, I might add, some of its contents."

Isaiah had visited the Havener sisters at their home and knew firsthand that it contained many valuable treasures.

"Yes," Madras said. "Your house contains many things of value, and if you determine to sell those things, then you would have the capital to buy a smaller house and enough left to invest to give you a modest income for the rest of your lives. But it's wise to find ways to bring in additional income by other means, such as Persia's mittens."

Madras stood by the fireplace, one elbow resting on the mantel. He thought suddenly of the day he had come to call on Fanny to ask for M's hand in marriage, when he had stood in this very place in this very room. He glanced at M and smiled fondly at her. She knew exactly what he was thinking and blew him a kiss.

Sam and Ellis Harding nodded in agreement with what Madras had said. Zulema, Fanny, and M let out a collective sigh of protest.

"No, certainly not," they said, almost in unison.

"Surely not," Elizabeth said emphatically. Though she had grown older, she was as beautiful as ever, her face only lightly etched with lines, her hair sparsely threaded with silver. She wore a dark blue dress of her own making, the bodice embroidered in an intricate floral design, and over it a white shawl she had knit of fine wool in a complex lace pattern.

"I am sorry to disagree, but they are right, Elizabeth," China said, "quite right."

"Oh, dear," India said, suddenly overcome, pressing the handkerchief to her eyes once again.

"Let me ask you, Isaiah—have you any thought as to where we might find someone to buy our house and the *Empress*, and where we might find a smaller house?" China asked.

"I can place advertisements about the ship in several marine newspapers, and we can advertise your house in others. As for a smaller house, I happen to know of one for sale in Searsport. It belongs to a cousin of mine; it's in good repair and might suit. I'll arrange for you to see it soon."

India dabbed at her eyes, a furious expression on her face. For a moment, China feared her sister might stalk out of the room in extreme agitation. But she remained seated and gained control of herself, except for a few shuddering intakes of breath. It pained China to see India in such distress, and stirred in her a need to shed a few tears of her own, though she would do so in the privacy of her own bedroom. Meanwhile, she kept her emotions firmly damped down.

"Why do I feel as if I have just been swallowed by a whale?" India demanded of everyone in the room.

"Because you have," Persia said, matter-of-factly. "We three have been swallowed by the great whale of domestic economy."

"Amen," Sam said.

"India, my dear, we will grow used to the change in our circumstances, just as we grew used to not being in command of the *Empress* and not going to sea anymore," China said. She got up and went to sit on the sofa beside India, hoping to console her. "Dry your eyes, dear. We are not alone in this."

"I know," India whispered. "But I am not certain I can endure so much change all at once."

"Of course you can, India," Persia said gently. "You have survived many a storm at sea, including two long weeks in a lifeboat when you were barely ten years old. In this situation, rough as it is, there is no ship to founder and sink. We have our feet firmly on the ground. All we have to do is make up our minds—and do it."

3.

The talk soon turned to other matters.

India tucked her handkerchief into the sleeve of her dress, excused herself, and went in search of the Mitchell children. She found them in the kitchen with their great-great-aunt, Honoria Cobb, who hovered near the pantry door, cradling a jar of molasses cookies in her arms as if it were a stand-in for the infant she had never given birth to. She was in her eighties, still thin as a rail, her mind sharp and clear. She was an odd little woman. She had never married, and always had lived in the shadow of her older sister, Augusta Mitchell, Madras' grandmother.

"Cookies, oh, my yes, those little ones," Honoria said softly, aiming a wan smile at India. She disappeared into the pantry, more shadow than substance. She doted on the children, often spent prolonged periods of time with M and her family, and was invited to all their excursions, even though she hovered on the fringes of things, flitting in and out of sight as if she were a little brown bird hiding in a tapestry of foliage. India understood and respected Honoria's shy, retiring ways.

The children adored Honoria, for when they were with her, they might talk as much as they liked about anything, they never heard a cross word from her, and she never told them to be quiet or sit still. Indeed, she would listen, nod her head, smile at them fondly, and touch their faces gently with her soft fingers. Sometimes the children begged her to dance with them. She would lead them through the steps of a reel she had learned as a little girl in the early 1800s.

The Abbott's Reach kitchen was large enough to accommodate an oval oak table in the center of the room. It also was furnished with a rocking chair, a wood-burning cookstove, several low stools for the children, and a few well-placed wool rag rugs.

India seated herself in the rocking chair.

"Miss India, are you ready to tell us a story?" Blythe asked. She was a small copy of her great-grandmother Fanny, with reddish hair waving softly around her face, a sprinkle of freckles across her cheeks, and an endearing personality. Her eyes, unlike her grandmother's, were brown.

"Sea monsters, sea monsters!" Lex chanted, dancing about and waving his arms. He favored neither his mother nor his father, but was a pleasant combination of both.

"Me, too, me, too!" Samuel echoed. He looked so much like his grandfather Isaiah that M and Madras declared he had been misnamed.

"Very well, then. Samuel, come sit here in my lap. Blythe and Lex, bring the stools and sit here near me." India smoothed Samuel's hair, breathing in his clean, little boy smell, and tears came to her eyes because she had missed out on motherhood, would never be a grandmother. She smiled at the children and began, "Once upon a time, there were three seafaring sisters—"

"Who looked exactly alike," Blythe said, interrupting.

"—who lived aboard a beautiful ship with their mother and their father, the captain," India continued.

"The *Empress!*" Blythe whispered to Lex.

"Shhh!" her brother said.

"The sisters loved living on the ship, for it took them to many parts of the world, and they saw sights most children never see."

"Like what?" Samuel asked. "Giraffes? Elephants? Alligators?"

"All of those things. And they saw huge flying fish that leapt out of the sea and threw droplets of water as big as silver coins into the air. They saw giant waterspouts whirling and skimming across the ocean with such force and fury that if one had ever touched the ship, the ship would have gone down to Davy Jones' locker. They looked down into the deep water of an evening and saw creatures glowing green, as if the water itself was lit from within."

"That's called phosphorescence," Blythe said. "Papa told me about it. Of course, I've never seen it, though someday I expect I will."

"But what about the sea monsters?" Lex demanded.

"Well, truly, the sisters did encounter sea monsters, but those monsters lived both in the sea and on dry land. One day as they were sailing in the Pacific Ocean, headed for Cape Horn—which is where?"

"Cape Horn is at the very tip of South America, where the Pacific meets the Atlantic, and the two oceans don't get along very well. Mama told me that when she made her first passage around the Horn on her honeymoon voyage, she had to lash herself to her bunk. Both ways!" Blythe's blue eyes grew wide as she imparted this information to India.

"Yes, quite right. Well, as I said, the ship was sailing good and steady, and the sisters, though they had been around the Horn, both directions, many times in their young lives, were, in fact, dreading it just a bit."

"Because of sea monsters?" Lex asked.

"Because of seasickness!" Blythe declared.

"Well, yes, on both counts," India said. "But their father, the captain, knew of their fears, and wanted to give them something else to think about, so he looked at the ship's course and saw that with a bit of a detour he could steer the ship toward Ecuador, which is . . . "

"A country on the northwest side of South America," Blythe supplied.

"To a group of islands known as the Galapagos. It was evening when they arrived, and the sisters were fast asleep, rocked in the cradle of the deep, as their mother liked to say. The next morning after breakfast the captain, the three sisters, and their mother rowed to one of the islands. It was a beautiful day. Everything was green and leafy, and blue and watery. The breeze was light. They had a picnic lunch. The sisters were in for the surprise of their lives, however, for it wasn't long after they had landed on the beach that they heard something stirring against the sand, against the foliage. And all of a sudden, what they saw made their mouths drop wide open. What do you think they saw?"

"Sea monsters!" the children shouted in unison.

"Oh, yes, sea monsters. These monsters were six feet long and they weighed as much as eight hundred pounds. And they moved as slow . . . As . . . molasses . . . on . . . A . . . January . . . day . . . in . . . Fort . . . Point . . . Maine. They were giant tortoises, believed to live for more than a hundred years. So it is very possible that the tortoises they saw that day were the very ones Mr. Darwin, the scientist, saw when he visited the island in the 1830s."

"Did they bite?" Lex asked.

"No, they didn't. They were very well-behaved tortoises . . . As all children ought to be."

"Did they hiss or make rude noises?" Blythe asked.

"No, they were seen, but not heard."

"Like Aunt Honoria," Samuel said solemnly.

"What happened after they saw the tortoises?" Blythe asked.

"They ate their lunch and the tortoises ate theirs. They watched the tortoises all day, and when the sun began to set, they rowed back to the *Empress*. They sailed away that night. The sisters were very sad to say good-bye to such magnificent creatures, but they spent many happy hours on the voyage, talking about the tortoises, writing stories and drawing pictures of them."

India reached into her skirt pocket and drew out a piece of folded paper. "See?" She showed them one of the sketches she had made of a tortoise on that long-ago voyage. "I made this drawing when I was a little girl and I have kept it all these years."

"Can we draw tortoises?" Blythe asked.

"Yes, indeed; go ask your Great-Grand Fan for paper and pencils." India watched the children scamper out of the room.

Honoria slipped out of the pantry and back into the kitchen, her eyes darting back and forth, not focusing on anything for more than a second. This time she held in her hands a plant pot containing a trailing ivy. Her fingers fluttered over it as if blessing the plant.

"Sweet. Like honey. Those three. Oh, my, yes," she said, a tiny trill of laughter underlining her words. She smiled shyly and disappeared soundlessly through the kitchen door into another part of the house as if she were a wraith from some other dimension.

Telling the story to the children had set India's mind to thinking about the many other adventures she and her sisters had had in their years at sea. Someone ought to write our story, she thought, as she went back to join the others.

4.

After everyone had waved good-bye to China, India, and Persia, Fanny put her arm through Isaiah Mitchell's and led him to the far side of the porch so they could talk privately.

"I'm going to go your proposal one better, Isaiah," Fanny said. "Several years ago, the house where I grew up—the same house where Elizabeth was raised by my sister, Mercy—was for sale. I bought it. It's been rented since then, but the tenants are moving to Bangor soon. It's a fine house with a lovely view of the bay and ten acres of ground. It has five small bedrooms, a large kitchen, a sunny parlor, and several other rooms, including a summer kitchen, with shed chambers above it. And a porch. There's a small barn, too. The taxes on the property are not high, and it's in good repair.

"I'd like you to arrange for the Havener sisters to see the place, but don't let on it has anything to do with me. If they like it, tell them the owner lives away and wishes to rent it for a nominal sum, just to have reliable tenants in it, and that they may have it for ten dollars a year. If they insist on buying it, tell them they may have it for one hundred and fifty dollars. Will you do that for me?"

"Very well," Isaiah said. "Though my cousin's house had not been sold yet, he has had an offer on it—not one he plans to accept —but it will do as an excuse not to show the sister's that house."

Fanny's proposal did not surprise Isaiah. She had a reputation for acts of kindness, paying for wood to heat the village church, making it a point to know what families were in need and sending baskets of food at Christmastime, tucking in scarves, hats, and mittens she, Maude, and other women of her acquaintance had knit. If there was sickness in a family and no money to pay the doctor, Fanny took care of it—or mentioned it to Sam and Maude, who then paid a call on the family to see how they could help.

Although there were many of a certain age in the vicinity who still recalled stories they had heard about Pink Chimneys and Fanny, and the notorious reputation she had made for herself many years ago, they kept still about it, for the most part. Fanny had proven her worth by her kindness, and they saw no reason to muddy the waters by resurrecting old gossip.

"Of course, Fanny. I'll do everything I can to see that the Havener sisters get through all this with as little to-do as possible," Isaiah promised.

"I knew I could count on you, Isaiah. You, Madras, Ellis, and Abner will help, too, I know. But I'd like the knowledge of the financial aspects to stay between you and me . . . And Zulema, of course."

"Very well," Isaiah agreed.

"In the meantime, I'll find someone to give the house a good cleaning, and I'll ask Ellis to hire a man to paint the woodwork and put up fresh wallpaper in the rooms so it will look extra appealing. Now, I must speak to Zulema."

Fanny went back inside, remembering when she had first come to Abbott's Reach after the disastrous years of her life as the much-talked-about madam of Pink Chimneys in Bangor. That life had given her money, which she had saved and invested wisely. It had made it possible for her to buy the boardinghouse and start another life. And then, miracle of all miracles, M had come to stay with her. That had changed everything, made it turn out all right. It was, she believed, far more than she deserved.

Fanny also recalled the bittersweet day of M's wedding aboard the Boreas. And that dreadful business with Augusta Mitchell, Madras's grandmother, when they had confronted one another and finally cleared the air between them. But all that was in the past. She and Augusta had mended their fences; though they still sparred from time to time, it was never serious. Augusta was an old lady now and didn't get out much anymore, but Fanny visited her from time to time to challenge her to a game of cribbage.

These days, Abbott's Reach was filled with M's and Madras's children, with family and with old friends, including Sam and Maude; Lancaster Treat, who had been a mate aboard the Boreas, and his wife, Dr. Matilda Drew, who lived in Old Town; Lex Nichols, former first mate of the Boreas; and the Havener sisters. Never in her wildest dreams, when she was young and in the thrall of Joshua Stetson, would Fanny have believed she would be part of such a splendid crowd of family and friends.

Fanny found Zulema in the kitchen, wiping cookie crumbs off the kitchen table.

"I'm going to need your advice about wallpaper patterns and fabric for curtains," Fanny said, outlining for Zulema the plans she had made with Isaiah about the house.

"We'll take the boat to Belfast next week. I know just the shop," Zulema said. "The Havener sisters don't go in for anything too ornate or showy. I am certain we can choose patterns and colors they would like. We should ask Elizabeth to go with us; her taste is infallible."

5.

Isaiah found a buyer for the *Empress* more quickly than China, India, and Persia had anticipated, and he got a fair price for it, more than they had dared expect. He also showed them Fanny's house in Fort Point, located just a few miles away from Abbott's Reach. They had agreed that is was the perfect house for them and decided to buy it. And to gild the lily further, a merchant from Boston bought the sisters' house in Castine to use as a summer home. Isaiah set a good price on it and the merchant had not haggled over the sum.

Now their course was set, and China, India, and Persia had plenty to do to bring about the transition from one house to another. They began in the attic.

"This sea chest contains all of Father's ship's logs, and the letters our friends and relatives sent to us and Mother," India said as she pulled envelopes and books from the chest. A large apron with a bib front covered her cotton dress, and she had tied a kerchief around her hair to keep straggling strands corralled. "This sea chest must go with us. If we part with it, it will be like taking away a piece of ourselves. It's our past, our history—all of it right here in this chest."

China and Persia agreed, but it was beginning to dawn on them that divesting themselves of the house and its contents, deciding what to keep and what to part with, was not going to be as simple and straightforward as they had supposed.

"That spinning wheel—it belonged to Grandmother Havener. It must go with us. I intend to have a sheep or two and try my hand at spinning my own yarn when we move to the new house," Persia said.

"Really, Persia," China said, shaking her head. "You are carrying this knitting thing way too far."

Sometimes when she spoke to her sisters, she had the distinct feeling she was talking to herself—her other selves, so to speak—but if she said so, Persia would remind her that although they were identical in looks, they were not identical in their thinking or their sensibilities. India, on the other hand, would insist they had identical souls. Time would be lost debating the point. Better to keep still and get the job of cleaning out the attic done and over with.

Persia gave China a look of dismissal and abandoned her interest in the sea chest to begin sorting through a trunk containing their mother's old clothing. Soon, tears began to roll down her face.

"These things still smell like Mama," she whispered between little sobs she tried to stifle.

Such behavior was so unlike Persia that China and India stared at her. Then they began to cry, too, leaving China to wonder if perhaps India was right after all—that they did, indeed, have identical souls.

"I can't do it! I just can't do it," India said, storming down the stairs, her hands fluttering in the air over her head, as if her emotions were annoying blackflies she was swatting away.

"Oh, Persia, now see what you've done," China said, going after India, drying her own tears as she went.

"You always blame me for everything!" Persia declared.

There were other rough waters the sisters had to navigate in terms of temper and sharp words, but gradually they cleared the attic and stored things in the summer kitchen against the day when a man who dealt in antiques and used goods would come to make them an offer.

The task became increasingly complicated as they moved to other rooms in the house. It was easy to decide on some things to sell, such as pieces of furniture that would not suit the scale of smaller rooms in a smaller house. It was much more difficult to determine what to do with other items.

What would they do with the portrait of their father, resplendent in a high white cravat and black coat, a parrot on a perch beside him? Or the grand painting of the *Empress*, which took up a great deal of space over the fireplace mantel? Both had been painted by Chinese artists who specialized in such fine and beautiful work. Or the picture of their mother wearing a lovely blue gown, done in London? Their father had been so proud of those paintings.

In the end, they decided that things deemed too precious to part with, such as the paintings, would be taken with them anyway, even if it would be impossible to fit them in the new house.

"We'll ask Ellis Harding if there is a way to build a small store-room in the summer kitchen, safe from mice and rats, where we can store such things," China said. This small plan went a long way toward softening the pain they felt at parting with other things.

It had not been difficult to say yes to their new house, which was the last of several houses Isaiah had shown them.

"There's room for a small flock of sheep," Persia had said when they saw the house at Fort Point for the first time. She had gazed at the meadow that ran all the way to the bay across the road from the house—the very meadow, though neither she nor her sisters knew it, that Elizabeth Giddings had traversed, taking her toward her future with Abner Giddings, after her aunt Mercy's death all those long years ago. It was the same meadow Fanny Abbott Harding had walked through on a moon-filled night to meet Robert Snowe, setting the course for the rest of her life.

"The light is nice in all the rooms," India had observed, "and I see there are apple trees and raspberries in the backyard." Already her mind was on the batches of jam and applesauce she could make from the fruit, and perhaps sell.

"And the view of the bay is more than I had dared hope for," China had said.

"The rooms are not nearly as small as I had supposed when I first saw the house," India had said. "I don't know what we will do with five bedrooms when we need only three."

"Perhaps some of our old friends will come to stay, as they have in the past," China had said.

It was clear, Isaiah and Zulema had reported to Fanny, that the Havener sisters, from the moment they first saw the house, envisioned themselves living there.

The move was accomplished with a minimum of fuss by early fall, and the sisters settled in. Within a very few weeks it seemed as if they had always lived there.

When they held a housewarming, M and Madras brought their children, including their new baby son, Isaiah, born in early May, just as Maude had predicted.

6.

China, India, and Persia passed what seemed to them an endless winter as they adjusted to life in a new house in a new village on the other side of Penobscot Bay. The habits of their former days in the much larger house at Castine cropped up in their new home, and they found themselves reaching for a pot in a place that did not exist in the new house. Sometimes, it seemed as if the house and its configuration were determined to frustrate them. Items they thought they would not want or need were the very ones they could not do without. They made many trips to the summer kitchen to rummage through the boxes and barrels stored there to retrieve a favorite bowl or a set of antique silver teaspoons that had been a gift to their mother from their father after she had given birth to the girls.

Snowfall was heavy the winter of 1881, and temperatures were so cold the bay froze solid. Weeks went by where the sisters barely went beyond the dooryard. Visits from the Abbott's Reach family were few, the nights were long, and time itself often felt encased in ice.

In her spare moments, Persia read books about raising sheep and chickens. She knit endless pairs of socks and mittens, which she packaged up and mailed to Castine whenever the mailman made it through the drifted road in his sledge. From time to time she received a small check from the sale of her knitted goods which she put aside until she could get to the bank and deposit it into an account earmarked for the purchase of chickens—if spring ever arrived.

Grandmother Havener's spinning wheel had been stored in the unheated summer kitchen. Persia looked forward to warmer days when she could experiment with spinning her own yarn, provided she could find an elderly lady to teach her the intricacies of the craft.

India wrote endless letters to all their friends and acquaintances far and near, a correspondence that spanned the world, asking if they recalled any stories of the Havener family at sea. She also spent a great deal of time rereading the *Empress's* logs and family letters from years gone by. She talked frequently of doing something with them of a literary nature, but wasn't sure how to begin, until Persia told her, somewhat sharply, to stop talking about it and just do it.

India heeded Persia's advice and spent several hours every afternoon making notes, organizing the material she had at hand, and penning the opening paragraphs of what she hesitantly hoped would become a book.

China, to her sisters' surprise, turned inward and didn't talk much that winter. Nor, when they asked, could she account for the mood that had settled upon her, except to attribute it to the cold, the snow, the lack of daylight. India and Persia did not believe a word of it; they knew her far too well. China was dwelling on something, but nothing they said could wrest it from her.

China, too, knew her mood had nothing to do with the weather. The truth was, after all these years she still missed the travel, the adventure of going to sea, being in command and responsible for the safe navigation of the *Empress*—being in command of herself. She thought longingly of those days, knowing they would never return, yet wanting them to. She often left rooms abruptly, hoping India and Persia did not see the tears in her eyes as some vivid memory of a port of call or a storm at sea floated unbidden into her mind. Sometimes her mood was so sour she spoke sharply to her sisters, leaving them stunned and wondering what on earth ailed her.

China realized after a few weeks that she was, for the first time, grieving the loss of the *Empress*, understanding fully, after so many years, that her livelihood was gone, never to return. She grieved for loss of time, loss of her parents, loss of a way of life, loss of her youth.

Even so, what troubled her went deeper. A question kept forming in her mind. Who am I without India and Persia? Where do they leave off and I begin? Who am I apart from them? She thought at first that she was going mad, and kept herself busy with housekeeping, cooking, doing the accounts—anything to push away her perverse, mutinous thoughts.

Then, China began to think about light . . . how it made shadows . . . its color and essence. During those weeks, she sorted through photographs and other images pertaining to their lives at sea, gazing at them as if attempting to discern something in each one that had escaped her scrutiny only the day before.

There were sketches, tintypes, and photographs of her parents aboard the *Empress*—her father wearing his cap at a jaunty angle, her mother clad in a white dress and straw hat with a wide brim; a picture India had sketched, not long before their mother died; photographs of crews, of harbors and ports they had visited, of friends they had called upon in harbors on the far side of the world. The images haunted her; not only their content, but their composition of light and dark, shape and shadow. Moments in time, she thought, the times of my life, of our lives. Memories given substance, memories to hold in the hand.

She often went to stand by the south window, remarking to India and Persia on the quality of the light, how it glinted off the snow, how the shadow of the barn lay across a drift, tinting it misty blue. At other times she stood in the east window, gazing at the frozen bay, absorbed in her thoughts. Sometimes she stood in the west window, watching the sunset until darkness had settled around her.

India and Persia stared at China's back, exchanging concerned glances and later, conferring privately. Should they consult Maude and Fanny?

"I think it may be the change," Persia whispered to India one morning when China had moved restlessly from window to window, one of those days when she seemed unable to focus on any task for more than a minute, and could not sit still.

"I thought of that," India whispered back. "But I am more inclined to think she may be hankering for the sea and the feel of a deck rolling under her feet."

"After all these years alongshore?" Persia said. "I think not, India."

In fact, they were both wrong.

Each time India and Persia tried to draw China out about what ailed her, or to include her in their daily habits of housekeeping, reading aloud to one another, or playing games of cribbage, China showed no interest, and instead would wander to a window to gaze out into the yard.

China knew India and Persia were baffled by her behavior, but she was not yet ready to let on to them that she, too, was baffled by her inability to fall in with their usual pastimes. It was as if selling the house in Castine and losing the *Empress*, touchstones that had anchored her securely in life, had set her adrift, as if she were alone in a small, leaky boat with no land in sight, no hope for even some small island of safety to appear.

Something had to change. She had to change. She had to set a new course, a course of her own, one she would navigate by herself. Alone, without India and Persia—a thought that was almost impossible to consider. How could she possibly entertain such a betrayal?

7.

When at last winter showed signs of abating by the end of March 1882, China, pushing away a sense of guilt, and without consulting her sisters—most unusual for her, for they always talked things over before doing anything—sent away to Boston for a Blair Tourograph camera. She had seen the camera advertised in a magazine:

PHOTOGRAPHY HAS RECENTLY BEEN SO SIMPLIFIED AS TO BE ABSOLUTELY BROUGHT WITHIN REACH OF ALL, MANY LADIES AND CHILDREN HAVING BECOME VERY SUCCESSFUL AMATEURS. ALL THAT IS NECESSARY IS ONE OF OUR LIGHT, PORTABLE CAMERAS AND A FEW DOZEN OF OUR SENSITIVE PLATES. THE PLATES ARE FURNISHED READY FOR EXPOSURE, AFTER WHICH THEY ARE PACKED AWAY AND DEVELOPED WHENEVER IT MAY BE CONVENIENT. THE TOUROGRAPH IS ESPECIALLY ADAPTED FOR TRAVELERS, AS IT CARRIES SIX OR EIGHT PLATES IN ONE HOLDER.

Intrigued, she had written to request a brochure. When it arrived, her interest quickened. Photographs taken by the camera illustrated the brochure, the cover of which showed a lady, stylishly dressed and wearing a hat ornamented with a plume, standing on a path in the wilderness. A mountain loomed in the background. The company's motto was "Photography in a Nut Shell."

Much to her private shame, China managed to conceal the arrival of the brochure from India and Persia. And when the camera arrived late in April, as bare ground began to show on the south side of the house and the Penobscot was once again free of ice, her sisters had gone for a walk, making it possible for China to take the package immediately to her room. She did not mention the camera to them, adding guilt to the long list of feelings she now kept from India and Persia.

The camera weighed approximately six pounds and folded into a compact carrying case. The tripod that came with it folded into a useful walking stick. It was everything China had hoped it would be. She also had ordered several dozen dry-plate negatives. The entire outfit cost more than forty dollars, making it a somewhat substantial purchase.

China knew she must tell her sisters what she had been brooding about all winter. She could not go on pretending nothing was wrong; she was obviously not herself. One morning, she summoned them to the front room and told them about the camera.

"A camera?" Persia said. "Why have you never said a word about it?" She was trying to conceal her alarm at this turn of events. There had never been a time when China had not consulted them about so large a purchase.

"Yes," China said, shame turning her cheeks red. But something alien possessed her. She wanted to tell India and Persia that for once in her life, she had given in to the urge to figure out where they left off and she began, to behave in a way that did not take into account the fact they were triplets, and that they had never in their lives lived apart from one another. For once, she wanted to make up her own mind without consulting them. Worst of all was her urge to be away from them; she knew perfectly well India and Persia had never experienced such a need to be alone.

"A camera doesn't strike me as something we need," India said, trying to add a practical, calm note to the conversation, although her tone was a bit sharp. "Especially since you were the one who determined we had to economize." China decided not to be pulled into an argument or to go on the defensive.

"No, we don't need it, but I do," China said, emphatically. And with that enigmatic remark, she went to her room, taking the camera with her and staying there until Persia called her down to supper.

India was so miffed that she had to vent her emotions to Persia before shaking out the rugs with a certain savage fury.

The next day, Persia asked China and India to join her in the front room.

"Dear heaven, what next?" India muttered under her breath.

"I have something I wish to say to both of you," Persia said. She had not slept well the night before for thinking about what she would say, and it showed. Her eyes were puffy and the lines in her face seemed deeper.

"High time," India remarked, looking directly at China.

China fully expected a severe reprimand from Persia. India rather looked forward to hearing Persia give China what for.

"As you know," Persia said after China and India had sat down on the sofa, "I spent much of the winter reading about raising sheep and chickens. I have written to Ellis Harding and asked him to find out where I can buy three healthy ewes and a ram. I've also asked him to get me some chicks so I will have eggs to sell this summer and fall. I have calculated the cost." She handed China a piece of paper with some figures on it. "Be sure to check my addition, China. I will pay for the chickens with the money I earned from selling my mittens, but the sheep will have to come out of the household accounts, if you think we can afford it. And I'll need a dog—a collie, I think—but I shall write to Isaiah and Zulema Mitchell about that. I feel certain, with their help, that I can find a dog someone will want to give away."

India was shocked. Now, instead of one sister keeping to herself, there were two! She glanced at China. India knew her emotions were written large all over her face. She trembled with the utter outrageousness of it all.

But calm prevailed.

China and India looked at Persia's figures and approved of them. There was a brief, awkward silence. China knew it was time to speak again about the camera, and what that meant. Otherwise she might never find the courage again.

"Since we are discussing our future endeavors, which require the outlay of funds, I'd like to tell you about mine," China said. "As for the camera, well, I did not tell you about it because I was not certain how to talk about what has been on my mind all winter. Indeed, I have not been certain myself, but now that I have the camera, it's wrong of me to keep you in the dark any longer." She took a deep breath. "I have decided to take up photography."

"Clearly," Persia said drily.

"Why, China," India said, feeling her anger and uneasiness subside, "I think that's a perfectly reasonable pastime for a woman. The little front room would be a perfect place for people to come and sit for you. It's a good way to earn something."

"I have no intention of setting up a photography studio here at home—at least, not at this time," China said.

"Then in the village, perhaps?" Persia asked, mystified.

"No. I am going to travel to places in Maine I have never been . . . inland places in Somerset and Penobscot counties. Places north and west of here. I know nothing about Maine except its seaports along the coast. I want to visit villages and take pictures of houses and streets and scenery and people. And, eventually, I want to make those photographs into postcards people can buy and send to their relatives."

India and Persia looked at China in stunned silence.

"But, China," India said softly, dread growing within her, "that means you would go away. Without us!"

The alarm in her voice was genuine. It was precisely what China had feared. She could not meet the accusation in India's eyes. She looked down at her hands folded quietly in her lap.

"Yes," she said, "that is true," confirming India's worst fears.

India and Persia stared at one another before turning their gaze back to China. This turn of events surpassed anything they had even dared imagine might be the trouble with China.

"But we've always been together, China. Since before we were born. We've never been apart," India said. The thought caused in her a feeling of being wrenched, cleaved, reduced to parts instead of a whole.

"We won't be the same with you gone. We'll be . . . incomplete," Persia said, losing for a moment her usual steady-headedness.

"But that's just it," China said. "I want to know who I am away from everyone and everything I love. Just for the summer and fall. I won't be away forever, and you will always know where I am. I'll write to you. I'll send telegrams."

"But what about the expense, China?" Persia asked, her practical nature reasserting itself. "You have to eat and . . . Where will you stay? Hotels cost money. And then there will be money for traveling. Do you know how much you will need?"

China rose abruptly from her chair and began to pace the room.

"No," she said. "I don't have an answer to those questions. Yet. But I will get them. I have planned where I want to go, I've charted a course just as if I were at sea . . ."

"Not precisely the same thing, China!" Persia said, feeling more and more outraged at this turn of events.

"China," India said, "is there more to this than you are telling us? Are you tired of being around Persia and me? Have we injured you in some way? Can you account for this . . . This idea of yours?" She was on the verge of tears.

China reached for India's hand and held it fast.

"Do you recall when we were at sea and we'd be in port somewhere on the other side of the world? We'd find lots of ships sailed by people we knew, people from home. And we'd hear news about men who had retired from sailing? Those men did extraordinary things. . . Some went west to Iowa and settled, became farmers, or opened stores. Others settled in California or Colorado, started ranches or operated hotels. Why, Captain Grover went to Cambridge, Maine, way inland in Somerset County, bought a store, and went into business there. Those men did not let the sea define them completely. Do you understand? They tried something new. They didn't look back."

"But they are men!" Persia said.

"Precisely," India chimed in. "Women cannot do what men do. Look at us! We are perfect examples of that."

"But, sisters, we have done what men do. We sailed Father's ship; we ran the ship's business. And we did it well and successfully. I see no reason why I, why any of us, can't embark in a new direction even if we are middle-aged and old maids."

"China, you know I do not like those terms," India said, hearing in her words a tone of primness that surprised her.

"Well, it's the truth," Persia said.

"I want a new truth," China said, "because before too long I will be an old lady, and my ability to go out into the world, near or far, will be gone."

Neither India nor Persia could argue with that.

8.

It took a lot more talking before India and Persia began to comprehend even a little why China was so set on spending the summer and fall away from them. Even so, they could not refrain from trying to persuade her to stay. Persia offered to give up her idea of raising sheep if China would cash in her idea of wandering the wilds of Maine, taking photographs. But China had made up her mind and was determined to go.

Whenever she was not engaged in duties the household required, China pored over a map of Maine, tracing roads and railways with her finger, noting the location of towns, taking into consideration the rivers and mountains. She would go first to Somerset County, to Cambridge, to call on Captain Grover, the retired mariner who operated a store there. She would go to Bingham, situated on the banks of the Kennebec, one of Maine's great rivers.

From there she would go to Greenville in Piscataquis County to see Moosehead Lake, Maine's great inland sea. She would go to northern Penobscot County to Patten, to photograph Mount Katahdin.

Her destinations chosen, China wrote to inquire about stage routes and train schedules. She wrote to town clerks to ask about hotels and boardinghouses, and inquired about cost. She factored in the price of boat tickets to get her upriver to the railroad station in Bangor, and home again in the fall. When she added up the numbers, it came to nearly two hundred dollars. She shared that information with India and Persia, dreading their reaction.

"That's rather a large sum," India said disapprovingly as she mixed a batch of bread in the big tan-colored bowl. Her apron was dusty with flour. She stirred the dough in a particularly aggressive way, signaling that she still held a substantial reservoir of doubt about what she called China's mad idea.

"More than I'll pay for my sheep," Persia said, pressing her lips together and keeping her eyes on her knitting. She drew in a sharp breath. "Now see what you've made me do, China . . . All this worry! I've dropped a stitch."

China saw how vexed they were, and tried to ease their feelings of anxiety and disappointment.

"We can afford it," she said. "I've checked my bookkeeping thoroughly. We ended up with quite a bit more than I expected from the sale of our house and some of our things. And I'd like to point out that some of those things did, indeed, belong to me, so it's only fair that I spend my share of those funds as I see fit."

"You'll never sell enough photographic postcards at a penny apiece to recoup an expense of that magnitude," India said tartly, with more venom than she intended. "Oh, if you must do this, why can't you take pictures around here? Down in the village, in Searsport, over to Castine? Make portraits that people will be glad to pay for?"

"I think we already know the answer to that one," Persia said, looking sadly at China. "She wants to be away from us." She found the dropped stitch, knit backward until she could place it back on the needle, and resumed knitting. She was working on yet another pair of mittens, in seed stitch.

"Persia, India, don't," China said, appeasement in her voice. "You seem to think I made my decision in some cavalier way, with no thought for your feelings. But I didn't. I thought long and hard about this. Mostly what I thought about is that none of us are getting any younger. I'm still hale and hearty, so it seemed to me that now would be a good time to pursue my interest in photography, even if it does take me away from you for several months . . . oh, all right, four months. I'm not throwing you over or abandoning you. I'm just . . . shipping out by myself, for a short period of time."

"Forgive me, China," Persia said. "I know India and I are being difficult. It's just that we don't entirely understand all of this—and I don't know what we shall do without you."

"I know exactly what you will do without me, Persia. You will raise sheep, gather eggs from your chickens, and knit. And I believe it will do you good to be interested in something that India and I are not interested in. As I recall, it was you who had that pet lamb when we were . . . What, eight or nine? Wasn't that the time we made a passage to Rio? You loved that little lamb. Mother taught us all to knit during that trip. I think sheep remind you of those good times."

"Yes, I suppose that's true," Persia conceded. "I can see that little lamb now, frolicking around the deck. I named it Lily."

"It followed you around like a puppy."

"As I recall," India remarked drily, "Lily ended up as lamb chops."

The sisters looked at one another and burst out laughing, the sound easing the constraint they all felt.

"One more reason we will miss you, China—all that you contribute to our collection of memories of those days."

"But what about you, India? What will you do while I am away?" China asked.

India thought a moment before she answered. The fact was that she, too, had spent a lot of the winter thinking about the future, and had begun to apply herself to it.

"I'm glad you asked, China, for I have wanted to say something long before this . . . but your news put what I had to say in a somewhat lesser light. I believe Mother and Father's story—and ours, for that matter—is worth telling. We are part of an age that is passing. The age of sail. Remember how, as children, we loved hearing the crew sing sea chanteys? We heard the same songs all over the world, no matter where we shipped a crew. Sometimes we sang along with the crew. I don't know if those old songs have ever been written down, so I thought I might do that." She hesitated, wanting to add something, but not sure if she should.

"Oh, for heaven's sake, India, spit it out," Persia said.

"I've already started writing down the sea chanteys. And I'd like to think that if I combined them with the story of the *Empress* and our family, I'd have a book someone might want to publish—that people would want to read."

"A noble endeavor, India," China said warmly. "And very impressive. You were always the best scholar of the three of us."

India nodded and did not try to deflect China's praise, she was so relieved and happy to have it.

"But there is one other thing that worries me," Persia said. "Mother always said that ladies of good family and reputation don't travel hither and yon alone. It's just not done. And you know it, China. Why, it might even be dangerous. We don't know a thing about the state of the roads or the cleanliness of the hotels and boardinghouses in the wilds of Somerset County. Or what ruffians you might encounter in a railway car or a stagecoach on your way to the North Country."

"Persia, look at me," China said. "What do you see?"

"I see a tall, slender woman of a certain age who has white hair and blue eyes who looks exactly like India and me."

"Very true. But do I—or the two of you—look like someone a man would accost because of our beauty or our . . . our sensuousness?"

Persia drew a sharp intake of breath and fixed China with an astounded look.

"Well?" China demanded.

"No. No, you do not. You look like someone's grandmother. I suppose we all do," Persia replied.

"Which means, Persia, I have reached the age where I have become all but invisible to members of the opposite sex. It's like a magic cloak. It will enable me to go wherever I like in relative safety and free-dom. Other women may disapprove of my solitary status, of course, but they will have no idea who I am, so it really doesn't matter. Nor do I care one iota."

"Then it's settled. You will ship out in May and we will stay here in port, to mind the ship, so to speak. But you must promise you will return by October at the latest," Persia said.

"Yes, I promise. And you must promise that you won't fret day and night about me," China replied.

India and Persia promised, but China could see their hearts weren't in it. They already were fretting.

That night China lay awake, thinking about leaving. Moonlight gave the room a pale, ghostly wash, banishing sleep and inviting the mind to dash wildly about, letting fear and doubt nip at her thoughts. Her journey would in no way resemble that of setting forth on the ocean. She had never sailed alone. She had always had charts and navigational aids. There were sextants and the sun and stars, and they had always had their father; even though he was not sober in his later years, he could still be counted on for his knowledge of the ship, the weather, the very sea itself. And their mother had anchored them securely as a family, her trust that all would be well teaching her daughters not to fear. China realized that traveling alone for the first time would take some getting used to. Nonetheless, the lure of traveling in an unknown inland region excited China as nothing else had in a very long time. Wasn't the unknown merely the unknown, she thought, whether it was the unexpected storms that blew one off course, or the unfamiliar inland villages where people might view her with suspicion because, heaven forbid, she was a woman of a certain age traveling alone with a camera in tow?

She tossed and turned, her thoughts aswirl like a thousand leaves blasted off a tree in an autumn wind. How they tumbled and whirled, impossible to catch even one for more than a moment. Her last thought before she fell asleep was I must see for myself.

She dreamed she traveled bumpy roads in a horse-drawn coach equipped with sails that carried the vehicle easily up and down the steepest mountain, across the widest river, the deepest lake. Her fellow passengers were children who begged her to tell them stories of life upon the deep, but instead she sang, "Blow the man down, bullies, blow the man down," the chorus of one of her father's favorite sea chanteys.

In the ensuing weeks, she studied the workings of the camera. She exposed a negative or two and familiarized herself with the process of taking a picture. She knew the ins and outs of the chemical process, the mysterious concoctions of liquid developers and fixers involved in transforming negatives into photographs, would have to wait until her tour of inland Maine was over. There simply was not time before her departure to set up a darkroom and experiment.

9.

The first day of May was M and Madras's tenth wedding anniversary and Fanny had organized what she termed a "frolic" at Abbott's Reach. It was a family affair, the last one they'd have until the end of October, for Fanny and Ellis would be much occupied with running the boardinghouse during the summer and fall.

At the gathering, China informed her friends she would be leaving soon to begin her travels in Somerset County.

"I don't understand the urge to travel," Fanny said as she, Maude, and China walked down the road that led to the boat landing. "Oh, I was hell-bent to see any place but here when I was a girl . . . And look at all the trouble that got me into."

"Yes, I remember those days quite well," Maude said, recalling how Fanny had run away with the ne'er-do-well sailor, Robert Snowe, had found herself in the family way and abandoned in Portland. Maude had delivered Fanny's baby, Elizabeth, who was M's mother, and Blythe's grandmother. "Ah, those were the days," she sighed. But the fact was, she had never had an urge to travel; she was content to live quietly and happily at Fort Point.

"It's not as simple as that," China said. "It's not just an urge to see new places; it's also a hankering to learn something new, such as photography. To discover whether or not I can fend for myself, get along without India and Persia. Know more about myself." She hesitated, then said, "India and Persia are concerned about me, a woman, traveling alone. What do you think?"

"I traveled alone many a time up and down the river on both sides of the Penobscot," Maude said. "And so did Fanny. Just around these parts, of course. We still do, in fact. I never saw the slightest reason why women ought to be compelled to travel around together like some great school of fish."

"China, you must do as you see fit," Fanny said. The wind lifted her dark green skirt and it billowed like a sail.

"Hmmm," Maude said. "There's a bit of the change mixed up in this, too, I suspect. The change is about a lot more than a woman passing beyond her monthly affinity with the moon. The heart and mind are affected, too, in ways that can't be predicted. Your heart and mind are telling you to go forth and make your mark before it's too late, that's what I think."

She walked slowly, with a slight limp because of her cranky knee. Fanny and China amended their pace every so often to allow her to catch up.

"Are you tired, Maude?" Fanny asked. "Perhaps we should go back to the house now."

"Yes, I'm ready."

"Then you don't think I have taken leave of my senses?" China asked.

Fanny and Maude exchanged glances.

"Quite the contrary, my dear," Maude said. "I'd say you've just come to your senses. Wouldn't you agree, Fanny?"

"Indeed, I would, Maude."

"Oh," China said.

"I know you will write to us while you are gone, China," Fanny said. "And do so often. We will be interested to hear about the people you meet, the things you see, the stories you hear."

"We will miss your company, of course, but we look forward to seeing you again in the fall," Maude said.

Their words, China thought, were as good as a blessing.

10.

China stood at the rail of the steamboat, known locally as "the Bangor boat," as it pulled away from the wharf near Abbott's Reach. Her sisters and friends had seen her aboard and waved farewell from shore. India and Persia had not shed a tear until China stepped from the wharf to the steamboat deck, then tears had rolled down their cheeks—partly because China was leaving, partly because they weren't going with her, and partly because seeing her embark on her journey had stirred in them memories of the many journeys they had taken together all those years ago. It stirred in them a sudden and long-buried yen to travel again, too.

Maude mother-henned India and Persia, offering handkerchiefs and words of consolation.

I don't feel sad, China thought, inventorying her emotions as she watched the shore of Fort Point recede. I ought to feel sad, but I don't. She had not shed one tear, nor felt the least inclination to do so.

Embarking on the journey buoyed her, there was no mistake about that. Yet, as the steamboat's churning paddle took her away from the landing, regret surfaced in her heart, and a small niggle of guilt at her selfishness and self-indulgence seeped into her thoughts.

It was the first time in her life she had closed a door against her sisters, she realized with a rill of shame. She suspected India and Persia also saw it that way.

Dear me, dear me, she thought, attempting to turn her mind away from the quicksand of guilt and back to the adventure at hand. I am simply taking a trip alone. I will come home in the fall, and no one will be the worse for it. We all will profit from it, I am certain.

China had dressed carefully that morning, choosing a simple blue cotton dress with just a bit of flare in the skirt, and over it, a double-breasted linen jacket of navy blue, with a high neck and silver-colored buttons. Its cut and style reminded her somewhat of the jacket her father had worn when he was master of the *Empress*, which was why she had chosen it. Her hat was a plain, round toque in navy blue felt, decorated with just a bit of matching tulle. Fanny had commented that the hat really needed a jaunty white feather to set it off properly.

China knew her traveling outfit was not fashionable when compared to current modes. It had no ruffles or bows, no pleats or delicate lace. She wore a corset, of course, all ladies did, but it was not tightly laced, and she could breathe and move with ease. Her outfit was very much along the lines of what she and her sisters had worn when they were at sea—practical clothing providing comfort and the least amount of bodily restriction. Besides, it didn't matter in the least whether or not her clothing was stylish. She wasn't angling for a man, going to a party, or trying to impress anyone. She merely was traveling to a new destination, both literally and figuratively. Serviceable clothing was by far the best choice.

The steamboat sounded its horn as it pulled out into the channel and got under way. The wharf and the people on it receded until China saw them no more, a pattern so familiar for so much of her life that it caused in her another wave of excitement. The force of old habit made her want to give a few orders as to the running of the vessel. Indeed, she even looked around to see if there was a mate nearby to whom she could give a command before she came out of her reverie and reminded herself she was only a passenger on the trip upriver.

It was a sunny morning and the steamboat had a full complement of passengers. Some of the ladies popped open silk parasols, the fringe trembling in the light breeze. These women stood at the rail, talking with their traveling companions. A few children escaped their mother's surveillance and frolicked around the deck.

Spring had touched the banks of the Penobscot with pastel fingers. Patches of blue, yellow, and white flowers carpeted the meadows bordering the river. The air smelled fresh and new, full of promise and possibility. China spotted a pair of osprey wheeling overhead, just off Verona Island, and heard their cries, a note of auspicious music to underscore the start of her journey.

She found her way forward and stood in the bow, turning her face upriver, toward whatever it was that lay ahead. Out of habit, she looked at the sun, her mind schooled to take a reading for the purposes of navigation, even though it was too early in the day. She almost felt the cool brass of a sextant in her fingers, almost heard the wind luff in the sails. Ah, she thought, those were the days.

She did not know any of the other passengers, but clearly the captain recognized her. He made a point to seek her out and speak to her after they were under way.

"I'm Captain Rawley. It's a pleasure to be shipping with you, Miss Havener," he said. "I once had the pleasure of meeting your father many years ago when I was just a young lad wanting to go to sea. He didn't have a berth for me, but he helped me find one, and I went as cabin boy on the *Defiance*."

"Thank you, Captain Rawley. My father helped many a youngster who wanted to follow the sea," China said.

The captain touched his cap visor in a salute and went aft.

When the steamboat arrived at the wharf in Bangor, China arranged for her trunk to be transported to the train station. Oddly, it was the first time she had traveled by train, although she had read about and seen images of them. She was not by nature fearful of new things and situations; her years of traveling the world had seen to that. What daunted her most—and this surprised her—was that none of the faces on the steamboat, the street, or the train were familiar to her. She was just another person in an endless sea of humanity on her way to somewhere else. The absence of India and Persia struck her with sudden, unexpected force, and almost took her breath away. She had never before experienced such a feeling, as if she had been torn asunder, like a scrap of paper ripped from a whole sheet. So this was what it meant to be on her own, by herself, no longer a daily part of the trinity that was the Havener sisters.

She calmed herself, boarded the train, and took a seat by the window. She watched the swiftly passing scenery slide by mile after mile as the train chugged toward Skowhegan.

At the depot, she asked for directions to the Elm House, had supper, and stayed the night, the first time she had ever slept under a roof that did not also shelter India and Persia.

I can't turn back now, she thought as she drifted off to sleep, but in her heart she wanted to.

11.

In the morning, China boarded the stagecoach for Cambridge and arrived in that town in the late afternoon.

Cambridge, with a population of four hundred and seventy-two, was little more than a cluster of white frame houses located near a stream, situated along a narrow road punctuated with tall elms and maples. A lumberyard took up space just beyond the bridge spanning the narrow upper end of Cambridge Pond. The sound of a steam-powered saw rose above the clip-clop of the horses' hooves, and the rattle and jangle of wheels and harness.

The melodious call of an oriole floated over the din, and China smelled the clean odor of freshly-sawn pine boards.

The other five passengers in the coach were men dressed in black jackets, vests, and pants. These men, with gallant politeness, had handed her into and out of the conveyance at stops along the way. During the journey, they had inquired after her comfort, and assured her that Mrs.

The Havener Sisters

Buzzell's boardinghouse in Cambridge set a good table. As they left the stage, the men tipped their hats to China and went their separate ways.

So there she was, a stranger alone in a strange town, her trunk standing on end, and the wooden carrying case containing her camera sitting beside it, across the street from the boardinghouse where she had arranged to stay.

"These yours, ma'am?"

The voice belonged to a boy who looked to be twelve or thirteen, China surmised. He was thin and looked as if he never had quite enough to eat. His boots were scuffed and worn, and his clothing did not fit him well. He had about him the unmistakable odor of horses, as if he had just come from the barn. His head was covered by a wide-brimmed wool felt hat that had seen better days. His eyes were a clear shade of blue. He met China's gaze forthrightly, almost challengingly, as if daring her to say no to his inquiry.

China smiled at him and nodded, starting toward the house. A woman came out on the piazza, beaming the sort of good-natured smile that encompasses everything and everyone. She was short and somewhat stout. A clean white apron covered her calico dress. Her hair must have been red once, China surmised, but had faded to the color of straw. Her eyes were hazel and her voice was pleasant.

"I'm Mrs. Buzzell," she said.

"Miss Havener," China replied.

"I understand you will be staying for several weeks?"

"Yes, I expect so. Two weeks at the most."

"Well, let's not stand out here in the dooryard. You must be tuckered out after that long ride up here. Clint, you have a care with that trunk; don't you be banging up my woodwork with it. You can leave it in the back bedroom."

The boy nodded assent and dragged the trunk toward the piazza steps. Then, with a strength China could not believe he possessed, he lifted the trunk and carried it to the room she would occupy.

"That's Clint Remick," Mrs. Buzzell said, raising her eyebrows and giving China a long look, as if that explained everything. China had assumed the boy belonged to Mrs. Buzzell's family. Clearly not; he was much too bedraggled to be kin to Mrs. Buzzell.

"You have a lovely place here," China said as she went inside. The house smelled of freshly baked bread, molasses cookies, and meat stew. Everything was neatly arranged and not a speck of dust showed on any surface. The house, inside and out, was well kept and inviting, the furniture arranged with an eye to comfort.

"The gentlemen who were also passengers on the stagecoach said you set a good table and keep a nice house. I see they were right," China said.

"I'm a widow lady. No man to muss things up once I've neatened the rooms. But I must say, I do miss Mr. Buzzell, even after all these years. He was killed at Gettysburg." Mrs. Buzzell imparted this last bit of information in a matter-of-fact way.

"How terrible," China murmured, recalling that while the Civil War raged, she and her sisters had sailed the Seven Seas, more or less unmindful of it, although it meant they could not put into any ports in the American South during those years. She remembered how she and her sisters had read accounts of the battles, including Gettysburg, how they had wept when they saw in the newspapers the long lists of the thousands of men who had died or were wounded in battle, for some of the names were familiar to them, boys from Searsport and nearby villages.

"Well, not as terrible as you might think. Mr. Buzzell wanted to go in the army, wanted to join the Twentieth Maine, wasn't like he'd have bought a substitute even if he'd had the money to do it. He believed Abe Lincoln was doing right by those poor, pitiful slaves. He wanted to do his part. We were married a few months before he left, and he died two years later. Never saw him again. But it all worked out just fine. Mama and Papa needed me back to home, and I looked after the young ones, my brothers and sisters, until they grew up, and then took care of Mama and Papa until they died. They left me this house so I could set up for myself and not be a burden on anyone or have to go to the poor farm." She spoke as if she had no regrets and was content with her lot.

China hesitated, curious, before she asked, "You had no desire to marry again?"

"Not in the least. Mr. Buzzell was the only man I ever had eyes for, and I never saw anyone else that measured up. So here I am. Supper will be on the table in half an hour. Clint, you git on out to the barn and don't let me see you hanging around here in the morning."

"Yes, ma'am," Clint said as he went out the door. He glanced at China and something deeply sad and full of need in his glance made her heart constrict with pity for him.

"Hasn't got a soul, that one, mother and father dead, no living brothers or sisters," Mrs. Buzzell said. "Not even any near cousins or aunts and uncles. Now that's a tragedy. No family—at least I still have plenty of cousins. I give the boy what work I can in return for food, but it's not much. Don't know what will become of him, but I can't think but what it won't be good."

In her room, the back bedroom off the parlor, China removed her dusty clothing and put on a clean cotton dress. She tidied her hair and went out to the dining room to eat the hearty meal Mrs. Buzzell had prepared.

Mrs. Buzzell had spread the table with a white cloth and napkins in what appeared to be silver rings. An oil lamp with a pretty globe painted with blue flowers had a place of honor in the middle of the table. It cast a large circle of light, giving the room a pleasant, cozy atmosphere.

"What brings you to these parts?" Mrs. Buzzell asked after she had sat down and dished up stew for China and herself. She passed a plate of biscuits. "My good dishes," she commented proudly, indicating the table settings. The dishes were decorated with a design of pink rosebuds and blue forget-me-nots.

"Very nice," China commented. She tasted the stew, found it to her liking, and buttered a biscuit. "I've come to call on Captain Grover."

"Captain Grover? You must mean Mr. Grover who runs the store up the road. Kin, is he?"

"No, we've never met."

Mrs. Buzzell took in this information and apparently did not know what else to say except a somewhat disbelieving, "Oh?"

"Captain—that is—Mr. Grover, in his former occupation, was a seafarer from Searsport, not far from where I live. When he left the sea, he came here to Cambridge to settle. I want to talk to him about that and perhaps take his photograph."

A surprised expression crept over Mrs. Buzzell's face. "My heavens," she said. "A photograph. And you've never met the gentleman. Hmm."

China felt her heart sink. India and Persia had been right about the stigma attached to a woman traveling alone. She hoped Mrs. Buzzell wasn't about to collapse in a state of shock. Instead, Mrs. Buzzell leaned across the table toward China and said expectantly, "Well, now, thereby must hang quite a tale."

"Yes. You see, I was born at sea and lived most of my life on my father's vessel, the *Empress*. Since my father died a few years ago, I no longer go to sea. Now I have an interest in making photographs, and am curious to know why a former sea captain would come inland to run a store in a village he had never been to before."

"Why, you don't say! I never heard of a woman living on a ship."

"It's quite common in Searsport where my people come from. It's a town on the Penobscot, downriver from Bangor."

"Oh," Mrs. Buzzell said, her face lighting up. "I know where Bangor is. I went there once by stage years ago to visit my mother's youngest sister. She was sick, and needed help. She's gone now, God rest her soul. But I remember that trip. Over hill and over dale. I thought to heaven I'd never get there. Of course, that was back long before the train came and getting from one place to another was a quite a chore."

"This is a lovely supper, Mrs. Buzzell. I think I might put one of these biscuits in my pocket . . . in case I wake up in the night and want something to eat. That is, if you don't mind."

"Oh, my yes, you go right ahead," Mrs. Buzzell said, pleased to hear her biscuits were so appreciated. She removed the soup plates and dished up a dessert of gingerbread with fluffy mounds of whipped cream. While she was occupied with cutting the cake, China slipped three biscuits into her pocket.

When the meal was over, China pleaded fatigue, the rigors of travel, the long day bouncing and jouncing in the stagecoach.

"If you would point me in the direction of the necessary house, Mrs. Buzzell, then I believe I will retire for the night."

"Right through the kitchen, out the back door, and follow the path," Mrs. Buzzell said in a low voice, as if reference to bodily functions ought only to be made in whispers.

Outside, China made a detour and went into the barn. She saw Clint leaning against the side of a stall, rubbing the forehead of a gray horse. He looked up when he heard China's step. Overhead, swallows flitted in and out of the barn. The horse lifted its head and gave a low nicker of greeting.

"Thought you might want a little bit of supper," China said. She handed Clint the biscuits.

"Thank you, ma'am," Clint said, reaching for them eagerly with a grubby hand, the fingernails unkempt and broken. He avoided her gaze, and she knew it cost him his pride to accept even this small handout.

"My pleasure," China said, and went back to the house.

12.

Captain Eben Grover's store contained just about anything anyone in Cambridge might require, including animal feed, tin dippers, soap, kerosene lamps, harness, seeds, and bolts of cloth. Bucksaws hung from nails driven into the ceiling beams, and kegs containing nails of all sizes stood along the far wall. The store smelled of leather and the oil used to preserve the wooden floorboards. A tall, round stove occupied the corner nearest the counter, and nearby a table held a checkerboard and a cribbage board. Several chairs drawn up around the table indicated that local farmers probably met there to talk politics, challenge one another to a game, hash over the news of the town, discuss the weather, and smoke their pipes.

China introduced herself and stated her business.

Eben Grover was a tall man in his fifties, his side whiskers threaded with gray. His black hair was neatly combed away from his brow. He regarded China with friendly dark eyes full of good nature and a great deal of curiosity.

"I don't believe I ever met your father, Miss Havener, but I've certainly heard of him . . . And of you and your sisters. Wasn't a port anywhere in the world where someone didn't mention the *Empress* and talk about the Havener sisters. I'm happy to make your acquaintance. Imagine finding you here so far from salt water." He took her hand when she held it out in greeting, his grip firm but gentle.

"I might say the same about you, sir. We are, indeed, a long way from the sea, Captain Grover."

"Aye, that we are, that we are."

China explained her purpose for being in Cambridge and why she wanted to talk to him.

"Then ask away, Miss Havener. I'd be happy to answer any questions you might want to put to me."

"Do you miss going to sea?"

Captain Grover leaned against the counter and gazed out the window. His face wore an expression China could not quite decipher. It was a mix of the rueful, the mirthful, and perhaps even a bit of ambivalence, as if he did not know precisely how to answer her question.

"No, can't say as I do. This will sound odd, but I didn't choose the sea. I was born to it, just as you were, born in the middle of the Atlantic Ocean halfway from Cork, Ireland, bound for Boston. My father expected me to follow in his wake and so I did. I made a good life of it, too. Married and took my bride with me. Raised our sons and daughters the same way I was raised. Then the young ones grew up. Not a one of them cared to go to sea. Then, a few years ago, my wife died. And that was when I told myself I was going to stay alongshore.

"One of my brothers married a woman from Cambridge . . . met her in Portland when she was visiting her sister . . . And they came here to settle so she could be near her family. When I went to visit them, they told me about the store, that it was for sale. So we bought it together, my brother and I, and I've never looked back."

"Do you think that is a commonplace thing—that those born to the sea can easily move on to other things?"

"Well, I'm not saying I didn't have some doubts. But here's the thing: what we were born to is more than just the sea; it's also the ability to move on with great ease to other ports of call, other places in the world."

"I hadn't thought of it that way, but I see your point. Seafarers are good at adapting themselves to wherever they find themselves in the world."

"Yes. And how about you, Miss Havener? How is it you come to be alongshore after all your years at sea?" It was a polite question, a way of learning more of her story, a way to compare notes with her.

China hesitated before answering, though the answer she had worked out for herself over the past few years boiled down to a few basic sentences.

"When my father died, my sisters and I, as I am sure you are aware, given the circumstances, had no choice but to stay alongshore. Recently, we were obliged to move to a small house on the other side of Penobscot Bay. This past winter I began thinking about doing other things. I realized I still wanted to travel, but on land this time, and to parts of Maine I've never seen. I brought a camera with me— photography is a new interest I have taken up. I'm hoping you will allow me to photograph you and your store."

Captain Grover raised his eyebrows in mild surprise, the expression on his face quickly evolving to one of pleasure, as if he had just won a special prize.

"Well, I don't see why not. Anytime you want."

"I was thinking tomorrow morning would be the ideal time, when the light is still soft."

"That will be fine," Captain Grover agreed, smoothing his beard thoughtfully with one hand. "But first, I want to know one thing. Is it true that while you and your sisters sailed the *Empress*, you bested the record of the old clipper ships sailing from China to Boston? Every turtleback I ever put to sea with claimed it was the gospel truth."

"That is true, Captain Grover."

But she didn't elaborate. It was one of the vilest passages the *Empress* had ever made. The crew was a scabrous assemblage of wharf rats who knew seamanship, but were of a brawling nature. The only way to keep them in line was to promise them a bonus if they bore down and applied themselves to shaving off the time it took to get a shipment of tea from Hong Kong to Boston, in order to be the first in port. And they had done it. By beating out the competition, they had obtained top price for the tea.

The door opened and a customer came in.

"Thank you, Captain Grover. I enjoyed talking with you," China said.

She stepped out onto the dusty road and walked in the opposite direction from Mrs. Buzzell's boardinghouse. New leaves adorned the trees and spring birds flitted and called. The air was sweet in a way the salt air of the sea never was. China breathed it in as if each breath were nourishment, as if inland air were a delicacy she had craved for a long time without ever knowing what it was she had longed for.

Cambridge, she discovered, contained a number of businesses, including a Mr. Rogers who made boots and shoes; Lucius Gilbert, wheelwright; John Cole, harnesses and trunks; I. D. Wentworth, Soule, and Morrill, blacksmiths, each one with his own forge; Albert Small, shingles; Nathan Clark and Co., sawmill and gristmill; John Russell, carriages; Philip Mason, painter; Mrs. Ira Horne, dressmaker; Frederick Bardin, coffins and caskets; N. L. Hooper and David Morrill, stonecutters; and two other general stores, one owned by J. B. And G. Mitchell, and the other owned by Ham and Whitney. There was also a hotel, the Island House, Stillman E. Bailey, proprietor.

Small though it was, Cambridge appeared to be a prosperous and growing place.

China had not gone far when she realized Clint Remick was tagging along behind her. She stopped to let him catch up.

"Good morning," she said, noting again the ragtag appearance of his clothing.

Sensing her scrutiny, Clint refused to look at her. He thrust his hands in his pockets and stared at the ground.

China turned her attention away from him and continued on her way. Clint walked a step or two behind. After they had gone a half-mile or so, she stopped again to let him catch up. This time he looked directly at her.

"You got any young ones, or anybody else with you?" he asked.

"No."

"No one to help you lug that camera stuff?"

"It's not heavy. I've managed heavier things in my time."

"Driving horses, maybe?"

"No. A ship."

Clint stared at her, then astonishment registered on his face. He was almost as tall as China, and she surmised that one day, when he was full grown, he'd be close to six foot in his stocking feet. He was a nice-looking boy with red-brown hair, what she could see of it, that curled around his ears. His clothes, the same he had worn the day before, were roughly patched and crudely mended, as if he had done the work himself.

"You mean like Mr. Grover? He's told me stories."

"And did he tell you that boys your age went to sea as cabin boys to learn the work of sailing the ship?"

"No." Clint paused, considering what he would say next. "Did you have cabin boys on your ship?"

"Yes, over the years we had many on the *Empress* . . . That was my father's ship."

"Oh." And with that Clint walked off in a different direction, leaving China to her own thoughts.

She wondered what Clint Remick would be like with his rough edges smoothed away, with his face and hands washed, and a decent pair of boots on his feet. Perhaps the guarded, unapproachable look in his eyes and in the bowed set of his shoulders would disappear.

"No business of mine," China murmured to herself as she fixed the camera to the tripod and aimed it toward the commercial heart, as it was, of Cambridge.

It was the first photograph she had attempted to take in Cambridge, and she felt a little foolish standing there in the middle of the dusty road, reading the fine print of the camera's instruction manual and following each step as indicated. Even though she had practiced some at home, she still needed to consult the manual. She thought about the light, looked through a small aperture in a wooden wing that pulled out of one side of the camera case to see if she liked what she saw, removed the lens cap, and then replaced it. It didn't seem as if she had accomplished very much. Indeed, she had no way of knowing if what she had done would yield an image that was clear, interesting, and of a quality anyone would want to look at, let alone buy if it was ever reduced to the size of a postcard. Yet, it seemed to her that instead of marking time as she had every since her sailing days had ended, she was moving toward something —mastery of the camera, eventually, and who knew what else.

Still, maybe India and Persia were right, she thought; maybe I should have stayed home and tried my hand at portraits.

13.

When China, with camera and tripod in hand, stepped off Mrs. Buzzell's piazza the next morning, Clint was there waiting for her. He wore the same grubby clothes and beat-up boots he had worn the day before. She knew now that he had nothing else to wear, and suspected he had eaten little or nothing for breakfast. She wished she had some more biscuits in her pocket to give him, but Mrs. Buzzell had served oatmeal and toast for breakfast which precluded leftovers.

Clint reached for the camera. China let him take it.

"I'm gonna be your cabin boy, ma'am," Clint said, with a determined tone in his voice. "Don't know what they do on a ship, but on land I think a cabin boy would carry heavy things for someone. So I'll carry this thing."

"It's a camera," China said. "Handle it gently, if you please."

"Never saw a camera before, but I have a picture of my folks, so I know what a camera does, even if I don't know how it works."

"Well, you're about to see," China said as she went about setting up her equipment in front of Eben Grover's store.

Clint watched with eager curiosity. "Now what do you do?"

"I look through this aperture to see what the camera sees, and decide if I like it. If I don't, I move the camera a bit until I see the details I want to include in the picture. The store sign, for example. Then, I remove the lens cap, wait a couple of seconds, then replace the cap on the lens."

"And that's it?"

"Not exactly. There's much more to it, but that will happen later, in a darkroom, with chemical baths. The light has fixed an image of Captain Grover's store to the glass-plate negative inside the camera. The negative has been treated with a light-sensitive solution . . . it comes that way. But in order to use that glass plate to make a photograph you can put in a frame or in an album, there is a procedure involving various chemicals I will need to do when I return home to Fort Point in the fall. It's called developing, and it's something I have not yet learned how to do. Indeed, the first photograph I ever took that might count for anything was yesterday morning. I still have a great deal to learn."

"So if the glass plates get broke, there won't be any pictures."

"Yes, that's right. Nor will there be a picture if too much light, or too little, strikes the negative."

She saw that he was quick to learn, and suspected he wanted to learn more.

"You want to take a picture of where I stay?" he asked suddenly, gazing intently at her, as if her answer mattered a great deal to him.

China glanced at him sharply. She had assumed, based on what Mrs. Buzzell had said, that Clint didn't stay anywhere except in the barns of kindhearted people.

"I'd be happy to, but first I must speak with Captain Grover. Wait here."

China heard the tone of command in her voice, was surprised to see that Clint responded to it.

She found Eben Grover dusting shelves inside the store.

"Good morning," she said. "I've just taken a photo of your store, and now I need one of you standing out on the steps. If you'd write down your mailing address for me, I'll see that you have a copy sometime next winter, or whenever I find time to make a print—provided, of course, it comes out the way I hope it will."

"Why, that would be something to have, Miss Havener. I thank you." Captain Grover scribbled his address on the back of an envelope and handed it her. "I notice you got yourself a helper."

"Yes. He has appointed himself my cabin boy."

Captain Grover laughed out loud. "You don't say. Probably not a bad idea. He hasn't got a soul, and you're all by yourself. Might be good for both of you. I've thought more than once of taking him in myself, but my brother and I have been talking about taking a trip out west this summer, and if I like it out there, I might stay a while, might even settle there."

"Captain Grover, what kind of people were Clint's folks?"

"They were good people. They had a nice place just beyond the village. But Jim Remick got sick and died, and then his wife, Lila Remick died, too, a few months later. That was a couple of years ago. Clint stayed on the place until the town took it for unpaid taxes. The selectmen thought Clint ought to go to an orphanage down to Waterville, but when he got wind of that he disappeared into the woods. Then, after they caught up with him, they thought maybe he ought to work somewhere—that working in the woods might suit him, so they farmed him out to a lumberman. No one saw hide nor hair of him for a while, but a few weeks ago he turned up in town again. People do what they can for him, let him sleep in their barns, pay him to do a few chores, feed him."

"Can't anything else be done for him?"

"Well, there are a couple of families that would take him in exchange for his labor, and they'd probably treat him right, but Clint won't hear of it."

"I see. Thank you for that information, Captain Grover."

"Well, he seems to have taken a liking to you, Miss Havener."

"Yes, it seems so."

After China took Captain Grover's picture, Clint led her up the road, past one of the blacksmith's shop where a beautiful, dappled black Percheron horse was getting a set of shoes, and past the church. He carried the camera and she carried the tripod. His strides were long, and every so often, he stopped to wait for her to catch up.

"It's not too far," he said encouragingly.

Little puffs of dust rose with each step China took, sullying the hem of her navy blue skirt. But at last they came to a lane, just two rutted tracks with grass growing between. They walked a short distance until they came to a crude lean-to of evergreen boughs and a circle of rocks enclosing the remains of a fire.

"This is where you stay?" China asked.

"Yes, ma'am, I do. I just built this camp a couple of weeks ago. Before that it was too cold to sleep in a lean-to. And of course pretty soon the blackflies will be too fierce for me to be outdoors at night, but it will do for now. This used to be part of our land." There was pride in Clint's voice.

"I see. Well, Clint, let me set up the camera. Would you like to be in the picture?"

"Why, yes, I would." He struck a pose, hat held in one hand, his head up, his eyes looking toward the distance beyond China's shoulder.

"Just be yourself, Clint. Stand very still. Don't breathe until I say so." She removed the lens cap and replaced it. "You can breathe."

Clint grinned. "Never thought I'd have my picture taken."

"I'll send a copy to Mrs. Buzzell, probably sometime next winter. She'll see that you get it."

"If I'm still around these parts."

Clint crawled into the lean-to to retrieve a battered knapsack. He reached into it and pulled out a tintype. He held it out for China to see. "Ma and Pa," he said.

The photograph showed a young man and woman, perhaps newly married, dressed in their best clothes. The man was seated and the woman stood behind him, her hand on his shoulder. The woman's eyes were like Clint's, and China noted a resemblance between the man and Clint.

"A handsome couple," China said. "You look like them."

A single tear rolled down Clint's cheek. He snatched the photograph from China's fingers and ran off into the woods.

Instinct told China it would do no good to go after Clint. In truth, it was none of her concern. The world was full of waifs like Clint, well beyond babyhood, or, indeed, childhood. She had seen them in ports from Portland to Shanghai, children with no parents, no homes, no comfort. She had always been drawn to them, always wanted to do something to ease their plight, but her parents had admonished her to avoid them; there was no telling what diseases they carried, or what base behaviors they had fallen prey to. She had obeyed her parents and lived by the information they had imparted to her, even now. Yet part of her knew it wasn't right. She hated to stand by and do nothing, but what else could she do? She picked up her equipment and walked back to Mrs. Buzzell's.

That night she dreamed she was aboard the *Empress*, captain of the ship, the sole person responsible for the safety of every soul under her command. At first the seas were calm, but soon a storm came up and waves tossed the vessel about in a savage way as she stood intrepid at the helm. In the dream she heard someone calling for help above the clamor of the wind in the rigging. She saw Clint clinging to the ratlines, barely hanging on, and suddenly, in the way of dreams, she was alone on the ship, the only one who could save him.

She remembered the dream the next morning and it troubled her, though she tried to put it out of her mind. Clint was not the first—nor would he be the last—child who had fallen on hard times. He was bright and strong enough to make his own way in his own good time. Residents in Cambridge, including Captain Grover and Mrs. Buzzell, would look out for him as best they could. But would that be enough? She feared it wouldn't.

That afternoon, she wrote a letter to India and Persia, briefly mentioning Clint and his plight, describing the kindness the townspeople had extended to him. She walked to the post office to mail the letter and then returned to Mrs. Buzzell's. Against her better judgment, she looked around for Clint, but saw no sign of him.

"I will take the stage back to Skowhegan, then up to Bingham at the end of the week," China told Mrs. Buzzell after breakfast several days later. She had spent most of her time in Cambridge walking around the town looking for places to set up her camera, enjoying being outdoors, visiting with Mrs. Buzzell, talking with Mr. Grover and other townspeople, and taking pictures. Two weeks had flown by. "I'll be sorry to see you go; you've been pleasant to have around here," Mrs. Buzzell said. "Entertaining, too, what with you wandering around with that camera and Clint Remick dogging your footsteps. Folks have remarked on it. Gives us all something new to talk about."

China wanted to ask if Mrs. Buzzell had seen Clint of late, but she held her tongue. No sense adding to the talk already going around the village.

She laughed to herself at Mrs. Buzzell's comment. Here she was, the focus of idle talk, just as India and Persia had said she would be. Yet, for a good part of their lives, she and her sisters had been a frequent topic of talk in seaports. They must have surmised it would be no different in the middle of Maine than it was in the middle of the ocean. The talk during those years had upset them, and had been one of the many reasons they had mostly kept to themselves when they were in port. They had not wanted to add any more fuel to the fire than was absolutely necessary. Instead of being annoyed, China did not find Mrs. Buzzell's remark offensive. She would be gone by the end of the week, so it really didn't matter. But she did know she would be haunted by the memory of her encounter with Clint Remick.

14.

China spent her remaining days in Cambridge photographing several houses and barns with interesting facades—with the farmers, their wives, horses, cattle, and children lined up in the yard. She walked to the top of a hill on the Mainstream Road to photograph a particularly scenic view that included the pond, and she also photographed the sawmill and some of the business establishments in Cambridge.

China looked for Clint as she went about the village, but he did not appear. She began to worry. Perhaps something had happened to him; perhaps he was ill. She asked Captain Grover if he had seen the boy but he hadn't, nor had Mrs. Buzzell. Fallen out of the ratlines, swallowed up by the tides of life, China concluded gloomily.

China spent her last evening in Cambridge sitting on the piazza chatting with Mrs. Buzzell as the May evening light fell softly on the landscape and the perfume of lilacs scented the air. After giving the excuse that her hair wasn't properly arranged, then removing her apron, Mrs. Buzzell agreed to let China take her photograph. China posed Mrs. Buzzell near the lilacs at the corner of the house. She included a corner of the piazza in the frame and a glimpse of the barn. Mrs. Buzzell chose not to smile, but the expression on her face, as she gazed toward the camera, revealed her for the woman she was—kind, friendly, and good-hearted.

"Not too much happens here," Mrs. Buzzell commented after China put away the camera and they sat down to watch the sunset, "but it's a nice little town. People are easygoing, they go to church regular, the men work hard to earn a living for their families, and us women work hard to lead good lives." She wrapped a shawl, crocheted in off-white yarn, around her shoulders.

"Yes, that is very evident, Mrs. Buzzell," China replied. "I suppose the church has done a great deal for Clint."

"Oh, the minister tried, but Clint wouldn't give him the time of day. Then word got around that Clint wasn't in the least what anyone could call the deserving poor . . . boy like him is strong enough to work, or could go to the home for orphans where there would be a roof over his head and he'd be fed regular. Nothing much the church could do anyway except maybe see that he had food to eat, and would have, but Clint wouldn't come a-near to eat what they had to give, and the ladies that were cooking it weren't about to hike all over town looking for him. So, everyone just left him to his own devices and did for him as much as he would allow. Which wasn't much."

"Such as sleeping in your barn."

"Yes. And doing chores here and there, or haying or chopping wood, odd jobs, that sort of thing, in return for some food and a bed in the haymow."

"Well, I'm sure he will get by just fine with so many kind people to look out for him, even if he doesn't want them to," China commented.

"So far he has," Mrs. Buzzell replied. "But I worry what he will do come winter. Won't be warm sleeping in a barn."

"No, it certainly won't."

That night China's sleep was disturbed by thoughts of Clint and his plight. When at last she drifted off, she rested well and did not dream of the boy falling out of the ratlines.

The next morning, when the stagecoach rumbled into town, China was ready and waiting, her baggage beside her. She had hoped Clint would show up to carry it for her so she could give him a dollar or two for his service to her. She expected him to show up at any moment, to say good-bye, but there was no sign of him.

China climbed aboard the stagecoach, took her seat, and discovered she was the only passenger. The driver spoke to the horses and with a jangle of harness and the crunch of wheels on the dirt road, the journey back to Skowhegan began.

"Well, here I am," China murmured to herself, "my course marked and set for Bingham." She settled back against the seat, feeling again a sense of being a small piece torn from the whole.

The stagecoach was barely two miles down the road when China saw a solitary figure walking along, headed in the same direction as the stagecoach. She knew at once it was Clint. Over his shoulder he carried a stick, and tied to the end of it was a tattered cloth that she assumed held his few belongings.

On impulse, China leaned out the window and called to the driver, "Stop! Please, stop the stagecoach!"

The driver reined in the horses and the conveyance came to halt a few yards beyond Clint. The boy kept walking with his head down and showed no interest in the stagecoach or China.

"Where are you going?" China said as she stepped out into the rutted road to intercept him.

"Wherever this road takes me," Clint said softly, scuffing the toe of his boot in the dirt, not looking at her, the brim of his battered hat hiding his eyes.

"I see," China said, pausing to think for a moment. "There's room in the stagecoach. I'm the only passenger."

"I can walk wherever I want to go," Clint said gruffly, still not looking at China.

"Well, I will need a cabin boy to help me with my heavy baggage once I get to Skowhegan, so perhaps you'd do me the honor of letting me get you a ticket. I will be happy to have you see to my trunk, and I'll pay you something for your efforts." She did not yet know how her interest in Clint's welfare would play out. She wanted to find a way to see that he had a little money, but in a way that wouldn't injure his pride.

Clint looked at her, then a faint smile spread across his face, the first time she had ever seen him smile. China spoke to the driver and learned she could pay Clint's fare when they reached Skowhegan.

As China turned back to the vehicle to mount the high step, Clint, with perfect manners that surprised her, handed her into the stagecoach, then climbed in behind her.

They rode in silence for a while, Clint curled up in a corner. Some of the tense wariness China had noted in him melted away with the sway of the stagecoach and the lulling sound of the horses' hooves on the road.

Had she done the right thing? Now that she had offered to pay him something for his help, China had no idea what would become of him once they reached Skowhegan. If he wished to continue on to Bingham with her, as her helper, she would need money for his food and lodging. Moreover, she could not allow him to tag after her wearing shabby, dirty clothing—and he needed a bath and a haircut.

She made up her mind to send a telegram to India and Persia requesting additional funds. She wouldn't need a lot. She would write and tell them more about Clint. She hoped they would not become alarmed or leap to any conclusions. She knew they understood the cabin-boy aspect of it, for many a time they had signed on boys to ship with them who were alone in the world and needed work so they could fend for themselves. Sometimes it was the making of those boys; China had seen it happen more than once. Sometimes, of course, it went the other way, and the boys fell into bad habits that did not profit them, or anyone else.

China glanced at Clint. He was dozing. Instinct told her he would profit from her care. He had been well mothered and fathered. He had been loved. He was seeking love and safety; that was all. China knew she could keep him safe. She wasn't sure about love, especially not the maternal kind a child needed. But she knew what it was to love her sisters, her parents, and friends. She knew what it was to be loved by kin and by friends. Surely, this was not so different. Clint had chosen her to be his friend; there was no doubt about that. Wasn't that where love began—with choosing one another?

At the beginning of her journey, on the steamboat headed up the Penobscot, China had expected to arrive at various destinations, meet a few people and get to know them a bit, engage in interesting conversations about the region, take photographs, and travel on to her next port of call, as it were. Never in her wildest imaginings had she expected to acquire a traveling companion, especially not a thirteen-year-old boy.

She did not think India and Persia would begrudge her extra funds for Clint's room and board, if it came to that.

When they arrived at the Elm House, Clint refused to allow China to pay for a room for him. "Costs too much money," he said. "You already paid my ticket here. Anyway, I'm not clean enough to sleep in a bed with sheets."

China made sure Clint had a good supper, which he insisted on eating outside, before he went off to spend the night in the big barn behind the hotel.

In the morning, just after dawn, China got up, dressed, and went to find Clint. She half-expected he would be gone. She found the stable hand already at work, cleaning stalls. He was a small man with kind gray eyes, and it was clear from the way he handled the horses that he understood them and loved being around them.

"You must be looking for the boy," the man said quietly. China nodded. "He's in the haymow. Still asleep, I guess. He yours? Grandson, maybe? Funny place for a kid to sleep."

"No. He's no relation. He has no family, but he traveled here with me, to help with my trunk and other baggage. I just wanted to make sure he is all right and to see that he has a good breakfast before I go on my way."

The man raised his eyebrows in sympathy.

"Well, if he's got no place to go, I could use a hand here. Not a big wage, but there'd be room and board . . . little room in back, off the kitchen."

"That's very kind of you."

China heard the hay stir above her head and Clint came backwards down the loft ladder. Clint looked the stable man in the eye. "Heard what you said, mister, and I thank you for the offer, but I already got a job with Captain Havener here. I'm her cabin boy, and I help her carry things."

"That so?" the man said. He glanced at China. She shrugged her shoulders. "Well, if you change your mind, lad, you let me know." He grabbed the handles of a wheelbarrow and headed for the dung heap just beyond the back door of the barn.

"Well, then, Clint, now that's settled, we have a big day ahead of us, and we can't do much until we have a decent breakfast. Shall we?" China said.

"Might be better if you brought me something to eat out here."

"No. You will come inside and sit at a table with me. But first, go to that water barrel over there and wash your face and hands. And let me pick these spears of hay off your shirt."

After he was as clean as he could be under the circumstances, Clint followed China inside to the dining room. He ate as if he'd never eaten before or ever would again, consuming eggs and fried potatoes, pancakes with maple syrup, biscuits with butter, and applesauce spiced with nutmeg. He drank a big glass of milk and then a mug of tea, well laced with cream so fresh it most likely had come from the cow that very morning.

China watched Clint eat with a sense of satisfaction, knowing that after weeks, perhaps months, of not having enough to eat, he was getting his fill.

"Are we leaving for somewhere today?" Clint asked after he'd scraped the last bit of egg yolk from his plate with the last crumb of a biscuit.

"No. Today you are going to have a bath and get your hair cut, and I'm going to buy you some clothes that fit," China said. "You may consider those things as part of your wages for this month."

Surprise registered on Clint's face, and China couldn't tell if he was pleased or simply shocked at the prospect of having a bath or getting new clothes, or both. She glanced at the watch pinned to the lapel of her jacket. "It's seven o'clock. By now there is a tub of hot soapy water in my room where you will go for your bath. Follow me."

China led Clint to her room on the second floor, unlocked the door, and let him enter. She glanced at the setup, noted that soap and towels had been provided, that steam rose from the water in the big tin tub. Satisfied, she stepped back into the hallway.

"Lock the door, Clint, and enjoy your bath." China handed him the door key. "You will find me downstairs in the ladies' parlor when you have finished."

The desk clerk told China that Holbrook and Hawes's store was the place to buy clothes for Clint. She stopped at the Western Union Telegraph window in the hotel lobby to wire her sisters, asking them to send twenty dollars to her, care of the Bingham House, in Bingham, the next stop on her journey.

That done, she sat down to write them a letter that more fully explained the situation. As she wrote, she found herself enjoying the story she told about Clint and his situation. She told it without embellishment, sticking to the facts as she knew them, adding many details she had not told them in her previous letter. She assured them in plain terms that there was no need for alarm. Nonetheless, she could not help wondering what they might say to one another, and to all their friends at Abbott's Reach, about her request.

15.

Clint emerged almost shiny from his bath, his wet hair combed back away from his face. His skin was very white just below his hairline where his hat had blocked the sun. By contrast his nose and cheeks were almost ruddy. He grinned and his eyes shone with happiness.

"That was nice. I smell like soap," he said.

"You clean up good, Clint," China said. "There's a barber here in the hotel. Here's a quarter. Go get your hair cut." She handed Clint the coin. He stared at it, at a loss for words.

"I never had my own quarter before," he said.

"Not even when you worked in the woods last winter?"

"No. I worked for room and board. That's why I left the woods camp. The boss paid the men, but he wouldn't pay me. Just gave me a bed to sleep in and three meals a day. I told him I needed money, too, but he wouldn't give me any, no matter how hard I worked."

"Well, now you have a quarter. You earned it carrying my things. Go spend it on a haircut."

Clint turned the coin over in his hand, examining it. "It's pretty. It's got Lady Liberty on it. Hate to spend it. If you cut my hair, we could save this."

"I don't know how to cut hair, Clint. Go to the barbershop. That's an order."

Clint grinned at her again. He raised his hand in a salute, came to attention, and said, "Aye, aye, Captain!"

"Hmm. You are improving as a cabin boy. That makes it hard for me to do without you," China said, smiling back at him. There was more than a little truth to her statement. Already, she found herself relying on him—not just to carry things, but to talk to, and take care of. Surely, there was no harm in that—just for the summer, until he could find a place he wanted to be—or someplace where he was wanted, with someone who would be good to him.

While she waited, China made a list of what Clint would need for clothing. He would need two of everything—underclothing, stockings, shirts, trousers. He would need a jacket, a cap, a good pair of boots, and a small valise to carry his things in. She estimated those things would cost at least ten dollars, if she did not pay top dollar. But she would not skimp on the boots. A boy as lively as Clint needed boots that would take a lot of hard wear.

The change in Clint was striking as he acquired new clothing. He carried himself with more confidence. He seemed taller, and he certainly looked a great deal better with the dirt scrubbed off him and his hair nicely trimmed.

"Very fine," China said, as she surveyed him wearing his new finery when he came out of the dressing room at the store.

There was such gratitude in Clint's eyes when he saw himself in the big plate-glass mirror, China's throat constricted with sudden tears, which she choked back, lest she embarrass the boy.

"What kind of jacket would you like, Clint?" China asked, when she dared speak again.

"I want one like a cabin boy would wear."

"Then it will have to be navy blue wool with a flat collar and lapels and deep slash pockets. Very warm. Probably too warm for summer, but if you don't need to wear it, you can keep it rolled up in your valise." China turned to the salesman. "Do you have anything like that, in a lightweight wool?"

The salesman did. He even had one that fit Clint perfectly. It had been ordered for the son of one of the man's customers, but it didn't fit the way the boy's mother thought it ought to, so she had refused to pay for it. The jacket was at least a year old, the salesman said, and he was willing to let it go for one dollar, far less than its actual value.

"Boy!" Clint said when the salesman held the jacket for him to slide his arms into the sleeves. "Oh, boy!" The jacket fit as if it had been made for him.

Clint chose a new cap, but refused to give up his own battered, broad-brimmed hat.

"Belonged to my father," he said quietly, not looking at China, a heavy mood cast in the lines of his body.

At China's request, the clerk placed the old hat in a box, so Clint, wearing a new cap and new clothes, could take it with him. China asked that Clint's old clothes be wrapped in brown paper and sent to the Elm House. She did not want to discard them—ragged though they were, they were pretty much all that Clint owned.

"And tonight, Clint, you will sleep in a room of your own in a bed with sheets," China said. "No more barns."

Clint ducked his head, turning away from her. China knew why. There were tears in his eyes, and he did not think it manly to weep, especially not in front of her.

They spent the remainder of the day walking around Skowhegan. The town had three photography studios, one belonging to C. A. Paul, another to Bridge and Merrow, and a third run by S. F. Conant.

"Shall we go in?" China asked as they passed the establishment of Bridge and Merrow.

Clint nodded. He held the door open for her and bowed, playfully, as China entered the store.

Photographic portraits of men, women, and children hung on the walls of the studio. China looked at them closely and took note of the details in the photographs, the lighting, the props, facial expressions, what the subjects wore, and the backdrop the studio had provided.

"Can you do photographs like that?" Clint asked.

"Don't know. Haven't really tried making photographs indoors. My sisters thought I ought to have a small studio like this and work at home. But since I am only just beginning to learn this craft, I thought I would have better luck outdoors, with natural light."

A young man came out of a back room and asked if he could help them.

"We just wanted to look at your work, thank you," China said.

"I'm Mr. Merrow. I'm between appointments. I could take a portrait of you and your boy right now, if you want," the man said. He was neatly dressed, his brown hair brushed smoothly away from his brow.

China almost said yes, so she could get a look at his camera and studio setup.

"No, thank you. We're just passing through town," she said. "But I must say, I do admire your portraits."

"Nice of you to say so, ma'am," Mr. Merrow said.

The door opened and a young woman carrying an infant came in.

"Ah, my next appointment," Mr. Merrow said. "If you will excuse me . . ."

China and Clint went out to the street and wandered along, looking in shop windows.

Eventually, they found their way to the outskirts of the business district and to the banks of the Kennebec, where the river made a ninety-degree turn, known locally, they had been informed by a storekeeper, as The Eddy.

"This is one of Maine's mighty rivers," China commented. "Before now, I had only seen the mouth of it. Another of Maine's great rivers is the Penobscot. The early settlers in Maine used the rivers as a road, to get far into these regions where they built houses and farmed and went into lumbering. Perhaps your ancestors came up this very river in a canoe."

"Don't know," Clint said. "But I do know this: We should have brought a lunch so we could sit here and eat, and listen to the river. Look up there. That's a bald eagle."

16.

The stagecoach ride upriver to Bingham did not follow the Kennebec River as China had anticipated. It wound through East Madison, past the eastern edge of Wesserunsett Lake and on toward a crossroads where they turned west and lumbered up a long hill and down the other side to yet another crossroads. Here, they turned north and the horses leaned into the harness to pull the stagecoach up yet another steep hill. The driver halted at the summit.

One of the passengers, traveling alone, a woman China thought might be in her seventies, smiled and said, "This is Robbin's Hill. Irving Young, the stagecoach driver, always stops here a few minutes to rest the horses. It's a fine view, the best there is." She opened the door and the stagecoach driver helped her out. China and Clint followed.

"Over there, all those blue mountains," the woman continued, "that's the western mountains over to Kingfield and Rangeley and places such as I've never been. And that there, that mountain that looks like it's holding up the sky, that's Moxie Mountain. That's the mountain that tells us we're almost home." She put her hand atop her hat to keep the breeze from blowing it away. The ends of the pale blue ribbons tied under her chin streamed out behind her and her voluminous black skirt threatened mutiny. For a moment, China thought, the lady resembled a character out of a Jane Austen novel.

"Are we going to those mountains?" Clint asked.

"No," China replied, as she consulted a guidebook published by the railroad company. "But we are going in the direction of Moxie Mountain."

The woman leaned on China's arm as they made their way back to the stagecoach to resume their journey.

Soon, the stagecoach rolled into Solon village and stopped at the Caratunk House, a hotel of three and a half stories with green shutters framing the windows on the first and the third floors, and with a two-story ell jutting at a right angle from the main building. Few vehicles were about, and no one stirred in any of the yards of the houses lining the main road. Clint descended from the stagecoach, stretched his long arms, and looked around.

"Pretty little town," he said. "But awful quiet."

"Shouldn't be," China answered. "More than a thousand people live here, so I was told."

China reached for her camera, walked across the road to set it up, and aimed it at the hotel. Just as she was about to expose the plate, Clint walked into the frame, which also included the stagecoach. Clint, unaware he was about to become part of the photograph, turned his head, as if something just out of the camera's view had caught and held his attention. The brim of his cap cast a shadow over his face, rendering him suddenly anonymous.

China registered all that in her mind even as she removed the lens cap to expose the negative, then replaced it. She knew instinctively this photograph was one she would be proud to have made—providing she had calculated the timing correctly. Someday, she thought, I will be glad I have this picture—if, indeed, it proved to be technically correct, and if when she processed it, she didn't make a mess of the chemicals. She almost laughed aloud at the thought. Here she was, pursuing ghost images made by light on a plate-glass negative, and without an iota of confidence that what she was doing actually would turn out to be anything worth even a minute of the time she had spent on it. No wonder India and Persia had protested. At least their pursuits were solid and tangible, creating things they could see and touch even as they went about producing them.

It was not the first time it occurred to China that the photographs she was taking would serve as a kind of memory, recording details of light, shadow, and form, giving shape to what her own mind and eyes failed to register. This particular photograph today would serve to nudge her ability to recall what had happened at the very moment Clint had stepped into the frame, turned away from the camera, and she had recorded his image.

This is what life is, she thought—a series of fleeting moments, moments in time, impossible to recall individually, which somehow make up what we know as the fabric of daily life. This is what defines who we are. Her photographs, she saw, would serve as a more reliable kind of memory, reminding her of what even now she was beginning to forget.

After a fine meal of deer steak, potatoes, and applesauce, with gingerbread and cream for dessert, the passengers climbed back into the stagecoach for the eight-mile trek upriver. It was late afternoon when they came at last to the final leg of road that wound down a hill and along the Kennebec River to Bingham village.

The town, which had a population of eight hundred and twenty-eight, lay on a flat plain of ground not far from the river. The Kennebec was no longer visible once they had passed the meetinghouse sitting on high ground a short distance from the graveyard. The long main road had but one slight curve, and as they rode along, China saw how the streets ran west toward the river and east toward what she presumed was a street parallel to the main road. Bingham was a town laid out in a grid, so very unusual in Maine, where roads often led from a hub and fanned out in all directions like the spokes of a wheel, or simply meandered along with no apparent rhyme or reason, rather like a cow path.

Green ridges, their gracefully rounded tops resembling the backs of woolly sheep, cradled the town of Bingham, giving China the sense of being swaddled in the folds of a very gigantic quilt. She had never experienced anything like it. All that soft green light, the intervales glimpsed between the ridges and threaded with lines of mysterious dirt roads, which surely led to outlying farms. Those roads intrigued her. She glanced at Clint, who was equally absorbed.

"There's something about this place ...," he remarked, his thought trailing off as if he could not find words to express how the sight of the town affected him.

A farm wagon rumbled by, driven by a man wearing a straw hat with a wide brim. Three small children with blond hair sat in the back of the wagon. They smiled and waved as they passed the stagecoach.

China spotted three nicely dressed women chatting in front of a general store. A group of girls and boys ran alongside the stagecoach until one of the women called to them to come away.

"I may need to send for more glass-plate negatives," China said to Clint as her eyes drank in the angles of rooftops, the colors of the ladies' hats, the rigs and wagons tied up in front stores.

"Maybe a whole crate," Clint said, grinning, understanding at once how the beauty of Bingham's landscape made China want to record it all. "Good thing you got a cabin boy."

"Guess you'll earn your keep now," she retorted, making Clint laugh, a happy sound that endeared him to her all the more.

17.

The stagecoach rumbled to a halt in the dooryard of the Bingham House, a three-story structure with a two-story piazza across the front, similar in architecture to the Caratunk House in Solon, though somewhat smaller. It was a well-kept building, its shutters freshly painted green. Two elderly men dressed in black jackets and pants sat on the deacon's bench on the piazza. They looked up, only mildly interested as the stagecoach passengers stepped to the ground. The hotel had an air of stolid respectability about it. The curtains at the windows looked as if they had been washed and starched only recently, China noted with approval.

Giant elms, like the columns of an ancient temple, stood on both sides of the main road, as if holding up the blue sky over the town, blanketing the road with lulling shade to shield it from the hot, sunny summer days that were to come.

As China looked around, she felt the colors, the shapes of the hills, the taste of the air seep through her skin into her heart. She couldn't stop smiling. Her eyes darted here and there, already picking out spots where she would set up her camera to photograph the village.

The hotel lobby smelled of cedar oil furniture polish and dried balsam fir. It was empty except for an old lady wearing a ruffled white cap, its strings untied, a type of headdress that had not been fashionable for more than forty years. The woman's black dress, with narrow sleeves and a boned bodice, was of shiny, cotton sateen and bespoke an era many years past. She sat with an air of quiet majesty in a wing chair drawn near a window, crocheting lace edging. She looked up as China and Clint approached, and smiled in a friendly, welcoming way.

"We're all in an uproar here today," the woman confided. "The parrot just flew out the door. Buster nipped a man that was in his cups and he's all a-lather, and we just heard that one of the ropes that pulls the ferry across the river has frayed and broke. Mr. Robinson the ferryman hasn't another, and it will be into next week before he can get a new one. Don't know how folks will get back and forth across the river except by canoe. Well, be that as it may, not a thing I can do about it at my age. Now, if I may ask, who be ye, and what can I do for ye?"

She spoke with an odd lilt that reminded China of the burr in the voices of stevedores and other men she had heard conversing with one another in harbors along the coast of England. Her interest in the town sharpened. In some respects, being here felt as if she had taken a few steps back in time.

"I sent a telegram to a Mrs. Chase a month or so ago, asking to reserve rooms. I am Miss China Havener, and this is my . . . factotum . . . Clint Remick," China said.

"I gathered that might be who ye be," the woman said. "Just sign the book over there on the desk. Mrs. Chase who runs this establishment—I'm her mother, Mrs. Sawyer—is out back, trying to coax the parrot out of a tree. Don't know how long it will take. First time the parrot ever took off like that."

"Thank you," China said as she signed the guest register. "Is there anything I can do to help?"

"Not unless ye know anything about parrots or how to splice rope, or how to get that great larrup of a man the dog bit to quit acting like he was about to die."

"Where might I find the gentleman with the nipped ankle?" China asked.

"Oh, he's there in the parlor, moaning and groaning. I'd have sent for the doctor, but he's over to Concord on the other side of the river. It's not likely he's going to be home anytime soon, what with the ferry rope broke. I don't suppose ye know how to charm blood to make him stop bleeding all over the carpet?"

"No, I can't say as I do."

"Well, probably he don't need that, or even believe in it, seeing as how he's wanting a doctor."

"I never heard of charming blood. How does that work?"

"No one knows for sure, but around here, more than a few folks can do it. I've seen it done myself. Man up Moscow way, lived on a farm up in the hills, sliced his leg deep and bad while he was out back splitting wood with a dull ax. As luck would have it, the woman who was his nearest neighbor knew the blood charm. We'd come to spend the afternoon with the man's wife.

"So the neighbor worked the charm, the bleeding stopped, and we were able to get him down to Bingham village where we found the doctor home. We'd no sooner got to the doctor's house and the bleeding commenced again, but the doctor took some fancy stitches in the man's leg, and he was all right. But he wouldn't have been if the neighbor hadn't come along when she did."

China smiled at the old lady. "That's a very interesting story."

"No story. Fact," Mrs. Sawyer said, fixing her dark eyes on China's.

China turned to Clint. "Wait here," she said.

"Wait," Clint whispered. "What's a factotum?"

"A handyman."

"Oh. Well, that explains the 'tote 'em' part."

China laughed at Clint's verbal quip. "Wait here," she said again.

In the parlor she found a bearded man with a narrow face and ruddy cheeks sitting in an overstuffed chair with his foot propped on a stool.

"Blasted dog," the man muttered as China came into the room. "Boston terrier. Came right for me, took a chunk right out of my shin. And where's the doctor, I ask you? What kind of place is this, anyway? Look, I'm bleeding bad."

"Yes, you do seem to be," China agreed. A red stain had soaked through the man's stocking, but fortunately, China noted, not on the carpet, as Mrs. Sawyer had feared.

"I'm waiting for the doctor. Do you know when he will get here?"

"No. He's stranded on the other side of the river. Ferry rope broke, so I am told. If you would allow me, Mr. . . . ."

"Ferguson."

The man eyed China with distrust, as if it were her fault the ferry rope had broken, stranding the doctor on the far side of the river.

"Mr. Ferguson, I have some small experience with wounds, and will do my best to help."

China had, more than once, bound up a sailor's gashed hand or bashed head, and once she had helped her father splint a broken leg when they were far out to sea and weeks from landfall. Basic doctoring was one of the many skills she had acquired living aboard the *Empress*.

Mr. Ferguson sat up straighter in the chair.

"The doctor's not coming, you say?"

"That is correct. So if you would undress your foot ..."

Mr. Ferguson removed his shoe and stocking with a show of irritation and reluctance, accompanied by moans and groans. China inspected the wound.

"You are in luck, Mr. Ferguson; I don't believe the bite is as bad as it appears. The dog's teeth pierced the skin, no doubt about that, but the wound is a puncture rather than a slash. It's deep enough, by the looks of it, to disturb a few veins. In the meantime, until the doctor can get here, the wound ought to be washed and bandaged."

China called to Clint and told him to ask Mrs. Sawyer for a basin of warm water, a small towel, and some bandaging material. With those items in hand, she cleaned and dressed the wound.

"I hope I don't get the rabies," Mr. Ferguson grumbled.

"Well, I can't vouch for that, Mr. Ferguson, but since the dog was merely frightened and reacted accordingly, so Mrs. Sawyer said, it is unlikely you have to worry about rabies. However, that is a question you ought to put to the doctor when you see him."

Mr. Ferguson drew a flask out of his pocket, removed the cap, and downed a big swallow.

"I thank you, ma'am," he said, raising the flask in salute.

"You are quite welcome," China said, drawing back to avoid breathing in any alcohol-laced fumes. She gathered up the basin, washcloth, and scissors and returned to the lobby.

"Mr. Ferguson has been tended to," she said to Mrs. Sawyer. "Now, how do I get out to the backyard?"

Mrs. Sawyer pointed to a corner of the lobby. "Right through that door," she said, with a wave of her hand.

"Come along, Clint. This won't take long," China said.

"Your factotum is right behind you, Miss Havener," Clint said gravely .

China gave him a long look. "How very droll of you to say so," she replied.

"You're the one who called me that. And all this time I thought I was just a cabin boy."

China shook her head in mock exasperation.

A large green parrot, perched on the limb of a tall maple, shifted from one foot to the other and bobbed its head up and down. Beneath the tree, a woman China assumed was Mrs. Chase gazed up at the bird. Mrs. Chase wore a brown dress, the hemline falling just to the tops of her black shoes. Her dark hair was threaded with gray and her hands were planted firmly on her hips. The expression on her face was one of pure disgust.

"That cussed bird! This never happened before," she said. "I blame it all on Mr. Ferguson, lurching around like he did, tromping on poor Buster and causing an uproar. And the door left open and out flew this blasted bird! If I can't get him in, he's going to be supper for a bald eagle, you mark my words."

"I'm Miss Havener," China said. "Just arrived."

"Pleased to meet you. I'm Mrs. Nyra Chase. I run the hotel. Whatever are you doing out here in yard?"

"Helping," China said.

To Clint's and Mrs. Chase's very great surprise, China made distinct parrot-like vocalizations that sounded like clicks and whistles, with an occasional "or-auk" thrown in for good measure. After a few moments, the parrot cocked his head toward her and appeared to listen.

"Pretty boy, pretty boy," the bird said.

China whistled and clicked her tongue again, then she held out her arm. To Clint's and Mrs. Chase's amazement, the parrot lifted his wings, flew down from the tree, landed on China's arm, and walked up it to perch regally on her shoulder. It uttered chirring sounds near her ear.

"How did you do that?" Clint asked, his eyes wide with wonder and admiration.

"We often had parrots like this one on the *Empress*. Once, one flew to the top of the rigging and wouldn't come down. None of the crew could catch it either. I took it into my head that if the bird thought there was another parrot around, it might come down on its own. So I improvised. It worked then, and it seems to have worked now." China stroked the bird's head and walked back to the hotel. Clint and Mrs. Chase followed in her wake.

"His name is Percy," Mrs. Chase informed Clint. "He's been in my family at least seventy-five years. He came up the river in a canoe with my grandsir. He'd been a seaman, but took it into his head he'd rather be a farmer. He fought in the War for Independence, so when he was given a hundred acres for his service, he came here to settle. He always said the parrot once belonged to a British seaman who was captured during a battle, but that may have been wishful thinking on my grandsir's part."

After Percy had been restored to his cage, China said to Mrs. Chase, "I understand the ferryman is in need of someone who can splice a rope."

"Why, yes, indeed," Mrs. Chase said, regarding China with even greater interest.

"And how do I find him?"

"Plato Robinson? Well, you take the road right by the meeting-house and it will take you to the ferry landing. It's a bit of a walk, but if your boy can harness the horse, you can take my buggy," Mrs. Chase said.

China looked at Clint. "Well?"

"Of course I can harness a horse," Clint said, giving her look. "Been doing that since I was barely five years old."

"As a factotum, Clint, your skills constantly surpass my expectations," China said.

Clint grinned at her.

"Let me warn you, though," Mrs. Chase said. "Buster will want to ride along."

18.

Clint took the reins, China sat beside him, and Buster squeezed in between them.

"Driving a horse is another thing I'm pretty good at," Clint pointed out to China.

"A man of many parts," China agreed. It pleased her to see Clint having a good time, to banter with him, and to see his interest in everything around him. It was almost as if he were coming back to himself after a long time away.

At the landing, the ferryman reached for the horse's bridle. He was a good-looking man, China noted. Unlike most men who sported lavish mustaches and side whiskers, he was clean-shaven. His eyes were as blue as the sky, and he looked directly at her when he spoke. His glance was friendly and unassuming, the expression on his face open and engaging. He spoke gently to the horse and stroked its nose.

"Ferry's not going today, ma'am. I got a broke rope, and you'd think I'd know something about how to splice in a new piece to get me through until I can replace the frayed one, but bless me if I don't know how," the ferryman said. He wore gray wool pants, a red cotton shirt, black leather boots with wooden soles, a battered hat with a wide brim, and leather gloves. "I see you have Buster with you—you must be staying at the hotel." He patted the dog's head and Buster wagged his stubby tail happily.

The situation, China surmised, was a delicate one. Here she was, a woman, a stranger, about to reveal that she did know how to splice in a new section of rope, a job that fell firmly into the realm of man's work, not woman's.

"You must be Mr. Robinson," China said, determined to approach the issue with as much diplomacy as possible.

"Why, yes, I am—Plato Robinson at your service." Surprise registered on his face that she should know his name. He touched the brim of his hat in a kind of salute conveying politeness, friendliness, and unmistakable interest.

"Mrs. Chase at the hotel told us about your dilemma—"

"This is Miss Havener," Clint said, a tone of respect in his voice. "She used to sail a ship around the world."

"You don't say?" Plato said, looking at China with even greater interest.

"This is my young companion, Clint Remick. He, on the other hand, has never been to sea," China said.

"Nor seen it either," Clint commented.

"Miss Havener, this sounds to me like a story I want to hear sometime," Plato said, smiling warmly at her.

"It would take too long to recount here, Mr. Robinson, but what Clint says is true. I was born at sea and lived all my life aboard my father's ship. I learned many things from that experience, including how to splice rope. I wonder, Mr. Robinson, if you'd allow me to . . . To have a look at the offending rope, to determine if I have the necessary know-how to be of any assistance."

Plato took off his hat, revealing wavy gray hair. He thought a minute. "Well, I can't see any harm in that. Maybe I'll learn something in the process." He gave a little bow, held out his hand, and helped China alight from the buggy. He ushered her with something akin to gallantry to the ferry to show her the rope.

China inspected the rope carefully, noting its number of plies and assessing whether or not a splice was possible.

"Yes, I see . . . not as bad as I feared. I believe I can mend this so it will serve until you can get a new rope, Mr. Robinson. I will need a length of rope the same size as this section and a nail . . . I'd prefer a marlinespike, such as seamen use, but a good-size nail will do. And I will need some stout twine and a bit of warm tar or pitch. Either one will do."

"Well, let me go see what's in the shed," Plato said as he headed for the house just down the road from the ferry landing.

"If you don't mind, Miss Havener, I'd like to point out that splicing rope is going to mess up your dress something awful," Clint said.

"That's true, Clint, which is why I will instruct you and Mr. Robinson in what to do. That way both of you will learn something about rope splicing."

Plato returned with a tapered, hand-forged nail with a finer point than China had dared hope for, a small pot of tar, a brush, the required length of rope, and a ball of cord.

China showed Plato how to use the nail to loosen the strands of both ends of the broken rope, and demonstrated how to weave the ends of the new rope securely into the old one. Then she took it apart and helped Mr. Robinson do the weaving. When that was done, she instructed Clint in the task of wrapping the whole together with the cord. He held it in place while Plato coated it with tar. He handled the tar carefully so no one's clothing was soiled in the process.

"This should last until you can get a new rope," China said. "But check it frequently to make sure it doesn't weaken. Even the best splice can fray and separate when you least expect it."

Plato swept his hat from his head and made China an elegant bow.

"Perhaps you and Clint would do me the honor of crossing the mighty Kennebec on my ferry to test this rope repair."

China was drawn in by his courteous manner and almost giggled like a schoolgirl. She hadn't had this much fun in a long time.

"We'd be honored," she said, with the utmost courtesy, not looking at Plato and hoping he had not noticed the high color she felt burning on her cheeks.

Clint checked to make certain the horse was secured to the granite hitching post before he, China, and Buster stepped aboard the ferry.

"This won't be just a frolic of a trip," Plato said. "I see Dr. Piper coming along the road across the river; that's the Concord side. I'd say we timed it just about right."

The Kennebec was, China estimated, only a hundred feet wide at that point, with a strong, smooth current. A light breeze blew upriver and the air smelled sweet and damp, devoid of the salt tang and fishy low-tide odor so familiar to her. The sun warmed her shoulders, and she felt completely at home on this odd watercraft that in no way resembled the sleek, graceful lines of the *Empress*.

She glanced at Clint and saw that he was absorbed in helping Plato work the ropes to move the ferry smoothly over the water. Buster sat off to one side out of the way, his nose sniffing the breeze. Clearly, it wasn't his first ferry ride.

The water is wide, China thought, and hummed a few bars of that old song.

"Now, that's as pretty an old tune as I've ever liked to sing," said Plato.

The ferry fetched up gently against the Concord side of the riverbank. Dr. Piper tipped his hat to China, led his horse and buggy aboard the ferry, and paid Plato the five-cent toll. The doctor was neatly dressed in a white shirt, a black suit, and a vest. He had about him an air of calm and confidence, as if he had seen much of the highs and lows of life and remained unswayed by either extreme.

"Doc, this is Miss Havener and her boy, Clint. They're traveling in these parts and staying up to the Bingham House," Plato said.

"She knows how to splice rope," Clint volunteered.

China gave him a look that said, "Be still." Clint's eyes gleamed with mischief.

"An unusual skill in a lady," Dr. Piper said. "Though one I surmise would come in handy some time or other."

"Well, it did today, Doc. Otherwise, you'd have been on the other side of the river until the middle of next week," Plato said.

"You don't say?" Dr. Piper replied. "Well, maybe my horse and buggy wouldn't have made it across, but I'd have hired Lonzo Bean to paddle me home in his canoe in return for the use of my rig until the ferry was fixed. A lot of folks on both sides of this river depend on me, you know."

"Including a Mr. Ferguson at the hotel who had the misfortune to annoy this little dog. Buster here abandoned his manners and bit Mr. Ferguson's ankle. I cleaned and bandaged it, but he would like you to take a look at it, Doctor," China said.

"I'll go there directly," Dr. Piper replied.

"Tell me, Dr. Piper, is this region considered good for the health?" China asked.

"Indeed it is, Miss Havener. Good air, clean water, and plenty of it, far enough from the centers of civilization to have a low rate of infectious diseases, though from time to time I see epidemics, fevers, and other ailments that put more than a few in the graveyard. But those are soon replaced by an abundance of new babies, so things tend to even out, eventually."

"I see."

"Am I to assume you are here for the improvement of your health?"

"No. Merely traveling to see something of inland Maine."

"Then you have come to the right place. There are lakes and ponds aplenty not far from here, and pretty little farms on roads that run up and down these hills. And the town itself, as you already have seen, is most pleasing to the eye. As for food and lodging, you can't do much better than the Bingham House."

"I've also heard that the region has people who know how to stop blood, which I believe is the term Mrs. Chase used.

"That is true. Some believe it works, some don't. As for me, I've seen a lot of things in my time when it comes to sickness and other ailments, so I'm not one to scoff at what seems to be a tradition in these parts. In fact, I have been a witness to blood stopping. I even know of one man who could work his blood charm from a distance of several miles. He even could work it on animals. To this day, scientific explanation for it eludes me. Still, I don't dismiss it as mere superstition."

"Then how do you account for it?"

"That, Miss Havener, I cannot say. Some things, as you know, must be taken on faith. Blood charming is one of those things."

When the ferry slid up to the Bingham side of the riverbank, Dr. Piper climbed into his buggy, tipped his hat to China, spoke to the horse, and drove away.

"Thank you, Mr. Robinson, for the ferry ride," China said, offering him her hand. "I wonder if you might allow me to take a photograph of you and your ferry tomorrow morning?"

"Why, I'd be honored. But there's one condition," Plato said.

"And what is that?"

"That you and the boy eat supper with me at Mrs. Chase's this evening. I board there, you see."

China felt her cheeks grow warm again, and noted that the color in Plato's face had heightened, too. His eyes were smiling at her again, and looking deeply into hers.

"Why, thank you. We'd be honored. What time should we meet in the dining room?"

"Well, they set down to the table around five o'clock at Mrs. Chase's."

"We will be there," China said.

Plato helped her into the buggy, and Buster jumped in behind her. Clint took the reins and they drove away.

China could not resist a backward glance at Plato. He gazed after her in a way that had occurred only a very few times in her life.

"Are you all right?" Clint asked. "You look funny."

"It's been a long day," China said.

"And interesting. The most interesting day I've had since . . . Well . . . since my folks went." Clint gazed at China with something akin to reverence.

"And why is that?"

"Well, I heard you talk to a parrot and it understood you. And I learned how to splice rope."

Clint clucked to the horse as they turned onto the main road, heading toward the hotel. Buster barked several times, apparently just for the fun of it.

"And Buster likes me."

China felt a rush of affection for Clint. She wanted to hug him fiercely and assure him that he could trail around in her wake as long he wished. Instead, she laughed aloud with such abandon it made Clint laugh, too, and Buster bark more loudly.

19.

"You have some letters," Mrs. Chase said when China and Clint returned to the hotel. "Came this morning."

China looked eagerly at the return addresses on the letters. One was from India and Persia. The other was a fat envelope from Fanny Harding. China surmised it contained messages from everyone at Abbott's Reach. The third piece of mail, addressed to Clint, was a postal card featuring the Bangor boat. China held it out to him.

"What's that?" Clint asked, his eyes wide with disbelief.

"Mail," China said.

"Can't be for me. I don't know anybody."

China turned the card over and read the address. " 'Master Clint Remick, care of Bingham House, Somerset County, Bingham, Maine.' I believe that's you."

Clint reached for the card, held it carefully as if he feared it might sprout wings and fly away, as the parrot had, to the top of the highest tree.

"I never got mail before," he said. He looked at the picture of the Bangor boat, turned the card over, and stared at his name. "Master Clint Remick. That's me. What does 'master' mean?"

" 'Master' is the proper way to address a boy who is not yet a man. When you are grown up you will be addressed as 'mister.' " China watched him read the postcard. Then he read it aloud, as if to make certain it was real.

"It says, 'Dear Clint, I understand you are serving as cabin boy to Miss China Havener, lately of the *Empress*. I commend you for choosing so wise and worthy a captain. Though you and I have never met, I look forward to the day when we shall. Yours most respectfully, Dr. Samuel Webber.' I don't know who that is."

"No reason why you should. Dr. Webber and his wife Maude are dear friends of mine. They live at Abbott's Reach at Fort Point, near where my sisters India and Persia live."

"But why would he write to me? I don't know him."

"I wrote to my sisters about you and told them you have joined me on my travels. No doubt they shared my letter with Dr. Webber and the others at Abbott's Reach. I think this is his way of saying, welcome aboard. Come. We must go to our rooms and spruce up a bit. It's less than an hour until suppertime."

"Do you think Dr. Webber would want me to write back?" Clint held the card gently, as if it and the writing upon it bore the invisible, but palpable, essence of the writer.

"I'm sure Dr. Webber does not expect it, Clint, but the courteous thing would be to send a reply."

Clint said nothing until they reached the top of the stairs. He stood by the door to his room for a moment, as if trying to decide something.

"I've written letters before . . . To my mother and father . . . but they were . . . gone, so there was no place to send the letters, even if I'd had a penny for the stamp," Clint said, his gaze turned downward. China noticed he never used the word died when he referred to his parents; in fact, he didn't mention them much at all.

"Did you keep the letters?" China asked softly, moved by what he had said.

"I burned them, thinking maybe the smoke would go all the way up to heaven and my folks would know it was from me, and that I was . . . Thinking of them."

And missing them terribly, China sensed. She resisted an impulse to enfold him in her arms to shield him from the hurt he had suffered, which still affected every moment of his life. But she was not his mother, she was his captain. He expected direction from her, to obey her commands. Indeed, she feared making such a gesture might cause him to bolt and run off forever. It was hard to know how much care Clint would accept from her, beyond providing a room for him to sleep in, food, and clothing. She did not want to impose on him any familiarity beyond what he wanted to accept. She knew anything she did for him had to be on his terms, a tacit agreement between them.

"Well, then, it seems to me you've had good practice in writing letters, and if you are inclined to respond to Dr. Webber's card, I know you will make a good job of it. Wait a moment." She hurried into her room and returned with a sheet of paper, an envelope, and a pencil for him. "I'll rap on your door in a little bit, Clint. Don't forget to comb your hair."

Clint nodded and looked up at China with what she thought was guarded affection, which startled her, since she hadn't expected any such thing.

In her own room, China tossed her hat onto the bed, settled in a chair by the window, and opened her first letter eagerly. One of the best parts of any journey, she had learned as a child, was receiving letters from cousins, aunts, uncles, grandparents, friends and acquaintances containing news of home.

Fort Point, Maine, June 2, 1882

Dear Sister,

You have been much on my mind since your departure, and not a day—indeed, at times, not even an hour—has gone by but what I don't find myself wishing for your advice, or needing to ask you about some detail of our life at sea. I have begun to compile a collection of sea chanteys, interweaving it with recollections of our life at sea, and with excerpts from old letters sent and received, and from the Empress's ship logs. Often there are things I can't quite recall, nor can Persia, and I am certain you would be able to supply what is missing. Nonetheless, I am happy to say I am making some small progress in my endeavor. I am corresponding with old friends from our seafaring days, and writing letters to librarians at various universities. I also will need to read the dusty tomes I have requested from said libraries. There is, of course, the expense of postage, which I have included in my budget for this project.

Already I have discovered that few books dealing with the subject of sea chanteys, or indeed, the lives of women who were born and lived at sea, even exist. Apparently, I am about to become a pioneer in the subject, though it's a bit like landing on a desert isle.

I began my project by talking with Sam Webber, who was most helpful. He has a sharp memory, and even consents to sing the sea chanteys that he remembers. Thus I was able to play on the piano the tunes he supplied and notate them, which is of the greatest importance. Having the words without the tunes would not serve my purpose at all.

Our friends are well, and there is much visiting back and forth between us and the folks at Abbott's Reach, one of the things I especially like about living here at Fort Point, even though there are times when I miss our dear house in Castine. Fanny and Ellis are busy with summer guests—the season of the rusticator is upon them. Fanny has added our house, because of Persia's work, to her list of outings for her guests, but I will let Persia tell you about that.

Not a day goes by but what we do not miss you and wish for your company.

Your loving sister,
India

⚬✍⚬

June 3, 1882, early morning

My dear sister,

India is not yet awake, but that is not unusual. She often stays up late reading and making notes for her sea chantey project. I rise early because the animals demand it. I speak, of course, of the sheep. I have four ewes and a ram now, a small flock of chickens, and a collie dog named Swan. I also *have a garden I planted to peas, potatoes, corn, string beans, cucumbers, beets, pumpkins, radishes, lettuce, and squash. I like to be up before the blackflies in order to inspect my rows to see how things are growing. The apple blossoms have gone by, and I believe we will have enough apples for sauce and jelly in the fall. The raspberry bushes are thriving, and already I can taste the pies and jam I will make from them.*

The sheep are out to pasture, of course, but I pen them at night to protect them from stray dogs and such. Thus, I must clean up behind them each morning.

When the "heavy" work is done, I go to my wheel and spin for a while.

India and I have worked it out that I will cook breakfast and she will cook the noontime dinner. For supper we make a lunch of what is left from dinner. We have divided other household chores accordingly.

But I digress. I am about to acquire a loom from an old lady in Stockton Springs. She said it belonged to her grandmother, so it is of a venerable age. This lady recalls how to "dress" the loom, and will work with me to get it set up in the summer kitchen. She will teach me a few of the basic points of weaving.

Fanny is so enthusiastic about my knitting and spinning, she recommends outings here to her guests. Later on when the garden comes in, I will sell vegetables. Fanny said I must sell my produce only to her, so I will have a ready market when the time comes. However, I will make sure to preserve most of it for our own use.

When India wants to rest her eyes, she takes a turn with the hoe in the garden—a great help to me.

India and I have talked about your association with the boy, Clint, and we are glad to know you have someone to help with your baggage. Perhaps somewhere on your travels he will find a suitable home where he will be happy and can go to school. We are relieved to know you have a companion, even though he is a child, to keep you company in the wilds of Somerset County.

*We are following your progress on a map, putting a pin in the towns
you mention in your letters.*
With affection, your devoted sister,
Persia

~~~

China folded the letters and tucked them back into the envelope.
How quickly things had changed, she thought—all those new developments in India and Persia's lives, and all because she had wanted to
go journeying on her own. How odd it was that so small a change in
the order of things had sent out ripples that enabled other changes to
spring up and take hold.

So much had happened, and it was barely a month since she had
left! Many things would not be the same when she returned, she realized with a small sense of uneasiness. Persia and India would not be
the same, and neither would she. They would be changed by time,
new interests, new associations, and by other, intangible things.

"Dear me, what have I done?" China said aloud to herself.

The thought, though startling, was not entirely troublesome. China
knew with utter certainty that she and her sisters were anchored to
one another by love, affection, and memories of their shared life. That
anchor would keep them steady, allow them, as it always had, to ride
out any storms that might arise, to float with confidence when the
seas were calm again. It also would allow them to alter course, though
for some reason that had only just occurred to her. By the time she
returned in the fall, the changes in all of them would be evident.

China glanced at the clock and put the letters away. She put on
a simple white cotton dress with long sleeves embellished with a bit
of lace. She tidied her hair and went across the hall to fetch Clint.

"Look what I did," Clint said, handing China the sheet of paper she had given him. On it he'd written:

❧

Dear Dr. Webber,
I received the postal card and I thank you for thinking of me. Miss Havener runs a good ship.
Yours truly,
    Clint Remick

❧

"Very nice, Clint. You write an excellent hand. Here's a penny for a stamp. Tomorrow you can walk to the post office and mail your letter."

Clint put the penny in his pocket and went back into his room to put the letter in a safe place.

Three of the four tables in the dining room, each set with places for eight, were full. Mr. Ferguson, the man who had been bitten by Buster, sat at a table with seven other men. He nodded to China. She returned his nod politely, barely looking at him. Mr. Ferguson was not the sort of man she wished to encourage.

Mrs. Chase, well turned out in a soft gray dress that rustled with each step she took, ushered China and Clint to the fourth table, which was empty. The food had not yet been brought in.

China glanced at the other tables, looking for Plato Robinson, but he was not among the diners. Perhaps he had changed his mind, China thought, with a little stab of disappointment.

But just as Mrs. Chase and her two hired girls came in with tureens of chicken stew, plates of biscuits, and platters of fried trout and potatoes, Plato sauntered into the room, nodded to China, and sat down beside Clint.

"A fine evening," he said, smiling at China. He was dressed in a black jacket and trousers, black boots shiny from polishing, a clean white shirt, and an old-fashioned cravat similar to the ones Sam Webber still wore, even though cravats were many years out of date. Somehow on Plato it did not seem archaic; rather, it seemed poetic, and suited him. He was not wearing a hat, and there was, China thought, something noble about his brow. In the lamplight, his features were sharply delineated, and she saw strength of character in the planes of his nose and cheeks. It was obvious he had spent time on his appearance, as if he had intended to impress her.

Oh, dear, she thought, I do like the cut of his jib. She suppressed a sigh and looked down at her plate, trying not to stare at him. He did indeed impress her with his looks, his manner, his intelligence and kindness.

"Yes, a very fine evening," China murmured, feeling shy and ridiculous, a seasoned woman beset by girlish emotions.

"Is that rope splice holding, sir?" Clint asked.

"It is, indeed, and a finer piece of rigging I've never seen. I am most obliged."

An awkward silence settled over them for a moment as the hired girl set pitchers of water and platters of food on the table.

"Boy, don't I like trout," Clint said.

"Help yourself, Clint," China told him. "Mr. Robinson, will you have stew or trout?"

"I think I'll start with stew and move on to the trout." He held out his bowl and China ladled the steaming stew into it. As if he were my husband, China thought, her cheeks suddenly warm.

The food, though simple, was as good as any China had ever eaten, and she remarked on it.

"I've been eating here ever since my wife Lephie died years ago. She was a fine cook, but here to Mrs. Chase's, it's almost as good. I think my Lephie had a lighter hand with a biscuit, but beyond that I can't complain."

"Do you have children, Mr. Robinson?"

"Had. We had children, my Lephie and me, five in all—two pretty girls and three rugged boys." Plato paused, laid down his spoon, and dropped his head a moment, as if to catch his breath. "But when the diphtheria came, it took them all . . . even my Lephie."

Tears pricked China's eyes and she wanted to reach for his hand— a strong, capable hand—to offer comfort and condolence. Instead, she folded her own hands tightly in her lap.

"Oh, I beg your pardon, Mr. Robinson; I didn't mean to stir up sad memories. I should not have—"

"Not at all, Miss Havener. I wasn't the only one in Bingham to suffer such a loss. It was one of the worst epidemics to come upriver. I was sick with it, too, but I was spared. Don't know why, but I keep hoping I will find out one day."

"My folks are . . . gone, too," Clint said, looking at his plate.

Gloom hovered over them, a spell that threatened to take the pleasure out of the evening.

"Perhaps we should turn our conversation to other subjects which will make it easier for us to digest this good supper," China said gently. "There will be other times, I do hope, to . . . To discuss melancholy matters."

Plato's eyes caught China's with a glance that said "Thank you."

"What I want to know," Clint said, "is how you got to be a ferryman."

"Now that's an easy question, my boy," Plato said, rising to the topic. "My father was a ferryman and so was my grandsir and my great-grandsir before that, he being the one who came early to this part of the river and helped settle the town." Plato talked easily with Clint, and China knew without a doubt that he had been a kind and loving father to his children, a good, dependable husband to his wife.

By the time dessert arrived—warm rhubarb pie—China felt as though she had known Plato all her life. In the time it took to eat supper, she learned that he had been educated by his mother in the evenings by the light of a candle and the fire on the hearth—that he had worked with his father on the river during the day. When he was fifteen, an uncle in Skowhegan offered him room and board so he could attend Bloomfield Academy to further his education, something his father wanted for him. When he finished school he worked as a clerk for a lawyer.

"It was during those years that I lost some of the burr of how I talked. Stopped saying ye for you, for one thing. That was the old way of talking, the eighteenth-century way. I was a man of the nineteenth century, and wanted to sound that way," he remarked.

He had married, settled down, and had children.

When the South fired on Fort Sumter, Plato was thirty-five years old and his oldest child was eight, with four more behind him. But in spite of his wife's pleading, he had enlisted and gone off to do his part to save the Union. After he nearly died from dysentery, never seeing any action, he was mustered out and sent back to Skowhegan. By that time his father was ailing and wanted him to come home to Bingham to run the ferry. So that's what he did.

His story was neither epic, dramatic, nor unusual, and he told it slowly—a sentence here, a sentence there, until China had gleaned the bare bones of it and could dress it with insights and assumptions of her own. Plato was a good man, kind, intelligent, even a bit philosophical—as befit his name, she thought. Moreover, he was a man of large character. He was not interested only in himself as she had observed many men often were. He had a genuine interest in others, their thoughts and ideas.

When they had finished supper, they sat for a while on the piazza watching night fall, listening to the sound of orioles sending flute-like notes high into the elms. Their talk took them to China's life at sea, to talk of her sisters, to her interest in photography, to information about Bingham and its residents, and to the life and times of a ferryman on the Kennebec River.

Clint listened closely to the talk, contributing comments of his own, but saying nothing much about his past.

When the full moon showed its silvery face over the tops of the elms, Plato rose and held out his hand to China. She slipped hers into his, and it seemed as if their hands knew one another. But it was merely a handshake. Plato bid her and Clint a good evening. Then, almost as an afterthought, he said to Clint, "If it's all right with Miss Havener, and you'd like to do it, I'd be glad of your help on the ferry tomorrow, Clint. Buster can come, too. Mrs. Chase won't mind that."

Clint turned to China, a big grin on his face.

"Of course you may go. When would you like him to be there, Mr. Robinson?"

"Well, I'm on the river by six, but the boy can show up at eight if he's so inclined."

Plato set off down the road. China stood on the piazza and watched him go, taking in his long, easy stride, the way he tucked his left hand into his pants pocket and swung the other in time with his step, with something akin to military precision. She wondered if he sensed how intently she was watching him. And in that instant, he turned his head for one last sight of her.

She heard soft footsteps behind her, turned to find Mrs. Chase at her elbow. Mrs. Chase breathed a soft sigh.

"Now that one . . . every maiden lady and widow up and down the river have set their caps at him. He's considered quite the catch, but he always eludes the net," Mrs. Chase said, looking directly at China, as if in warning.

China felt her cheeks flush, glad the dark hid her face. "I believe he was very devoted to his late wife," she said. "There are men who never recover from such loss. Perhaps he is one of them." She thought of her father, how he had never recovered his equilibrium after he was widowed.

"Yes, that is so, but it's such a terrible waste," Mrs. Chase said, shaking her head sadly. "Why don't you and the boy come into the parlor? I thought we might sing. I play a bit, and Mr. Chase plays the fiddle some."

China and Clint spent the remainder of the evening tapping their toes and singing *Rock of Ages, Blessed Be the Tie that Binds, In the Gloaming, Barbara Allen, Camptown Races*, and *Greensleeves*.

When there was a lull in the music, and it was clear the evening had come to a close, China gazed out the window at the dark. We are all in boats of our own making in this life, she thought. Most of us are good sailors and will weather tempests well. Plato is one of those. I am one of those. She suspected Clint was, too, given the fact that he already had endured so much heartache for one so young, and that he had not foundered on any of the rocks and shoals that had beset the course of his young life.

20.

Later, as she prepared for bed, China gazed at herself in the mirror. The face she saw was indeed that of China Havener, but it was also India and Persia. She recalled times when she had wanted more than anything to look only like herself. Once, as a child, she had cut her hair, causing her mother to weep. She had wanted to be different from her sisters, to stand out, to be China, not China-India-Persia.

After that, to spare her mother any more tears, she merely imagined how she might alter her appearance to look only like herself, although she thought about blacking her hair with shoe polish or rubbing the juice of beets on her cheeks. Instead, after her hair had grown out again, she insisted on wearing it in a fashion of her own devising. Let India and Persia wear braids, the ends tied together with a large silk ribbon bow; she wore her hair unbraided and tied back with a length of white cotton bias tape, though there were times, at her mother's request or her father's command, when she dressed and wore her hair exactly like India and Persia, though that was a rarity.

There was no getting around the fact that the Havener sisters looked exactly alike, right down to the lines in the palms of their hands, prompting China to embroider her initials on her clothing against the awful chance that they suffered some ghastly fate. The initials ensured that when they were found—dead, of course—the searchers would know her from her sisters.

China's childhood rebellion had caused them all to think, and by the time they were young ladies of thirteen, India and Persia, too, wanted to dress and wear their hair according to their own tastes and inclinations. As they grew to adulthood, it became increasingly clear they were not identical when it came to their interior landscapes.

China's long white hair, loosed from its pins, fell like a cape almost to her waist. Her face was lightly lined, and she looked years younger than fifty-five. Her blue eyes shone with vitality and were her best feature. Her nose—our noses, she thought—was a trifle too long, her mouth a trifle too thin. But even though her youthful prettiness had dimmed somewhat, she wasn't too hard on the eyes. Did Plato Robinson see her that way? What, indeed, did he see when he looked at her?

"Oh, bother!" she said aloud, suddenly impatient with her silly mooning over a man she barely knew. She gave herself a mental shake and reached for the letter from Abbott's Reach, which she had not yet read.

As she expected, it was a compendium of greetings from the members of Fanny's "clan," as China always thought of them.

❧

Dear China,

Rest assured that India and Persia are well and not pining for your return. Someone, usually Ellis or Madras, but sometimes M and Maude, or myself, check on them every few days. This comes about naturally since we covet Persia's yarn, her knitting, and the vegetables from her garden we expect to enjoy later this summer.

Sam especially likes talking to India of seafaring days; he gets to sing endless verses of the sea chanteys he remembers while India writes it all down or plays it on the piano. It's lovely to watch and to hear.

Business at Abbott's Reach is picking up now that the weather is so fine. Many come just for the day to wander about the beach and the woods, and some come on the boat for cake and lemonade on the piazza in the afternoon. Many are from Bangor, and they come with a certain curiosity about me; no doubt my past bad reputation is still out there after all these years. I often marvel how a few years of bad behavior can mark one for life, never completely canceled out by the many years of living an upright life. Why is that? Still, I can't help but wonder if it isn't something of a privilege to become a legend in one's own time.

Everyone here misses you, but we understand the need to set one's sails to explore new territory. We enjoyed reading your account of all you have seen and done so far, especially about Clint Remick, and look forward to fall when you return.

Affectionately,

Fanny

❧

Dear China,

The days at Abbott's Reach flow by most agreeably. M and Madras are often here with the children, and they keep me wonderfully entertained. They like to hear the story about my encounter with the British when they invaded Hampden and Bangor back in 1814. The little boys take up sticks and pretend to be fighting with swords and the little girls run off shrieking as if their brothers really were Redcoats intent on mischief at the door.

My aches and pains keep me from being as useful as I would like to be, but Fanny always finds things for me to do—a bit of mending, pie dough to roll out, or helping with the accounts.

Fanny has said so already, but I want to underscore it: You are missed, and we look forward to your return. But in the meantime, see all you can, do everything that pleases you, and enjoy it.

Fondly,
Maude

❧

China, my dear,

Although Maude did not mention it, we all are most interested in the boy, Clint. He sounds like a good lad, one who would fit in nicely around here. As you know, there are children everywhere who through no fault of their own are thrown on hard times and need a hand up. I hope you will let him stay with you throughout your tour; who knows, there may be dragons. Though I rather think not, for it has been my experience that most people are good, and only a very few are intent on doing evil.

*We look forward to your letters and especially enjoy your descriptions
of the people you meet and the sights you see. We eagerly await the day we
will have the privilege of viewing the photographs you are making.*

Yr. obed't servant,

Sam Webber

❧

Dear China,

*The children are clamoring for me to go with them down to the beach,
but I have put them off for a few minutes while I add my two cents' worth
to this "log." I feel fortunate to have called the very day Fanny was organizing the writing of it. Later, I will take Blythe and Lex out in the Zephyr
to give them a sailing lesson. Sam offered to stay behind with his name-
sake, Samuel, and they will engage in digging large holes at the water's edge,
searching for pirate treasure. I feel certain Sam already has "planted" some
artifact for young Sam to discover. Maude has offered to tend the baby while
I am out on the bay with Blythe and Lex.*

Madras joins me in sending you our best love.

M.

❧

As China put the letters away, there was a knock at her door.

"Who is it?" she asked.

"Clint." He opened the door and stuck his head in.

"What do you need, Clint?"

"I know I wrote a letter to Dr. Webber, but I wanted to write
him a postcard, too. I bought one down in the lobby with a penny I
had left over from that quarter you gave me in Skowhegan."

"That's very nice, Clint. You can show me in the morning. Go to bed now. It's late."

"Aye, Captain Havener." He closed the door quietly behind him.

China heard the soft fall of his footsteps in the hallway, then the opening and closing of the door to his room.

She lay quietly in the dark, feeling as if some invisible thread connected her and Clint, a cord they were in the process of spinning into being. Would it hold? Would it fray and snap like the ferry rope? Would splicing be possible if the cord parted in the middle? She didn't know the answer to any of these questions, but it seemed quite likely she would find out one way or another, when she least expected it.

21.

The postcard Clint chose to send depicted the Bingham House.

"I don't know if I wrote the right things; I'd like you to read it," he said as they sat down to breakfast the next morning.

China took the postcard and held it a moment before she turned it over. Clint had written:

❧

Dear Sir,

It was a pleasure to hear from you. Miss Havener is good to me. Mr. Robinson asked me to work with him on the ferry. I've never been on a ship, but I am a good cabin boy.

Sincerely yours,

Clint Remick

❧

"That is well put, Clint."

Clint's face lit up with a smile at the praise.

"I always liked writing. My mother showed me how to make the capital letters fancy," he said. "Later today, I want to buy my own stamp and stick it on and everything. I want to walk uptown to the post office and mail it myself."

"Don't forget to take the letter you wrote last night," China said, noting that his mention of his mother had not clouded his mood, that he was filled with buoyancy at the prospect of spending the day on the ferry with Plato Robinson.

Clint nodded and turned his attention to the plate of fried eggs and potatoes one of Mrs. Chase's hired girls had set in front of him.

"There is a falls not too distant from here, Clint, on the other side of the river, and I am going to visit it," China said. "Mrs. Chase's hired man, Mr. Franklin Moore, will drive me and a few others there. We will leave at ten this morning and be gone until suppertime. Mr. Moore will help me with the camera, if need be."

"By then, my letter and my postcard will be in the mail. And I will help Mr. Robinson ferry you across the Kennebec," Clint said with pride and enthusiasm, his mind already on the adventures of the day. He finished eating a last slice of toast, pushed his chair away from the table, and headed off to the post office and the ferry. China waved good-bye from the piazza and went upstairs to write a brief note to India and Persia. Then she went down to the yard to wait for Mr. Moore to take her on the expedition to the falls.

Franklin Moore drove up in a buckboard that had room for six people. He was a small man with a shy smile who handled the horses with a firm but light hand. He helped China into the buckboard with great care, tucking her skirt safely around her feet and making certain none of it trailed against the wheel.

The other members in the party were Mr. And Mrs. Ashford of Boston and Miss Spencer, the village schoolteacher, who confided she had grown up at The Forks, a village twenty miles upriver.

Miss Spencer sat down beside China and they exchanged pleasantries, remarking on the fine weather and the beauty of the ridges that enfolded the village. Miss Spencer confided that she was a birdwatcher and knew a great deal about the species inhabiting the Bingham region. She mentioned the bald and golden eagles, orioles, bluebirds, wood thrushes, and Canada jays she had seen. China also loved watching birds, and had seen many exotic kinds during her seafaring years, recalling most vividly a toucan with a bill of many colors she had seen in a cage in South America. Miss Spencer wanted to hear more. China was pleased to have such an agreeable companion for the trip.

Miss Spencer seemed much too young to be a teacher, but assured China she was eighteen years old, and had passed with nearly perfect marks the test to receive a teaching certificate two years before. She had taught at The Forks, at Brighton village, and at the Concord school across the river. Now she was teaching the younger children in the Bingham school. She was making the trip to the falls so she could better inform her students about it. She wanted to have something of a local nature to add when her class studied the geography of Maine. She very much believed that children should learn about the town and region they lived in.

Bingham could boast of a mill that made calks, the pointed metal parts for the soles of boots worn by log drivers, several sawmills, a carriage maker, a harness maker, a shingle mill, and a cabinetmaker who also fashioned coffins. The town also had general stores operated by S. A. Dinsmore, Willis B. Goodrich, and Warren Colby; a millinery and fancy goods store owned by S. T. Goodrich; a clothing and dry goods store owned by M. Savage; a store owned by B. Smith that sold drugs and furniture; a hardware store owned by Calvin Colby; a furniture store owned by H. J. Abbey; E. W. Moore, a jeweler; and A. B. Chase, who owned a meat market.

"Bingham is a very prosperous town," Miss Spencer said. "I want my pupils to know there is much to be proud of here."

The Ashfords, China learned, were on their honeymoon. They trailed a haze of happiness that was almost visible, and had eyes only for one another. They had chosen Bingham as the destination for their wedding journey after reading an article in a newspaper extolling the virtues of the area. They were so pleased with their choice, they had already made plans to return next summer and bring their parents.

When they arrived at the ferry landing, Clint, wearing his father's battered hat, similar in style to the one Plato wore, strode toward them with pride and confidence in his step to lead the horse onto the waiting ferry. He tethered the animal to an iron ring fitted to the side of the ferry and set chocks against the wheels of the buckboard to keep it from rolling. Then he helped Plato with the ropes.

It didn't surprise China to see how quickly he had learned his duties, how easily he had stepped into the role of ferryman. It pleased her to see that he was no longer the dirty, hopeless boy who had followed her around Cambridge; he had useful work to do, and took pride in it, and in himself.

When they reached the landing on the Concord side of the river, Clint led the horses onto the riverbank. By then another conveyance was waiting on the Bingham side. Clint waved to China and jumped back on the ferry.

China glanced at Plato. He gave her a nod and a warm smile.

"Mr. Robinson is much admired around town," Miss Spencer confided quietly, taking in the silent exchange between China and Plato. "Especially by the ladies."

"So I was given to understand," China said, sounding somewhat prim.

Miss Spencer seemed to expect more, but her good manners prevented her from asking questions when China did not elaborate.

They drove for more than an hour upriver on the narrow road, following the riverbank until they reached the Spaulding farm in Pleasant Ridge, where they stopped to rest and eat an early dinner. After a good meal of deer meat China asked the Spaulding family to line up in front of the house in order to take their picture. It was the first time the Spauldings had ever been photographed, Mr. Spaulding commented. China said she would send him a copy. She jotted down his address in a small notebook she carried in her pocket for just that purpose.

Mr. Spaulding, dressed in a faded blue shirt with the sleeves rolled up and brown wool trousers, served as their guide. He drove the party up a narrow track winding upward through the woods until they came to a stopping place. They could hear the distant commotion of the falls. He tied the horses to a tree branch and helped the ladies out of the buckboard.

The air smelled of evergreen, damp earth, and wildflowers. The trill of birdsong reached their ears, and Miss Spencer, serving as interpreter, identified the species making the sounds—wood thrush, blue jay, chickadee.

"The trail is steep in places, but it's not far to the falls," Mr. Spaulding said. He reached for China's camera to carry it for her.

He was right about the steepness of the trail, and China was glad she had worn sturdy boots and a skirt that came only to her ankles. She used the tripod walking stick to hold aside brush growing close to the trail, clambered over rocks that thrust up from the ground, and tramped around muddy spots where water appeared to seep from the ledge. The beauty of the falls was not to be found in its height; rather, it was in the way it cascaded into a grotto-like pool, then spilled over the ledge through shallow channels until it tumbled another few feet into a chasm that bore it down the side of the ridge toward the

Kennebec River. On either side of the falls, tall cedars trembled in a light breeze. Beneath the dense curtain of branches, it was dim and cool, the earth spongy with evergreen needles accumulated for untold centuries.

The three men in the party set aside their jackets and climbed a very steep path leading to the top of the falls.

China set up her camera and made a photograph of the men standing triumphant on an outcropping of granite more than forty feet above her. None of the ladies wanted to attempt the climb, although China wished she were Miss Spencer's age, with the strength and vitality to climb the nearly perpendicular path and explore the upper reaches of the brook.

Mrs. Ashford and Miss Spencer obligingly posed with the falls behind them, and China took their photograph, too. What she saw in the frame delighted her—the ladies in their tailored linen jackets decorated with dark bands of cloth tape, the shadows created by the folds of their skirts, their hats adorned with fluffs of tulle and artificial flowers—framed by the natural setting of the falls and the trees. Both Miss Spencer and Mrs. Ashford had confided to China that they never wore hats trimmed with feathers once they'd learned of the indiscriminate slaughter of millions of birds to satisfy the constantly changing demands of millinery fashion.

Everywhere China looked there was something more she wanted to photograph—a spot where the cedars thinned and sunlight filtered through in a visible haze; Mrs. Ashford and Miss Spencer sitting primly, back to back, on a rock—Mrs. Ashford looking serenely downstream and Miss Spencer, her face lit with delight, gazing at the falls as if enchanted.

I'm going to need to order more glass-plate negatives, China thought, not for the first time, as she joined the ladies to await the return of the men and to begin their return trip to Bingham.

At the ferry landing, Plato, with a certain audacious air, winked at China, then stood back to let Clint guide the ferry across the Kennebec to the Bingham landing. Clint carried out the operation with grave dignity, and China saw in the planes of his face the man he would become, saw, with pride, that he would be a good man. It came to her, then, that her feelings must be akin to those a mother would feel, and it startled her, for she had never expected to feel anything of a true maternal nature.

That night, Clint shared the adventures of his day with her.

"In a way I wish I'd gone to the falls with you, Miss Havener, to carry your camera, but I just had to see what it was like to be a ferryman, and I'm glad I did. I liked how Mr. Robinson wanted to teach me things, and how he was so patient about it. He told me my first job was to see that the splice held, so I checked it every hour. It's such a strong mend, it will last a good long time. But Mr. Robinson thinks the new rope will come on the stage tomorrow morning, so he said if I wanted to, I could help him get it rigged up, if that's all right with you. Of course, that means—"

"You will be derelict in your cabin boy duties," China finished for him. "That is quite all right, Clint. Tomorrow, I'm going east to the top of Babbitt Ridge, the height of the land around here, where there is a magnificent view of the western mountains, so Mrs. Chase has told me. Mr. Moore will drive again. And I also want to walk around the village streets, looking at houses and taking photographs."

Clint helped himself to another piece of spice cake.

"Then you don't mind if I help Mr. Robinson? Because I really want to."

"Then that's what you must do."

China glanced around the dining room, hoping to see Plato coming in late for supper.

Clint saw that her attention had wandered from the conversation.

"Mr. Robinson doesn't come to supper every night," he said.

China, embarrassed that Clint had noticed her inattention, opened her mouth to protest, to say she wasn't looking for Mr. Robinson, but thought better of it. It would have been a lie.

"Well, that is a shame," she said. "He makes for pleasant company."

"Oh, I forgot! He told me to tell you he wants us to come to his place for supper some night this week, and I said I'd ask you, and tell him tomorrow what you said."

A smile reshaped China's mouth from a disappointed line to a curve of pleasure. But when she replied, it was with decorous reserve as befit her status as a single lady of a certain age speaking to the boy in her care.

"You may tell Mr. Robinson we would be happy to accept his invitation, at his convenience." She saw no reason to decline the inviation, which included Clint, who now counted Plato as his friend. Indeed, she was eager to spend time with Plato. If eyebrows were raised, then she would only have to endure it for the length of her stay in Bingham.

"Oh, boy!" Clint said, grabbing a cookie.

China didn't know if he was commenting on the abundance of food or the prospect of eating supper at Plato's house. Probably both.

Later, when China was alone, getting ready for bed, she wondered what Plato's house would be like. Would she feel at home there? Was he the sort of man who had never quite figured out how to see to himself after his wife died? She thought not. One had only to look at the ferry, or at him, to see the neatness about him.

Her last thought before she fell asleep was that Plato had winked at her.

22.

The next morning dawned fair, a high June day with the sky so blue it seemed to define the very idea of the celestial. Thick pads of white clouds rose over the surrounding ridges, and the sheer beauty of the day threaded light into China's mood.

"You forgot your hat," Mrs. Chase observed as China made her way through the lobby to the piazza where Franklin Moore waited with a buggy.

As a rule, a woman never went anywhere without a hat settled prettily on her head. To go forth without one was akin to throwing caution to the wind, a state of mind rare for China. But on this day, her mood was buoyant, her thoughts free of clutter. She felt airy and weightless, as if bubbles filled her veins. Everything she saw delighted her—the quality of the light, the intensity of the blue sky, the rounded sides of the Kennebec Valley hills. It crossed her mind how limiting it was for photographs to be only in black and white. Perhaps someday, someone would invent a camera to record those colors in all their gorgeous subtlety.

"It's such a glorious day . . . ," China said, leaving Mrs. Chase to fill in what she had left unsaid.

Mrs. Chase raised her eyebrows, smiled knowingly, and said nothing. China realized she was not casting aspersions on her lack of a hat; she simply could not refrain from making conversation about everything that passed within her range of vision. Mrs. Chase was the sort of woman who noticed everything, took interest and delight in it, and could not refrain from commenting on it.

China wasn't wearing a jacket either, even though current modes of fashion dictated that she should. To complement her gray skirt, she wore a high-necked white cotton shirtwaist with sleeves that stopped at the elbows. She had, however, pulled on a pair of white lacy gloves Persia had crocheted for her. She carried a pretty pale blue shawl, although she felt certain it would not be needed.

Frank Moore, driving a buggy equipped with an umbrella to provide a bit of shade, with China seated beside him, made slow progress along the main road. He nodded to acquaintances he passed along the way. Frank knew everyone for miles around, and made a great ceremony of tipping his hat to the ladies and saluting the gentlemen going about their errands either in rigs of their own or on foot.

Frank let the horse take its time after they crossed Austin Stream bridge and started toward Moscow, a settlement close to Bingham.

"All uphill from here," he said. "A mile or so of hard pulling up to the Pomroy place, and the best view of the valley and the western mountains."

The narrow road, hardly more than a wagon track, ran in a nearly straight line up what Frank referred to as Babbitt Ridge.

Frank stopped by a road that swung to the left to let the horse rest, checking its harness to make sure nothing chafed or had come loose.

"Worst is yet to come," he said.

And so it was. The road grew steeper, then went downhill for a short distance, before it rose steeply again. When they gained what appeared to be the summit, Frank stopped and told China to look behind her. Spread out in a broad panorama, she saw the blue contours of distant mountains.

"Western mountains, over Kingfield and Rangeley way," Frank said with pride in his voice, as if the view belonged to him. He clearly took satisfaction in showing it to someone who had never seen it before. He turned onto a grassy track which opened out into the dooryard and fields of the Pomroy place.

Mrs. Pomroy, a woman in her mid-forties, China judged, came out of the house to meet them in the dooryard. Her hair was parted in the middle and pinned up at the back. She wore a long white apron over a mustard-yellow calico dress. Behind her stood a Cape Cod-style house of a story and a half, and beyond that, a barn with its doors and a long row of narrow windows set into its side, marking it as a structure from an earlier time. In newer barns, doors were placed in the gable end.

Frank helped China out of the buggy and led the horse into the barn to let it rest and cool off. He reached for a cloth under the buggy seat and wiped sweat from the horse's neck, back, and sides. He went to the well in the yard and drew up a bucket of water for the horse.

"Mrs. Chase, good soul that she is, sent word you'd be coming today," Mrs. Pomroy said to China. "Come along into the house and I'll pour you a glass of cool water. I fetched it from the well not ten minutes ago. We have a nice spring just down the road, too."

When China stepped through the door and into the house, it was as if she had gone back in time at least a hundred years. As Mrs. Pomroy led her into a narrow passage with a steep stairwell to one side, China caught glimpses of two front rooms furnished mostly with what appeared to be handmade pieces, including chairs and candle stands, some of pine, some of maple. On the walls of one room she spotted stencil decorations of red and green motifs she knew dated back to the early 1800s. The walls of both rooms were finished with wainscoting and chair rails.

"They say a traveling man came through years ago and put that decoration on the walls," Mrs. Pomroy remarked when she saw China's interest in it. "My husband's grandmother always thought highly of it. My husband wanted to paint over it when he brought me here as a bride some years back, but I wouldn't hear of it. Those dark red scrolls and those big green leaves . . . such a pretty pattern. I never get tired of it, even if it is a little faded."

In the kitchen, a large hearth with a baking oven built into the chimney took up most of the back wall. The smell of baking beans escaped from a cast-iron pot hanging over a bed of coals. The hearth was equipped in the old-fashioned way with a crane, fire dogs, tongs, a reflector oven, and cast-iron skillets in several sizes.

A large spinning wheel occupied one corner by the hearth. Several braided wool rugs and two hooked rugs covered the floor. A drop-leaf table with six chairs around it occupied the center of the room.

"It's not much, but it's homey," Mrs. Pomroy said with shy pride in her voice. "This house was my husband's grandsir's place, built when he first come here to Moscow in 1815. A lot of the furnishings were his, but I made the rugs. I make my own candles, too, in the fall. It's a chore, but it saves buying lamp oil."

She poured water from a pitcher into a teacup, in a blue willow pattern, and handed it to China.

"It's a lovely room, so cozy and homey," China said. "I brought a camera with me, Mrs. Pomroy. I'd like to photograph the view from here, but I wonder if you would also allow me to photograph this room, and perhaps the one with the stencils on the walls."

"This old place? It's not much to see," Mrs. Pomroy said with genuine modesty, although she seemed pleased at China's request.

"Perhaps you would do me the honor of standing at your spinning wheel and being in the picture."

Mrs. Pomroy thought about China's suggestion for a moment. "Would I have to smile?"

"Why, no; you could simply stand by the wheel while I record your image."

China wasn't at all certain there was enough light in the room for a successful photograph. She consulted her camera manual, decided to try a long exposure, and hope for the best. Until that moment, all her photography had been done outdoors. Now, suddenly, a whole new aspect of what she might do with the camera opened up to her.

Mrs. Pomroy, persuaded that her hair was in order, that she didn't have to smile, and that she didn't need to change into her "better" dress, went to the wheel and placed her hand on it.

"It's a walking wheel, for spinning wool—no sitting down with this one," she explained.

"Now, Mrs. Pomroy," China said, "if you would stand very still until I tell you otherwise . . ."A golden shaft of sunlight gleamed through the east window and illuminated the fine bones of Mrs. Pomroy's face. China removed the lens cap, glanced at the tall clock standing against the wall by the door, and waited until, by her estimate, thirty seconds had passed before she replaced the cap.

"Just be still one more moment, Mrs. Pomroy, while I expose another plate," China said, wanting to try a shorter exposure time. Then, "Thank you, Mrs. Pomroy; that will be all."

"It's all took?"

"Yes."

"Imagine that."

"We live in an amazing age, Mrs. Pomroy."

They moved to the room with the stenciled walls and China photographed that, too.

After they had finished with the inside photographs, Mrs. Pomroy said, "Well, everyone that comes up here always wants to see the view, so you'd best come along with me. I've got a jug of switchel to take out to my husband and the boys."

Switchel, she explained, was a drink made of water mixed with vinegar, sweetened with molasses, flavored with ginger, and drunk in the fields during haying time. It was not a beverage China had ever heard of, but when Mrs. Pomroy offered her a taste, she took a sip and found it rather pleasant.

Mrs. Pomroy led China through a side door and out across the barnyard to a split-rail fence. "There you have it," Mrs. Pomroy said. "Wait here a minute while I take this switchel to my husband. He'll be looking for it right about now." She strode off across the field toward her husband and sons, who halted their work to drink the cool, sweet concoction.

China had viewed many mountain ranges in her travels around the world. She had seen the Andes, the Alps, the Himalayas, and the volcanic mountains of Hawaii. But the vista that lay before her, blue-green in the clear June light, charmed her as no other mountains ever had, spreading before her in layer after layer. She had no idea why, but there was something about the landscape, the pale indigo blue of the distant peaks, the rounded contours, that made her feel as if she were safely home. She photographed the view first with her eyes, staring at it for a long moment as if she were mesmerized.

The first layer of the view was the field where Mr. Pomroy and his sons scythed the first crop of hay of the summer. The team of red-brown horses hitched to the hay wagon shook their heads and stamped their feet, jingling the harness rings and buckles, impatient to move the load to the barn. Beyond the field lay a border of hardwoods that fell away with the contour of the landscape. In the middle distance, China spotted the Kennebec River as it flowed just south of Bingham village, where the valley widened into a floodplain.

At various points along the ridges she saw farm buildings surrounded by pastures, and what appeared to be patches of moving snow.

"Sheep," Mrs. Pomroy said, returning to stand beside China at the fence. "More sheep than people in these parts."

"And do you have sheep?" China asked.

"Oh, a few, but just for wool. I won't let Mr. Pomroy use them for meat. Anyway, they are mine, given to me by my father when I married Mr. Pomroy, so what I say goes. Not that he cares. All he has to do is shear them every year and I do all the rest. And in the bargain he always has good warm socks, mittens, and hats."

"My sister Persia keeps a small flock of sheep. She has just taken up spinning and weaving. Perhaps if I give her your name and address, she might write you for advice should she need it."

"Why, that would be nice. I always like finding a letter in the mail. Not too many people around here, or anywhere else, I guess, spin their own yarn anymore."

While they talked, China set the camera on its tripod and photographed the mountains. She made certain Mr. Pomroy, his sons, the horses, and the hay wagon were in the frame, to give a sense of perspective.

"Do the mountains have names?" China asked when she had finished taking pictures.

Mrs. Pomroy lifted her hand and pointed. "Well, that one is Saddleback; then there's Sugarloaf, and over there is Bigelow. Those are the main ones. Some call the whole of them the Longfellow Mountains, and that's how I like to think of them. Seems like a good name, considering as how everyone I can think of learned by heart the verses Mr. Longfellow wrote . . . 'Paul Revere's Ride,' 'Hiawatha,' 'Evangeline,' 'The Wreck of the Hesperus.' "

China smiled. "My sisters and I were especially fond of 'The Wreck of the Hesperus.' I have no idea why, being at sea as we were, and knowing full well that shipwreck can easily befall seafarers. Indeed, we once were shipwrecked, though after a few dreadful days in the lifeboat we were rescued." She added a few more details about her life at sea.

"My goodness, to look at you, one would never know it."

"That's the thing about people, isn't it, Mrs. Pomroy? You'd never guess, just by looking at someone, what they have experienced."

"Truer words were never spoken, Miss Havener."

When China and Mrs. Pomroy walked back to the house, they found Frank Moore waiting.

"I enjoyed your visit, and if you expect to be in these parts a while, I'd be honored if you'd call again sometime. I'm always here,"

Mrs. Pomroy said, her last sentence holding a note of wistfulness. She waved as Frank and China drove away.

"Mrs. Pomroy is a very amiable woman," China commented.

"She was a Baker. Good-hearted lot, all of them," Frank replied, as if that explained everything, which apparently it did, for he said nothing more.

23.

China spent the next few days walking around Bingham, taking photographs of the buildings that lined the main road. Some of the buildings were no larger than a cottage, while others rambled a bit or had false fronts to make them appear larger than they really were. Dull yellow-brown paint covered some of the buildings, although most were white. All were veiled by the shade of lofty elms.

China trained her camera on the old meetinghouse, at a large white house of three stories on the northern end of the main road, and at many of the structures in between. Before she removed the camera's lens cover, she waited until someone walked into the frame, a new idea she was experimenting with. She set the camera up in front of businesses where horses and wagons were tied, in order to include them in the photograph. People stopped to ask what she was up to and wanted to know how they could get copies of her photographs. A few ladies, seeing her with her camera aimed at their houses, invited her into their homes for a cup of tea, invitations she gladly accepted, eager to see what the rooms of the houses looked like and to get acquainted with those who lived there.

Franklin Moore, who confided that he was descended from one of the Moores who had settled in the town in 1812, drove China to view what was known locally as the dugway, a narrow road carved out of the sides of the hills rising steeply from the Kennebec. The road, also known as the Old Canada Road, Frank said, ran through the townships of Moscow, Caratunk, The Forks, and eventually into Quebec Province, Canada. He told her the story of how Benedict Arnold and his men marched through the region to Quebec in 1775 during the War of the Revolution. A relative of Mrs. Chase's husband, who had lived to tell the tale, had been on that march, he said, and had kept a diary of the hardships the soldiers had endured. Mrs. Chase had shown him the diary. Holding it in his hands, he said, was like touching the very fabric of history.

He drove her to Gulf Stream Gorge and she looked down into the chasm where Austin Stream flowed far below.

"There's talk of the railroad coming through here," Frank said, "and if it does, they will build a trestle bridge across this gorge—quite some feat. I doubt if it will happen in my lifetime, though I wish it would, for I'd like to see that trestle when it's done."

On the return trip, Frank was in a talkative mood. China asked him about stopping—or charming—blood.

"There was a family in the township of the Enchanted region, to the north," he said, "who had the gift of stopping blood—didn't have to touch the person bleeding, no tourniquet, nothing. I know a lumberman who hurt himself bad with an ax. A man was sent for—though sometimes it was a woman, because the gift of charming blood is passed in one family from man to woman to man. He did the charm and the wounded fella was taken down to Bingham to see a doctor. The very minute the hurt fella was at the doctor's front door, he started to bleed again. The blood charm had worn off by then, you see. The doctor stitched the fella's wound, and he's still around today to tell the story. If it hadn't been for the blood charm, that man would have bled to death."

"I'd never heard of such a thing until the first day I came here, and Mrs. Sawyer asked me if I knew how to charm blood. I had no idea what she was talking about."

"Quite a few people around here know how to stop blood. We don't think much about it."

"Do you know how it is done?"

"Some say the blood charmers quote a certain verse from the Bible, some say they don't. Some are even able to charm blood from a quite a distance, without being near the one that's bleeding. And they can do the same thing with animals, especially horses."

"The power of prayer . . . ," China commented.

"Apparently so," Franklin replied as they pulled up in front of the Bingham Hotel.

During her stay, China heard many other stories of Bingham's past, and sometimes wished she had the ability to write those stories down to go along with her photographs. Perhaps someone in the distant future would write those stories, she thought, for surely, they ought to be written down.

She continued to make photographs, and the more she saw, the more she found herself looking around more keenly, more discerningly. She found herself being more selective rather than merely pointing the camera at just anything, without thought, because what she saw appealed to her sense of beauty. Beauty, she began to realize, really was in the eye of the beholder.

This came home to her one afternoon when she found herself photographing a flea-bitten dog of mysterious ancestry as it lay in the sun beside a rickety picket fence, the paint peeling. It was the light that drew her interest, the way it sculpted the dog's form, how it caused the curls of paint to cast strange shadows, how the dog lifted its head and stared mournfully at her just as she removed the lens cap. In that moment, she felt a new kind of excitement possess her. I am educating my eye, she thought.

It was all about the light, of course—the sun illuminating the pickets of a fence, the shadows on the north side of buildings, the shady branches of elms hanging over the street, the contrast and interplay of light among the shadows. She began to see how shape and shadow informed what she was looking at, and began to seek it out. She did not know if her skill was increasing, or even if any of the photos she had taken would turn out to be anything more than blotches. She didn't mind not knowing; that was part of the mystery and attraction of the craft. It reminded her, somewhat, of being at sea, where the unknown lay at all quarters. Going to sea required faith in one's aptitude for survival, in one's endurance, in one's navigational skills, knowing how to pull the right ropes at the right time, how to use the wind. Taking pictures, she discovered, was also an exercise in faith. When the time came, the images would appear and show that what she had seen and what the camera captured were in harmony, if not in precise agreement.

The hours passed quickly and agreeably. As she grew more confident and more absorbed in her task, it sometimes startled her to realize that she had not given one thought to anything beyond photography while she was wandering around Bingham. It was only at suppertime that her thoughts returned to Clint, India, and Persia, the daily matters of life—and Plato Robinson.

One evening at the hotel as she ate supper with Clint, she looked around for Plato. She did not see him and felt a sense of restlessness, of disappointment, as if the day were incomplete.

After supper China and Clint sat on the piazza with Mrs. Chase and the other guests. They talked about books they had read, what was going on uptown, or the news that Old Lady Goodrich, thought to be nearly a hundred years old, and who had come to Bingham as a young girl, had died that day.

When at last the day came to go to Plato's house for supper—the time and day had proved somewhat difficult to arrange—China felt her heart expand in a way so new, she wondered if she was imagining it. She spent more time than usual seeing to her hair and selecting a shawl she knew intensified the blue of her eyes. She even pinched her cheeks and chewed on her lips to bring color to them, a trick she and her sisters had employed when they were young and hoping to find husbands.

"You look, I dunno . . . different," Clint said when she came downstairs.

"It's midsummer," she said as they walked toward Plato's house. "Longest day of the year. The long light of evening plays tricks on the eye."

"This time of year Pa would have been haying, and I'd have ridden to the barn on the hay pile in the wagon," Clint said, softly. "Ma would have been cooking all day for the men that came to help, mixing up jugs of switchel. And after we got our hay all cut and into the mow, we'd go and help the men who came to help us." It was the most Clint had ever said about his parents. China listened quietly and respectfully.

"You had a good life, and kind parents," she said when Clint stopped talking, reflecting back to him the sweetness that infused his memories.

Clint nodded soberly, and she knew he was feeling an upwelling of grief. She never knew how to gauge the depths of his sadness, so she put her arm across his shoulders, a tentative gesture. He did not shy away from her touch, and they walked that way a little while until his mood shifted and she sensed something lighter in him.

Plato met them at the door.

"It's not much, but it's home," he said modestly as he led them inside his Cape Cod–style house, so like the Pomroys', except for an ell, which the Pomroy house did not have.

China's immediate impression was one of neatly kept rooms furnished with simple tables and chairs, the floors covered with well-worn braided rugs scattered here and there. He led them into the large kitchen, with its dull red wainscoting and white plaster walls.

"Very nice," China said as she looked around. She liked the spareness of the furnishings, the lack of useless bric-a-brac. It reminded her of a ship's cabin, with a place for everything and everything in its place. A pot of ivy sat on a windowsill, its trailing fronds touching the floor. A child's doll, carved of wood and wearing a blue-checked dress, sat on a windowsill.

"I kept everything the same after my wife and children were gone," he said. "It keeps them close. My father-in-law made this pine table, and the doll. He was a good man with a piece of wood. He knew how to make something that would last. The only thing I wish I had is a picture of Lephie and my young ones."

"But you must have many pictures of them in your mind," China murmured.

"That I do, that I do," he replied. "And I have a silhouette cutout of Lephie, done right after we were married."

For supper Plato set out fried trout and potatoes, biscuits, field strawberries, and a small pitcher of fresh cream. Clint ate his fill, excused himself, and went outside to walk along the river, leaving China and Plato to clear the table and stack the dishes.

"A lovely supper, Mr. Robinson," China said.

"Well, it will keep body and soul together," he replied. He ushered China out to the yard to sit in chairs he had placed under the apple tree. The river made a constant murmur, a lulling, restful sound. A light breeze riffled through the leaves and the songs of robins, orioles, and other birds floated in the air. Twilight settled agreeably around them, reminding China of evenings at Castine when she and her sisters had sat under a rose arbor to talk over the day's events.

But this evening held much more for her. It was the beginning of something—of exactly what, she did not know, except that it had something to do with a shifting of allegiance away from India and Persia. The thought stalled and she brought herself firmly into the moment, away from such foolish imagining.

"I'm very grateful to you for letting Clint work with you on the ferry," she said. "He's been through a lot, has lost so much, and he needs the company of a levelheaded man to give him balance."

"He's a good boy, willing and able, and he has a good head on his shoulders for one so young. He's about the age my youngest, Seth, would have been had he lived to grow up."

A shadow came across Plato's face for a split second, then disappeared. China wanted to reach out and take his hand, but she let the impulse pass.

"I wonder, Mr. Robinson, if I might draw on your experience as a father. Am I doing the right thing by Clint . . . letting him stay with me instead of finding a good family to take him in, perhaps adopt him?"

Plato drew a deep breath and stared out over the river before he turned to China.

"First of all, Clint's got a mind of his own. He's not going to let anyone tell him what to do, or who he should live with, or where. By the looks of him, I'd say you are doing everything right. He's young to be left so alone, but he has shown that he can fend for himself if need be. He didn't fall into any trouble after he lost his folks, and when he tagged along after you, he showed good judgment. I think he wants to make something of himself; otherwise, he'd have done something different, got into all kinds of mischief, maybe ended up in jail. But, no, he sized you up and figured he'd be all right with you."

"I've done little except provide him with a few of the basic necessities of life. He needs much more than that. He needs education to fit him for the rest of his life. He's a bright boy."

"That he is. He catches on quick."

"Mr. Robinson, would you . . . given the fact you are alone . . . might you consider taking Clint as your . . . Apprentice? He likes you, and if he stayed with you, it would be because he wanted to . . ."

Plato gave China a long look before he answered. For a moment she worried she had offended him, and wished she had kept her mouth closed.

"That's not a simple question."

"No, it is not."

"There's no doubt Clint could learn to run the ferry, and be doing it all by himself by the end of the summer. But here's the thing: This ferry isn't going to be around forever. One of these days there will be a bridge. Don't know when, but there will be, and that's the future. So it makes no sense to fit Clint for a job that won't be around by the time he's grown up. He'd be better off to get schooling as an engineer that will design and build bridges."

"Ah, yes, I should have thought of that. The future. Just as the future means the replacement of sail with steam, it also means the replacement of ferries with bridges, and building a trestle bridge across Gulf Stream Gorge. It's young people like Clint who will bring those things to pass."

"True. And another thing . . . Clint picked you."

"But he also picked you."

"For now, perhaps, but I don't expect that to last, considering as how you'll only be here another week or so."

"Yes, that's true."

"I don't suppose there's any chance you'd stay on a while longer?"

Plato's eyes locked onto China's, and she saw in his face a long-ing, and a hope.

China weighed Plato's question before she answered. She did not want to read into his words something that wasn't there. But if his words did contain a deeper meaning, and she was certain they did, was she ready for that, ready to give up the freedom of her wanderings for the anchor of being loved and cherished? She did not know. All she knew was that when she was with him, it felt right. She felt alive in his presence, and worthwhile, as if she mattered to him more than she had ever mattered to anyone, including India and Persia.

Yet, something about the need to surrender into his keeping fright-ened her. She had been, for all intents and purposes, along with her sisters, the captain of a ship. She was accustomed to taking charge, to giving orders and having them carried out. She was now the captain of her own life. Did she want that to change? She honestly did not know.

"No, but there's a very good chance I will come back to Bing-ham one day."

"When?"

"I don't know, Mr. Robinson. I embarked on this journey to see things I had never seen before, and to see if I could make something of myself as a photographer. It never occurred to me that in the pro-cess I would meet interesting people . . . such as Clint, and yourself, people I would . . . grow fond of . . . so very quickly." Plato sat back in his chair and dropped his gaze to his big, capable hands.

"Well, I wish you good traveling, Miss Havener, and hope you know that if you come this way again, my door is always open to you."

The expression on his face was one of tenderness, tempered by what China believed was disappointment. He, too, China realized, quickly put up a shield when it came to matters of the heart.

"Mr. Robinson, I charted a course for this summer and fall. After that, I will have to chart a new one, and for the moment, I cannot say for sure where the wind will take me."

"Well, if there's one thing I know, the weather always changes . . . A lot of times for the better. I'll bear that in mind."

"I hope you will."

By now the sun had dropped behind Old Bluff, directly across the river.

Clint drifted back to China and Plato, saying, "It's going to be a fine day tomorrow. And look up there—it's the first star of the evening."

"Then you had best make a wish," China said, rising and turning to Plato. "It has been a lovely evening, Mr. Robinson, one of the happiest of my time here. I thank you for your company and your kindness." She knew she sounded formal and stilted, but she hoped he heard the warmth in her voice.

"It was my pleasure," Plato said, taking her hand as she held it out to him.

She was struck by how strong his fingers were, yet how gentle. Suddenly she wanted to close her fingers tightly around his and never let go, even though the impulse terrified her. Her sudden need filled her with uncertainty that was in direct conflict with her desire to shake off all fear and stay with this man forever.

She released the pressure of her fingers and reluctantly withdrew her hand from his. She felt her mind grow calmer, more sensible. She was no longer a girl who followed her heart and never her head—quite the reverse. She was in command of herself as any woman her age ought to be. It would not do to make rash decisions.

She turned to Clint. "Come along, Clint. It's late. We have much to do tomorrow."

Plato lit the candle in a pierced tin lantern and walked with them to the main road. Clint kept up a steady commentary about the ferry and its workings, the number of stars in the sky, pointing out how pretty the houses looked with lamplight or candlelight gleaming from windows, and the hills beyond, glowing in the moonlight.

At the main road, Plato handed the lantern to Clint. "You can return this to me tomorrow," he said.

Clint took the lantern and started up the road, assuming China was right behind him.

As China turned to Plato to say her final good night, he looked deeply into her eyes.

"And if I ever wanted to find you?" he asked softly.

In an instant, China's firm resolve not to let her heart get mixed up in anything of a romantic nature melted away almost completely.

"I will write to you," she said. "You will always know where to find me."

"I'll look forward to that."

Plato reached for her hand and brought her fingers to his lips. In that instant China felt the air go out of her body. He let go of her hand and as she turned to leave, he bowed ever so slightly, as if paying homage. He turned to go, but changed his mind and faced her again.

"Just remember this, my dear . . . We are too old for somedays," he said softly, and walked away.

China drew in her breath sharply.

"Clint, wait," she called, and hurried toward him.

They walked in silence for a few minutes beneath the overarching branches of the elms, where the lantern did little to pierce the darkness.

"I think he's sweet on you," Clint said, an odd note in his voice.

"Mr. Robinson is our friend, Clint. So it stands to reason that he holds me . . . And you . . . in high esteem."

"Oh."

"We will leave at the end of the week, Clint, on Friday. I thought you might spend the mornings at the ferry, then in the afternoons, we can pack and get ourselves organized for our departure."

"Aye, aye, sir."

Somehow, China didn't think his heart was in it. Nor, she thought, was hers.

24.

The journey to Greenville required some backtracking, there being no well-traveled roads in the Bingham region to take them directly to Moosehead Lake. The stagecoach from Bingham would take China and Clint back to Skowhegan, and from there they would take the train back to Bangor. They would take another train to Old Town and then all the way to Monson, where the track ended. Finally, they would take a stagecoach through Blanchard and Shirley to Greenville, China explained to Clint.

On the morning of their departure, Mrs. Chase, Mrs. Sawyer, Miss Spencer, Mr. And Mrs. Ashford, and Franklin Moore stood on the piazza at the Bingham House and waved good-bye as the stage-coach driver spoke to the horses and headed south. Buster the dog, chased along behind for a short distance, barking, before he gave up and trotted back to Mrs. Chase.

China looked for Plato as they came toward the old church, hoping she might see him standing at the corner of the ferry road to wave as the stagecoach passed. But he wasn't there. She sat back in the seat, hiding her disappointment from Clint, glad there were no other passengers in the vehicle.

At times, the stage road followed the Kennebec River, then veered away before coming back to it. On either side of the road, the hills rose steep and green.

"It's like riding through a leafy green loaf with a deep slice through it," Clint remarked. He had not been especially talkative since their departure.

"Yes," China said, "a very large, very green bun."

"Is that what Greenville will be like?"

"I don't know, Clint. I've never been there. But Mrs. Chase said she'd heard that Moosehead Lake is surrounded by mountains, and the village sits at the head of the lake. The lake is so large, a steamboat carries passengers to and from a very fancy hotel called the Kineo House some miles up the lake."

"Will we stay there?"

"The Kineo House? No, it's much too grand for people like us. Are you looking forward to seeing Greenville?"

"I suppose so."

"Clint, would you rather have stayed in Bingham with Mr. Robinson?"

"Maybe. But he didn't say anything about it, and there's no way I could let you go off by yourself without a cabin boy to look out for you."

"Clint, although I very much enjoy your company, I am not your responsibility, and there is no call for you to travel with me if you do not wish to."

"I know that. It's just . . . I really liked the ferry."

"Mr. Robinson and I talked about that, Clint. He said the ferry will be replaced by a bridge in not so many years, certainly before you are grown up, so fitting yourself to be a ferryman is unwise. It was his opinion that you should go to school and perhaps take an interest in building bridges, since that is where the future lies."

"Mr. Robinson said that?"

"He did."

"But if I was to go to school, I'd have to . . . live somewhere. Belong to someone."

"Yes." Clint seemed to shrink back into himself.

"Well, there's no need to think about that if you don't want to. We are on an adventure, perhaps the last I may ever have, given the fact I am somewhat past my prime. It seems to me the best thing to do is for both of us to enjoy it while we can, and for as long as we want to."

Clint was silent and didn't look at China for a few moments.

"Do you think we'll take the steamboat up that lake?"

"I have every intention of doing so."

"I bet you'll start acting like the captain, giving everybody orders." Clint's voice had a slight edge to it, and China feared his words had a deeper meaning. Then, he grinned, and China saw that his mood had become less introspective. Her own mood was somewhat less than buoyant, though she took care not to let on to Clint.

She had felt a deep sense of loss when she had said her final good-bye to Plato the night before, when he had come to the hotel for supper. He had brought her a posy of wildflowers, handing it to her in front of everyone, even though he knew Mrs. Chase's sharp eyes had seen the gesture and would chatter about it to all and sundry. Tucked into the bouquet was a slip of paper with Plato's post office box number so China could write to him, if she wished. In return she had slipped him the names of the hotels she expected to stay at so he could write to her. She also included her approximate itinerary and her Fort Point address.

After supper, Plato had pushed back his chair, wished her a good journey, shaken hands with Clint, and walked away.

China had wanted to go after him, to tell him that someday she would come back to Bingham to see him. But she recalled what he had said about "somedays." The future for them, she thought, was not some vague destination hovering before them like an insubstantial dream, with plenty of time ahead to attain it. They were no longer young. Someday no longer existed for them. Perhaps they had already waited too long. The thought annoyed her.

"Clint, although I told you we would have to go back through Bangor in order to get to Greenville, what I did not tell you was that I sent a telegram to my sisters to say I would be in Bangor overnight, and if it was convenient, they should meet us at the Bangor House for supper."

Clint turned to stare at China, his mouth slightly agape. Then he clamped his lips shut, folded his arms across his chest, and would not look at her. He even scowled.

Dear me, thought China, as she waited for him to speak. His sudden dark mood alarmed her. Only moments before he had been happy enough.

"You're going to leave me there, aren't you? You're going to make them send me to school somewhere while you go off to Greenville and who knows where else! You're going to leave me just like everybody does!" he said in a tight, angry voice.

China reached out and touched his shoulder, but he shrugged her hand away. His mouth settled into a grim line.

China waited and did not speak until she saw his jaw muscles relax a bit.

"Mr. Remick," she said sternly but kindly, "as your captain it is my responsibility to chart the course that will take us safely to our destination. It is I, the captain, who will decide what ports of call we will make. But without the trust of my crew, and my cabin boy in particular, my job becomes very difficult. Firstly, even though there was no formal signing of papers to enlist you into service aboard my vessel, as it were, you did, indeed, volunteer. Which means you may leave whenever you choose. However, as long as you wish to retain your position as cabin boy, you may do so. It is not, I assure you, my intention to hand you over to my sisters like some sort of pirate's booty so you can be sent to school. And secondly, I have no authority to make any decision about your future or your education or anything else about your life. I wish you to meet my sisters because they wish to meet you. That is all."

Clint took a deep breath and turned his head to look at her.

"I'm sorry," he said quietly.

"And so am I."

"Why are you sorry?"

"Because I should not have assumed you would like to be surprised. Nor should I have assumed meeting my sisters would be a happy occasion for you."

"You must think I'm a baby."

"No, Clint. I think you are a boy who has seen too much heartache at too young an age, and sometimes it makes you cross."

After that, Clint settled down and seemed to enjoy the journey.

At Solon, several other passengers joined them, a couple with a boy near Clint's age and a girl of perhaps sixteen. They were a lively family and much inclined to talk and ask questions. The remaining hours to Skowhegan passed agreeably.

They spent the night at the Elm House and took the train to Bangor in the morning.

25.

As the train arrived at the outskirts of Bangor, Clint stared intently out the window. When he caught sight of the ships moored in the

Penobscot, heard steamboat whistles, and spied small boats ferrying people back and forth across the river, his mouth literally hung open.

China suppressed an urge to tell him about everything he saw. Better that he absorb as much of it as he could on his own, she thought. She would answer his questions as they arose.

Without turning toward her, he said, "You were captain of a ship like those?"

"Yes, in a manner of speaking, but not entirely on my own. As I have said many times during our travels, I shared that duty with my sisters." She couldn't resist an urge to point out which ship was a barkentine, which was a schooner, and the difference between square and gaff rigging.

That information caused Clint to tear his gaze away from the window and stare at China.

"Wow!" he said. "I'm going to write a postal card to Mr. Robinson and tell him all about this."

China laughed with delight, and other passengers in nearby seats, overhearing Clint's comments, smiled and exchanged friendly and knowing glances with China.

An elderly man sitting in the seat opposite them commented, "He's a sharp one, that young mister is." China smiled in agreement.

When the train pulled into the station at the end of Exchange Street, Clint was so excited he could not sit still, and was the first to reach the door and step out onto the train platform.

"Come, Clint, my sisters will be waiting for us at the Bangor House. We mustn't be late," China said, suddenly worried she would have to take Clint by the hand and drag him away to prevent him from bolting to the waterfront for a closer look at the ships and the small boats serving as ferries. "This evening after my sisters have returned to Fort Point, I will take you to see the ships. But for now, we have other business to attend to."

"What about our bags?"

"I've arranged to have them sent to the Windsor Hotel, where we will spend the night, and the rates are more affordable, although I thought eating supper at the Bangor House would be a nice treat and give you a chance to see one of Bangor's most famous buildings. President Ulysses S. Grant once stayed there. And, since we've been sitting some hours on the train, I thought we might walk to the Bangor House. It's not far. That way you'll have some time to look around."

"Never thought I'd ever come to Bangor," Clint said. He was fairly dancing with excitement.

Many people milled around the station as passengers got off the train and others waited to board. A man pushing a two-wheeled cart offered fruit for sale. The clamor of voices, the clip-clop of horses' hooves, the clatter of buggy wheels against paving stones, the clang of bells, the squawk of seagulls, and barking of dogs filled the air with a busy bustle. A breeze blew a stew of odors—smoke from the train engine stack, hot tar, wet rope, dirt, warm stones, river-soaked logs, sawdust, damp wool shirts, evergreen resin, and the funk of low tide. Clint drew it all in, embracing it, and in the process, canceling China's fears that he might be overwhelmed by the vitality of Bangor. Quite the contrary. Clint appeared to revel in it, asking questions nonstop about where the ships came from and went to, if she thought there would ever be a bridge across the Penobscot, what her sisters were like, and if he would like them. She answered each question briefly, except the last one.

"Everyone I know likes and admires my sisters. I have every reason to believe they will like you as much as I do once they have become acquainted with you," China said. She pointed up the street, indicating the Bangor House, then in the opposite direction to show Clint which was the Windsor Hotel, where they would stay the night.

At the Bangor House, China asked to be directed to the parlor. She had barely turned away from the front desk when she saw India and Persia striding toward her, their faces wreathed in smiles, their hands stretched toward her, skirts swishing with the effort to reach her as quickly as possible and enfold her in their arms.

Oh, how glad she was to see them! Tears of happiness pricked her eyes, and India and Persia reached for their handkerchiefs, too.

"India, Persia, may I present to you my cabin boy, Clint Remick. Clint, these are my sisters, Miss India Havener and Miss Persia Havener."

Clint, with a quick check to make sure it was clean, held out his hand, first to India, then to Persia.

"Pleased to meet you, ma'am," he said to each, a look of incredulity on his face. "You all look exactly alike! Three Miss Haveners and all the same, the very same! I can't tell one of you from the other!"

"That's because we're triplets," China said. "I told you that, I believe."

"I know, but . . . You mean like twins, but with one more?"

"That's one way to put it, though we never have been able to figure out who are the twins and who is the one more, as you put it," Persia said drily.

"My father's cow had twin calves once," Clint remarked, trying to make sense of three sisters who looked exactly alike.

"Not precisely the same," India remarked, fixing her gaze on Clint, then smiling at China. "Though we may be the same on the exterior, we are very different in other ways, which I expect you will discover upon closer acquaintance."

China knew then that India, at least, had already taken a liking to Clint.

"Well, shall we all go into the dining room and sit down?" Persia said, making motions with her hands to shoo them toward the door, as if they were sheep.

India inclined her head closely to China's and said, "Acting more like her sheepdog every day."

"I heard that, India," Persia said, but with no rancor in her voice. "I must warn you, Clint, I may coerce you into taking my side in this matter."

Her remark caused Clint to become suddenly quiet, a look of alarm in his eyes.

"She's having fun at your expense," China said in a loud whisper to him.

"Oh," Clint said, regaining his composure.

Her sisters' behavior startled China. They had changed, and it had only been a few weeks since she had last seen them. Then she noticed Persia's hair. The familiar coils of braids were gone.

"Persia! Your hair!"

Persia lifted her gloved hand to her head. "Oh, yes, that," she said. "Just a bit of a . . . Trim."

"More like a shearing," India said. "Now she even looks like one of her sheep."

"That will do, India," Persia said briskly. "We wouldn't want Clint to think one of us is in reality a sheep and the other a cat . . . now would we?"

China's mouth dropped open and she stared at them. Never in her life had she ever heard India and Persia address one another in such a way, at least not since they were children. Clearly, they held no acrimony toward one another, yet their jests—or whatever it was that had just passed between them—held a bit of an edge. Nevertheless, neither India nor Persia seemed at all perturbed by the exchange. Quite the reverse.

"The fact is," Persia continued, "those braids kept coming out of their pins or coming loose or just getting in the way. So one day, I cut them off. I still have enough hair to tie back or even pin into a small bun, just not so much as there was before. And I must say, it's so much more practical."

A waiter seated them, handed them menus, took their order, and brought food. Clint, never one to shy away from a beefsteak and baked potato, dug in as if he had not eaten three eggs and bacon just that morning.

"Well, Clint," Persia said. "China wrote that you grew up on a farm. Did she tell you that I keep sheep?"

"Yes, ma'am, she did."

"Were there sheep on your family's farm?"

"We had a few." He stopped to fork another bite of meat into his mouth, chewed, and swallowed. "My father took the fleeces over to Harmony to the spinning mill there, Bartlett's, and exchanged them for yarn. My mother knit me mittens and socks." He looked down at his plate and became silent.

Persia reached out and put her hand on his, a gesture of comfort and understanding. Clint did not shy away from the gesture, China noted.

"I should like to hear more about Bartlett's mill later on," Persia said.

Clint nodded.

"Perhaps, Persia, we might hear a bit more about your sheep," China said.

"They are Hampshires, very pretty to look at. Swan, that's the collie dog, works well with them and with me, though I am still learning how to instruct him. I'm just getting the hang of weaving, but I spin quite well now. I bought some fleece from a farmer in Stockton Springs so I could experiment. In fact, I knit Clint a pair of stockings and a pair for you, China, from some of the yarn I spun."

Persia reached into her reticule and drew out two packages, each one wrapped in brown paper and tied with string. She handed one to China, the other to Clint.

"A present?" Clint whispered, so taken aback he could barely speak for moment. He put down his fork and opened the package slowly.

He drew out a pair of finely knitted dark blue socks. "I thank you," he said. "They will keep my feet happy. Open yours, Miss Havener."

China undid the string and paper to find a pair of white stockings knit in a lace pattern.

"Oh, Persia! These are lovely!" China said.

"She's very clever with her knitting needles," India said. "My gifts to the two of you aren't on a par with Persia's, but I know how much you like my chocolate fudge, China, so I brought enough for you and Clint." She offered them a small box she had been carrying.

"Oh, boy!" Clint said, taking the box from India. He removed the cover and helped himself to a piece of fudge. "This is good."

The sisters laughed together and suddenly, for China, it was like old times, as if she hadn't been away for six weeks, as if she wouldn't be away for another eight or ten.

"Oh, sister," India said, reaching for China's hand, "we have missed you."

"But not so much that we want to deter you from your adventure, China. India and I have talked it all over quite a bit, and have come to a better understanding now of why you wanted to go off without us. But we miss you enough to look forward to the day you come home," Persia added.

China thanked her, then said to India, "How is your work on the sea chanteys coming along?"

"Right now, all I have is a large stack of notes and pages of music I have transcribed as I played the ditties on the piano, or sang them to myself or with Sam Webber. But with each song, I have copied out sections of Father's log, or sections of Mother's journal, or passages from letters they received, so one gets a sense of what was going on when those chanteys were sung, or where in the world the *Empress* was at the time. Sam Webber insists on reading what I have written so far, and he says it's good reading. He often has excellent suggestions on how

I can improve the text, or points out places where I need to expand the information. So with that small encouragement, I have written to a publisher in Boston, though I think I may be ahead of myself there."

"I will look forward to reading what you have written, India," China replied.

"Look at her fingers," Persia said, taking India's hand and holding it up for them to see. "Ink stains!"

"Better that than indigo-blue hands from dying wool!" India retorted, laughing with Persia rather than at her.

After they had eaten, they retired to the ladies' parlor to drink tea. Clint, still considered a child, was allowed to go into the parlor with them.

The sisters talked about the practical things of life—China's travel budget; India's interest in Ticknor and Fields, the publisher that had published Hawthorne, Longfellow, Stowe, and Whittier; and Persia's plan to increase the size of her garden next year.

India and Persia gave China the latest news of their many friends and acquaintances, and they became absorbed in their talk.

Clint feigned interest, but he was restless, and wandered over to the window to gaze out at the many wagons, rigs, carriages, horses, and pedestrians going up and down Main Street.

"By the way, Abner and Elizabeth Giddings gave this to us, to deliver to you," India said, passing a note to China.

"They have invited Clint and me to stay at their house over on Summer Street," China said as she read the note. "How very kind of them. Clint, we won't be staying at the Windsor Hotel after all. I'll write a note and cancel our reservation, and have our bags sent on. Perhaps you could take the note to the hotel manager at the Windsor. Do you remember which one it is, just up the street from the train station, on the corner of Exchange Street?"

Clint perked up, glad to have somewhere to focus his energy.

"Aye, aye, Captain," he said with enthusiasm. "I certainly do remember."

Even so, China gave Clint detailed instructions on how to get to the Windsor Hotel.

"And, Clint, since you will have to walk along the waterfront, back toward the train station, have a care. Don't talk to any of the layabouts or let yourself be accosted by sharp-tongued shills who think you have money they can part you from. Come back immediately, and we will go to Summer Street where Mr. And Mrs. Giddings live."

Clint tucked the note China had written into his pocket, pulled on his cap, and set off.

The sisters talked until the clock chimed the hour. It was nearly six o'clock.

"Clint should have been back by now," China said, suddenly aware of how much time had passed.

Persia stood. "We've sat here long enough," she said. "We'd best go find him."

"Dear me, yes," India agreed. "It's very easy for a boy to go astray on a waterfront. Press gangs, you know, never go out of fashion."

"I don't believe press gangs intent on coercing innocent boys into serving aboard a ship against their will still exist," China scoffed, refusing to entertain the notion. "Clint is a capable boy and knows how to fend for himself. Perhaps he was delayed at the hotel for some reason."

"Perhaps press gangs don't exist anymore," India said, "but I'll wager there still are those who might attempt it if there was a dollar to be made from it."

Persia agreed on that point.

The sisters settled their hats more firmly on their heads, gathered up reticules, umbrellas, the socks, and the box of fudge. They sallied forth, their long strides carrying them down Washington Street and into the heart of the comings and goings of Penobscot River commerce.

They said little to one another as they peered into store windows, hoping to see Clint, and scanned what shipboard activity they could see from the street.

Anxiety ground in China's stomach. But no, Clint was level-headed. He wouldn't get into trouble. At least not on his own. But what if trouble found him, trouble in the guise of a smooth-talking agent whose job it was to supply ship crews to captains with bad reputations who couldn't get anyone else and were willing to pay the going price? There were laws against such practices, but laws never stopped bad people from doing bad things if the right amount of money was involved.

"I think we should split up," Persia said as they approached Exchange Street, opposite the train station. "China, you inquire at the hotel. I'll search the train station, and India can look over at the ferry landing."

"Persia, that's it! The ferryboats!" China exclaimed. "Clint is greatly interested in ferrying. That's how he spent his time when we were at Bingham. He helped Mr. Robinson operate the ferry across the Kennebec."

They reversed direction and headed toward the ferry landing. They walked faster now, overcome by an urgency fueled by the hope they would soon find Clint. They recalled to one another the stories their father had told of men who been beaten up, drugged, and sold to ship before the mast. Those men had never been to sea before, had no way of letting their families know what had become of them until three or four years later, when they turned up on their own doorsteps to find their sweethearts married to someone else or the infants they left behind now grown into children they did not recognize.

"Outrageous!" China muttered, for no particular reason, except to vent her growing worry that something terrible had happened to Clint.

At the ferry landing, the sisters found a young man wearing a flat-topped cap. His smile was friendly.

"We're looking for a boy," China said. "Comes to about my shoulder, thirteen years old, wearing a navy blue jacket and a cap. Perhaps you've seen him?"

"Can't say as I have. Would he have taken one of the ferries?" he asked, indicating a yawl propelled by men wielding heavy oars. It cost a penny to be ferried over to Brewer, and that particular boat was owned by Captain Henry Leach, the young man confided.

"We don't believe so."

"Then I wouldn't have seen him."

"Then who might have?" Persia demanded. "Especially if the boy just wanted to see what the ferry was all about."

"He a runaway?" the man asked, sensing that these were ladies with a purpose and not to be trifled with.

"No, but he's a country boy, never been to Bangor before, and we fear he might have been . . . Appropriated," China said, pointedly.

"If you mean what I think you mean, you should get the police," the man said. "Let's go ask Jake. He helps passengers in and out of the boat, the ladies and little kids, and he ties up and casts off the mooring lines."

Jake, a middle-aged man with gray side whiskers, stood on the pier, gazing across the Penobscot, keeping an eye on the boat just embarking from the Brewer side of the river.

"Excuse me," China said. "We're looking for a boy, thirteen, about this tall."

"I've seen a lot of boys today, ma'am. Some of them just as you describe," Jake said.

"This one would be wearing a navy blue coat, probably asking questions about ferrying, or just hanging around, say, within the last hour or so," India said.

Jake thought a minute, pursing his lips as he did so.

"Come to think of it, I did," he said. "Nice-appearing boy. But he wasn't alone. There was a man talking to him. Didn't like the looks of him, though. Can't say why for sure. I heard the man say something about taking him to talk to a ferryman over at Slade's saloon. That's over in the Acre. No place I'd want my boy to be."

The sisters looked at one another. It was worse than China had feared. The Acre, known locally as Hell's Half-Acre, but often referred to as the Acre to avoid saying the word 'hell,' was the sordid side of Bangor where, in spite of Maine's law against the sale of intoxicating liquors, saloons flourished, and with them, the shadier side of life.

"Thank you, sir," India said.

Although the sisters had never been to the Acre, they knew it by reputation. Maude Webber had told them stories about some of her midwifery excursions there, many details left out, of course, but told in such a way as to to let the sisters know that it was a place where the seedy and seamy sides of life were always present.

Temperance was the law in Maine, but liquor was sold more or less without police interference, though there were sporadic raids from time to time, just to keep the saloon keepers guessing.

Persia gripped her parasol handle more firmly, as if she felt the need of a weapon.

"You don't have to go if you don't want to," China said to her sisters as they retraced their steps and regained the street. "But I'm going." The look on her face was set and determined, and India and Persia knew better than to try to talk her out of it.

"If you think for one minute I am going to let you go off to the Acre alone, you are quite mistaken, China," Persia said. "India, you can find your way up to Summer Street to Abner and Elizabeth Giddings's house, if you like. I am going with China."

"I most certainly will not," India said. "This may turn out to be one of our finest adventures, the last we may ever have in our declining years. I certainly wouldn't want to miss it." And with that she strode ahead of her sisters. "I believe this is the direction we must take," she said over her shoulder.

China and Persia stepped up their pace to catch up with India, and shoulder to shoulder they marched toward the Acre and Slade's saloon.

26.

"What will we do when we get there?" India asked, stopping suddenly, overcome with the enormity of the situation, her bravado of a few moments ago ebbing. Ladies never went to places where spirits were sold, and they most certainly did not draw attention to themselves by getting into any kind of public fracas. She had seen firsthand how drinking too much rum had helped to sour the last years of their father's life. She, China, and Persia sometimes took a glass of dandelion wine as a tonic, or a bit of grape cordial to build the blood—purely medicinal, of course. But a place where men went to drink to get intoxicated, to drown their sorrows in a pail of beer? Certainly not! India tended to vacillate when she found herself in unfamiliar waters she deemed too deep for her notions of propriety.

"We will inquire politely about a lost boy. That's all," China said firmly, not in the least swayed by India's momentary trepidation. Clint was in danger, perhaps led astray by thugs, prevented from leaving. He would be frightened, perhaps threatened with violence if he did not put pen to paper. She wasn't going to stand by and let that happen, even if she had to march into that saloon all by herself.

"What if we find them, but not Clint, and they refuse to tell us anything?" Persia asked.

"Then we will find a police officer," China said.

"China, I really think . . . ," India began, her chin trembling a bit.

"India, if you have lost your nerve, then take Persia and go up that way, which will bring you to Summer Street, where you will find Abner Giddings's house. But I am going to Slade's whether you— either of you—wish to or not."

And with that, China marched forward, leaving India and Persia a few paces behind.

Persia gave India a withering look that brooked no nonsense, hooked her arm through India's elbow, and propelled her along until they caught up with China.

"There is safety in numbers," she said firmly.

"Thank you, Persia," China said. "I wouldn't want to do this without you . . . Though if I had to, I certainly would."

But more than that, she realized with sudden clarity, doing without them was an impossibility—even though she would spend another twelve weeks away from them. As she strode along the street with her sisters—the other parts of herself, one on either side of her—she sensed an old feeling, one she had known, most likely, since birth. She felt complete, whole, entire. And she saw that India and Persia felt that way, too.

"I'm all right now," India said. "I had a sudden fit of faintheartedness, that's all."

Wooden buildings, some two or three stories tall, some low and squat, lined both sides of the street. The clapboards had weathered dark gray, and cedar shingles curled with age covered the rooftops. Doors stood open to the fine weather and the sound of singing, the plaintive wail of a fiddle tune, and the clink of crockery drifted out to them.

Laundry, hanging on lines strung between some of the buildings, shivered slightly in a sudden breeze, the legs of trousers and hems of skirts jumping and dancing, creating a macabre dance, sending a sudden rill of dread jangling along China's spine. More than anything she wanted the impending encounter to be over and done with. She straightened her shoulders and kept on walking.

Women clad in ill-fitting clothing and well-worn shoes walked with a weary stride, one carrying an infant, another toting a basket, a third herding four young children, their faces streaked with dirt.

Men strode along purposefully, alone, in pairs, or groups of three or four. They wore work clothes, heavy boots, and battered felt hats, though here and there a man wearing a neat black jacket and a bowler hat threaded his way along the street.

Wagon and dray traffic added to the confusion.

The sisters stayed their course and soon found themselves at a loss. No sign indicated which establishment was Slade's.

"I shall ask," China said, determination in her voice.

India's eyes grew large. "Oh, dear," she murmured, anxiety getting the best of her again.

China ignored her, detached her arm from her sisters', and approached a nice-looking man wearing a dark jacket and good shoes.

"Excuse me, sir, but could you tell me which place is Slade's?"

The man tipped his hat in polite greeting even as he raised his eyebrows in surprise.

"That's no place for ladies," he said. His eyes darted from China's face, to India's, then Persia's, taking in their identical features, clearly wondering what errand these respectable looking ladies were on.

"Yes, we are quite aware of that, but we are on family business . . ." China deliberately let her sentence trail off, hoping that it would satisfy the man's curiosity.

The man regarded her steadily for a moment, as if making up his mind. He inclined his head in the direction of a building just up the street. "It's that one there, the one with the black horse tied out front."

"Thank you."

The man gave a curt nod and continued on his way.

China, India, and Persia looked at one another, took a collective deep breath, and started toward Slade's. There was no hesitation in their step now, though India's heart was hammering and Persia felt her face flush with sudden warmth. When they reached the building, China opened the door and stepped through, with India and Persia close behind, a triumvirate of indignant, mature, don't-meddle-with-us womanhood.

The barkeep, hearing their footfall, not at all like the heavy tread of the boots men wore, looked up from his task of drying a tumbler to stare at them. He was a small, bald man, suspicion glowing in his eyes. It had been some time since his establishment had been raided by the local authorities—Maine was, by law, a temperance state—and he was ever on the alert for any tricks the law might play on him. As for women, he had no use for them at all. They were bad for business, stirring up trouble of one kind or another, which usually resulted in the law showing up.

Pipe and cigar smoke, the odor of tobacco, and the sour smell of beer clotted the air in the tavern. Curious male eyes, shadowed by hat brims looked up and stared. One old man grinned, as if he relished the excitement he felt certain was bound to ensue if these tall, determined women didn't beat a hasty retreat.

"We don't serve women," the barkeep said in a rough voice, meant to intimidate them. He flicked the bar rag in the air, motioning for them to be gone.

China ignored him, her eyes scanning the gloom, her gaze landing on an alcove furnished with a dark booth where two men sat talking, apparently, to a third person who was not visible owing to the height of the back of the booth and the configuration of the nook.

"Wait here," China murmured to India and Persia. She walked with a confident step, her umbrella held firmly in her hand, across the room to the booth.

"Hey!" the barkeep snarled, coming out from behind the bar. India and Persia moved suddenly to intercept him.

"How dare you speak to us like that!" India fumed, anger replacing her fear, causing the barkeep to hesitate.

This brought a ripple of ragged laughter from the men sitting at the tables.

"Excuse me," China said to the men in the booth, "but I believe that boy you have with you is my . . . son. Clint, I'm quite ashamed of you, going off like that . . . " The tone in her voice was a reprimand, a tone she had learned from her mother, when as a child, she had come up against a parental rule she had disregarded.

"You best hold your horses, lady," one of the men said in an oily voice. "You've mistook this boy. He's signed on to go as cabin boy on the next boat headed downriver. Fair and square. Got the papers right here." The man tapped his dirty finger on some rumpled, ink-smeared sheets of paper.

"Clint, did you sign those papers?" China demanded, not taking her eyes off the men.

Clint, his face white, clearly frightened, a bruise visible on the side of his face, shook his head briefly, almost imperceptibly, a motion China perceived out of the corner of her eye.

"My son looks older than he is, gentlemen. He's barely twelve," she lied, silently asking her mother, father, and all the saints in heaven to forgive her. "I believe it's customary for a boy to be at least fourteen before he's considered of legal age to ship out. So, sir, if you would be so kind as to get up and let my son out of this booth, I will be on my way and trouble you no more."

The other man stared at China, as if weighing his options, gauging her likelihood to back down, betting she wasn't being any straighter with him than he was with her, figuring that since she was a woman and hadn't already called the police, she would be easily cowed.

"We say he signed, and he said he's fourteen."

With a sudden move, China planted the sharp pointed ferrule of her umbrella just beneath the spot on the man's neck where the jawbone begins its L-shaped ascent. The other man stared at her, taken aback.

"You better back off, lady," he said in low, menacing tone.

"Mister, I weigh a good one hundred and fifty pounds. If I lean just the slightest bit more on this umbrella, your mate will find himself skewered and bleeding like a pig fit to die," China said, a steely tone in her voice. To demonstrate, she pushed the ferrule just a bit harder into the man's neck, causing him to emit an ugly growl of panic and pain.

Almost at the same moment, Clint, sensing his opportunity, sprang up to stand on the booth seat, stepped onto the table, and kicked the other man in face. The man sagged into the corner.

"Don't you ever sass my mother again!" he screamed, his face contorted with a level of rage that surprised her.

India and Persia, umbrella points raised like rapiers to fend off the barkeep, backed toward the door, shouting in unison, "Fire, fire! Help! Help! Fire! Police!" Almost immediately a few people, including two police officers, hastened through the door, shoving India and Persia out of the way.

By that time, China, with Clint firmly by the arm, India and Persia beside her, pushed her way through the door, gaining the safety of the street.

The last thing they heard was an old man's voice cackling, "I knew it! I knew it! I shipped once on the *Empress*. The Havener sisters, that's who they are, the Havener sisters! Did you see that? How they look exactly alike? Them sisters never took no guff. Oh, no, oh no," he said, punctuating his words with a cackle of laughter. "They never took no guff off any man that went to sea on their ship."

China, India, Persia, and Clint, not looking back, hurried up the street, intent on putting as much distance as possible between themselves and Slade's saloon.

When a police officer caught up with them to inquire about the situation, China assured him she did not intend to press charges or make any further fuss. She explained how she had extricated a boy from what she perceived to be a serious dilemma. He was safe now, and no more needed to be said about it.

"If you must arrest someone, I suggest you begin with me, Officer. I was the one who threatened one of the men with his life if he didn't hand over my son," China said, her arm protectively around Clint's shoulders. She felt him tremble and lean against her.

"Those boys play a rough game. They won't take this kindly," the officer said. "We'll put them in the cooler for the night—otherwise, they might make more mischief for you."

"That will suit us quite well, Officer, for we will be on the early train in the morning, out of Bangor. I thank you."

The officer lifted his hand in a quick salute and went back to Slade's, where the knot of bystanders, still staring after Clint and the Havener sisters, was beginning to thin now that the excitement was over.

27.

"Nothing much changes over in the Acre, no matter what part of the waterfront it takes hold in," Abner Giddings said as he sat by the fire in the parlor of his house on Summer Street.

Clint sat beside him, awestruck that Abner had spent his life at sea from the time he was a boy.

"I remember times when the authorities raided those dives and the gutters ran brown with the whiskey they poured from barrels hidden in all manner of places," Abner said, ruffling Clint's hair. "And a very long time ago, when I first went to sea, I was a cabin boy, sailing with Captain Job Bailey, in those days one of the best seamen around these parts."

Elizabeth, in her usual gracious and efficient way, handed around plates of cake and poured cups of tea, which China, India, Persia, and Clint enjoyed as they provided details of their adventure at Slade's.

Elizabeth took her place in the chair near Abner, her eyes, filled with affection, finding his every so often.

"Bangor was a much more uncivilized place then," Elizabeth said. "But some things never change."

"I was shanghaied once, by Captain Joshua Stetson," Abner went on, glancing fondly at Elizabeth. "That was back in the days when Stetson ran most everything on the waterfront his own way, had his own ships, including the *Fairmount*, of which I was the master."

He hesitated, thinking how to edit his tale so as not to say anything about Fanny Abbott Harding, then known as Fanny Hogan, whose reputation in those days had left much to be desired.

Clint's eyes grew round as he stared at Abner. He had recovered his composure, but his face was still pale. "So this Stetson fellow wanted to . . . To steal you, like those men were trying to steal me?" he asked.

"Yes, he did. He was a man of perverse nature, and thought only of himself and what he could do to make himself richer. I was in the coasting trade in those days and wanted to stay in it, but he wanted to put me on the *Venerable*, in the China trade. When I turned him down, well, that went against the grain of things for him, so to teach me a lesson, he had me shanghaied. When I woke up I was on the *Venerable*, all right, one of the worst-run ships there ever was, with a brute for a master. I shipped before the mast as a common seaman for a year or so before I jumped ship and found my way back home to Elizabeth."

"We were keeping company then," Elizabeth said quietly, smiling at Abner. He returned her gaze with equal loving kindness, and reached for her hand. He kissed it quickly. In fact, they had been estranged from one another during that time due to a terrible misunderstanding. But that was something Clint did not need to know.

The talk turned to other stories of the sea, both humorous and dramatic, and the evening passed pleasantly.

With the excitement of finding Clint, India and Persia had missed their boat back to Fort Point. Elizabeth had insisted that they stay the night, too.

China's and Clint's bags had been sent from the Windsor Hotel to the Giddings home. Clint had accomplished that errand before he had been accosted by the men who had forced him to go with them to Slade's saloon.

Elizabeth settled Clint in a room by himself, and put China, India, and Persia in a large room at the back of the house. After India and Persia were asleep, China got up and knocked on the door of Clint's room.

"Come in," he called softly. He was propped up in bed, his lamp burning brightly, as if he feared what might lurk in the dark if he turned the light out. He looked drained of energy, as if the stress of his ordeal had manifested itself only then.

China sat on the edge of the bed, folded her hands in her lap, and said, "I want to apologize to you for saying something that was untrue, Clint. I told those men I was your mother only because I thought they would be more likely to take me seriously, to listen to my case; I thought it would appeal to what little kindness may have been in them, which turned out to be none at all."

To China's surprise, Clint placed his hand atop China's and let it rest there.

"I know," he said softly. "I don't mind." Tears filled his eyes, but did not fall.

China kissed his cheek and pulled the covers more snugly around him, even though the night was warm. She brushed his hair out of his eyes. It was not the first time she had ventured to touch him, but it was the first time he had seemed to welcome it.

"You are very dear to me, Clint. Never doubt that. Now get some sleep; we make an early start in the morning."

"More adventures," Clint murmured as his eyelids drooped.

"But none, I hope, as exciting as what transpired this evening. Good night, Clint," China said softly. She turned the lamp down, but not out, knowing he needed the comfort of that small blaze.

"See you in the morning," he whispered.

She closed the door softly behind her.

She slid into the trundle bed Elizabeth had pulled out from under the big bed where India and Persia lay sleeping.

China felt her heart hammering for several seconds, skip a beat, then settle into its usual rhythm. She stared into the darkness, her thoughts returning to the moment they had found Clint—how relief had flooded through her, the way her heart had almost stood still when she thought how easily, how quickly Clint might have been lost to her, vanished without a trace, forced to work like a beast of burden, perhaps ill-fed or beaten.

She had called herself his mother thinking it might serve as a lever to make those scoundrels sit up and take notice. It hadn't made a dent in their hearts, but it had made one in hers. Clint was her son—not because biology or a court had decreed it, but because she had made a place for him beside her, had seen to his clothing and comforts, had informed her sisters and friends that he was her responsibility. Everyone she knew accepted and approved of it. Without exception

they welcomed him, even those who had not yet met him. They had
reached out to him, and supported her in this new reality in their lives.

As for Clint, he had said he didn't mind that she had called herself his mother, had called him son. When he saw his chance, he had
leapt from danger to her side, where he knew he would be safe. That
alone told her that she also mattered to him—that he looked to her
for comfort and protection.

And now, for the first time, she had kissed his cheek and tucked
him in, the things a mother did to comfort a child who has suffered a
terrible fright, to make him know he is loved, that he matters.

How very odd, she thought, as sleep drifted toward her tired mind,
that I should become a mother without ever being a wife.

28.

China and Clint boarded the train the next morning. Abner,
Elizabeth, India, and Persia stood on the platform to wave them off.

Although China's good-byes with her sisters were hasty, she felt
the visit with them had been successful. They were more understanding of her need to continue her travels, and she had seen how they had
gained confidence in their own endeavors during her absence. Because
Clint was now her traveling companion, they were less inclined to
fret about her safety.

Their adventure of the night before, when they had rescued Clint,
had brought it home to them that as a unit they were not to be trifled with, something they had forgotten during their years alongshore. Their encounter with the ruffians at Slade's saloon had done
much to increase the strength of the bond they had shared all their
lives. It had also endeared Clint to them.

China left the glass-plate negatives she had exposed in Cambridge and Bingham in India's and Persia's care. They promised to store the negatives until her return in the fall. Abner had accepted the duty of buying more glass-plate negatives, and would send them on to Greenville by train in a few days' time.

The train engine blew its whistle, and precisely at seven-thirty a.m. it lurched forward, pulling the cars along the tracks of the European and North American Railway. China and Clint waved farewell as the train chugged out of the station and up the track along the edge of the Penobscot River. After a twelve-mile ride, they arrived in Old Town, where the cars bound for Greenville were attached to another engine. From there, they went on the tracks of the Bangor and Piscataquis Railroad.

The journey was uneventful except for one brief incident when the train slowed to a stop because a cow, complacently chewing its cud, stood in the middle of the track. With Clint's help, that bovine obstacle, much to the boy's intense delight, was encouraged to step off the track so the journey could be resumed.

The weather, fine and clear, allowed views of Mount Katahdin as they passed through South Lagrange and Milo. Even though it was nearly July, Katahdin still had snow on its peak. China pointed out the mountain to Clint.

"Once we have photographed Moosehead, Katahdin country will be our next destination," China said.

"Will we climb it?" Clint asked, eagerly.

"Katahdin? No, we aren't equipped for a mountain-climbing expedition, and I am no longer spry enough to attempt it."

Clint looked disappointed.

"But think of the photographs you'd get standing up there on top. You'd be able to see all the way to . . . To I don't know where."

"I am certain there will be other expeditions to Katahdin for you, my boy."

She had almost said my son.

"How do you know?"

"I know because it's within the realm of possibility, and because one day you will grow up and be able to do as you wish. And if you wish to climb Katahdin, you will."

"Oh. That's a long time to wait."

"In the meantime, you will see Moosehead Lake."

The other passengers in the car were a mix of what China took to be local folks and well-to-do families from away, intent on spending the hot weeks of high summer far from the torrid heat and unhealthy climes of Boston and New York. These people, China knew, would stay at Kineo, the grand hotel in the wilderness where they would sail, bowl, waltz to the music of live bands, and be conveyed to wilderness ponds where they would "rusticate" for several nights. Their every need would be taken care of by experienced guides who would pitch tents, cook food on an open fire, and even provide entertainment by playing harmonicas or singing ballads in two-part harmony.

As they neared Blanchard, a fellow passenger pointed out to them the outline of Russell Mountain, reigning over the Piscataquis River valley. The track took them along the brow of a ridge east of the valley, which offered many scenic, panoramic views of the country.

It was nearly noon when the cars arrived at Blanchard station.

"That was quick!" Clint said. "Just in time, too, because I'm hungry."

"Then we'd better feed you," China said.

They ate a good dinner in the boardinghouse at the depot, then, along with the other passengers, boarded stagecoaches for the five-mile run to Shirley, much of it uphill, where the driver stopped to rest and water the horses. From there it was seven more miles over somewhat less hilly terrain to Greenville.

The scenery in the distance unfolded before them in a series of hills, valleys, and mountains. As they neared Greenville and descended a long hill, the last leg of the journey, the driver called out to them to look left or right to view Squaw, Lily Bay, Baker, Elephant, Indian, Rum, and White Cap peaks.

Greenville, a town of five hundred and eighty-six residents, lay at the bottom of Indian Hill, at the southern end of Moosehead Lake, Maine's great inland sea.

China had read in her guidebook that although the village was pretty enough, it held nothing of interest to strangers in the town. The statement struck her as arrogant in the extreme, and she concluded the guidebook must have been written by someone who had only passed through, never staying long enough to become acquainted with the town.

As China looked around, she saw, indeed, how beauty always resides in the eye of the beholder. The town impressed her as being somewhat rough around the edges, a state reflected in its remote and wilderness character; clearly, it had been part of the frontier in the not-so-distant past. Yet she noted that the buildings were in good repair, yards were neatly kept, and storefronts gleamed with fresh paint. Such things reflected pride of place, she believed.

But it was the quality of light that caused her to draw in a sharp, delighted breath. In spite of the summer warmth, the air was clear and pure, scented by water, earth, trees, grass, and sunshine.

Water lapped against wharves and the rocky shore. It was the voice of the lake, a watery music playing constantly in the background.

The lake itself stretched northward in a wide swath of indigo blue for nearly thirty-eight miles. It varied in width from one to ten miles.

"Gosh," Clint said as he gazed out over the water.

"Indeed," China replied, already thinking about the challenges of photographing it.

The stage stopped at the Lake House, one of only two hotels in town; the other was the Eveleth. Most of the other passengers boarded a steamer up the lake to the Kineo House, the palace in the wilderness.

The Lake House consisted of a large frame building of three and a half stories. Piazzas wrapped around it on three sides on the ground and second-story levels. It put China in mind of the Bingham House, though the Lake House was much larger.

The lobby contained an assortment of comfortable chairs arranged in companionable groups to take advantage of the light streaming in the many windows. An assortment of side tables, their surfaces covered with crocheted doilies, held oil lamps or vases of wildflowers mixed with evergreen boughs. A large music box, waiting for someone to turn its crank to set its mechanism going, stood in one corner.

"Guess they don't have a parrot," Clint remarked, grinning at China as he looked around.

"Behave," China said, giving him a look but smiling back at him.

The front desk, fashioned of oak, occupied a niche by a wide flight of stairs that turned back on itself, its underside forming a slanted ceiling over the area. A man in his forties, China judged, stood behind the desk. He was of middle height, with sandy hair and a quiet manner full of efficient practicality. He indicated a large, open ledger.

"Sign there, if you please. Room twenty for you, madam, and young mister is in twenty-one," he said. "Up those stairs, turn right at the top, first two doors on your right. Rooms with a view and access to the upper piazza. Supper is at six o'clock in the dining room, through that door over there. Breakfast is at seven, dinner at noon." He glanced at the clock, which said quarter of six. He handed China the room keys. "Oh, one moment; I believe there is a letter for you. Arrived yesterday." He handed China an envelope, glanced toward the others waiting to check in, and said, "Next."

"Who's it from?" Clint asked, overcome by curiosity, though he knew it was not polite to ask.

"There's no return address, but the postmark is Bingham. I assume it's from one of our acquaintances there."

The handwriting was not feminine, and she knew instinctively it was from Plato Robinson. A ripple of pleasure consumed her as she tucked the letter into her black leather reticule. He must have mailed it several days before she and Clint had left Bingham, in order for it to coincide with their arrival in Greenville. Clearly, he did not want her to forget him.

Clint gave China a strange look, but said nothing.

"If the letter concerns you in any way, Clint, I will let you know. We'd better hurry. Supper will be on the table soon."

There would be no time to read the letter until later.

After they had eaten and made the acquaintance of several of the other guests, Clint succumbed to a pressing need to burn off some energy. He wanted to explore the grounds of the hotel and visit the large barn situated behind the hotel. China watched him lope across the grass.

China strolled to one end of the piazza and sat down in a wicker chair to read the letter. She opened the envelope with steady fingers, taking care to tear only a narrow strip off one short end.

❧

Dear Miss Havener,

Quite a few people have remarked upon how much they enjoyed your company while you were here, and wish you'd come back through town again. I nod my head in agreement. You are remembered with affection by many.

Tell Clint the ropes on the ferry have caused me no trouble, but I must say that being a ferryman holds somewhat less excitement without his help and many questions.

The weather holds fair here, and the Goodrich boys have commenced to haying their fields along the banks of the river.

I hope this finds you and Clint in health and enjoying your journey. I am, yours sincerely, Plato Robinson

PS: Tell Clint I will write a note to him soon.

China read the letter again, turned the page over to see if anything was written on the back. It was blank and she felt cheated, as if there ought to have been more, though she knew she had no right to expect anything other than what he had written. She had hoped for a letter from him and she had received one. Yet, here she was feeling disappointed because he had not written in a more intimate manner—and entertaining toward him a great many feelings that had nothing in the least to do with mere friendship.

"Botheration!" she muttered under her breath, annoyed with herself for such contrariness.

She tucked the letter into her pocket and strode off across the piazza to stroll the uneven ground peppered with small chunks of ledge that served as the hotel's front yard.

It felt good to stretch her legs, to find herself enveloped by the vista of Moosehead Lake and the dark green solidity of the mountains that provided a backdrop to the great body of water. The evening was warm, yet a hint of cool air coming from the water brushed her face.

Far out on the lake she spotted a plume of smoke from one of the steamers returning, she assumed, from Kineo. She began to register the subtle changes of color emanating from the lake and the sides of the mountain, and from the sky above—so many shades of blue and green. She began to look more intently, focusing on shapes, light, and shadow, the difficulties she would encounter as she attempted to photograph the grand panorama that lay around her.

She rounded the corner of the building and spotted Clint standing beside a slim girl a few inches taller than he. Their backs were toward China. The girl, with a graceful sweep of her right hand, was telling Clint, China assumed, about the distant mountains—their names, perhaps. The girl wore an ankle-length dress of blue-and-white-striped cotton, and black leather boots. Her pale brown hair, falling untidily to her shoulders, was tied back with a narrow blue ribbon.

They turned when they heard China approach. Clint, with manners China did not know he possessed, introduced the girl.

"Miss Hardy, I would like to present to you Miss China Havener. Marm, I'd like you to meet Miss Fannie Hardy. She's from Brewer, across the river from Bangor, and she knows how to hunt and trap!" Clint said. "Her name is almost the same as your friend at Fort Point— Mrs. Fanny Harding."

China raised her eyebrows in surprise. Clint had chosen a name to call her by. He had called her "Marm."

She extended her hand and said, "How do you do, Miss Hardy."

"Pleased to meet you, Miss Havener." Fannie Hardy's voice was pleasantly light, and something in her poise and self-possession put China instantly at ease. Clearly, she had good manners and an open disposition. China judged the girl to be seventeen or eighteen.

"Clint said you two have never been to Moosehead before. I was just telling him about some of the places you ought to visit while you are here."

"I'm sure your knowledge will be very helpful to us."

"I'm here with my cousin, Mrs. Margaret Wheeler, but I've traveled this country, especially north and east of here, with my father, Manly

Hardy. He's a woodsman and a fur trader. He knows this country like the palm of his hand," Fannie said. As she spoke she lifted her arm in emphasis, pointing toward the mountains, her hands underscoring her words. She moved with a quiet poise bordering on the otherworldly, as if everything she saw, heard, and sensed pertaining to the wilderness held deep meaning for her. Her countenance was serene, which gave her face an unusual beauty. Yet, there was about her a down-to-earth quality, mixed with a practical turn of mind. She did not have any of the guile and silliness often associated with young ladies of her age. She glowed with health and self-confidence.

It was as if the girl's soul was permanently attached to the spirit of the good Maine earth, China thought—as if the two were kindred.

Clint seemed unable to say much of anything. He simply stared at Fannie Hardy, his mouth slightly agape, eyes filled with something akin to adoration.

Dear me, China thought, the boy is smitten!

She touched Clint's shoulder gently. "Come along, Clint. We need to unpack. It was lovely to meet you, Miss Hardy. I hope Clint and I will have occasion to spend more time with you and Mrs. Wheeler."

"No doubt about that, Miss Havener. I already told Clint I'd take him out in a birch-bark canoe and show him the finer points of paddling, and how to read the lake." Clint grinned. "Tomorrow?" he asked Fannie.

Fannie looked at the sky, studying it, reading what it said.

"Better make it the day after. The wind has changed, and I see some fishbone clouds. It will rain tomorrow," she said.

And with that she stepped off toward the hotel, turning once to wave to them.

29.

Just as Fannie Hardy had predicted, it rained the next day. A series of boisterous thunderstorms swept in from the northwest, creating a level of darkness that made it necessary for the hotel staff to light the lamps early in the afternoon.

Clint stood in the window of China's room, watching for lightning strikes.

"Look at that, Marm! Wouldn't it just be something if you could photograph that! Miss Hardy would take notice of that, I bet."

"Well, then, let's try it," China said, happy to fall in with Clint's desire to impress his new friend.

She set the camera on its tripod, adjusted the lens, and pulled back the curtains. Since she could not predict when the next fork of lightning would occur, or where, she decided to remove the lens cover at random intervals several times in a row, making a double exposure on the same negative.

"Now!" Clint said, some instinct telling him that another spear of lightning was about to slash across the dark clouds hanging over the lake. He was right. China pulled the cover away from the lens, counted to ten, and replaced it.

"I let in a lot of light on purpose," she said. "I have no idea what sort of effect that will produce. Next time I'll try it another way and let in much less light."

"Try it again in a minute or so," Clint said. "Even if you don't get the lightning bolt, you might get the flashes, and certainly all those jumbled-up thunderclouds."

"Perhaps you should be the one to expose the negative this time, Clint. Want to try?"

She placed a new negative into the holder.

Clint's face registered delight.

"All right, I will."

He stepped over to the camera, glanced out the window, waited a minute, and removed the cover from the lens. He counted aloud, One, two, three.

"Marm, do you think you could mark that negative so we'd know it was me that took it?"

"Why, yes, Clint. I'll write your name in pencil on the negative frame."

"Wish I could see it tomorrow," he said.

"So do I," China replied.

The next day dawned bright and clear, with no humidity. The black fly quotient seemed to have abated overnight.

"By the Fourth of July, next week, there won't be many black flies around," Clint informed China, "but watch out for the mosquitoes," as if he knew something she didn't already know.

At breakfast, Fannie Hardy introduced her cousin, Margaret Wheeler, a small woman dressed stylishly in a gray skirt, matching vest, and a white shirtwaist with many pin tucks ornamenting the front. A cameo brooch set off the garment's high neckline. She wore her hair, threaded with many strands of silver, coiled neatly atop her head.

"Fannie tells me she has invited your boy to go canoeing. I want to assure you that Fannie is an expert canoeist. Your boy will be quite safe with her. I wondered if you might allow him to go on the lake with her tomorrow after breakfast," Mrs. Wheeler said.

"Well, Clint, what do you think?" China asked.

"I'd like to go." Clint wore eagerness in every line of his body.

"What time do you want him to be ready, Mrs. Wheeler?"

"Around seven-thirty," Mrs. Wheeler said. "Later in the day Fannie and I want to go on a shopping expedition to Saunders's store, and then we will call on some of our acquaintances here."

Fannie grinned at Clint. "See you soon," she said with a wave of her hand. "We'll be using the birch-bark canoe the Tomah brothers built for me last summer. The Tomahs live over there by the lake. I'll take you to meet them when we get back. They tell wonderful stories about their people, the Micmacs."

30.

The day of the canoe excursion dawned bright and warm. Clint leapt out of bed and ran to the window of his room to see what the weather was like. The sky was clear, the sun shining. The lake lay placid and calm, its surface dark and mysterious. In the distance, smoke coiled out of the stacks of a steamer headed up the lake, leaving a wispy smudge behind.

Clint smiled as he stood in front of the mirror, combing his hair. Miss Hardy had said morning was one of the best times of day to be on the lake in a canoe; the other time was evening. That was when the lake was smooth as glass.

The thought of Miss Hardy made Clint grin wider. He'd never known a girl anything like her. Once, back in Cambridge, Mrs. Buzzell had introduced him to her niece, but she was dull compared to Miss Hardy. Miss Hardy knew things and talked about them, and she could do things he never knew a girl could do—paddle a canoe and camp out, go fishing and tend traplines.

He looked quickly around the dining room, hoping Miss Hardy would be there already with her aunt. She wasn't, and disappointment and gloom squelched some of his high spirits as he ate breakfast.

"I had a note from Mrs. Wheeler last night, Clint," China said. "Miss Hardy will meet you down at the town dock."

A smile found its way back to Clint's face, but disappeared again when he realized that China had her camera with her and was rigged up to go with him. He had all he could do not to break into a run, but he matched his step to China's, carried the camera, and tried not to be impatient. When they arrived at the dock, Fannie was nowhere to be seen.

"Is there more than one town dock?" Clint asked.

"No, it's this one," China said as she set up the camera and aimed it toward the lake. "If I am not mistaken, that little white dot headed this way is a canoe, with Miss Hardy handling the paddle."

And so it was.

Clint wished he had binoculars, but gradually the white dot coalesced into a magnificent birch-bark canoe propelled by Fannie Hardy, who wore a straw hat with a broad brim and a simple gray cotton dress. She wielded the paddle with such dexterity and deftness that Clint felt suddenly shy; he feared he would be so inept and clumsy, she would laugh at him. He didn't know a thing about paddling a canoe, had never even been in one, though he had seen them when he was a little boy and remembered being intrigued by them. But he sure didn't want to make a fool of himself in front of Miss Hardy.

As the canoe glided beside the dock and touched the shore, China took pictures. The light was splendid, and she knew instinctively that these photos would stand out, perhaps from all the others she had taken so far.

Clint didn't quite know how to convey to Fannie how inexperienced he was. He stood uneasily by the bow of the canoe, not quite sure what to do next.

"When you step into the canoe, Clint," Fannie said, sensing his uncertainty, "take hold of the gunwale, one hand on either side, and keep low. Move slowly and stay centered. There you go. Nicely done.

Now take your seat, get the paddle, and let it rest across your knees for now. Miss Havener, if you will give us just a bit of a push, we'll be off."

It didn't take much effort to release the tip of the bow from the shoreline, and within seconds, the canoe glided past the dock. With several precise and expertly executed strokes of the paddle, Fannie turned the canoe and headed out on the lake in a westerly direction.

"When you apply the paddle, Clint, don't lean out over the side; just dip the paddle slowly and rhythmically, and keep your back straight. I'll match my paddling to yours for now, until you get used to it. Every so often, when you feel like it, paddle on the other side of the gunwale. That will help us keep going in a straight line, more or less—not that it matters. This is a pretty big lake, and as you can see, we have it to ourselves for now."

At first, Clint dug in too deeply. He felt the water resist, as if the lake were fighting him. He took a deep breath and made himself slow down, counting one-two-three, as if he were learning a dance. Soon, he felt his efforts settle into a pleasant, predictable rhythm.

"It's easier than I thought," he said, turning his head so Fannie could hear his words.

"Yes. It's a bit more complicated when you have the stern seat and must figure out how to steer, but we will leave feathering and other paddle techniques for another day. For now, let's just follow the shoreline for a while and see what there is to see," Fannie said.

Their voices drifted back clearly to China as she stood on the shore watching them. She was about to pack up the camera and transform the tripod into its walking-stick mode when she heard the lowing of cows behind her. She turned to discover six dairy cows making their way slowly toward the boat landing. A dog, barking with authority, raced back and forth to keep the cows moving in the right direction. A barefoot boy with a switch in his hand seemed to be in control of the situation.

China grabbed her camera and the tripod and stepped hastily aside. The boy smiled at her. When the cows reached the water's edge, they stepped in daintily, putting their heads to the water to drink.

China set up the camera again and aimed it at the herd, waiting until the boy and the dog were in the frame. There was a lot of motion among the cows, and she knew some part of the image would be blurred, but she was certain at least some of it would be in focus. She had never seen anyone in Maine drive cows to a lake to drink, and wondered if it was unique to Greenville. It seemed a very sensible thing to do.

The boy tipped his hat and smiled at her.

"Nice cows you have there," China said.

"I bring 'em every morning and every evening," he said.

"How far is it to your farm?"

"Up the hill a ways, mile or so."

"And in winter, when the lake is frozen?"

"Well, I lug a lot of water then; melt snow, too."

"A lot of work."

"Not if you like cows."

And with that the boy whistled to the dog, tapped one of the cows on the neck with his switch, and turned toward the steep road from whence he and the cows had come.

China gathered her camera equipment and made her way to the center of the village. She stopped in front of Saunders's store. The window displayed canoe paddles, sturdy boots, rucksacks, fly-fishing rods, cotton plaid shirts, lanterns, a small tent, and several straw hats with broad brims. She decided to keep walking along the main road to the top of Indian Hill, where she'd have a wonderful panoramic view of the lake and the mountains surrounding it.

As she walked she thought about the past—how for good and ill, even though it no longer existed, it stayed like a faded, indelible stain, an inevitability no one could escape. She had only one regret about the past, and that was that she and her sisters had never married. Marriage ensured the growth of a family, guaranteed that its elderly were cared for, brought a greater measure of joy than sorrow. Yet, she was glad for the unusual freedom the lack of husbands had afforded her and her sisters—how it had taught them to think for themselves, to learn a level of self-reliance few women of their time ever attained. What lay ahead was, for the most part, unknowable. What determined the future was what one did—or did not do.

It occurred to her now that the last few years of living along-shore—all those quiet years, when she'd had so much time to think—had resulted in her decision to travel in Maine, to learn the art of photography, even if it proved to be a colossal failure. But what was failure? It was merely a point at which one was given the opportunity to reconstruct the old path or find a new one. I am finding a new path, she thought, and the idea pleased her.

Her thoughts drifted to Plato Robinson, and she let the image of his face rest in her mind's eye. She liked him, was attracted to him, that much was certain. Beyond that, there was no need to go. At least not on this day, at this time.

At the summit of the hill, China scanned the lake and spotted what she thought might be Clint and Fannie in the canoe, but she couldn't be certain. Even so, she pointed the camera in that direction and made a photograph. She pointed the camera to the left and to the right, attempting to photograph the mountains and the sky.

It was mid-morning by the time she made her way back toward the village. Greenville's main road had begun to stir with pedestrians, horseback riders, and excursionists in open wagons and carriages. The men wore bowler hats and the ladies, wearing small hats that reminded China of candied confections, held fringed parasols over their heads. The men driving the conveyances were a good-looking lot, dressed in red shirts and wool felt hats folded into a single point. Almost to a man, they sported drooping mustaches that hid their mouths. They tipped their hats as they passed and China nodded a greeting in return.

The men reminded China of Plato Robinson. They had that same air of quiet independence and self-possession, of being at ease with themselves, of belonging to the lake and the mountains, just as Plato belonged to the river and the Kennebec Valley hills, just as she belonged to the sea.

China had not yet replied to Plato's letter. She knew she must not put it off much longer, or Plato would think she cared nothing for their—she did not know what to call it . . . Acquaintance? Friendship? Certainly they were more than acquaintances. But they hadn't known one another long enough to be called friends. Their friendship, if indeed that's what it was, had consisted mostly of sharing a table at a hotel at suppertime and conversing. That was all. His feelings toward her remained unstated, though he had made it clear he admired her, and she had indicated her admiration for him. Was there anything beyond that? Would there be? She did not know. And not knowing vexed her. Yet, something in her heart said she would not be ready for an attachment until she had finished her travels, until she knew for certain whether or not her photographs amounted to anything. And, there was Clint to add to the equation, another unknown quantity if ever there was one.

So many new paths before her, all in a tangle, impossible to determine where one began and another left off.

Enough, she thought. Enough of this foolishness.

31.

It was nearly noon, time for dinner, when Clint came back to the hotel. China had spent the last hour pacing slowly back and forth along the piazza, or sitting on a wicker sofa reading a newspaper, waiting for him, eager to hear about his excursion.

"Marm," Clint called, as he ran lightly up the piazza steps. "I caught a big trout!"

He placed a newspaper parcel on a nearby table and unwrapped it.

"Eight pounds! Biggest fish I ever saw, let alone caught. Miss Hardy sure knows a lot about fishing and paddling a canoe." Admiration and awe tinged the tone of his voice. "I never thought I'd say that about a girl."

"It may come as a surprise to you, Clint, but girls are quite capable of catching very large fish, and can even guide the progress of a ship, as I have told you many times."

Clint grinned. "I know, I know." A mischievous gleam came into his eye. "Bet you never caught a whale, though."

China laughed. "Quite right. No whales. Come along; dinner must be ready by now. Bring the fish. You can ask the desk clerk what to do with it."

"That's easy. I want to eat it for supper. But first, Miss Hardy said to trace around it. Tomorrow she's going to bring some birch bark and show me how to cut the shape of this very fish from it. I can write my name and the date I caught it on the back of the bark and hang it on my wall to remind me of this day, and everything that happened. But I would like to hang on to this fish long enough for you to take my picture with it. Would you do that?"

China pulled his hat off his head and handed it to him as they entered the hotel. "Yes, of course, I will," she said.

After finding out from the desk clerk that he could store his fish in the hotel kitchen, Clint joined China at their table. He dug into his food with the hearty appetite of a growing boy who had just spent a few hours outdoors.

"This is good," he said between forkfuls of roast chicken, boiled potatoes, and gravy.

"Tell me about your canoe outing," China prompted him.

"Not much to tell. Miss Hardy showed me how to handle the paddle, and I got the hang of it pretty quick. Then we headed up the lake. She said we'd stay close to shore because it was my first time out. I don't know how far we went, but it was way out of sight of town. Then we fished. She has a fly rod and knows how to cast. But I was the one who caught the big fish!" He took a bite from a big wedge of custard pie. "She's going to college in the fall. I didn't know girls did that."

"Miss Hardy is a very unusual and very bright young lady, Clint. Many young ladies in this modern day and age go to college."

Clint nodded, put his fork down, and pushed his plate away. He regarded China with a serious look.

"Can anyone go to college?"

"Yes, if they study hard, earn good grades, and can pay the tuition."

"Oh."

"Do you like school, Clint?"

"I used to, but I had to stop going after my folks died." He looked down at his plate. "So I guess that lets me out when it comes to college."

"Not necessarily."

"What do you mean?" China detected a spark of curiosity in Clint's eyes.

"I'm not sure yet. But when I am, I will let you know. Come, let's go outside and photograph you with that fish of yours."

After the picture was made, Clint returned the fish to the kitchen, where he was assured that it would appear on his plate at suppertime.

China suggested they walk up the road to Saunders's store. She wanted to purchase socks for him and a new pair of gloves for herself. She made the purchases and was ready to leave, but Clint lingered. He stood in front of a display of camping gear arranged in a rustic setting, gazing at it. The display included evergreen boughs, a deer, and game birds—products of a taxidermist's art—a tent, firewood ready for a flame, fishing rods, canoe paddles, and a variety of canvas stools and cots.

"Someday, I'm going to have me a fly rod, a canoe, and a tent, and I'm going to camp beside a lake where I can catch monster fish," he said. "What I'd really like to have is a birch-bark canoe like Miss Hardy's, but she said those are hard to get now. She did say that the Tomahs and other Indians she knows still make them."

"A lofty ambition, Clint," China said. "Well, let's go back to the Lake House. I have something I wish to talk to you about."

As they walked slowly back toward the hotel, China turned over in her mind exactly what she wanted to say. She wasn't sure she was picking the right time, and fretted over whether or not she was doing the right thing.

At the hotel, China found a quiet spot on the far end of the piazza and sat down on a wicker sofa.

Clint, leaning against a pilaster, looked at her questioningly, reading something in her face that seemed amiss to him.

"Did I do or say something I shouldn't have?" he asked, a look of apprehension clouding his eyes.

"No, Clint. I want to talk with you about your future. And by extension, mine. You are alone in the world. You need to go to school, and you need someone to look after you. What I propose is that I be the one to stand in your parents' stead and guide you in a way they would approve of, and most likely would have done were they still here to do so."

"What do you mean?"

"I mean . . . I can't ever replace your mother and father, but I can be appointed your legal guardian, or adopt you—which means you would live with me until you were eighteen, or twenty-one."

"Live with you at Fort Point?" Clint interrupted.

"Yes."

"With you and your sisters?"

"Yes."

"They wouldn't mind?"

"I haven't discussed this with them yet, but I have indicated to them in my letters how much I have come to depend on you, and how I believe you have come to depend on me. When they met you in Bangor, they liked you very much and got on very well with you. For the past week or so I have been thinking about the idea of becoming your guardian or adopting you, and trying to figure out the best way to present it to you. This seemed as good a time as any . . . What do you think?"

Clint's gaze shifted from China's face, and she saw that he did not want to look at her—did not want her to look at him.

"Don't know what to say." Clint's voice was very soft, almost gruff.

"Then say nothing for now, Clint. Think about it and let me know. There's no hurry. However, if you decide in favor of the idea, we could return to Fort Point at the end of the summer . . . in time to get you enrolled in school for the fall term. The decision is entirely yours. I won't try to talk you into it, or pressure you in any way. To me, it simply makes sense, and I hope it will make sense to you, too."

Emotion worked visibly on Clint's face, but he brought it under control. He drew in a deep breath, seemed to consider what she had said, turned his back to her, and stood with his spine pulled into a rigid line.

"I thank you, Miss Havener," Clint said, his words formal and polite. And with that he walked off toward the lake.

He had called her Miss Havener, not Marm.

China felt her stomach knot up. She wanted to go after him, but she let him go, knowing her talk of adoption and guardianship had stirred sad memories of all he had lost, of all he had endured in the aftermath of losing his parents. Perhaps he already had firm ideas about what he wanted his future to be—and it didn't include her. The thought brought tears to her eyes.

Even though she intended to travel until early October, she felt no qualms about going back to Fort Point at the end of August if Clint wanted to go with her. If she was to be his guardian, or his adoptive mother, she would need the support and advice of others—India and Persia, and the people at Abbott's Reach, especially Sam Webber, Madras Mitchell, and Ellis Harding, men who still remembered what it was like to be boys, men who had experienced much of what the world had to offer, men who had learned patience and wisdom, who would teach Clint by example all he needed to know to become a good, steady man.

Dear heaven, what have I done? China thought, suddenly regretting that she had spoken to Clint about adopting him.

She felt a wave of anger engulf her. She wanted to leave Greenville that very moment, to flee from Clint and the strange notion that she might take him permanently into her life and family. Too bad the rooms at the Lake House were paid for through the next week. Had they not been, she would have taken the next stage out of town.

Why, at this point in her life, had she suddenly taken leave of her senses? Was it the change—the need to leave behind her something beyond her name, birth, and death dates carved on a slate stone? Better off, she thought somewhat savagely, to have foundered on a reef and gone down with the ship. Neat and tidy—fish food.

"Damnation!" she said aloud, disliking herself for having such hateful thoughts.

She wandered back to her room and lay down on the bed, intending to rest, to clear her mind.

When she woke it was late afternoon and she was in a better frame of mind. She fixed her hair, went to Clint's room, and knocked lightly on the door. No answer. She turned the knob, but the door was locked. She called softly to him. No answer. Had he locked himself in to keep her out? The thought pained her.

She went down to the lobby to inquire of the desk clerk if he had seen Clint. The clerk shook his head. Nor had he seen Miss Hardy or Mrs. Wheeler.

China wandered around the hotel grounds in search of Clint, went to the barn, and walked to the boat landing, hoping to see him. There was no sign of him. It was as if he had vanished into thin air.

When the supper hour came and Clint had still not appeared, though his nicely fried trout did, China began to worry in earnest.

She spoke to the desk clerk about her worry, and he sent a boy to fetch Henry Boyd, Greenville's constable.

Boyd looked more like a river driver than a man of the law. He wore a battered wool hat with a wide brim. His dark green wool pants were "stagged"—cut even with the tops of his leather boots. His shirt sleeves were rolled up, and he sported a mustache. In spite of his rustic appearance, China saw immediately that he was efficient, intelligent, and had much experience with tracking down wayward boys.

"He can't have got too far, unless he had money for the stage," Boyd said.

"He had no money," China said. "What worries me is that he may have taken it into his head to go into the wilderness to fish. I must also tell you that he is not my son or my ward. He has no family. He attached himself to me some weeks ago, in Cambridge. Earlier today, I asked if he might consider allowing me to become his guardian, or to adopt him. He disappeared soon after that conversation."

"Do you think he's run away, then?" Boyd asked, giving voice to the question China dreaded to hear.

"I don't know, but I fear that's a possibility," China said.

"Any particular reason to be worried? He acting out? Or maybe you spoke sharp to him?"

"No, nothing like that, Mr. Boyd. I only suggested guardianship or adoption, and that he come to live with me and my sisters in Fort Point, downriver from Bangor."

"Well, that's no reason for running away. Maybe he's just out rambling along some of these roads up in the hills. Lot of nice views around here. Pretty little farms, too."

As China talked with Henry Boyd, she spotted Fannie Hardy and Mrs. Wheeler coming toward the hotel.

"Excuse me, Mr. Boyd. I must speak to those ladies." China hurried out to tell them Clint was missing. Fannie listened carefully, her demeanor calm and not in the least alarmed.

Mrs. Wheeler, too, was self-contained and not worried. "I'm sure there is some logical explanation," she said, her voice soothing.

"Clint seemed to me a very practical boy, and not at all inclined to mischief."

"Auntie," Fannie said, "I'm going to step across to the boat landing where I tied up the canoe. If it's gone, then I think we can presume Clint is in it. He was very taken with the canoe, and talked about wanting to go camping and to sleep outdoors under the stars."

"Go along, then, Fannie," Mrs. Wheeler said. "I'll stay here with Miss Havener."

Boyd joined them. "I asked around. No one here at the hotel has seen him—not since noontime, anyway."

"My niece is checking to see if her canoe is missing," Mrs. Wheeler said. "If it is, she thinks he may be out on the lake in it."

"God help him if he is," Boyd said. "There's a thunderstorm brewing, and once that bears down on us, being out on the lake won't be a pretty place to be."

Fannie came hurrying back. "The canoe is gone," she said. "I'm going to see Mary Tomah. If her sons can't find Clint, no one can."

"Who is Mary Tomah?" China asked.

"One of the Indians who live here," said Fannie. "She will know what to do." Fannie turned to her aunt. "I don't know when I will be back."

Mrs. Wheeler's face registered alarm. "Fannie, I think you can leave this to others who are more experienced in these matters—"

"Well, I can't," China interrupted. "I'll come with you, Miss Hardy. If we can't search in canoes because of the storm that's coming, then surely we can search from the deck of one of the steamboats."

And with that China strode off toward the steamboat landing with Fannie close behind, until she went her own way to ask Mary Tomah and her sons for assistance.

Only one steamboat was tied up at the wharf. No one appeared to be around, but China stepped aboard and found her way forward, calling "Ahoy!" as she went.

A man wearing a flat-crowned black hat with a visor came from below and intercepted China near the wheelhouse.

"We're done with excursions for the day, ma'am," he said. "Come back in the morning."

"I'm not here for a boat ride," China said. "My boy has gone off in a birch-bark canoe, there's a storm coming, and I want to . . . To charter this boat to go in search of him."

"Good heavens," the man said. "I'm Captain Abel Gower. No need to charter this boat."

China held out her hand to shake his, and introduce herself. "I'm China Havener. Pleased to meet you, Captain Gower," she said.

"The difficulty, you see, Miss Havener, is this: I'm low on wood for the boiler, and without fuel to burn, there won't be steam . . . "

"But you do have some wood?"

"I do."

"How long does it take to get steam enough to move this craft?"

"Well, I haven't been tied up more than a half-hour, so most likely we could be off fairly quickly. But I'll need a man to keep stoking the fire."

"Will a woman do?" China asked.

Captain Gower was taken aback. "I should think not—"

"Mr. Gower, I spent more than forty years of my life aboard my father's sailing ship. For many of those years, my two sisters and I were in complete command of that ship. I know how to be of use."

"I appreciate your offer, Miss Havener—"

He was interrupted by the appearance of Constable Boyd coming aboard. Close behind him were two young men he introduced as brothers Louis and Joseph Tomah, small, handsome men of quiet demeanor, their dark eyes moving from face to face, as if everything they saw imprinted itself in their very being. They nodded politely to China.

"I've got a couple of men lined up to throw junks of wood into your boiler, Abel. They'll be along directly. Show me to the working end of this floating palace and we'll get the fire started."

Almost immediately several other men arrived, each one pushing a wheelbarrow filled with sticks of wood.

Soon, the steamboat was on the lake, the paddle wheel churning a wake of froth behind it. Louis and Joseph Tomah took up posts at the rail in the bow.

"Not a good time to be out there in a canoe now," Louis remarked.

The wind had increased in velocity, and in the distance, far up the lake, flashes of lightning illuminated dark gray clouds. Already, whitecaps were forming on the surface of the water.

It grew dark rapidly. China stood in the bow and scanned the lake and shore on either side, looking for a slash of white to tell her it was Clint in a birch-bark canoe. She prayed he had stayed close to shore and not risked the middle of the lake, that he had seen the storm coming and headed toward shore. Her head began to clog with "ifs" and "if onlys," and tears pricked her eyes. If only she hadn't said anything about guardianship and adoption.

The wind picked up and rain began to fall heavily. Captain Gower urged China to go below, but she would not leave her post at the forward rail.

"I intend to stand this watch," she said above the noise of the wind, the rain dripping off the narrow brim of her hat.

Louis and Joseph Tomah pulled their hats down firmly on their heads as the wind lashed rain into their faces.

When China realized she was soaked through, she knew the only sensible thing to do was to retreat to the wheelhouse.

"If this were my father's ship, the *Empress*," she said to Gower, as she swallowed her pride and went in out of the rain, "I'd have reefed sail to ride it out."

Captain Gower smiled. "Never knew a seafaring woman before," he said.

"Where I come from, down around Searsport, it's a common thing for women to go to sea with their husbands or fathers. Some of us were born at sea. We don't think anything of it."

It was impossible to see much of anything with the rain lashing against the wheelhouse window, creating a gloom that only added to China's dark mood.

Although she was free from the driving rain, China found she could not stay in the wheelhouse for long. It was one step too removed from Clint, out there somewhere on the heaving lake. She spotted a sou'wester hanging from a peg, reached for it, and pulled it on.

"I need to watch for him out there," she said by way of explanation as she went back to the bow.

Now, she watched for Clint and watched the weather, too, looking for signs that the storm was passing, and to her relief she felt the wind abate a bit, noted that the time between lightning flashes had increased. She spotted along the distant horizon a thin band of gray lighter than the dark scowling clouds rolling overhead.

Louis and Joseph noticed the change, too, and signaled to Captain Gower. In response, the captain altered the steamboat's course and aimed it toward a small island on the port side.

"We keep a canoe there," Joseph told China. "Abel Gower knows."

Much to China's surprise, as the steamboat neared the island, Louis and Joseph grinned at her, handed her their hats, kicked off their boots, and dove into the lake. She leaned over the rail and watched them swim safely to the island. They disappeared into the trees and soon returned carrying a birch-bark canoe which they pushed into the water and began paddling toward the west side of the lake. The canoe breasted the waves and the Tomahs paddled with a skill and grace that was a joy to see.

China returned to the wheelhouse.

"We've come up the lake a good three miles, Miss Havener," said Captain Gower. "We can't go any farther, or we'll run out of what little fuel we started with. I'm going to make a swing toward the east, and head back to Greenville. Louis and Joseph will hug the west shore. If Clint is anywhere out there, they will find him. Meanwhile, now that the storm is beginning to wear itself out, you can keep an eye straight ahead . . . just in case."

He meant, of course, in case they encountered an empty canoe, or worse, Clint's body floating facedown in the water. The thought made China want to howl like a mad thing.

The dim gray band of light in the sky widened rapidly and the clouds became white again. The surface of Moosehead grew smoother.

There was no sign of Clint.

32.

It was nearly dark when the steamboat reached the wharf. Fannie and Mrs. Wheeler waited at the lake's edge amid a cluster of men and women who had heard the news that Clint was missing.

Captain Gower took China's elbow to steady her as she stepped ashore. When he saw her safely landed, he saluted to her and turned to confer with some men he knew.

Fannie and Mrs. Wheeler hurried to China, and with one on either side, steered her to the Lake House. She saw the question in their eyes.

"No sign of him," she said, weary and on the verge of tears.

"Which does not mean, Miss Havener, that he won't be found," Mrs. Wheeler said gently, her tone so positive and hopeful that it grated on China's nerves.

But dead or alive? That was the question China didn't utter, the question none of them wanted to speak, though it was there in the very air they breathed.

"A lot of men have put out in canoes and boats now," Fannie said. "There's a bright moon . . . That will help. The search can go on all night. And it's mild, so there's no danger Clint will suffer from the cold. The hotel put out food and coffee for the searchers. It will do you good to have a cup of tea and something to eat."

"Yes," China agreed, because she couldn't bear to rebuff their kind intentions. "All right, a small piece of custard pie and a cup of tea," she said, even though she knew food would be like sawdust in her mouth.

"The thing to remember is that Clint could not have got very far," Mrs. Wheeler said. "The canoe is large and heavy, and it's not easy for one inexperienced boy to paddle. He could not have made much headway. The other thing is, Clint is sensible. He would have known the storm was coming; he would have seen the signs. And I believe he would have headed for shore. I am equally certain he would have stayed fairly close to shore, making it easy for him to get off the water and to shelter in time."

Fannie agreed wholeheartedly.

China wanted to find comfort in Mrs. Wheeler's words, but she could not. She was wretched with fatigue, with worry, wretched with her own imaginings of what horrible things might have befallen Clint. And worse, she had caused his flight. She had failed to keep him safe.

Light from oil lamps made the dining room bright, holding the depths of night at bay. In the distance, a loon cried, and the sad, lonely sound went straight through China's heart. For a moment, she was undone and tears rolled down her cheeks and dripped off her chin. Mrs. Wheeler handed her a dainty linen handkerchief scented with lavender.

"Are you sure you don't want to go to your room and lie down, Miss Havener?" Mrs. Wheeler asked, taking China's hand in a gesture of comfort.

She shook her head.

"Well, at least you must get out of those wet things," Mrs. Wheeler said. "Come, let me take you upstairs."

She helped China change into dry clothes, then returned with her to the dining room. Throughout the rest of the night, the searchers came to the hotel to drink coffee and eat doughnuts before going back out on the water to continue searching. They had seen no sign of a canoe, no sign of anything to indicate whether Clint was dead or alive.

The Tomah brothers had not been seen either, but that, the searchers said, was to be expected. Louis and Joseph could read the lake, the weather, the woods, the birds and animals, in ways other men could not. If anyone could find Clint, it would be the Tomah brothers, they reassured China.

When dawn broke, Mrs. Wheeler and Fannie went to their rooms to rest. But China stayed in the dining room, pacing, staring out the window at the lake. She knew she must rest, must sleep, if only for an hour. She must eat something, wash her face, change her clothing, fix her hair.

She went up the stairs slowly and reluctantly, leaning on the banister, feeling old and bruised, longing for India and Persia, for all her friends at Abbott's Reach. She longed, too, but only for a moment, for Plato Robinson.

She gave herself a mental shake, recalling one of the many times the *Empress* had had a nasty passage around Cape Horn, when towering waves had hurled the vessel from side to side, how the sails and rigging had become coated with ice, making the ship seem like a crystal copy of itself. She had faced such dangers, and she had weathered them. She was not a coward.

I must remember that, she told herself.

In her room, she lay across her bed, intending to take a short nap. She fell asleep immediately. When she woke, the sun was high in the sky, and she knew it must be noon or later. She made herself presentable and went down to the dining room.

Dinner was on the table. She made herself eat some stew and a slice of bread. She drank a cup of tea. She did not ask if there was news of Clint; she knew there wasn't. If there had been, someone would have summoned her.

Mrs. Wheeler joined China at the table.

"Fannie has gone out on the lake with one of the search parties," she said. "I didn't want her to go, but I knew if I refused her permission, she'd go anyway. Fannie is quite strong-minded—a trait her father has fostered in her, and one that will enable her to do many things women rarely have the opportunity to do, I suspect."

The afternoon passed, and all China knew for sure was that the search for Clint was still on. She had never felt so helpless, so useless in all her life.

Mrs. Wheeler refused to let China out of her sight. At last, feeling confined and stifled, China made her excuses and said she needed some exercise, and would walk to the top of Indian Hill. Alone.

Mrs. Wheeler, with compassion and understanding in her eyes, retreated graciously, though her hands fluttered toward China, wanting to comfort her.

When China reached the summit of the hill, she turned to survey the expanse of the lake below. The thin line of buildings that was Greenville lay scattered like toy blocks at the head of the great inland sea. She saw several steam-propelled craft on the water, spumes of smoke coming from the stacks. Smaller boats—canoes and rowboats, and an occasional sailboat—also plied the water. She stood, taking in deep breaths of the high summer air, blotting her face, damp with the exertion of walking up the hill, with a handkerchief.

As China scanned the lake and the mountains surrounding it, she felt encased in beauty, and took comfort in it. Then, she spotted a dot of white, a dot that moved with smooth, certain grace. She stared at it for a few long moments. And then she knew.

It was the Tomah brothers. She knew, too, that the search was over, and that Clint would be with them. But dead or alive?

Her mind let the question in and just as quickly slammed the door in its face.

33.

China started back to the village, uncertain for a moment what her destination ought to be. Then she made straight for the boat landing.

She had never in her life shrunk from difficult situations. If Clint was injured, she believed he would want to see her, no matter the unpleasantness that had passed between them. If he were . . . her mind refused to admit the word . . . she would want to see what remained of him.

Suddenly, she felt ill and wanted to sit down in the grass and cry. Where is your backbone, she chastised herself, lengthening her stride until she was almost running.

By the time she arrived at the boat landing, men, women, and children had gathered to see what was happening.

"If that boy is alive, it will be a miracle," one woman said. "I heard he was a runaway, a bad seed if ever there was one."

It took every fiber of China's being not to round angrily on the woman and speak sharply to her. She wanted to shout at her, tell her that Clint was a boy who had fallen on hard times, a boy who sometimes could not bear up under the weight of confusion and grief that tore at him when anyone least expected it, a boy who was good and true.

As China approached, the knot of people stood aside to allow her to get as close as possible to the place where the canoe would put in.

"I am here if you need me, Miss Havener," said Mrs. Wheeler, who had just arrived. She touched China's arm gently, then stepped back a few paces to allow China as much personal space as possible, given the number of people assembled. Mrs. Wheeler was not the sort of woman who usually hovered, though she was always ready to be of assistance in both small and large ways, as the occasion demanded.

"Thank you," China murmured.

As the canoe drew near, China strained to count the people in it. There were two—Louis Tomah in the bow and Joseph Tomah in the stern. They plied their paddles with muscular grace and a beautiful efficiency that reminded China of the men she had observed many years ago in Hawaii as they paddled outrigger canoes.

Men stepped forward to grasp the bow of the canoe and pull it ashore. Louis stepped out first. His eyes found China's. He gave a brief nod, and she knew she was about to learn Clint's fate. Joseph bent forward and touched something that looked like a pile of old blankets in the bottom of the canoe.

China's heart hammered and her lips trembled with fear.

The bundle of blankets stirred. Clint, with Joseph's help, sat up, blinking in the bright sunlight.

China's hand went to her mouth to stifle a sob of relief, to brush away the tears sliding down her face. She stepped close enough to the canoe to touch it, to kneel in the mud beside it. Clint's hair was every which way, his face sunburned and swollen with mosquito bites. He was barefoot, his clothing muddy and torn. He seemed dazed, but did not appear to be injured.

"You've had quite an adventure, Clint," China said, keeping her voice calm, almost whispering to keep the crowd from hearing her words. "You must be hungry."

Clint gazed at her briefly, then hung his head—weary or ashamed, or both, she could not tell.

"I am happier to see you, Clint, than I was on the day I saw you walking along the road to Skowhegan," China murmured, keeping her joy subdued, not wishing to overwhelm him with too much emotion.

Clint moved his head slightly, as if to say *I know*.

Constable Boyd came forward and took command.

"Bring that wagon over here. Come on, son, we're going to take you over to the hotel. I've sent word to Dr. Shaw, and he's going to come and look you over."

Louis and Joseph helped Clint out of the canoe and carried him, one on either side, to a waiting wagon. They laid Clint down, arranging the blankets around him.

China, not wanting to impose on Clint's sense of personal dignity, walked beside the wagon, speaking to him in low tones to let him know she was close by. A small group of people, including Mrs. Wheeler and Fannie, followed respectfully behind, creating a kind of parade.

Thank God this isn't a funeral procession, China thought. Not a funeral, not a funeral . . . The thought stuck in her head and would not depart.

Once, Clint glanced at China, the expression in his eyes unreadable, then his eyelids drooped as if weariness had suddenly overtaken him.

In response, China gently touched Clint's shoulder and he emitted a long, wrenching sigh, leaning into her touch.

One of the hotel staff helped Clint out of his clothing and into a tub of hot water, after that he was put in bed and examined by Dr. Shaw. The hotel kitchen had sent up a mug of nourishing beef broth and an egg custard, which Clint ate slowly, with China's encouragement.

After he had eaten, China helped him settle down under the covers, smoothing the sheets and blankets over him. Mary Tomah had sent a salve to alleviate the itching and help heal the insect bites and sunburn Clint had acquired, so China dabbed some on the boy's face. By this point, Clint was barely awake, but he knew she was there, sitting by his bedside. She leaned close to his ear, tears dripping down her cheeks, and whispered, "Don't ever do that again."

"I'm sorry," Clint said as he drifted off to sleep, aided by a potion Dr. Shaw had given him.

Dr. Shaw assured China that Clint had suffered no lasting damage from his ordeal.

"He's a good rugged boy, Miss Havener," Dr. Shaw said. "A good night's sleep, some hot food, and a couple days' rest, he'll be right as rain."

China was exhausted, too, but she went to Mrs. Wheeler and Fannie Hardy to thank them for their help and support. She told them Clint would be all right. Then she walked to Mary Tomah's house to thank her and her sons for searching, for the ointment, for their kindness.

"Sit," Mary said. "Drink tea." She handed China a crockery mug containing a hot liquid that tasted something like tea, but wasn't. They sat in silence and China felt an odd peace descend on her.

"Go home, now. Sleep," Mary said. "Tomorrow, all better."

She smiled, and her face creased with grooves that made her seem ancient, as if she were the keeper of great wisdom, the very foundation of the universe, the mother of all mankind.

34.

When morning came, China went down to the dining room to find Mrs. Wheeler and Fannie Hardy sitting at a table by a window in the pleasant morning light.

"We're so glad to hear Clint is none the worse for wear," Mrs. Wheeler said as she poured cream into her cup of tea and spread field strawberry jam on her toast.

"I'm sure he will have a lot to say about his adventure when he wakes up this morning," Fannie said.

"No doubt," China replied.

In fact, she dreaded the moment when she would ask Clint why he had gone off without telling her. She wanted to know, and yet she didn't. Perhaps his answer, if he answered at all, would not be to her liking.

And then what? Could she return to Fort Point as if nothing had happened, as if Clint had never been? She knew she could not. Clint had become a part of her life, and she would do everything in her power to see that he was provided for, in spite of his wishes, if need be, even if he decided to pack his things and strike off across country on his own.

China drank the last of her tea, her breakfast finished.

"I saw Louis and Joseph Tomah down by the landing earlier this morning," Fannie remarked. "They told me they wanted to talk with you."

"Thank you," China said. She excused herself and walked to the lake.

She found Louis and Joseph inspecting their birch-bark canoe for damage.

They nodded a greeting as China approached. "Clint is still sleeping," she said. "Thanks to you, he's alive, and safe."

The Tomahs nodded again, not looking at her.

"He was four, maybe five miles up the lake," Louis said. "He used his head. Saw the storm coming. But before he got off the lake, the canoe turned over and the wind blew it away. He got to shore all right. When the storm was over, he used his head again. He tried to follow the shore and walk back to Greenville, but there are places where he couldn't follow the shore. He had to go back and around."

"Swampy," Joseph said. "Blowdowns."

"He got turned around, walked the wrong way, away from the lake. Then it was night. But he used his head again. He stopped, sheltered under some pines. Built a little camp with boughs and brush. He stayed there, and we found him."

"He was easy to find. He broke little branches on purpose, walked in muddy places to leave footprints," Joseph said.

So, China thought. He had left signs. He had not wished to disappear.

"There is no way I can ever thank you enough," China said.

Louis shrugged his shoulders, as if to say it wasn't much of anything to get excited about. Joseph nodded, as if to agree with what his brother hadn't said.

China thanked them again and returned to the Lake House.

Clint was awake when China went into his room. He buried his face in the pillow, not wanting to look at her.

"No one is angry with you, Clint. Especially not me," she said kindly.

He rolled over and met her gaze. His face was slightly less swollen, though still lumpy from insect bites, but his gaze was clear and true.

"I don't know what to say," he whispered.

"Well, one thing you might say is that you are sorry for causing me so much worry," China said, her voice tinged with humor, hoping to get him to smile.

"I am sorry for that. But I didn't know I was going to be gone so long."

"Am I to understand that you didn't run away?"

"Run away? You mean, never to come back again?" Clint shook his head. "I just wanted to think about what you had said, because I didn't know what to think. I thought if I was out there on the water, where it was quiet and nobody could get to me, it would be just me and Ma and Pa, and maybe they'd let me know somehow what to think . . . But mostly I just wanted to go out in that canoe and paddle it all by myself. I knew if I told you that's what I was going to do, you wouldn't let me . . . And neither would Miss Hardy."

"Correct on both points. But you did it anyway."

"Yes, I did, even though I knew I shouldn't have."

"I see."

A feather of silence settled for moment.

"Did the Tomahs find Miss Hardy's canoe?" Clint asked. "Because that's the worst of it, you know, if my taking the canoe caused it to be busted up, or worse, lost for good."

"The Tomahs and some other men have gone to look for it today."

Clint drew a deep breath. "Well, I guess I better get up and get dressed, and go downstairs and face the music," he said.

"I think you will find Miss Hardy and Mrs. Wheeler as relieved as I am to know you are safe and unhurt."

A look of relief came over Clint's face.

"I sure don't want Miss Hardy to think badly of me," he said, "but I suppose she does now."

China kept silent, then asked, "Are you strong enough to be out of bed, Clint?"

"I think so."

"Very well, then; I'll leave you to it."

"I'd like to talk with Miss Hardy and Mrs. Wheeler by myself, if that's all right with you," Clint said as China reached the door.

She nodded.

China went to her room to write to India and Persia to let them know she and Clint would soon be back in Bangor for one night before taking the train to Patten, a decision she had made only that moment. She told them that on such short notice, she saw no reason why they should make the trip upriver to see her and Clint. She added a short account of Clint's adventure, folded the letter, and put it in an envelope. Then she wrote a brief note to Plato Robinson, telling him of Clint's ordeal.

35.

In the days that followed, Clint became a minor celebrity, and everyone in Greenville knew who he was. When they saw him on the street they stopped and asked him questions about his experience, told him they were glad he was all right, mentioned stories of others who hadn't been so lucky, and praised the Tomahs for their skill in finding him.

Clint called on the Tomahs to thank them, and they welcomed him into their mother's house. At China's suggestion, he brought a tin of tea as a gift. Mary Tomah looked deeply into Clint's eyes and spoke to him in a language he had never heard before.

"She says you have a good heart, a strong spirit, and you will live a long and useful life," Louis Tomah said. "Our mother knows these things."

The Tomahs had found Fannie's canoe the day before, fetched up against some rocks a few miles up the lake. It was scuffed and torn, but could be fixed.

"I want to help fix it," Clint said. "If you will let me."

Louis and Joseph seemed pleased with Clint's request, and took him to a shed beside the house to show him what needed to be done.

Clint spent the day stirring pitch as it heated over an open fire and learned how to patch the tears in the canoe. He listened eagerly to the stories Louis and Joseph told of hunting and fishing trips, of men who had disappeared in the woods north of the lake, and of others who had set out across the frozen lake in winter, never to be seen or heard from again.

"There was this logger, name of Roscoe Herrick," Joseph said. "He was carrying letters to Greenville, walking on the ice down the lake. He didn't show up back at the woods camp that night. Didn't show up in town, either, so we looked for him. Never found him. We found the place where he went through the ice. We found his fur hat; the letters were safe in it. Last thing he ever did was throw that hat onto solid ice so the letters weren't lost with him."

"And his people never knew what happened to him?" Clint asked, his eyes wide.

"Oh, they knew he went through the ice, that the lake took him. The woods boss wrote to his people. They lived in Harmony, south of here," Louis said.

"Harmony!" Clint breathed. "That's the next town to Cambridge where I'm from."

Louis and Joseph nodded their approval.

"Nice country down that way," Joseph said. "Trapped some good beaver there."

China saw that being with the Tomahs was good for Clint, and encouraged his visits with them.

Sometimes, Fannie joined Clint and the Tomahs in the shed, too, and took a turn at stirring the pitch pot.

"Fannie and I are leaving in a day or two," Mrs. Wheeler said one fine July evening as she and China sat talking on the piazza. "She must start thinking about getting ready to go away to school . . . Smith College in Massachusetts. There are new clothes to make, packing to do, and I know she wants to spend time on the Penobscot River with her father this summer. There is much to do. September will be here before we know it."

"It's time for Clint and me to move on, too," China said. "I want to photograph Katahdin. Perhaps we can take the train back to Bangor together. We will spend a night there and then take the train north the next day."

And so the plans were made. Before she and Clint left, China carried her camera to the Tomahs' house and took photographs of Mary, Louis, and Joseph, and of Clint and Fannie helping to mend the canoe.

In order to take those photographs, China drew on every bit of her experience as a photographer, even though it wasn't much, to make certain the photographs were the best she could make them. She assessed the quality of the light; she made certain no awkward shadows fell in the wrong places. She tried to catch the Tomahs in natural attitudes without asking them to pose in a certain way. She did ask Mary Tomah to sit outside in a chair to have her photograph taken. Mary obliged, bringing with her a collection of baskets she had woven. She held one small basket in her lap, placing the others on the ground by her feet.

China removed and replaced the lens cover. Mary got up and handed the small basket to China.

"To remember this place. Where the lake spirit smiled on you," Mary said.

36.

It was an odd thing, China thought as she and Clint said their good-byes to Mrs. Wheeler and Fannie Hardy at the railroad station in Bangor, how quickly the bonds of acquaintance were loosed when people found themselves once again on home ground.

From the moment Fannie spotted her father, Manly Hardy, waiting for her on the platform, she became a different person. She placed her hand on her hat to hold it in place, turned to wave to Clint, and grabbed her skirts to hold them away from her feet as she ran to meet her father, flinging herself into his open arms to be welcomed home. Mrs. Wheeler smiled her final good-bye and followed Fannie, though more sedately. They did not look back.

"Guess we won't ever see her again," Clint said wistfully, the expression on his face a cypher.

"I don't expect we will," China replied. "But I am quite certain we will hear a great deal about Miss Fannie Hardy in years to come."

"What do you mean?"

"Miss Hardy has a lively and rare intelligence, Clint. She is going to college, still quite a novel thing for a young lady to do, where she will learn a great deal more, including how to make useful what she already knows. I believe she will make her mark in the world."

"Well, I hope she writes to me."

"She will, Clint. Not only will she write to you, and to me, but I believe she will also write books about what she knows about the Maine woods, her canoe trips with her father, and about the Maine Indians, about things as they used to be, as they are now, and why they got to be that way. It has been our very good fortune to have met her. Come, let's get our things and go to the hotel."

As she expected, China found letters waiting from India and Persia, and the Abbott's Reach family, and one from Plato Robinson.

"Looks like you have letters, too, Clint." China handed the envelopes to him.

"These are all mine?" he asked.

"Well, your name is on them."

"By cracky!" he said, a term he had picked up during their stay in Greenville. "There's one from Dr. Webber. And one from Mr. Robinson and one from Mrs. Madras Mitchell—I don't know her—and one from the Miss Haveners, your sisters."

"It's only natural India and Persia would want to write you, Clint, since they are now acquainted with you. After all, you did provide us with a lively adventure when you were about to be shanghaied. Apparently, you made quite an impression on them. They will want you to write to them, too. Mrs. Madras Mitchell is one of the Abbott's Reach crew. She sailed around the Horn with her husband on their honeymoon voyage in 1872. They went to Hawaii and from there, as they made their way to California, the ship was pounded by a fierce storm. Captain Mitchell was badly hurt when a spar fell, and Mrs. Mitchell was left to navigate the ship safely to San Francisco. She never cared to go to sea much after that, though she did accompany him on runs down the coast now and again with her children in tow."

"You never told me that story."

"Not mine to tell. But Madras and M Mitchell will be more than happy to give you all the details one day, I am certain."

Clint nodded his head. "Marm, if I go downriver to Fort Point where you and your sisters live—I mean, just to visit for a little while— would I have to stay if I didn't like it . . . ?"

China turned to him and put her hands on his shoulders.

"No, Clint. I have no authority over you to make you stay where you do not wish to be. But it is my hope, once you have seen the lay of the land and the rise and fall of the tide, and have been swept up in the currents of life that swirl around my sisters and the Abbott's Reach clan, you will decide of your own accord to sign on for the voyage with all of us."

China saw tears start in his eyes, but he dropped his head in hopes they would not overflow and she would not see them.

"Well, let's find our rooms, read our letters, and rest a bit before the supper hour comes around. What do you say?"

Clint nodded, picked up China's camera and the largest of the bags, and headed up the stairs at the Windsor Hotel.

37.

China pulled the pin from her hat and tossed it on the bed. She unlaced her shoes and took them off, setting them neatly on a chair. She took off her jacket and loosened her shirtwaist. Then she fingered through her letters, seeking the one she wanted to read first—Plato Robinson's, written in beautiful copperplate.

She opened the letter slowly, hoping, but not hoping, it would contain more than the first letter he had written her.

Dear Miss Havener,

I was greatly distressed to hear of Clint's adventure on Moosehead Lake, but some relieved when I reached the end of your account and learned he was found alive and not too much the worse for his ordeal. He's a good boy, and I have no doubt he meant no mischief when he set off. He's had some rugged trials in his young life, as you well know, and being a boy, he's liable to do things that might seem foolish to us, but seem sensible to him—at the time, anyway. Boys at that age can be very notional.

Life goes on here as it always has, the folks coming and going across the Kennebec and me ferrying them back and forth. I suppose that sounds monotonous, but it isn't.

I have written to Clint, advising him that if he gets a notion into his head to go off alone into the wilderness north of Patten, he should first tell you, and be sure to take a good ax with him.

I remain your devoted friend,
Plato Robinson

When she finished reading the letter, China folded it carefully and put it back in its envelope. She felt the stirring of a familiar feeling—what she and her sisters had named "the longing for land" after many months at sea. Well, here she was tossed about in a sea of emotions she had experienced only once before in her life, when she was in her thirties and had fallen in love with a first mate who had shipped on the *Empress*, out of California. He was a tall man with ebony eyes, and when he smiled a single dimple had flowered in his cheek on the left side of his face. Despite the proximity of their lives aboard ship, distance and decorum had been maintained. He never knew how much she longed to know him better, and she never knew if he had entertained a similar notion toward her.

If Plato Robinson had formed any sort of attachment deeper than friendship for her, he had not said so, and his letters did not seem to indicate it. As for herself, even though she was very attracted to him, she was still confused about the precise nature of her feelings toward him. She loved his company, his looks, his sense of humor, the things he knew and talked about. She felt safe when she was in his company. Did that constitute love, or merely admiration? She did not know.

What prevented her from taking steps to attain for herself an affection greater than friendship? What was she afraid of—that she was the sort of woman men admired, but never loved? That love didn't last? That was a silly thing to think, for she was surrounded by people for whom love had lasted—Maude and Sam, M and Madras, Isaiah and Zulema, Fanny and Ellis. Her thoughts went round and round, getting nowhere.

She tucked the letter into her pocket, liked the thought of carrying close to her body something Plato had touched. She blushed at the thought, then became impatient with the turn of her thoughts, taking the letter out of her pocket and tucking it into her valise.

She reached for the letters from India and Persia, both in one envelope.

India had written:

༄

My Dear Sister,

Persia and I were glad to hear of the happy end to Clint's adventure. We spent some time discussing whether or not we should urge you to come home now and decided against it. We know you can take care of yourself, as you did when Clint was in danger of being carried off forcefully and put to sea against his will. But then, of course, you had Persia and me to help you right that wrong.

It is a busy season here, especially for Persia, but I will let her tell you about that.

I have been corresponding with the publisher Ticknor and Fields in Boston, which has expressed interest in my book. The work is going well. I expect it will be finished by next spring.

I have made the acquaintance of a music teacher who lives in Belfast. His name is Mr. Donald Quinn. He is most interested in my writing project, and often calls to assist me with musical notation.

I have learned from Madras Mitchell that his brother, Gordon, captain of the steamer Goliath, is something of an artist. He has agreed to furnish pen-and-ink drawings to illustrate the book. He was here a few days ago to look at the painting of the Empress, the portraits of Mother and Father, and the portrait of the three of us in our white dresses when we were still young. He is making line drawings of these.

The publisher has indicated that it can furnish illustrations of some of the ports the Empress visited to give the book "flavor," as it were. This is dependent, of course, on the publisher's decision to accept my book for publication, which I am certain is in the works.

Everyone at Abbott's Reach is well, though Mrs. Webber was somewhat low several weeks ago. She is up and about now and back to normal. Dr. Webber was, we are given to understand, quite concerned for a few days.

Write again soon, China, dear.

Your loving sister,

India

⁐

Donald Quinn? Why hadn't India said more about him? Perhaps for the same reason she hadn't said anything much about Plato Robinson. What in the name of heaven was happening to the Havener sisters? She unfolded the letter from Persia, wondering what revelations it contained.

✍

Dear Sister,

I might as well tell you this right now, rather than wait and let you be stunned by the news on your return to us. I believe I am being courted.

India says I shouldn't leap to such a conclusion, but I think that's because she doesn't dare to entertain one about her Mr. Quinn—though I really do not believe he is courting her, yet, and may never if she doesn't get her nose out of her book and stop long enough to hear the music Mr. Quinn is making. He plays the piano, and, of all things, the guitar.

It's like this: As you know, I take the boat over to Castine whenever I have enough socks or mittens to sell at a store there. And one day, not long after you left on your great inland odyssey, I happened to be there when Mr. Rufus Beaumont came in. He said he was very happy to meet the lady who had made such warm socks, and he bought all I had with me. Mr. Beaumont is a country lawyer. His father was a farmer, so he understands and appreciates the work of the soil.

Mr. Beaumont has visited India and me several times. Once we asked him to stay to supper because he had brought us a lovely mess of trout. And since lettuce from my garden was at a prime eating stage and the radishes were ready, I put together a salad and India whipped some cream for the gingerbread she had made that morning. Mr. Beaumont, I am happy to say, asked for seconds, and stayed until well after moonrise.

Aside from that, dear sister, we are well, in good spirits and health, and each day is filled with many things to do. I sent to Bartlett's mill for finished yarn—which Clint told me about—in Harmony, a little town not all that distant from Cambridge, where you first met Clint. I will use the yarn to make socks on the knitting machine I recently acquired. It's just dandy—all I have to do is crank the handle. I start after supper and by the end of the evening I have a sock made. I will, however, continue to knit socks by hand because Mr. Beaumont and many of those who buy my socks prefer that. I don't have enough sheep to produce enough fleece for the amount of yarn I need for socks and mittens.

We do miss you, China, but we have come to see that you were right about going off on an adventure of your own, for as it turns out, India and I are also in the throes of adventure—her with her book, and I with my sheep and my mittens.

Looking forward to your return, I remain, your loving sister,
Persia

✑

China tucked the letter back in its envelope. Why had it never occurred to her that men might want to court her sisters? Or that India and Persia would entertain such an idea? At their age! She had never thought about that, even as she had not, for many, many years, thought anyone would ever court her, or that she would ever be drawn to any man, especially so late in her life. They were being courted; and she was not!

Was this what happened when they stopped being a unit and looked to their own separate interests? How quickly things had changed!

But change was what she had craved, after all—what she had fled from her sisters to find. Well, now she had found it, and it had found them. This will take some getting used to, she thought, feeling as if everything in her life was suddenly out of kilter. And all because she had wanted to be on her own for a while!

China tucked the letters into her valise. It was time to go down to the dining room to supper.

A tap came at her door.

"It's me," Clint said.

China pinned her hat back on her head and went out to the hallway.

"Ready for supper?" she asked. Clint nodded.

"Dr. Webber said in his letter that when . . . if . . . I go to Fort Point in the fall, Mrs. Webber will tell me the story about when the British invaded Bangor in 1814 and she defied them. And Dr. Webber will tell me about the time he and the ship he was on came up against pirates!" Clint said. "And I got a letter from someone else I don't even know—Captain Gordon Mitchell. He said if I want to go on the train to Boston sometime, I can go aboard his steamship."

"Does that sound like something you'd like to do?"

"Well, maybe. Then, maybe not; you'd miss me too much."

And with that enigmatic remark, Clint raced down the stairs and into the dining room. He was waiting by a table for two when China joined him. He grinned at her. She sensed a new level of ease in Clint, something that hadn't been there before he was lost on the lake.

"Cap," China said softly, and Clint quickly pulled his cap off his head, rolled it into a tube, and stuffed into his back pocket.

38.

The next morning, China and Clint took the European and North American Railway train to Mattawamkeag. There, they boarded the Laing and Jones stagecoach for Molunkus, Benedicta, Sherman, Staceyville, and Patten.

Among the passengers were several respectable-looking men and a woman with a small girl in her care. The woman and child did not seem to like one another, China noticed, but since it was no concern of hers, she merely greeted the woman politely and smiled at the child. She made sure Clint had a seat by the window. Sitting between too many people made him feel hemmed in and fidgety.

The stagecoach set off with a jingle of harness, the smart clip-clop of horses' hooves, and the crunch of wheels in the dirt.

Clint's mood had brightened since their stay in Greenville, and China, too, felt a renewal of energy, partly because Clint was content, and partly because this was the final leg of her inland journey. The fact was, she had begun to look forward to going home to Fort Point to begin the task of learning how to develop her negatives. The only way she would know the worth of her work of the past several months was to spend time in the darkroom, where she would discover once and for all if what she had seen before she exposed the negative was anything anyone else might consider worth looking at.

It was oddly exciting, and somewhat dreadful, to think of those shadowy images living on glass-plate negatives. So much of what she had pinned her hopes on was imprinted on those fragile squares of glass. It would take so little to shatter them, and in the process, her hope of becoming a photographer.

If her experiment with photography failed—and that certainly was a very real possibility—what then? Well, she'd put the camera away and concentrate on seeing to Clint and what he needed—provided, of course, when they reached the end of their trail together, he wished to continue on and not go his separate way. That, too, was possible, and was always on her mind. During her sailing days, more than once the *Empress* had shipped cabin boys no older than Clint, boys who had no families and had to make a living. She never knew what happened to any of them after they left the *Empress*, and she had often wondered. She did not want Clint to disappear into the great gulf of time as those other cabin boys had.

Well, she thought, if I turn out to be a failure as a photographer, then I will find something else to occupy my time.

No doubt India and Persia would welcome her help in their endeavors, even though she had no interest in sheep or writing.

And then there was the matter of her sisters' gentlemen admirers; that would all bear watching, best done if she were at home to keep an eye on things.

China roused herself from her reverie and observed the other passengers—two men in dark jackets and pants who had about them the air of those who rarely left home for anything other than jury duty, and the woman and the small girl, who looked to be around five or six years old. Both were dressed in black. The woman's face registered anxiety, annoyance, rigidity. Every so often she gazed out the window, a sigh escaping her thin lips, before fixing a cold gaze on the little girl. No one seemed inclined to talk. Clint slouched into one corner of the coach, gazing out the window, thinking his own thoughts, perhaps dreaming of Fannie Hardy.

The little girl's blue eyes were red-rimmed from crying and she seemed disoriented, as if she had not quite grasped where she was, or with whom. She sat stiffly with her hands folded in her lap, her gaze lowered. Every so often she murmured something inaudible. Once, China thought she heard the little girl whisper Mama.

Assuming she could expect no pleasant talk from the lady, China gazed out the window at the passing scenery. The road wound through stretches of dense woods, uphill and down dale, with occasional views of distant mountains. Then, as they crested a particularly steep section of road and came into the tiny hamlet of Benedicta, the coach slowed and stopped. The driver jumped down from his seat, opened the door, and said, "Katahdin over there. We'll rest the horses for thirty minutes."

China and Clint stepped out of the coach to stretch their legs and take advantage of the view. The other passengers did the same.

"Oh, boy," Clint said as he gazed toward Katahdin. "The Tomahs told me the story about Pamola—how he lives on Katahdin. He's the thunder god, and he has the head of a moose, the body of a man, and the wings and feet of an eagle. He's the spirit of the mountain, and he doesn't like people to climb it. The Tomahs said their people would never do anything to get Pamola all stirred up, and none of them have ever been to the top. I'm with them. I'd never want to climb that mountain now, even though I thought I wanted to a while back."

"I'm glad to hear that, Clint," China said, raising her eyebrows at him.

"I know what you're thinking," he said. "But I learned my lesson when I was lost on the lake and in the woods. I'm not going to strike off for Katahdin. The Tomahs are my friends, and they wouldn't like it if they found out I did such a thing."

Nearby, the woman kept a tight hold on the little girl's hand even as the child tried to pull her hand away. Finally, the woman lifted the girl roughly back into the coach. Immediately, the child began to cry loudly.

"Maybe her mother died," Clint said softly, noting the little girl's distress and her black dress. His eyes filled with pity for the little girl.

"It's not our concern, Clint," China said. "There's nothing we can do."

"Well, neither was I your concern, Marm, but look how that's turned out."

"Point taken."

They resumed their seats. The child, curled up in a ball on the seat opposite them, cried softly.

"That story your boy told about Mount Katahdin must have scared her," the woman said to China in an acid tone.

Suddenly, the little girl sat up straight and opened her eyes to glare at the woman.

"Did not! I want my mother! You take me home!"

"Now, Adeline, you know your mother died, and I am taking you to your new home in Patten."

Adeline slumped back against the seat and renewed her sobs.

Clint shot China an I-told-you-so glance.

"How dreadful," China murmured.

"She's an orphan now. There's a relative of some kind in Patten, and I'm taking her there," the woman said. "My name is Mrs. Murphy. I was a neighbor to her mother, who had no relatives in Lincoln, where I live, so I took it upon myself to see what I could do. This relation in Patten is a cousin of some kind to Adeline's mother. He and his wife have quite a few children, but he said he'd take Adeline because his wife could use some help. Even though she's only six, she can certainly help with the younger ones."

"I see," China said. "You've never met the man and his wife?"

"Sit still," the woman said sharply to the child. "No, never met them; just wrote back and forth a few times until things were settled. That was a month or so ago."

"Perhaps Miss Adeline would enjoy looking out the window. I'd be happy to swap places with her," China said.

For the first time, Adeline looked up at China. Her mouth trembled and tears still misted her eyes.

Clint slid over on the seat until he was shoulder to shoulder with China. "Take my seat. That way when Mount Katahdin comes into view again, you can see it real good," he said to Adeline, a note of sympathy in his voice.

Without waiting for Mrs. Murphy's permission, Adeline shifted over to the place Clint had made for her.

"Now, Adeline, you behave yourself, or you'll have to sit here by me again where I can keep an eye on you," Mrs. Murphy said.

Adeline ignored her and looked out the window.

"My mother died a while back, too," Clint whispered to Adeline.

Adeline turned to look at Clint. "What did you do?" she asked, gazing steadily at him, as if his answer would make all the difference in the world.

"Found a new one," he said softly, not looking at China.

China pretended not to hear, but her heart filled with joy at his words.

"I don't want a new one," Adeline said crossly.

"Neither did I, but that's how it turned out. My name is Clint. This is Miss Havener."

"My name is Adeline Miles."

Adeline blinked away her tears. She seemed to be thinking about what Clint had said.

China knew Clint's remark had been meant as much for her as for Adeline. She smiled at him and patted his shoulder to let him know she understood and was happy for it.

As the stagecoach rumbled on, Adeline relaxed and continued to respond when Clint spoke to her. Mrs. Murphy, relieved for the moment of her charge, relaxed a bit, too.

After Adeline was settled beside Clint, one of the men turned to Mrs. Murphy and said, "I'm Reverend George Stearns of the Patten Congregational Church. I wonder if I might inquire what family the little girl is going to?"

Stearns was in his forties, China judged. He had a lean, pleasant face and a kindly manner. His hair had a reddish tone and his eyes were green.

"She's going to Mr. John Taylor Harvey."

"Well, that's a shame, because when I left Patten a week or so ago, Mrs. Harvey had taken a turn for the worse. They say it's consumption," he said. "Her sister and an aunt have come to see to the young ones. John Harvey's place is up in the back part of town. They don't get down to the village much, but they are a good family."

"How many children do the Harveys have?" China asked.

"I think eight, and one of them is a baby, along with a couple of others who are still pretty little."

Mrs. Murphy's face registered dismay.

"Oh, dear me," she said. "With Mrs. Harvey so ill . . ."

Clearly, China thought, other plans would have to be made for poor little Adeline.

The stagecoach rumbled on and the conversation turned to other things—haying, the terrible state of the roads, and the musical program Mr. Stearns had organized at his church, to take place later that week.

Lulled by the voices, Adeline leaned her head against Clint's arm and dozed.

39.

The stagecoach rounded a turn and rolled to a flat stretch of road at the top of a hill. On the left there was a grand, panoramic view of Mount Katahdin.

"Well, we're pretty near home now," George Stearns said. "The mountain is always the landmark. That and Finch Hill, which we are fast approaching."

As the stagecoach crested Finch Hill and began a slow descent, the town of Patten, containing seven hundred and sixteen residents, spread out below against a background of green mountains. Already, China saw in her mind's eye how Mount Katahdin would look through the lens of her camera. She was eager to discover what Patten was like, whether or not the town would yield scenes she'd want to photograph, and if she would make the acquaintance of friendly, pleasant people. Having conversed with Reverend Stearns, she felt she was off to a good start.

The stagecoach stopped in front of the Patten House on the main road. The town, China observed, as she, Clint, and the other passengers stepped out of the vehicle, consisted of the main road and several other roads running at right angles from it. She saw two women going into a milliner's shop up the road, and observed five other business establishments that carried general merchandise. A wagon loaded with newly sawn lumber rumbled by, indicating the town had a sawmill. Behind it came a buggy driven by a handsome woman wearing a pert chip of a straw hat festooned with a swath of white tulle.

"That's my wife, Lydia," George Stearns said proudly. "I enjoyed meeting all of you. I hope you will attend a worship service at my church while you are in town. It's up the road on the right a little ways, past the Baptist church, which is that steeple you see there on the left. This church here on the corner is the Methodist church."

He tipped his hat and waved to his wife as she brought the buggy to a stop. She slid to one side of the seat so Mr. Stearns could sit in her spot. He took the reins and spoke to the horse as his wife leaned affectionately against his arm, smiling up at him as they drove away. Mr. Stearns inclined his head toward hers, and China was certain they would kiss as soon as they were out of sight of prying eyes. She watched them as they drove down the road and out of sight, a wistful little ache in her heart.

Lively little town, China thought, wishing it had been possible to make a photograph of Mr. And Mrs. Stearns as they had gazed so lovingly at one another. Someday, she thought, perhaps I will experience such an affectionate exchange with someone who loves me—perhaps Plato Robinson. How silly of me to hang on to that illusion, she scolded herself, and turned her thoughts firmly to matters at hand.

A small, round man stepped out of the hotel to collect the passengers' bags. "I'm Bill Hackett, hotel proprietor. Nice to see you all. Come right in. Mrs. Hackett will give you the keys to your rooms."

The Patten House was not quite as large as the hotel in Bingham, China observed, but it had a mansard roof that accommodated a fourth story. Windows were arranged in rows of four across the front of the building and in rows of three across the sides, which meant its rooms would be filled with light. Piazzas ranged along the ground floor and second-story levels, giving the hotel an inviting air.

As the stagecoach driver and his helper unloaded bags and baggage, several boys, who looked remarkably like Mr. Hackett, carried the luggage into the hotel lobby.

Mrs. Murphy, holding tightly to Adeline's hand, looked around in frustration.

"Not a soul here to meet us. Though with Mrs. Harvey as sick as she is, that's not a surprise. Mr. Hackett, I'm Mrs. Murphy. Is there by any chance a message for me from Mr. Harvey?"

"I believe there is, Mrs. Murphy. Come right in, come right in," he said. He ushered her through the door, with China and Clint following.

Mr. Hackett handed Mrs. Murphy an envelope. She tore it open and her face went white.

"Oh, dear me!" she exclaimed. "Mrs. Harvey has died! Mr. Harvey can't possibly take on another child at this time!"

Adeline burst into tears even though she did not fully understand what all the fuss was about. Mrs. Murphy seized Adeline by the shoulder and gave her a rough shake.

"Be still, Adeline."

Clint's face darkened. China placed her hand on his shoulder to prevent him from saying or doing something he might regret.

"What will you do now, Mrs. Murphy?" China asked sympathetically.

"Stay the night, of course, and be on my way back to Lincoln on the next stage. I can't keep the child, of course. I'm no relation to her, and besides, I'm far too old. I suppose she will become a ward of the town of Lincoln, or the State."

Hearing Mrs. Murphy's words, though she did not comprehend their meaning, Adeline began to wail again.

"Clint, perhaps you would take Adeline out to have a look in the store windows," China said. "It will be good for both of you to take some exercise after all those long hours in the stagecoach."

Mrs. Murphy relinquished Adeline's hand with an air of relief. Adeline, her sobs subsiding, placed her hand confidently in Clint's as he led her outside.

China turned again to Mrs. Murphy. "What will happen to Adeline if she becomes a ward of the State?"

"Well, most likely she will be farmed out to some family who will be paid a little something for her keep. Or the State will find some people somewhere to adopt her."

"But you are not willing take her."

"Dear me, no, I cannot. My young ones are grown up and married, and I don't want to start over again with a stubborn little girl like Adeline Miles. Her mother spoiled her something awful. I've done my duty by bringing her all the way to here. I tended Adeline's mother while she was sick, and I was with her the night she died. She made me promise I'd bring Adeline here, even wrote a letter saying I had the right to sell what little she had so there would be money enough for the stagecoach fare and a room at the hotel. What was left was to be put into an account at the bank for Adeline—not that it amounted to much, only five dollars. I did all of that, so I've done my duty by Mrs. Miles and the child. I can't do any more."

"But surely you don't want to see Adeline sent away to live with strangers who might be unkind to her?"

Mrs. Murphy drew a deep sigh.

"No, I do not. But the world is a harsh place, and the sooner Adeline learns that no one owes her a living, a lesson we all have to learn, the better it will be for her. Where's that boy of yours? I need to get

Adeline fed and put to bed. It has been a long and wearying day. I'm worn out, what with Adeline carrying on so."

She went out and stood on the plank sidewalk, spotted Clint and Adeline, and motioned for them to come in.

Later, after China and Clint had gone to their rooms to unpack their things, and supper had been eaten, they went for a walk along the main road as dark began to settle over the town.

"What's going to happen to Adeline?" Clint asked.

China told him the gist of what Mrs. Murphy had said.

"She will turn Adeline over to the State? She can do that?" he asked.

"I believe so, Clint. She has no claim on the child and wishes none. She has fulfilled her duty as Adeline's mother wished her to. She doesn't want to take Adeline in, so the town or the State must assume responsibility for her."

Clint didn't reply immediately, and China could see he was deep in thought.

"There must be something you . . . We . . . can do," he said, after a few moments.

"Perhaps. I inquired of Mr. Hackett if there is a lawyer in Patten. He said there is . . . A Mr. Samuel Benjamin, who is also a judge. Mr. Hackett said he would arrange for me to speak with Mr. Benjamin tomorrow morning."

"But the stagecoach will have left by then."

"I will talk to Mrs. Murphy and ask her to delay her journey back to Lincoln for at least a day."

"Oh, boy!" Clint said, rolling his eyes. Clearly he thought China was asking for trouble when it came to Mrs. Murphy.

"Clint, I'm only making inquiries; nothing will be settled. But when it comes to making difficult choices, one needs the power of correct information. Don't ever forget that."

Clint nodded, and they turned back toward the hotel.

Here and there, between the large houses lining the road, they caught glimpses of Mount Katahdin, the deepening twilight casting it into a bold outline.

"I wonder if it's possible to photograph that entire scene with the mountain, just like that, in this light?" China mused aloud.

"Never know until you try. Only thing you got to lose is one glass-plate negative if there's not enough light," Clint replied.

"My very thought," China said, smiling fondly at him.

Clint went to his room and China rapped on Mrs. Murphy's door. She explained her wish to consult a lawyer about Adeline's plight, and asked the woman to delay her return to Lincoln for a day. Mrs. Murphy agreed.

Back in her own room, China drew a deep breath and leaned against the door as she closed it behind her. Now what am I getting myself into, she thought.

40.

Samuel Benjamin stood up as China entered his small office, tucked between two general stores just up the road from the Patten House.

A tall man wearing a suit of black broadcloth, China judged him to be in his sixties. His white hair was combed away from his brow and ears, and intelligence and good humor played in his gray eyes. Behind him stood an oak desk and a solid, square table with several stacks of official-looking papers on it. His handshake was firm but gentle. China noticed his hands had calluses, as if he were no stranger to an ax handle or a scythe.

"Do sit down, Miss Havener, and tell me how I may assist you," Mr. Benjamin said in a pleasant voice.

China, dressed in a white shirtwaist and navy blue linen skirt, said, "I need advice. But I must warn you that I am putting my nose into business that does not directly concern me." She gave him the details of why she had come to see him. "Mrs. Murphy has no wish to adopt the child, and there are no relatives, so far as anyone knows, other than John Harvey, who has just suffered the loss of his wife, so Adeline can't go to live with them as was planned. My question, sir, is what other choices are there for Adeline? What does the law permit?"

"There's adoption, guardianship by a private party, or making her a ward of the State of Maine," Mr. Benjamin said.

"And if she becomes a ward of the State, what would happen to her?"

"She might be sent to a home for waifs, or the State might find a respectable couple to take her in, or adopt her, or simply become her guardians until she turns eighteen."

"In other words, she would go to live with strangers."

"That is one way to look at it, although quite often these things work out well for all concerned. I'm afraid that no matter what happens, she will end up in the care of people she has never met."

"Yes, quite so. I hadn't thought of it that way. If, Mr. Benjamin, I wished to become Adeline's guardian, say, on a temporary basis, while the matter is looked into more thoroughly, what would be required of me, and who would decide if I were fit for that responsibility?"

"Inquiries would have to be made as to your character and your ability to support the child . . . food, clothing, seeing to her education. If those inquiries reveal that you are an upstanding individual, of which I have no doubt, I would decide whether or not it was in the child's best interest to live, for the time being, with you." Mr. Benjamin paused. "Miss Havener, clearly you are beyond those years when one seeks the joys of motherhood. Might I inquire as to what prompts you to contemplate, as I assume you are, becoming a mother to the child—even if only for a short time?"

China shifted in her chair, looked at her hands for a moment, and then met the lawyer's steady gaze. She had not, until that very morning, given any great thought to, as Mr. Benjamin put it, becoming a mother to the child.

"As it happens, Mr. Benjamin, I have already assumed maternal duties toward Clint Remick, a boy who has no family whatsoever. His parents died several years ago. He attached himself to me some weeks ago at the start of my journey to photograph inland Maine. It has been in my mind to seek advice about adopting him, and I have broached the subject to him. At first, he did not seem to embrace the idea, but since our stay in Greenville, I believe he has developed an interest in it.

"In fact, it was Clint who wanted to know what we could do about easing Adeline's situation. The child and Clint have taken a liking to one another; he understands her grief, and she senses that he understands, even though she is too young—only 6 years old—to be able to say so. I should also add that there is no legal arrangement between Clint and myself. I see to his needs and keep him in pocket money. In return, at his suggestion, he serves as a helper to me as I travel about, making photographs."

"Then, am I to understand you are contemplating the adoption of the boy Clint and the guardianship of the little girl, with the possibility of eventually adopting her, too?"

"Yes. Yes, I am. Despite my age and the fact I have never been married and have no expectation of ever being so. Will that hinder my chances of adopting Clint and Adeline?"

"Not necessarily. But I must say, Miss Havener, the gentlemen in your town must be blind not to see your worth."

China felt her cheeks grow warm at the compliment, which pleased her very much. She spent the next twenty minutes giving a brief history of her life, including the move to Fort Point and the subsequent developments.

Mr. Benjamin listened attentively, with great interest, asking a few questions here and there, clearly enjoying her story.

"May I ask if you consider yourself a woman of means, Miss Havener?"

"Certainly not. But my sisters and I have enough to live modestly for the rest of our lives. And enough to take care of Clint and Adeline. They would not go hungry, nor would they ever be in rags or without a home. I can, in a modest way, see quite satisfactorily to their needs."

"Very well, Miss Havener. If you will provide me with the names and addresses of those who might speak candidly of your character . . . or lack of it"—he grinned engagingly—"I will see what can be done. In the meantime, I will arrange for the child to become a temporary ward of the State, and have her placed in your care until the necessary paperwork and other procedures can be carried out. Efforts will be made to determine if there are other relatives, no matter how distant, who might wish to take her in. I will talk with John Harvey and secure his signature on a document, relinquishing any claim to the child. It will be my task to determine what will be in the child's best interests."

"Thank you, sir," China said. "I am staying at the Patten House, and expect to be in town for a month—perhaps longer, if necessary."

When China returned to the hotel, she went immediately to find Mrs. Murphy and tell her what had transpired.

"Well, you seem like a nice-enough person," Mrs. Murphy said. "I'm glad to know the State is involved now, and that I'm out of it. My husband will be glad when I come home without the young one. Now, who's going to tell Adeline . . . not that she will care a jot that she won't be going back to Lincoln with me."

"Leave that to me, Mrs. Murphy."

"I told Clint to take Adeline over to the parsonage to call on Mr. Stearns, that minister we met on the way here. I expect them back pretty soon," Mrs. Murphy said.

"Thank you, Mrs. Murphy, for all you have done for Adeline," China said. "I know it has been difficult for you. Perhaps you would sit with us at mealtimes today, and for breakfast before the stage leaves tomorrow. That way, Adeline can get to know Clint and me a little better, and you and I can become better acquainted. If it's all right with you, I'd like to write you from time to time to let you know how Adeline gets on."

Mrs. Murphy smiled thinly and nodded.

That woman, China thought, judging by Mrs. Murphy's sour disposition, has not seen much kindness in her life. No wonder it was difficult for her to give or receive it.

China went downstairs and out onto the plank sidewalk to look for Clint and Adeline. She spotted them down the road a ways. When they saw China, they broke into a run, Adeline clinging to Clint's hand, Clint adjusting his stride to fit the little girl's shorter legs.

"Marm, Marm! Mr. Stearns wants you and Mrs. Murphy to come to the music program at the church this evening," Clint said. He paused somewhat dramatically and said, "She sings!"

"Who sings, Clint?"

"Her. Adeline."

A satisfied smile spread across Adeline's face as she nodded enthusiastically.

China bent to smooth Adeline's hair where it had been ruffled by the breeze.

"You sing?" she asked.

"You should hear her. Mr. Stearns wants to know if it's all right if Adeline sings a piece at the entertainment this evening," Clint said.

"Would you like to do that, Adeline?" China asked.

Adeline nodded again.

"Well, then, that's settled. I'll let Mrs. Murphy know about the entertainment and invite her along."

Later, when it was time to attend the musical evening at the church, Mrs. Murphy came downstairs with Adeline in hand. The child wore the same black dress she had been wearing for days, and her hair, out of its customary braids, flowed in a crinkled wave to her waist, held back by a wide black ribbon.

"Did you know she could sing?" China asked Mrs. Murphy.

"Can't say as I did, but I know her mother, Caroline Miles—she was a widow—played the fiddle some."

"Violin," Adeline said softly.

"Oh. Well, one's the same as the other as far as I'm concerned," Mrs. Murphy said.

The violin had been one of the items she had sold after Mrs. Miles died, provoking Adeline into a fit of hysterical screaming. But it had brought the most money of what few possessions Adeline's mother had owned.

The Congregational church was a two-and-a-half-story edifice with a square bell tower jutting from one corner. Ornate fretwork adorned the gable facing the road. It was large enough, China thought, to contain a good part of the population of Patten.

The pews were filling rapidly as they entered the church. China, Mrs. Murphy, Clint, and Adeline found seats a few rows back from the front. China exchanged nods with Samuel Benjamin and Mr. And Mrs. Hackett.

George Stearns said a prayer of blessing for the event. He introduced each performer, and one by one, or in twos and threes, they materialized from the audience, made their way to the front of the church, and sang, played the piano, the violin, the trumpet, the guitar, or the accordion. Their musical ability ranged from amateur to fairly accomplished. The audience applauded enthusiastically for each performer.

Then, Mr. Stearns took the floor and announced, "Tonight we have a special treat. Miss Adeline Miles, who is visiting Patten for the next few weeks, will favor us with a song. Miss Miles?"

Adeline rose gracefully from her seat beside Clint and walked with quiet self-possession to stand beside the piano. Mr. Stearns sat down at the keys, played the opening bars of the song, and nodded to Adeline. The child gazed at him, her face lit up, and she began to sing.

"I dreamed I dwelt in marble halls, with vassals and serfs at my side, and of all who assembled within those walls, that I was the hope and the pride."

Her voice, though untrained, had a quality and timbre unusual for one so young. She sang with a confidence beyond her years, and with obvious joy. When the song ended, a few women in the audience wiped away tears, and the applause rang loud and long. China could not believe her ears—so much talent in such a small girl.

"Perhaps Miss Miles would favor us with another?" Mr. Sterns asked.

Adeline went to him and whispered in his ear. He played the opening chords of *Greensleeves*, and once again Adeline held the audience in her thrall. When she had finished the last refrain, Mr. Stearns smiled at her and nodded his head. Adeline made a dignified curtsy and went back to her seat beside Clint.

"I never heard such a thing in all my life," Mrs. Murphy said under her breath to China.

"Nor I," China replied, thinking how the child's natural talent would need to be nurtured.

"Looks like you have your work cut out for you," Mrs. Murphy said. "Glad it's not me."

After the show, people flocked around Adeline to praise her singing and thank her for entertaining them.

Later, at the hotel, China, Mrs. Murphy, Clint, and Adeline settled into chairs in the lobby. "I have some news," China said. "Tomorrow, Mrs. Murphy will return to Lincoln."

Adeline hung her head—whether from denial or despair, China could not ascertain. Clint reached for Adeline's hand and pulled her into his lap. She buried her face into his chest.

"The news also affects you, Adeline," Mrs. Murphy said.

Adeline turned her face to look at China and Mrs. Murphy. Tears filled her eyes and her lower lip trembled.

"I spoke to a gentleman who has made me your temporary guardian, Adeline," China said. "What that means is, instead of going to Lincoln with Mrs. Murphy, you will stay here with Clint and me for the next few weeks. What do you think of that?"

Adeline's face brightened. She nodded, yes, quickly, as if fearing China, or worse, Mrs. Murphy, would say it wasn't true at all—that it was all a joke.

Clint shot a quick, approving look at China.

"What I propose is that we all go to bed now so we can get up early to see Mrs. Murphy off," China said. "I hope, Adeline, you will remember your manners and thank Mrs. Murphy for her goodness to you."

For a moment it looked as if Adeline might rebel, but Clint gave her a little push. She slid off his lap and went to stand by Mrs. Murphy.

"Thank you for bringing me here," she said. "And for looking after me."

"Nicely done, Adeline," China said.

"It was the least I could do, Adeline. I had a duty to perform according to your mother's wishes. Now it has been done," Mrs. Murphy said. She leaned down and kissed Adeline on the cheek. "Miss Havener and Clint are kind people, Adeline. I hope you will be a credit to them."

"Come, Adeline, Clint—time for bed. If you wish, Adeline, you may sleep in my room tonight," China said. The child took China's hand and smiled.

China tucked Adeline into a cot near her bed, and soon she was asleep.

Poor little thing, China thought, as she made herself ready for bed. She has been stunned by losing her mother and being dragged all this way to a strange town, among people she doesn't know. Nevertheless, there's backbone in that little girl.

China's last thought before she drifted off to sleep was, I wonder what India and Persia will think. Her one comfort was that when Mr. Benjamin made inquiries into her character, he would not write to her sisters. He had required references who were not members of her family. She had directed him to write to Sam Webber, to a sea captain whose father had been a friend of her father's, and to the minister of the Congregational church in Castine.

41.

The next morning, the stagecoach bore Mrs. Murphy away.

After breakfast, China organized an excursion to Finch Hill. Mr. Hackett arranged for her to hitch a ride with Hiram Myrick, who lived out that way, and was in town to buy a sack of flour. Clint and Adeline claimed the back of the wagon, dangling their feet over the dusty, rutted road. China climbed up on the seat beside Mr. Myrick.

"My wife Nettie teaches at the school out on Happy Corner Road, where we live," he said. "Stop out there sometime and see us."

"Thank you, I will," China said. "Do you by any chance have a good view of Katahdin?"

."That we do. I heard you have one of those newfangled cameras and have been aiming it at the scenery around here."

China smiled. "That I have. And if you and your wife don't mind, I'd like to aim my camera at the two of you," she said.

"Well, I guess we could stand that. Nettie's been wanting a picture of us to hang on the wall. Can't say as we could pay you much . . . "

"There would be no charge, Mr. Myrick. I'm still learning how this . . . newfangled thing works, and I'm not sure if the photographs I've already taken will amount to a hill of beans."

"Well, as my mother likes to say, 'Life is an act of faith.' Guess that probably covers taking pictures, too."

"I believe you are right, Mr. Myrick."

The hill grew steeper, so Mr. Myrick drew up the horses to let his passengers get down and walk the rest of the way. He tipped his hat and continued on toward the Happy Corner Road.

A large pasture, where several horses grazed sedately, rolled out like a green carpet before China and the children. In the distance, Katahdin was an easily recognizable, purplish-blue shape dominating the horizon. Off to the right rose Mount Chase, encased in the limitless green of the equally endless forest. At the bottom of the hill lay Patten, a small oasis in the wilderness. The spires of the Baptist, Methodist, and Congregational churches rose white against the blue sky, signaling the safety and comfort of home.

"Come along," China called to Clint and Adeline, "let's go into the pasture and find the best spot to set up the camera."

Adeline hung back a bit, as if wading in the tall grass was not an activity she was familiar with and had no interest in experiencing.

"Come on, Adeline," Clint urged her, sensing her reluctance. "Let's go pat the horses. Come on, I'll take you piggyback." He scooched so Adeline could climb onto his back. She secured her knees in the crook of his elbows and he conveyed her across the pasture.

The photograph of Clint and Adeline with the horses, one white, one a pretty bay, with Mount Katahdin looming in the background, was the one China prayed would be perfect. A breeze played in Adeline's hair, in the horses' manes and tails, and in the tall grass. The light glowed along the white horse's flanks. Clint placed his hand on the bay horse's nose and Adeline placed her hand on the horse's neck. That was the moment China removed the lens cap.

Clint fashioned a daisy crown and placed it on Adeline's head, which made her look like a fairy child, China thought, as she exposed more negatives.

After they had eaten a picnic lunch, Adeline asked, "Miss Havener, will we have to walk all the way back to the hotel?"

"No, Adeline, Mr. Stearns said he'd come to fetch us, and if I am not mistaken, that speck I see just starting up the hill is that very gentleman. Which brings me to another matter. Mr. Stearns asked me if I might spare you for an hour each morning to practice your singing. I told him I certainly could spare you, but only if you wished it."

Adeline's eyes shone. "Oh, yes!" she said.

"Then I shall arrange it."

"So what am I going to do while she sings and you tramp around with your camera?" Clint wanted to know, an odd note in his voice.

"I assumed you'd want to go tramping with me, Clint."

"Well, sure, I do. But . . . "

"But what?"

"Well, I'd like to go fishing."

China thought about that a minute as she packed up the picnic things. It was the first time Clint had ever asked for anything for himself. Surely that was a good sign.

"I will ask someone how to go about arranging a fishing trip for you, Clint. Just for a few days. I understand Shin Pond isn't too distant, and I'm told there are guides here who know the woods and waters well. What do you say to that?"

"Oh, boy!"

"But in the meantime, I will need your help, not only with the camera equipment, but with Adeline."

"So when would I go?" Clint asked.

"As soon as I can arrange it."

Mr. Stearns, driving a buggy, came into full view, stopped the horse, and waved to them. Clint ran to the buggy and climbed onto the seat with him. China and Adeline took the seat behind them.

"I take it you found the view to your liking, Miss Havener," Mr. Stearns said.

"Yes. It quite takes my breath away. And, with the children in the picture, it was perfect."

"Clint and I liked the horses best, but I don't like tall grass. It's itchy," Adeline chimed in, and they all laughed.

As they descended the hill, Mr. Stearns hummed a familiar hymn. Adeline, China, and Clint sang the words: "Once to every man and nation, comes the moment to decide . . . "

Somehow, the words seemed to sum up the recent days of China's life.

"What are we doing this afternoon?" Clint asked China after Mr. Stearns had let them off at the hotel.

"I'm going to write letters and rest a bit," China said. "But you and Adeline may explore the town a little more, if you'd like. Those back streets look interesting. Mind your manners, now."

China watched for a few moments as Clint and Adeline strolled under the shade of the stately elms that lined both sides of the road. Adeline clung to Clint's hand. What pretty children they are, she thought, watching them with pride.

She sat down at the table by the window in the hotel parlor, and took up pen and paper. It had been her intent to write to India and Persia about Adeline, but instead she wrote Plato Robinson's name. She had resolved not to write him again, but her resolve had deserted her.

Dear Plato,

Since last I wrote much has occurred, but I will be brief. I have another child in tow—a little girl named Adeline, who lost her mother a few weeks ago and has no family to take her in. Adeline was destined to be farmed out or sent to an orphanage. It pained me to think what might happen to her. She has attached herself to Clint, and that seems to be doing them both good. I am hoping to be appointed Adeline's guardian, at least for the moment, until inquiries and other formalities can be carried out. There is the possibility that an as yet unknown relative may be found to take her in. Adeline sings, quite well for a child of six.

I have not yet written my sisters of the increase in my "family," and I hesitate to tell them just yet, in the event a relative comes forward to claim Adeline. It is also possible that Mr. Benjamin, the local magistrate, will decide the child would, indeed, be better off elsewhere. In the meantime, I will see to her needs, as she seems to feel at home with Clint and me.

I trust the ferry business is keeping you well occupied.

With kind regards, I remain your friend,

China Havener

As China walked to the post office to mail the letter, people nodded and spoke to her. At the post office, the postmaster introduced himself as Charles Bradford. He was a small man with rusty blond hair and eyes that were a powdery shade of blue.

"Samuel Benjamin said you were looking for someone to take your boy into the woods to do some fishing," Mr. Bradford said. "That so?"

"Yes," China replied, "that is so." She was not at all surprised to discover that word traveled fast in Patten.

"Well, Will Smallwood is going up to Shin Pond tomorrow, and you won't find a better man around. He knows the best streams to fish, and he's a good hand in the outdoors. Knows his way around a campsite and then some. He worked in the woods handling horses when he was a young pup, but now he makes harness. Always a demand for harness come September, when the men and the teams go back into the woods for the winter."

"Thank you, Mr. Bradford. That's excellent information."

"He heard you were looking for someone, so he won't be at all surprised when you stop by and inquire."

China nodded her thanks, went down the road to the harness shop, and struck a deal with Will Smallwood to take Clint on a camping expedition for a few days.

42.

With Clint on his camping adventure with Will Smallwood, and Adeline at the church practicing her singing, China carried her camera to the middle of the main road, set it up, and pointed it toward the Methodist church and Finch Hill. She exposed the plate, then walked up the road to aim the camera at a large white house with a piazza across the front and a big barn attached at the rear.

As China adjusted the tripod, a tiny woman with white hair, wearing an old-fashioned black dress with a wide billowy skirt, came out into the yard. She leaned on a cane and seemed as insubstantial as dandelion fluff. She smiled in a kindly way and lifted one of her hands, clad in knitted white lace mitts, in greeting.

China waved back. The woman walked slowly to the edge of the road.

"They call me Old Mrs. Reid, and I guess I am, because there are several much younger Mrs. Reids who seem to be related to me in one way or the other," the woman said. "Wives of my grandsons, I suspect, but I can never keep them all sorted out. It can be very confusing to have so many descendants. I've seen you and your boy and girl walk by a few times. I heard all about you, and that you take pictures.

"I always wanted a picture of myself standing in front of this house. When I came here way back in 1841, this house was only a few years old. I was close to forty by then, had a string of young ones, and a good, kind husband, too. We don't get many photographers around here. Could I get you to take a picture of me sitting here by my house?"

"I'd be happy to, Mrs. Reid, but I have to warn you—I'm new to photography, and I can't guarantee the result. Nor do I have the equipment, or the knowledge, as yet, to print pictures after they are taken. But if the photograph turns out to be a good one, I'll send a copy to you."

"Well, that's very obliging. And I'll tell you what I will do: When I get that photograph, I will send you fifty cents in the mail."

It was the first time anyone had offered her money for one of her photographs and her initial impulse was to gently refuse.

Mrs. Reid sensed her hesitation.

"It seems to me that anyone that goes around taking pictures must have to spend money on things—I don't know enough about it to say what—but I just wanted you to know that I think you ought to charge a little something. I don't know what your time and a photograph are worth, but I surely can afford to send you fifty cents," Mrs. Reid said.

"Then I accept your offer," China said. "I think, Mrs. Reid, that the light is best over here, toward the front of the house. I see you have a rosebush and a nice little flower bed. Perhaps if you stand there, with the window and the door behind you . . . "

Mrs. Reid limped slowly to the spot China indicated.

"I'm going to hide the most of this cane in the folds of my dress. No need for my great-great-grandchildren, years from now when I am long gone, to see how lamed up I am with the rheumatism. There was a day when I was pretty as a picture, or so my husband always told me."

On impulse, China picked a few daylilies growing by the door. "Hold these," she said.

Mrs. Reid took the flowers and, with a natural gesture, let her arm rest across her waist. China told her to lift her chin slightly toward the light, and Mrs. Reid complied without a trace of self-consciousness, as if she had had her picture taken dozens of times. She stood very still as China removed and replaced the lens cap.

"My, my, as quick as all that," Mrs. Reid said.

"We live in remarkable times, Mrs. Reid."

"That we do, according to the newspaper. Perhaps you'd like to come in and visit a while. I'll make us a pot of tea."

"Thank you, Mrs. Reid. I would like that."

"We might as well set in the kitchen, Miss Havener. It's my favorite room—very cozy."

From the moment she stepped inside, China felt at home in Mrs. Reid's kitchen. A square, drop-leaf table stood in the center of the room. A fireplace with a cookstove fitted to it took up one wall, while another held cupboards and a sideboard. A row of three windows ranged across the exterior wall, letting in the morning light. A basket containing Mrs. Reid's knitting sat on an armchair, drawn up by the windows;

it gave the kitchen a note of cozy utility, and China surmised Mrs. Reid spent much of her time sitting in this spot.

China also noted that the seats of the chairs around the table were covered with pads made in the manner of hooked rugs.

"This is a very hospitable room," China commented.

"Sit down, sit down," Mrs. Reid said, pulling out a chair. She reached into a cupboard for a teapot, measured loose tea into it, and poured in boiling water from the teakettle on the stove.

"Guess I ought to add a stick of wood," Mrs. Reid said, rattling the lid as she added fuel to the fire. That done, she seated herself at the table and poured the tea into cups that matched the forget-me-not design on the teapot. She offered the sugar bowl and China added a teaspoonful to her cup.

"I'm enjoying my stay here in Patten very much," China said.

"Patten's a nice town. Can't say as I ever wanted to live anywhere else. My husband, rest his soul, and I lived downcountry, out a ways from Bangor, before we came here. I was sorry to leave at first, but once I got here, I never looked back, and I was always glad we came."

"People are very friendly."

"That they are. Of course, when I first came here, there weren't all that many folks living here. But the town grew quick, and it wasn't long before we had plenty enough families to fill three churches!"

"Did you think of yourself as a pioneer?"

"Good heavens, no! We just wanted a better life for our young ones, and thought if we went to a brand-new town, we'd have some say in what it turned out to be."

"And was that the case?"

"It surely was. Mr. Reid was selectman many a time, and I helped get the Methodist Ladies' Aid going. And for a while, the first of it, I had a school right here in this kitchen, teaching the little ones their letters. But pretty soon, the town hired a real schoolteacher. As for my young ones, the girls found good husbands and the boys fitted themselves for work and found good wives, too. My oldest boy fought at Shiloh and lived to tell the tale."

She smiled serenely, as if recalling those years gave her pleasure.

"What about you, Miss Havener—what brings you so far up this way?"

Briefly, China recounted the details of her story.

"But as it turns out, Mrs. Reid, I had barely started my journey before Clint Remick attached himself to me, and almost as soon as I arrived here, I decided to become guardian to a little girl, Adeline Miles. So as you can see, not only am I not alone, I am one of three again. Only at this very moment did I realize that."

"It's meant to be," Mrs. Reid said, nodding sagely. "Some things are just out there, looking for you. Why, when I married Mr. Reid, he was a widower with three girls and I was a widow with three boys. And then between us we had another girl and another boy. And me, already past forty by the time Daniel was born. Wasn't exactly how I thought the rest of my life would go. But there it went, and I can't say as I regret a thing.

"You don't strike me as the kind who will regret having Clint and Adeline around either. Seems to me Providence saw your state of singleness and Clint and Adeline's state of orphan-ness and put one and two together, so to speak."

"I worry sometimes that I won't be able to provide for them properly," China confided. "My sisters and I must earn something to help keep a roof over our heads."

"You do your part as best you can, and Providence will do the rest."

Touched by Mrs. Reid's kindness and faith, China left that lady's kitchen in high spirits. All her senses seemed heightened, and everything she looked at appeared to be sharply delineated. No matter where she looked, she saw a photograph she wanted to make—a baby carriage parked outside a house in the shade of a towering elm, the facade of a store, the cascade of a vine with broad leaves clinging to one corner of a porch. But she knew she had to be selective. She already had taken more than a dozen views, which left her with a little over two dozen unexposed negatives.

As she made her way down the main road to the Methodist church, people she already knew by sight, if not by name, greeted her and inquired about having their photographs taken. China thanked them and said she'd consider it, though for the present she was confining her work to outdoor scenes in and around the village. Their inquiries made her think that perhaps India and Persia had been right about portraiture. It seemed that people in small towns such as Patten, who rarely if ever had an opportunity to be photographed, would indeed pay to have their pictures taken.

As they ate dinner at the hotel, Adeline was unusually quiet and only picked at her food.

"Do you feel well, Adeline?" China asked.

Adeline nodded.

"Missing Clint, perhaps?"

"A little bit, but not too much, because Clint promised he'd be back on Sunday, and I know he will," Adeline said firmly.

"You can count on that, Adeline. It seems to me that you might be thinking heavy thoughts. I wonder if you'd like to share them with me. Perhaps I could help."

Adeline heaved a sigh, as if she carried a great and wearying weight.

"I don't like wearing black," she said softly. "Everyone looks at me funny, and a boy said I look like a beetle. I don't look like a beetle, do I?"

"No, you certainly do not."

Though Adeline understood that she wore black to signify mourning for her mother's death, the color was not at all becoming to the child. China was not among those who believed children should wear black after a death in the family. Death, she believed, was a heavy enough burden to carry without adding to it the weight of endless months of wearing monotonous black dresses.

"I told that boy he was mean, but he just laughed at me. I stamped my foot at him and told him he was nothing but a snake in the grass!"

"I see," China said, trying not to smile. "What was your mother's favorite color, Adeline?"

Tears misted Adeline's eyes as she looked down at her plate.

"Blue," she whispered. " 'Blue as beautiful as my little girl's eyes.' That's what she always said."

"Well, Adeline, here's what I think we should do. Let's finish our dinner and go down the street to Mrs. True's shop and see if we can find your mother's favorite shade of blue. What do you say to that?"

The clouded expression on Adeline's face cleared and she nodded happily.

43.

Mrs. True's store occupied a corner on the upper end of the main road. A magnificent elm stood beside it, shading it like a dark green parasol. The screen door did not creak when China opened it to let Adeline go in ahead of her.

A curtain of heavy fabric in royal blue, surely an auspicious sign, separated the store and the back room from which Mrs. True emerged. She carried a white straw hat decorated with pale pink tulle and silk flowers, which she settled in the shop window. She was a fine-boned woman of indeterminate age with dark eyes that flitted from China to Adeline, as if taking their measure.

"We are searching for something very special for this little girl," China said. "She's looking for fabric and ribbon in a shade of blue that was her mother's favorite color."

A smile lit up Mrs. True's plain face.

"I think you ought to come through to my workroom," she said. She drew aside the curtain to let them enter. A large work table occupied the center of the room, and a New Home sewing machine stood near a window where the light was best. Several hat forms occupied a special place on a counter, and a dress form stood in the corner.

Mrs. True led Adeline to a cupboard and opened the door to reveal several dozen reels of ribbon arranged according to color, from light to dark.

"That one, that one!" Adeline exclaimed immediately. "Mama loved that color, Miss Havener."

"This shade is called Heavenly Blue," Mrs. True said.

"We will take two yards of that," China said.

Mrs. True opened another large cupboard containing many bolts of fabric.

"What I have for fabric right now is here; I just got a nice shipment in a week or so ago. A good part of it is woolen, because even though it's barely August, winter isn't so far away. But there's plenty of cotton and linen there, too, if it's a summer item that's wanted," she said. She pointed out which fabric was which.

"What do you think, Adeline? Do you see a color here that reminds you of your mother?" China asked.

Adeline ran her fingers over the bolts of fabric.

"This one," she said, her fingers stopping on a powder-blue cotton with a tiny white floral design.

"Two things," China said to Mrs. True. "I'd like a pillow slip and a dress for Adeline made of this fabric."

"Oh, Miss Havener!" Adeline exclaimed, throwing her arms around China's waist.

"I have a fashion pattern book here, if you'd like to choose a style," Mrs. True said. She pulled chairs up to the work table and opened the book.

"This has been a very popular style this summer." She pointed to a dress with rows of frills, puffed sleeves, and a wide sash.

"It's very pretty, but no," Adeline said, turning the page.

"I quite agree," China whispered in a droll tone in Adeline's ear.

The child giggled and turned more pages until her eyes lit on a simpler style. The skirt was gathered, the bodice had rows of pin tucks, the sleeves were not puffed, and the neckline was round, edged with lace. It also buttoned up the front.

"This one. With a dress like this, I could put it on all by myself," Adeline said.

"Very true," China replied. "Mrs. True, I think Adeline has made her choice. And a very good one it is."

Mrs. True smiled. "As it happens, that's one of my favorite designs for a little girl. It's pretty without being fussy."

She took Adeline's measurements, wrapped the ribbon, collected ten cents for it from China, and said the dress and pillow slip would be ready in two weeks.

When they returned to the hotel, China removed the black satin mourning ribbon from Adeline's braids and tied them up with the new blue ribbon. She also tied a length of ribbon, like a bracelet, around Adeline's left wrist.

"Left, because it's nearest your heart," China told the child. "So every time you look at the ribbon, you will remember that your mother will always live in your heart and will always be a part of you."

Adeline leaned her head against China's hip, gazed at the ribbon, and stroked it with her fingers.

Later, while Adeline occupied herself with drawing pictures, China wrote a note to Mrs. True telling her to make two more dresses in the same pattern for Adeline—one in white and one in pale yellow. It was an extravagance, but she figured that if she cut her time short in Patten by a week or so, her budget could stand the additional expense.

She did not mind setting an earlier time for returning to Fort Point. The fact was, she was looking forward more and more to developing her negatives, and learning whether or not she was any good at photography.

She asked one of the Hackett boys to deliver the note to Mrs. True, and then she began writing a letter to India and Persia to tell them about Clint's fishing trip, Adeline's new dresses, and her visit with Mrs. Reid.

She was halfway through the first page when Adeline looked up from her sketching, her small face still etched with the anxiety she had suffered in recent weeks. However, the smile she aimed at China was broad and genuine. She held up a sheet of paper.

"I drew this for you," she said. A stick figure of a woman with a halo and wings and wearing a blue robe hovered in the air. Below her, arranged in front of a house with smoke curling from the chimney and the sun beaming in the sky, were three other figures—a very tall woman wearing a hat, holding the hand of a small girl wearing a blue dress, holding the hand of a boy almost as tall as the woman.

Adeline pointed to the angel figure.

"That's Mama, looking down on us, Miss Havener."

"Thank you, Adeline," China said. "This is a very beautiful picture. I will treasure it."

Tears welled up in her eyes. The picture, China saw, contained everything Adeline felt but was too young to know how to say. She believed her dead mother watched over her, and that the bond between them was deep and true; yet, she also knew that she had found two people who would care for her and keep her safe. She had, with a few deft lines, made a portrait of her growing trust that all would be well.

"Why are you crying, Miss Havener? Did I make you sad?" Adeline asked, her mood suddenly somber.

"Adeline, my dear child, these are tears of happiness. I am so very touched to have this lovely picture."

A small smile of satisfaction turned up the corners of Adeline's mouth as she went back to her drawing. "One for Clint," she said softly as she took up her colored pencils.

China resumed writing her letter:

❧

Our stay in Patten is not an overly active one. I find it very restful, and I've been thinking often of the future. I realized something only today: I am not making my way these past weeks with loose sails filled with a wayward wind that pushes me hither and yon, as it seemed—and must have seemed to you—when I first embarked on this journey. Indeed, sisters, I have got my bearings.

I think, too, of Clint and Adeline, whose circumstances I described to you at the beginning of this letter. They are not precisely glass-plate negatives, but are made of an equally mysterious and precious material. Once they are grown, they will turn out to be creatures of light and shadow, molded, in part, by my eye being firmly fixed on their well-being.

I have come to the conclusion that the only way I can be certain Clint and Adeline will have a good life is to adopt them. As you already know, Clint is entertaining the idea of adoption, and I believe he will soon give his consent. As for Adeline, the details are still unclear, and will remain so until it is determined whether or not there are other relatives who might give her home. It is my fervent hope no one will be found, for I have become quite attached to her.

It may surprise you to learn that I look forward to being at home with you again, although I do worry that you may find the addition to our household of two lively children too much to endure. Yet, I know it's a ridiculous worry, for when we were at sea all those years, we lived in a small space among many. Thus, I see no reason why you would not welcome Clint and Adeline as permanent fixtures among us.

We have only to look at Fanny and the Abbott's Reach folks to understand how the addition (within reason) of children makes life richer, and more complete. A solitary person—or indeed triplets, like us, who view themselves as a solitary unit—need more people in their lives, especially as they grow older. Because of Clint and Adeline, more people will come into our lives; they will someday bring a wife and a husband, and, eventually, children, to whom we will be grandmothers. Just think of that!

I know you will talk about all this, and I have faith that when I come home with the children, you will take them to your hearts, just as I have. If you cannot, then it would make sense for me to establish a household of my own, somewhere nearby.

I know all of this is a great deal for you to absorb and I wish I could have broken it to you more gently. But be assured that I am being sensible and guided by common sense. I have every confidence that you will stand behind me in this matter as you have always stood by me, no matter what.

And now, dear sisters, I must set up my camera and make a portrait of Adeline. The western sun has slanted through the window and falls perfectly on the child, making her reddish-blonde hair glow. At this very moment, she is a picture of contentment, the lines of anxiety that frequently etch her face erased by the pleasure she finds in drawing a picture for Clint, who returns from his camping trip on Sunday.

When I expose the negative, it will be a double portrait—the one of Adeline, which can be seen (eventually), and the one of myself, which will

*be invisible, except for the fact that what the camera sees is what my eyes
saw first—the light in the room illuminating this lovely child in that beautiful and poignant way.*

Your affectionate sister,
China

❧

She reached for the camera, but instead of placing it on the tripod, she held it with one hand while she removed and replaced the
lens cap with the other. She knew she risked causing the image to
blur, but if she had gone through the rigmarole of setting up the
tripod, Adeline would have been disturbed, the moment lost.

All of my memories since I started on this journey are contained
in this square oak box, she thought, liking the idea, but feeling a stirring of anxiety that none of her photographs would come out right.

"Adeline, I'm going to walk to the post office to mail my letter. Would you like to come with me, or would you prefer to stay
here?" China asked.

"Go with you," Adeline replied.

"Very well. I thought we might also stop a minute to pass the
time of day with Mrs. Reid, who lives just down the road from the
post office. She is a new acquaintance and has expressed an interest
in meeting you."

They found Mrs. Reid sitting in a straight-backed kitchen chair
placed beside the kitchen door, knitting stockings.

"Good day to you, Miss Havener," she said. "And who might this
pretty child be?"

"This is Miss Adeline Miles," China said.

"Well, Adeline, this is your lucky day," Mrs. Reid said. She reached into the basket by her feet and took out a pair of red mittens. "These ought to fit you."

"What do you say, Adeline?" China prompted gently.

"Thank you," Adeline said, as she bobbed a small curtsy.

"Very prettily done, Adeline," Mrs. Reid said.

"My mother was going to show me how to knit," Adeline said shyly, "but she died." She said this last word softly, the first time she had used it in China's hearing.

"Now that is a great misfortune," Mrs. Reid said. She tucked her knitting in the basket. "Come in a minute." She led China and Adeline into the kitchen.

"It smells like . . . home," Adeline whispered, her chin quivering.

China took her hand in a gesture of comfort.

"Sit down at the table," Mrs. Reid said. She reached into an earthenware crock and arranged a dozen molasses cookies on a plate. "Have some of these. I'll be right back."

She disappeared into the main part of the house. When she returned, she carried a small doll carved of wood, a pair of knitting needles, and ball of pale blue yarn.

"These are for you," she said to Adeline. "This was my doll when I was a little girl, and these knitting needles my father whittled for me out of ironwood when I was just about your age, and wanted to know how to knit. I want you to have them."

She placed the doll, knitting needles, and ball of yarn on the table in front of Adeline.

A smile of pleasure and wonder spread over Adeline's face.

"Thank you," she breathed in a barely audible whisper.

"That is very generous of you, Mrs. Reid," China said. "Surely, the doll and the knitting needles should be handed on to one of your daughters, or granddaughters . . . "

"I already tried that, but the style today is china-headed dolls with elaborate dresses and little leather boots and such. And knitting needles today are either steel or bone, not wood. But your Adeline, she's an old soul—I can see that in her—and she will grow to appreciate the things of the past," Mrs. Reid said.

Adeline reached for the doll and smoothed its calico dress and white lawn apron.

"Look, Miss Havener—she has a little carved comb in her hair." She held the doll up for China to see, then turned to Mrs. Reid. "What's her name?"

"Well, I always called her Abigail, but you can call her whatever you want," Mrs. Reid said.

"What's your name?" Adeline asked softly.

"Why, bless you, child; my given name is Laura."

"Then I will call her Laura Abigail." Adeline cradled the doll in the crook of her arm.

"Somewhere up attic there's a little leather trunk, and it's full of dresses and such that my mother and I and my sisters made for the doll. Once I find that, it will be yours, too." Mrs. Reid smiled and smoothed Adeline's hair. "I'll send word to you."

After that, Mrs. Reid gave Adeline a knitting lesson, which at first resulted in a mighty tangle that made them laugh. But soon Adeline grasped the concept of bringing the yarn through the stitches on the needle in her left hand with the bare needle in her right hand. She did not yet understand how to apply proper tension to the yarn, but China knew that practice would solve that difficulty.

"When I can really knit without getting the yarn all tangled," Adeline said, "I'm going to make a shawl trimmed with blue ribbon for Laura Abigail."

44.

China and Adeline spent the remainder of the week happily as they went about each day—Adeline to singing practice and working at her knitting, China wandering around town, taking photographs of houses and yards she found interesting, walking to a farm on the outskirts of town, and going out to the Happy Corner Road to visit the Myricks, where the view of Mount Katahdin was so splendid, she spent more time staring at it than she did photographing it.

Everywhere she looked were scenes that drew her eye and filled her with energy and longing, infusing her very soul with light.

Life seemed to her newly rich and filled with greater promise than it had before she had left Fort Point, very unexpected so late in her life. When she had reached her mid-fifties, the age she was now, she had expected to find a dwindling of possibility, an ebbing of vitality bordering on the brutal. But now she saw the reverse was true. The camera had opened her life, her spirit, as if the light it took in found its way into the waiting negative of her heart, printing there an image of happiness unlike any other she had ever known.

Clint and Adeline were a large part of that light.

The only thing sending a ripple across her pool of contentment was Plato Robinson. Whenever thoughts of him floated into her head as she went through the day, or at night, after she had gone to bed, she felt restless and filled with an odd longing that was out of keeping with everything else in her life. He was the blurred image in her days, and she did not know how to bring him into focus. In spite of her doubts, however—in spite of her attempts to talk herself out of it—she knew he was fixed firmly in her heart.

At night, her mind roamed back to Bingham and the pleasant hours she had spent in Plato's company. It was amusing to think that when it came to a ship, she knew how to drive it and the people upon it, and had done so without fear or hesitation, but when it came to Plato Robinson, she was as helpless as a newborn kitten, and twice as brainless. Her inability to know what to do, what to say, her inability to sail serenely into his life, mystified her and filled her with frustration.

Absence, she concluded, did not make the heart grow fonder. It made the heart confused. It made the heart question and doubt itself. For surely, she thought, Plato Robinson was in the process of forgetting her. Perhaps he had already been drawn to an attractive summer visitor who had taken his ferry across the Kennebec and turned his head with her charms, snaring him with her pretty smile.

Perhaps the news that she now had two children in her care had caused his feelings toward her to change. Perhaps at his age, he was not interested in becoming attached to a woman of middle years with youngsters in tow. Perhaps that was why he wrote so seldom and said so little.

After a spell of such round-and-round thinking, China fell asleep.

When she woke the next morning, Adeline's smile and her immediate needs made any stray thoughts of Plato Robinson recede to a place where they did not command every iota of space in her brain.

"It's Sunday, it's Sunday!" Adeline proclaimed as she climbed out of bed. She threw her arms around China's neck. "Clint's coming home today! Wait till I show him my pretty new blue pillow slip!"

Mrs. True had finished that item only the day before.

"But first, Adeline, we must get dressed, have breakfast, and go to church."

"Oh, yes, I have a pretty hymn to sing—but I want to see Clint."

"Clint won't be here until later today. Here's what I think we will do after church. I'll hire a horse and carriage from Mr. Peavey, the blacksmith, and we'll drive out on the Shin Pond Road to meet Clint and Mr. Smallwood. Mind you, I have no idea if it's even possible to intercept them, but I thought it might be fun to drive out there anyway. We can take sandwiches to eat along the way."

Adeline's eyes shone with pleasure, and she stood very still as China tied the sash of her black dress since her new dresses weren't ready yet.

After church several people stopped to inquire when China expected Clint and Will Smallwood to get back. Samuel Benjamin took a moment to tell Adeline how prettily she had sung *Abide with Me.*

Village life was something China had missed out on as a child, and she found herself enjoying the daily contact with people whose faces were beginning to be familiar to her.

Armed with a picnic lunch Mrs. Hackett had packed for them, China and Adeline set off toward the Shin Pond Road.

It was a lovely August day. Trixie, the gray mare pulling the buggy, appeared to have a sedate disposition, and China had no qualms about her ability to guide the animal along the road. Driving a horse was a skill she had learned as a girl during those times when she and her sisters were alongshore for a few months. She had, for a change, left her camera in her hotel room in order to give Adeline her undivided attention.

The narrow road, rutted and rocky in places, took them past grassy fields filled with black-eyed Susans. China stopped several times to let Adeline collect a bouquet for Clint and one for Mr. Smallwood. "Because I don't want him to feel left out," Adeline said.

They proceeded slowly, laughing and talking. Adeline chattered about her new dresses, wishing they were finished, eager to see them, impatient to wear them.

Whenever they stopped for yet another session of flower picking, to admire a view, or to investigate a brook, China let Trixie browse the grass.

"May I drive?" Adeline asked, after a quick stop to pick a few ferns growing beside the road.

"Yes. Sit here in my lap," China said, showing Adeline how to place her hands on the reins. China kept hold of the reins, too, knowing that Adeline lacked the strength to control the horse properly. They went up a hill and started down another that took them through a stand of tall evergreens which cast a refreshing pool of cool shade across the road.

Suddenly, right in front of them, a deer jumped out into the road, then bounded away. Startled and frightened, Trixie shied, reared, and broke into a run, seemingly for her life.

Instinctively, China tightened her left arm around Adeline, retaining her grip on the reins with her right hand. She braced her feet against the dashboard and pulled with all her might. Trixie did not heed the signal, and China knew she lacked the strength, using just one hand, to pull Trixie to a stop.

The buggy hurtled on, bouncing and jouncing. Trixie's tail and mane fanned out in the breeze created by her headlong flight. Her hooves pounded against the dirt surface of the road.

Adeline screamed, causing Trixie to increase her speed.

"Be still, Adeline," China said firmly into the child's ear. Adeline closed her mouth and put her hands over her eyes.

China, her heart hammering, expected the buggy to overturn at any moment. But soon the trees gave way to meadow on both sides of the road, and she thought, if the worst happens—something that never crossed her mind when the *Empress* had plowed through a filthy storm, bucking, rolling, and pitching, the wind screaming in the rigging, the starboard rail awash. But then, she had been in command, in total control, not at the mercy of a fear-crazed horse.

Then the worst did happen. The right front wheel of the buggy fetched up against a rock, making the carriage buck and tip.

China cried, "Jump, Adeline!" as she pushed the child to what she hoped was a safe landing in the tall grass. It was too late for her to jump clear of the buggy.

With a sickening, terrifying lurch, the buggy overturned and China fell hard against the turf. She felt the side of her head strike something, then everything went black.

When the field stopped spinning and the sound of her own screams subsided, Adeline stared at the lovely blue sky and thought Mama! She blinked and said, "Miss Havener. Clint." Sobs convulsed her chest.

Then it occurred to her that she didn't feel any pain. She turned her head slightly, enough to see Trixie and the buggy with its broken wheel a little way down the road. Trixie was awash in sweat, sides heaving, her head drooping with weariness.

"Miss Havener?" Adeline called softly, then more loudly.

China did not answer.

Slowly, Adeline sat up and looked around for China. She stood up, calling and calling, "Miss Havener, Miss Havener." No answer. She took a few steps, turned to look down the road where the trees dimmed the sunlight, making it appear menacing. She looked up the road where the sunlight filled the meadow, where Trixie, blowing a great gust of air through her nostrils, turned her head to look at Adeline, as if to say Now what?

Only one purpose filled Adeline's mind: She had to find Miss Havener. She had gone only a few dozen steps when she spotted something gray—the hem of a skirt.

China lay all in a heap, blood smeared on one side of her face. Her hat was squashed beneath her, and her shirtwaist was torn at one shoulder. Adeline touched China's face, patted her arm, and took her hand.

"Miss Havener, Miss Havener," she said again and again, fighting down a terrible urge to scream. She knew instinctively that screaming would not help. There was no one to hear. Screaming had not helped when her mother died. It had not helped when she was taken to Mrs. Murphy's house. It had not helped the day they had boarded the stage-coach for Patten.

Adeline sat down on the grass beside China.

Once, China's eyes opened and she whispered, "My head hurts." Then she closed her eyes and spoke no more.

Adeline clung to China's hand and did the only thing she knew how to do. She sang. She sang every hymn she knew. When she ran out of those, she began on the other songs she knew by heart—*Shenandoah* and *Greensleeves*. And when she ran out of those songs, she started over again with the hymns.

She had no idea how much time had passed, but she watched as the sun sank lower in the sky, and knew the afternoon had worn on. Just as she began to despair of anyone ever coming along the road to help, she heard the jingle of harness and the rumble of wagon wheels coming from up the road.

Her first instinct was to run toward the sound, but she could not let go of China's hand. Instead, she figured now was the perfect time to scream. "Help us!" she shrieked. "She's hurt! She's hurt!"

Not two minutes later, Clint was there, cradling her in his arms, and Will Smallwood knelt at China's side, assessing what needed to be done.

"Nasty crack on the head, by the looks," he said. During his days of working in the woods, he had seen plenty of cuts, bruises, and broken bones. And though he was no expert on such things, he knew the basic signs to look for. The woman was breathing, but unconscious. Neither her arms nor her legs appeared broken. The bleeding from the wound where her head had struck the rock was not excessive. But she needed the care of a doctor, no doubt about that.

Clint, still holding Adeline, her legs wrapped around his waist and her face buried in his shoulder, stood nearby.

"Is it bad?" he asked, knowing the answer, his stomach in a knot.

"Bad enough. Set the girl on her feet and make a bed in our wagon with the camp blankets," Will said. "Lead the horse over this way so we don't have but a short ways to lift her. Don't want to hurt her any more than she already is."

Gently, with great care and some effort, they lifted China into the wagon bed. As they set her down, she moaned and her eyelids fluttered. Will covered her with a blanket. "Take that other horse and ride as fast as you can back to the village and alert the doctor. I'll have to take it slow so as not to hurt Miss Havener any more than she already is. Come on, Adeline, you can ride up here with me," Will said, indicating the wagon seat.

"No," Adeline said firmly, taking Clint's hand. "I'm going with Clint."

"Adeline, you can't. The horse doesn't have a saddle," Clint tried to explain.

"I don't care, I'm going with you! I'll hang on . . . I'm going!" Adeline insisted. She began to tremble and Clint could see she was on the verge of a fit of serious screaming.

Clint, in the process of unharnessing Trixie, looked at Adeline and said, "Okay, but when I put this horse to the run, Adeline, you better lay low over its neck and hang on to its mane for dear life, because there won't be any stops along the way. And if you whine even once, I'll stop and leave you beside the road, I don't care how dark it is. You got that?!"

Adeline's weeping came to a sudden halt. She wiped her tears away with the back of her hand and looked Clint straight in the eye. "Yes," she said firmly, her lower lip in a pout.

Clint tossed her astride Trixie and flung himself onto the horse's back behind her. Adeline wove her fingers into the horse's mane and laid herself along the horse's neck. Clint turned Trixie, grabbed the reins he had fashioned from the sash of Adeline's dress, and nudged his heels into horse's sides. And Trixie, despite her recent adventure, made tracks for Patten.

Adeline, much to Clint's surprise, hung on and uttered not one word of protest.

Clint had no idea how many miles it was to Patten, but he thought it wasn't more than two or three. Whenever Trixie gave the least sign of slowing down, he kicked her hard in the ribs and she resumed her pace.

Clint was beyond thought, beyond feeling. All he could do was ride and see to it that Adeline didn't fall off.

45.

When Clint and Adeline reached the village, Trixie was at the end of her strength. Her sides heaving with weariness, she had slowed to a walk. No amount of urging on Clint's part would make her go any faster.

Lamps were already lit in some of the windows of the houses along the main road, although the sun had not yet fully set.

As they came by Mrs. Reid's house, a voice from the piazza called out to them. "You young ones, what are you doing out at this hour? Is there trouble afoot?"

"It's Mrs. Reid! Put me down! Put me down!" Adeline insisted. "She'll know where the doctor lives."

Trixie, with no urging, stopped in her tracks. Clint helped Adeline slide from Trixie's back to the ground.

"Mrs. Reid, we need a doctor!" Adeline called as she ran toward the older woman, the story of the accident tumbling out of her.

Leaning on her cane, Mrs. Reid made her way to the edge of the road.

"Leave the horse to me, I'll put her in the barn," she said to Clint. "Run down to the hotel. Sometimes Dr. Woodbury has supper there on Sunday night. If he's not there, he'll be to home and someone can fetch him. Make sure it is understood that Miss Havener is to be brought to my house. Adeline can stay here with me and help me light the lamps and make up the bed in the back bedroom."

"Yes, ma'am," Clint called over his shoulder as he ran toward the hotel, where he found Dr. Burton Woodbury just finishing his supper. Within fifteen minutes, Dr. Woodbury, Clint, and several other men, carrying lighted lanterns, equipped with blankets and with a fresh horse tied behind, rode in a wagon along the Shin Pond Road. They intercepted Will Smallwood a little more than a mile from town.

Clint and the other men held the lanterns high as Dr. Woodbury quickly and efficiently assessed China's injury.

"Definitely a concussion, possibly a skull fracture," said the doctor. He didn't mention the possibility of bleeding and swelling within the cranium that may have already occurred, and could possibly prove fatal before the night was out. Will Smallwood's horse, Pete, was tuckered out from the long miles it had walked all day and evening. The men unharnessed the animal and put the fresh horse into the traces and the rescue party set off toward the village. When they arrived at Mrs. Reid's, Sarah Woodbury, the doctor's wife, Lydia Stearns, the minister's wife, and Mrs. True put China to bed. Dr. Woodbury did a more thorough examination of China's wound, and cleaned and bandaged it.

"All we can do now is wait," the doctor said.

What he meant, but did not say, was wait to see if the wound became infected, wait to see if signs of swelling in the brain appeared, wait to see if symptoms of bleeding within the skull cavity became apparent. Head injuries were unpredictable; they could go either way. The next twenty-four hours would determine the final outcome, for good or ill.

Dr. Woodbury exchanged a meaningful glance with his wife. Only she understood the full measure of his concern.

While the doctor, Mrs. Reid, and the others attended China, Clint and Adeline sat close to one another on a sofa in the front room, just outside the back bedroom. The lamp had not been lit and they sat in the dark. Adeline leaned against Clint, her breath coming out in occasional stifled sobs.

"You better stop crying, Adeline. Won't make any difference one way or another," Clint said, his voice rough and sharp.

"I know that!" Adeline said mournfully. "But it was all my fault." Another sob and more tears spilled down her face.

"I'm sorry, Adeline. I didn't mean to be hateful and speak so sharp. It wasn't your fault a deer jumped out and scared the horse."

"But I was helping Miss Havener drive."

"That's still not your fault. She let you because she wanted your help."

They heard the soft rustle of a long skirt against the floor and Mrs. Reid came in, lit the lamp, turned it low, and sat in a chair near Clint and Adeline.

"Now, children, I know this looks pretty bad, but things will look brighter in the morning. They always do. I thought maybe you should spend the night here so I can see to you. First, you'd best eat something. Come along with me to the kitchen. There's some stew and beans and biscuits. Some good food will make you feel better—help you sleep."

Clint felt suddenly numb, as if all the air had been sucked out of the room. He wasn't sure he could stand. He felt Adeline's hand in his. "Come on, Clint," she said softly.

"That's a girl, Adeline," Mrs. Reid said. "You take care of Clint. And, Clint, you look after Adeline. Be a help to one another. The rest of us will take care of Miss Havener."

The kitchen was warm and pleasant, the smell of food enticing. Already the women of Patten had risen to the occasion and brought in pies, loaves of bread, puddings, jellies, pots of baked beans, and cold sliced chicken.

Suddenly, Clint felt a little more hopeful, and Adeline, always willing to follow his lead, dried her tears, realizing that she, too, was hungry.

Dr. Woodbury joined them, taking the cup of tea that Lydia Stearns handed him. He sat down at the table with the children.

"Will she die?" Clint asked bluntly.

Adeline's eyes grew large and her mouth quivered.

"I'm sorry to upset you, Adeline, but I have to know. We have to know."

Dr. Woodbury had children of his own at home, and many times in the course of his years as a doctor he had seen children left motherless. Indeed, as he had been told, both Clint and Adeline were orphans. It was a terrible question for them to have to ask, considering what they had already lost. It was equally terrible to be asked such a question. He had long ago determined that it did no good to pretend everything would be all right, when in fact he did not know whether or not it would be.

"At the moment, there is no way to tell, Clint," he said. "Miss Havener has suffered a blow to her head which has left a wound. She is a strong and healthy lady. Time often does much to heal such injuries. I have seen people with worse recover to full health." He had also seen those with lesser wounds succumb far too quickly to their injuries. "The important thing, right now, is for you to have patience and let Mrs. Reid and these good ladies take care of you. Do you think you can do that?"

Adeline nodded. Clint looked down at his plate.

"If it . . . goes the other way, and you know it's coming . . . Will you tell me?" he asked in a voice devoid of emotion.

"Indeed, I will."

"She has sisters. And a lot of friends. Should I let them know?"

"As I said, Clint, let's wait until morning and see how things are then," Dr. Woodbury replied. By morning he would know several things—especially if the wound was becoming infected, and if there were signs of pressure on the brain. "Tonight we simply watch and wait."

Clint woke early the next morning in Mrs. Reid's shed chamber, a quaint room under the eaves of the house. Its rough-board walls were whitewashed, and the wide-board pine floor was painted a dull red. Adeline was still asleep in a cot across the room. Mrs. Reid had wanted Adeline to sleep in a small room at the top of the stairs, but Adeline had insisted she would not leave Clint.

Clint dressed quietly and went down to the empty kitchen. The fire in the stove was out. He kindled it and set a kettle of water on the back burner. He found biscuits and stew left over from the night before, which he set on the front burner.

He glanced at the clock ticking on a shelf and saw that it was just a few minutes past five o'clock. He paced back and forth impatiently, willing the water to boil so he could make tea. He knew it would take a while for the fire in the stove to get hot enough, then more time for the food to heat and the water to boil, so he went outside and into the barn, looking for the woodpile, found it, and carried several armloads to the woodbox in the kitchen.

When that was done, he took the broom and swept up the bits of dirt and bark the effort had left behind on the kitchen floor. That had been one of his chores at home in Cambridge when his folks were still alive. He recalled what his mother always said: "You're a good man with a broom, Clint." He remembered how proud her words had made him feel. That thought undid him, and hot tears of grief rolled down his face. He went back to the barn and up into the loft to hide in the hay so no one would see him cry. His thoughts became jumbled, and the pain of his parents passing, his descent into the circumstances of being a child without a family, became mixed up with feelings of rage and fear that China might die—that he would forever be adrift. Those feelings became enmeshed with such deep despair that he did not think he'd be able to stand on his own two feet ever again.

He had no idea how long he lay there, weeping, hating himself for being a crybaby, and furious with China for stopping that stagecoach and taking him to Skowhegan, and all that came afterward.

The thought came suddenly: He would to go to the hotel and get his things, strike off on his own, find his way back to Bingham to become a ferryman, or go back to Cambridge to his old campsite. Why shouldn't he do it? He didn't belong to anyone. There was no one to stop him from heading on down the road. He'd find rides along the way. Wouldn't be the first time he'd done it.

He sat up and dried his eyes with the back of his hands. That's what he would do. He would go.

Then he heard Adeline calling his name.

"Clint, where are you? Mrs. Reid said it's time to eat breakfast. Clint, don't leave me all alone!" Adeline said, a quiver in her voice, as if she sensed he was poised to go, to run, to flee.

He knew instantly that the sound of her voice saved him from acting in a way that would dishonor China—and himself. He stood up and brushed the hay chaff from his clothes.

"I'll be right down," he called gruffly to Adeline. "I was seeing to the horse; she needed hay." Trixie had spent the night in Mrs. Reid's barn. "You go back in the house and tell Mrs. Reid I'll be in directly."

When Clint heard Adeline go back into the house, he climbed down from the loft, gathered another armload of firewood, and went inside.

Mrs. Reid set a plate of fried eggs, a pot of oatmeal, and a small pitcher of cream on the table. She poured cups of tea, tucked a napkin into the neckline of Adeline's dress, and sat down at the table.

Clint gazed at her, a question in his eyes.

"She had a quiet night," Mrs. Reid said. "Other than that—no change."

Clint felt his mood sour, his appetite disappear. He stared at his plate.

Adeline sniffed and leaned her head against Mrs. Reid's arm.

"There, there," she murmured. "Now, then, you young ones, I don't want any moping. That won't help a bit. Adeline, my daughter Rose Alma found that little trunk of doll clothes up attic. Soon as you finish your breakfast, I'll get it for you. A little later this morning, Rose Alma will take you to Mrs. Woodbury's house, where you can spend the day with Jenny Bates, the doctor's niece, who is staying with them this summer. Jenny is a year or two older than you are, but she's a nice little thing, and I think you two will get along.

"As for you, Clint, you can take that horse Trixie back to Mr. Peavey. And once you've done that, stop by the hotel to see if any mail has come for Miss Havener that ought to be tended to right away. Then you can ask Mrs. Hackett to pack some of Miss Havener's things, which you will bring here. By then I may have other errands for you to do."

She paused a moment.

"We'll get through this. It will come out all right. In the meantime, we all must keep busy and do our part. Is that understood?"

Clint nodded, hiding the misery he felt.

Adeline, buoyed by the fact she was to have someone to play with, and the prospect of the trunk of doll clothes, was happy to do her part, but her eyes still sought Clint's for reassurance.

"You go have a good time, Adeline. If you're needed, I'll come get you," Clint said.

When Clint returned from his errands, Adeline had left for the day, and the ladies he had seen the night before were back, cleaning up the kitchen and preparing more food.

"Dr. Woodbury is with Miss Havener now," said Lydia Stearns, placing a comforting hand on Clint's shoulder. It took a great deal of effort on Clint's part not to shrug her hand away.

Clint nodded to Mrs. Stearns and took China's things to the front room. He had brought the camera with him. He loaded a glass-plate negative into it, just as China had taught him to do. Its inner workings interested him, and more than once, China had let him take a picture of something that had caught his eye.

On impulse, he went back to the kitchen carrying the camera.

"I wondered if you ladies would let me take your photograph? If you all went out and stood on the piazza, I think there's enough light for it," Clint said.

"Well, ladies, what do you think?" Mrs. Stearns asked her companions in the kitchen. The ladies agreed at once that they would like to be in a photograph. There was a flurry of untying aprons, peering quickly into a mirror to make certain no strands of hair were straggling, and the shaking out of skirts.

Outside, Clint lined them up—Mrs. Stearns, and Mrs. Woodbury, behind Mrs. Peavey and Mrs. True. They didn't smile, but something in their eyes, and the serene expressions on their faces, were better than smiles. Clint liked how they looked, in a cluster on the top two steps of the porch.

"Keep very still," he said. "Try not to blink until after I put the lens cap back on." He exposed the negative and replaced the lens cap. He had no idea what had possessed him to make the photograph, though as he did so, he felt a strong kinship with China, a feeling that sustained him.

Mrs. Reid came to the door and beckoned to them to come back inside. They returned to the kitchen where Dr. Woodbury was washing his hands in a basin of hot, soapy water. He spoke directly to Clint.

"She is still not conscious, but I see nothing alarming in her condition," he said. "The wound is clean, with no infection. She has no fever. I think it might be helpful if she hears voices she is accustomed to. I'd like you to go and sit with her for fifteen minutes this morning, another fifteen this afternoon, and another fifteen this evening. We'll see how she is tomorrow. At that point we might let the little girl see her for a few minutes at a time."

"When should I go in to see her?" Clint asked.

"Now, if you'd like. I'll come with you to observe."

China lay still in a maple bed with massive bed posts carved into large balls at the top. She was slightly propped up on a drift of pillows covered with off-white pillow slips. A patchwork quilt covered her to her chin so only her head in its white gauze bandage was visible. She seemed smaller than Clint recalled, as if somehow she had shrunk overnight. He walked softly into the room and sat down in the chair pulled up beside the bed.

Dr. Woodbury stood at the foot of the bed, his eyes on China's face, watching for any facial movement, any change in respiration the sound of Clint's voice might inspire in his patient.

"Marm," Clint said, speaking quietly, "you had an accident. You hurt your head. They brought you to Mrs. Reid's. Adeline wasn't hurt. Dr. Woodbury says you are getting well."

Clint paused and looked at Dr. Woodbury.

"Speak a bit louder, Clint."

Clint nodded and began again.

"I had the best time with Mr. Smallwood. We saw Katahdin, but we didn't climb it. I brought you a rock from up that way. And I made you a pretty flower holder from birch bark. It has a loop on it so you can hang it on the wall."

When Clint stopped speaking, Dr. Woodbury saw China draw in a deep breath, something he had not seen her do since her injury. He motioned to Clint to keep speaking.

"This morning I went to the hotel to see if any letters had come for you, but there wasn't anything. I was hoping we'd have one from Mr. Robinson . . . "

China's eyelids fluttered and she opened her mouth as if to speak, closed it, swallowed, and lay very still.

Dr. Woodbury beckoned to Clint and they stepped out of the room.

"I'm convinced she heard you, Clint, responded to the sound of your voice, to some of what you said, especially when you mentioned Mr. Robinson," Dr. Woodbury said. "You can talk to her again sometime after dinner. Now, I'd like you to go and ask Mrs. Woodbury to come in here with some water, some warm broth, and an invalid feeder. Hopefully, we can get a bit of nourishment into her now that I know she can swallow."

When Clint shared the news with the ladies in the kitchen, relief and hope shone in their faces. "Mr. Stearns has organized a meeting at the church this evening to pray for her," Lydia Stearns said.

"I'll tell Adeline; she will want to sing," Clint said on his way out the door. He was down the road before any of the ladies could offer him a doughnut or a molasses cookie.

As he ran, Clint tried to be hopeful. He remembered how he had hoped and prayed his mother would recover from the illness that had ended in her death. How he had bargained with the universe. How nothing had worked. She had died. So he ran and now he was still running. He slowed his steps to catch his breath. Running, yes. But not away anymore. Running toward, that's what he was doing now. Toward Adeline, who looked to him for comfort and safety. And if China died? Well, he would run toward Plato Robinson, or to China's sisters and her friends who had, through their letters, shown interest in him. He found the thought comforting as no other had since China was injured, since his father and mother had died.

How odd it was, he thought, how even though Mrs. Reid's house was filled with people who were helping China get well in every way they knew how, he felt alone in his misery. He blamed himself for what had happened. If only he had not gone off camping with Will Smallwood, China and Adeline would not have been out there on that road, coming to meet him. His logical mind told him such a thought made no sense whatsoever. Why, they might all have been out for a ride on that road and still a deer might have startled the horse and they all might have been injured. Might have. He realized the world was filled with far too many might haves, and if onlys.

With great effort, he put his thoughts in order—first, he must tell Adeline that China had shown signs of knowing him, then find out if she was having a good time with Jenny Bates. Then he would ask her if there was something she wanted him to tell China when he sat with her later in the day.

"Tell her I'm not hurt, that I love the pretty dolly Mrs. Reid gave me, and that I'm having fun here," Adeline said. Clint could see that. Mrs. Woodbury had given the little girls some old clothing to play dress-up in, and they were flitting about the yard like bright butterflies.

"I'll come and get you at suppertime," Clint said.

Then he walked back to Mrs. Reid's to get the camera. From there he walked to the blacksmith's shop and asked if he could take a picture of Trixie. Then he took one of Mr. Peavey wearing a leather apron and skull cap, hammering on a horseshoe, the sparks flying.

He went back to Mrs. Woodbury's and stood a ways off, setting up the camera to include the house in the frame. He took a picture of Adeline and her new friend arranged like pretty flowers in the grass.

When China is well, he thought, she will see those photographs and will know something of the moments she was insensible to. It will be like remembering, only through my eyes and not hers.

When afternoon came and he returned to China's bedside, he carried the camera into the room.

"I brought your camera, Marm. I'm going to leave it over there on the bureau, so when you get to feeling better you'll be able to see it. I took a few photographs this morning so you can see what Adeline's been up to. She said to tell you she wasn't hurt when the buggy tipped over. And she's over the moon—well, she didn't exactly say that, but that's what she meant—about that doll Mrs. Reid gave her. She's at Mrs. Woodbury's, spending the day with the little Bates girl. Maybe tomorrow Dr. Woodbury will let her come in here with you for a few minutes," Clint said. He continued to talk, watching her to see if she responded to anything he said. She did not.

Soon, Dr. Woodbury arrived and stood quietly by the doorway, observing China closely while Clint talked to her. He had been encouraged that morning when China had been able to swallow eyedroppers full of water and broth.

As Clint talked of Adeline, a faint smile flitted across China's face. It was so fleeting he wondered if he had imagined it. He glanced at Dr. Woodbury. He nodded to indicate that he, too, had noted the smile.

"Take her hand, Clint," Dr. Woodbury said softly. "Then ask if she can hear you."

Clint did as he was told. China's hand felt frail, the bones of her fingers birdlike.

"Marm, can you hear me?"

Immediately, he felt the slight lift of one of her fingers.

"Can you wiggle your finger again, Marm?" This time, he felt two of her fingers move. He took his hand away and asked her to move her fingers a third time so Dr. Woodbury could see.

"That's a very good sign," he said quietly to Clint. "Enough for today, I think."

That evening, Clint wrote to India and Persia describing the accident and assuring them that their sister was being well taken care of and that she was recovering, even though that was not yet entirely certain. He knew the letter could not possibly reach them for at least a week and by then, he felt certain, China would be much improved. He couldn't say why, but he just knew it would be true.

46.

Several days later, China's eyes fluttered open. She gazed at the morning light falling softly through the white curtain, was dazzled by it. She blinked her eyelids slowly.

"Who is singing?" she whispered, with no slur in her speech, which had been one of Dr. Woodbury's concerns.

Clint leaned over the bed and spoke softly.

"It's probably Adeline," he said, though he knew perfectly well Adeline was not singing. She was in the kitchen, helping Mrs. True make ginger cookies.

"Yes," China murmured, "Adeline." She turned her head until her eyes found Clint's face. "Clint. It's Clint? I had a terrible dream."

"Yes, it's me, it's Clint. You had an accident a few days ago, Marm. Hurt your head."

A confused look came into China's eyes. "I don't remember."

Mrs. Reid slipped out of the room, intent on sending someone for Dr. Woodbury, but discovered him just coming through the kitchen door. She told him that China was awake, and he hurried to the bedroom.

"You've turned the corner for the better, Miss Havener," Dr. Woodbury said after he had spoken with China and checked her various responses and reflexes.

"I don't remember what happened," China said in a worried whisper. Her fingers plucked nervously at the bedclothes.

"No reason you should," Dr. Woodbury said soothingly. "Your brain suffered a concussion when your head hit a rock. It's a natural aftereffect. Some of what happened may come back to you in time. But for now, it doesn't matter. I take it you know who this boy is?"

She nodded. "Clint."

"And what about this lady?" He indicated Mrs. Reid.

"Mrs. Reid. Is . . . is this your house?"

"Bless you—yes, on both counts. We have been on pins and needles waiting for this moment," Mrs. Reid said.

"Oh," China breathed, her eyelids drooping.

"Rest now. No more talking. You can talk more in the morning," Dr. Woodbury said. He told Clint and Mrs. Reid to go downstairs. He would sit with China for a while.

After they were gone, the thing he most wanted to see soon occurred. China fell into a natural sleep, her body relaxed. He knew then that she would recover with no lingering effects from the blow to her head. He went to tell Mrs. Reid, Clint, and Adeline.

"Can she eat cookies now?" Adeline asked. "I rolled these and cut them out all by myself. Mrs. True helped me put them in the oven."

"I see no reason why not," Dr. Woodbury said, smoothing Adeline's hair with his hand.

And, indeed, the very next afternoon, Adeline, with great ceremony, carried to China a ginger cookie on one of Mrs. Reid's best plates. The child stood hesitantly in the doorway, somewhat fearful, half-believing China had died and come back to life, even though she knew that wasn't true, for her mother had not come back to life. She stepped quietly to the bedside.

"Adeline, my dear child," China said softly. She was propped up in bed against a bank of pillows Mrs. Reid and Mrs. Woodbury had placed beneath her head and shoulders.

"I brought you a cookie, Miss Havener," Adeline said. "Dr. Woodbury said you could have one. I helped Mrs. True make them." Her face glowed with pride at her accomplishment.

Adeline held the cookie and China took a small nibble. "Best I ever tasted," she said.

And from that day forward, China recovered quickly.

Letters arrived from India and Persia, then a telegram asking if they should come, that they could leave on a moment's notice. China dispatched Clint to telegraph a reply telling her sisters there was no need for them undertake such a long journey, that she was recovering. She also wrote them a note, knowing they would be reassured when they saw her handwriting. By early September she was well enough to be up and around. Dr. Woodbury saw no reason why she should not undertake the journey back to Fort Point by the end of the month.

In the meantime, Mrs. Reid insisted that China, Clint, and Adeline stay on at her house. Her daughter and several granddaughters offered to assist with the cooking and housekeeping.

Clint, too, stepped in to do whatever he could to help Mrs. Reid. He worked on the woodpile, split kindling, and kept the woodbox full. He raked the yard, escorted Adeline to and from singing practice, and made himself useful wherever he saw a job that needed doing.

By early September, teams began to come through town on the way to the north woods for the winter's timber cutting. They came from near and far, a long parade of men, young and old, with teams of clever horses they would use for twitching logs into the woods yards, teams hitched to wagons of supplies, and sometimes a lone man leading a lone horse. Some of the men stopped in town overnight and sought shelter for their horses and themselves in the barns of the houses along the main road.

Town residents looked forward each fall to the time when the loggers headed back to the woods, for it was an opportunity to add something to the household coffers. In the morning, the woodsmen ate a breakfast prepared by the barn owner, paid for their keep, and went on their way.

"Why, back in 1871, we counted two hundred and ninety-eight horses and upwards of six hundred men that went through this town on their way to the woods," Mrs. Reid said.

Clint collected the money the men paid and turned it over to Mrs. Reid. It had been some years since she had had help enough to allow men and animals to stay in her barn.

"If it weren't for you, Clint, and those good women in my kitchen, I'd never have been able to earn anything from the woodsmen parade," Mrs. Reid said.

"Least we can do until Miss Havener can settle up with you, Mrs. Reid."

"Go along with you, Clint Remick. As if I'd charge her one red cent, her with her misfortune. But I am obliged to you and all you do to help keep hearth and home together. And besides, all this excitement makes me feel young and useful again."

Each day, China grew stronger. Finally, the day arrived when Dr. Woodbury said she was ready to leave her room and go to other parts of the house. That evening for the first time since her injury, she sat at the kitchen table and ate supper with Mrs. Reid, Clint, and Adeline.

China experienced moments of dizziness, but it was fleeting, and soon it no longer troubled her. She still had no memory of the accident, or even the hours before it happened, but Adeline told the story of the runaway horse and the wrecked buggy so many times, it almost seemed as if China did recall the event.

"Everything has changed," she said to Mrs. Reid one evening as they sat in the front room after supper, watching darkness fall. "It's as if everything has become more precious . . . Clint and Adeline, you and your kindness, and everyone who has made such an effort to see to my needs and those of the children. I have been thinking . . . I want to do something to let people in Patten know how much I appreciate all they have done, and continue to do for us. I want to make photographic portraits of anyone who would care to sit for me. I thought perhaps I could pose them beside your house, when the morning sun floods the yard. I'd send everyone a picture come next summer, after I have processed the negatives. It would be my gift to them."

"Now, that's quite a nice thing to want to do. Do you think you are up to that?" Mrs. Reid asked, a note of concern in her voice.

"Yes, I believe I am. Not everyone will want to be photographed, and I won't post a notice. I'll just let it be known by word of mouth that I will be available to take photographs for just one morning—or until my negatives run out. Clint can help me."

Mrs. Reid nodded in agreement. "Clint's a good boy."

"Yes, he is," China said. She was silent a moment, then said, "And after I finish that, I must return to Fort Point."

"Yes, my dear. The time is right around the corner. I'll miss you something fierce. But now that you have so many friends here, no doubt you will come back this way next summer. If you do, you will have a place to stay right here."

"I should like that," China said. "And now I must go and do what I have not been able to do. I must write to my sisters and let them know of my plans." China retreated to her room to write her letters, which, though she had not mentioned it to Mrs. Reid, included a note to Plato Robinson.

༄

Dear Mr. Robinson,

I won't go into details, except to say that I have recently recovered from a carriage accident. The horse was startled by a deer. I banged my head and was not myself for a while. However, I am up and around now, and doing well. I expect to return to Fort Point sometime next week.

Wishing you well, I remain, yrs. Truly,

China Havener

༄

It wasn't what she wanted to write, but it was the best she could do. She no longer knew where she stood with him. It had all become confused, as if the blow to her head had rattled her capacity to understand the nature of her feelings toward him right out of her mind. She still thought of him, still wished for his company, but so much had happened, so much had changed. The time when their attraction to one another might have blossomed into something more seemed to have ended. Her hope of love, of tender attachment, was simply . . . gone—as if the blow to her head had pounded that unpleasant fact into her being.

She folded the note, tucked it into an envelope, and affixed a stamp to it.

Then she wrote to India and Persia, telling them she would be home soon, though in her own mind she had not yet set a specific date.

The next morning, after she had helped to prepare breakfast, washed the dishes, and tidied her room, she put on her jacket and hat. Adeline had gone to play with Jenny Bates. Clint was in the barn sweeping out.

"I'm going to the post office to mail some letters," China told Mrs. Reid. It would be her first outing on her own since the accident.

"Are you sure you ought to, my dear?" Mrs. Reid asked, a concerned expression passing across her face. "Perhaps Clint ought to go with you."

"I'm quite all right, Mrs. Reid. It's hardly a stone's throw down the street. And it's high time I stretched my legs."

China knew that as soon as she was out the door, Mrs. Reid would alert Clint. She smiled at the thought. Sure enough, after she had dropped the letters in the slot and started back toward Mrs. Reid's house, she saw Clint sauntering—that was the only word for it—toward her.

"You don't have to pretend this is a casual meeting, Clint. I know perfectly well Mrs. Reid sent you to make sure I am all right. And as you can see, I am."

Clint grinned. "I told Mrs. Reid you didn't need me to check up on you, but she wouldn't take no for an answer. So here I am."

"Yes. And by the looks of you, you ought to get your hair cut. We'll be going home to Fort Point in a few days. I want us all to look our best."

Clint looked at the ground and scuffed the toe of his boot in the dirt. "I like it here," he said softly.

"So do I, Clint. I see no reason why we can't come back to visit next summer."

He looked up and smiled. "I'd like to go on another trip with Mr. Smallwood." He paused. "I'd like to go back to Bingham, too, to see Mr. Robinson."

"Yes," China said, linking her arm through Clint's. "We'll see what next summer brings."

The next day, Mrs. True delivered Adeline's new dresses, the making of which had been postponed because Mrs. True had spent most of her odd moments and evenings helping out at Mrs. Reid's while China lay abed, recovering from her injury.

Adeline, who had been expecting only one dress, and had described it in detail many times to her friend Jenny Bates, was dumbfounded to discover that she now had three new dresses rather than just one. At first she didn't know what to say, except to whisper, "Thank you, Miss Havener."

"Well, young miss, seems to me you ought to try them on," Mrs. Reid said to Adeline.

Mrs. True gathered up the dresses and beckoned to Adeline. They disappeared into the back bedroom and after a few minutes, Adeline, clad in the blue dress, stepped back into the room. She twirled and preened, modeling the garment as if she had been doing so all her life. Twice, she skipped back into the bedroom and returned wearing another of the new dresses.

"These are so pretty, it makes me want to sing," the child declared.

Everyone applauded, and Adeline made a sweeping curtsy. She threw her arms around China.

"No more black!" she said jubilantly. "I bet that makes my Mama even happier in heaven."

"Well, since you are so happy," China said, "perhaps you'd sing something for us."

Adeline was pleased to oblige.

47.

One the day they were to leave, China, in response to a note from Samuel Benjamin, arrived at the lawyer's office at mid-morning. She had walked from Mrs. Reid's house and felt fit and well. It was a sunny day, leaves were beginning to turn, and the air was crystal clear, as pure and sweet as springwater.

She had worried that her business with Mr. Benjamin would not be concluded before it was time to leave Patten. But he had assured her he would do his best to expedite the process.

The smell of ink and old books in Mr. Benjamin's office made a sharp contrast to the outside air, which held the tang of apples and the freshly turned earth of harvest time.

China took the chair Mr. Benjamin offered. "I hope this is good news," she said.

"Indeed, it is," Mr. Benjamin replied. "I made all the necessary inquiries, including of John Harvey, cousin to Adeline's mother, as I am sure you will recall. Mr. Harvey regrets that he is unable to offer a home to Adeline, given the fact he has a houseful of motherless children. He also assured me there are no other relatives to his knowledge who might want to take Adeline.

"Since no one else has come forward to claim kinship to Adeline, there are no impediments to adopting her. As for Clint, he's old enough to choose for himself. So I have drawn up the necessary papers regarding Adeline, which only you will have to sign, and another set for Clint, which both you and he must sign. Assuming, of course, that you still intend to go ahead with adopting both children . . . That your health—"

"My health was only temporarily sidelined by the accident, Mr. Benjamin. Dr. Woodbury says I have made a full recovery, and he sees no reason why I won't continue to be in good health. So, yes, it is still my intention to adopt both children. I would like Clint and Adeline to be present when the papers are signed. I don't want to do anything connected with their well-being that they are not aware of.

"Clint, naturally, knows that I have petitioned to adopt him, though he has not actually agreed to it yet. He knows that even if he does not wish to undergo formal adoption, he will always have a home with me, and I will abide by his wishes. As for Adeline, even though she is too young to grasp all of this, she is a bright child, and understands it is my wish to provide her with a home."

"Then it's settled; I will stop by this evening with the documents. Mrs. Reid can serve as witness," Mr. Benjamin said.

When she returned to Mrs. Reid's, China summoned Clint and Adeline to her.

"I have news that affects both of you," she said, without preamble. "Adeline, Mr. Benjamin has determined that you have no other relatives who could offer you a home, and because it is my dearest wish that you will come and live with me, I have been granted the right to adopt you. That means I would be . . . responsible for taking care of you, just as a mother would be responsible, but I would in no way replace your mother, or want to. However, adoption requires me to sign papers saying that I alone am responsible for you, and that you would live with me at my home in Fort Point. You'd go to school there, make new friends . . . "

"Would I be able to sing, Miss Havener?" Adeline asked shyly.

"Oh, yes, you would sing, Adeline. My sister India plays the piano. I am quite certain we could find a way to continue your music lessons. There is a church in the village where you could sing in the choir."

Adeline nodded, slid off the chair, went to China, and threw her arms around her.

"Clint said I'd find a new mother in the real world, but I would always have my real mama in my heart world."

"Then when Mr. Benjamin comes with the necessary papers, would you like me to go ahead and sign them?"

"Yes," Adeline said firmly. She grinned at Clint, then grew sober. "Does this mean Clint will be my brother?"

"Yes, Adeline, it does," Clint said, looking directly at China.

Adeline grinned at him again. "Well, that's good. But it doesn't mean you can start bossing me around!"

"As if I could, even if I wanted to," Clint said, giving one of her braids a gentle tug.

Adeline threw her arms around his neck and he gave her hug.

"I always wanted a brother," she said. "Just like you."

"Adeline, I believe Mrs. Reid is in the kitchen waiting for you to help her mix up some biscuits," China said.

Adeline skipped happily out of the room, her braids dancing on her shoulders.

"Clint, Mr. Benjamin will also bring papers pertaining to the legal matter of adopting you. I know this has not been a subject you have wished to entertain. And if that is still the case, I will say no more. But if there has been a change in your thinking, and you wish to . . . formalize our relationship, you will be required to sign the papers, too. In other words, it would be a contract between us. It will be my job to provide you with all the necessities of life, including education. It would be your job to let me do that. Do you understand?"

Clint looked at the floor. He took a deep breath. "I wasn't for it before because—well, it seemed as if I wasn't sticking by my folks. But then there was this whole thing with Adeline, and then the accident, and we didn't know if you'd live or die . . . " A tear dripped down his face, and he brushed it away roughly with the back of his hand.

China said nothing, letting him finish what he wanted to say.

"That night after they brought you in, and the next day, all I wanted to do was run as fast as I could . . . didn't matter where, though I thought of going to Mr. Robinson, or back to Cambridge, or just anywhere. But I didn't run because I couldn't leave Adeline alone, especially if . . . Well . . . You died . . . And well, because you needed me.

"And that was when I felt it for good and true—that you meant almost as much to me as my folks ever did. And between the three of us . . . You, me, and Adeline . . . We were as much to each other as if we were blood relatives. So signing that paper, to me, just means I'll be making it official, what I already know." Once again, Clint wiped his eyes with the back of his hand, then gained control of himself.

"Well, that's a relief," China said.

Clint looked up at her, their eyes met, and for no reason either of them could think of, they burst out laughing.

They signed the papers later that day.

Afterward, Clint took Adeline aside. "From now on you better think of something to call her besides Miss Havener. I call her Marm, and I think you should, too," he said, firmly.

"I'm not going to be bossed by you," Adeline said, tossing her head. "I'm going to call her Mum."

Early the next morning, half the town of Patten stood in front of the hotel to wave China and the children off as they began their journey back to Fort Point.

48.

China had telegraphed India and Persia to expect her and the children on September 25; she told them she did not know precisely what time they would arrive, or on which boat, and she hoped they would make no fuss.

As the stagecoach bowled along over the rough road back to Mattawamkeag, Adeline kept up a lively chatter. She wondered if she should have worn her yellow dress instead of her blue one, if the house they were going to was as pretty as Mrs. Reid's, if there would be any little girls to play with. After they had resumed their trip following the noontime stop, she sagged against Clint and slept.

Clint, mostly silent, stared out the window, turning to China now and then to comment on the scenery or to wish the journey wouldn't take so long. When Adeline woke, he entertained her, playing cat's cradle with a knotted string he took out of his pocket, and making up riddles for her to try to answer.

China passed the time of day with the other passengers, Mr. And Mrs. Weymouth, who had been rusticating all summer at a camp on Shin Pond. Mrs. Weymouth, who had delicate health, said she and her husband lived in Bangor and looked forward to getting home. They had missed hearing music and seeing plays at the Bangor Opera House. Mrs. Weymouth talked eagerly about shopping for new winter woolens at the shops along Main Street.

Such chatter helped to pass the time until they arrived at Mattawamkeag. While they were at the station waiting to board the train for Bangor, China sent a telegram to Abner and Elizabeth Giddings, informing them of the time of their arrival at Union Station, knowing they would invite her and the children to spend the night.

When they arrived, Adeline, with wonderment in her eyes, took in the bustle of Exchange Street, stared at the small boats plying the Penobscot, and gazed in awe at the tall masts of the many ships tied up at the wharves on both sides of the river.

The whine of sawmills, the jingle of harness, and the rumble of cart wheels filled the air. The train engine panted and hissed steam, and rigging creaked as the ships rocked in the river current.

"It's always good to come home again," China said, glad to discover she was, indeed, looking forward to getting home, to seeing India and Persia, to settling down with Clint and Adeline.

"I almost got shanghaied when I was through here a few weeks back," Clint informed Adeline, importantly.

"What's that mean?"

"It means," China said, "that my sisters and I had to retrieve Clint from a sticky situation."

"It means some bad men wanted to force me to sign papers so they could put me on a ship and send me to sea against my will," Clint said.

"Were they pirates?" Adeline asked breathlessly.

"In a manner of speaking," China said, smiling down at Adeline. She looked up and saw Elizabeth and Abner coming toward them.

"How happy we are to see you!" Elizabeth exclaimed. She wore a navy blue dress and a matching jacket with braided cord trim decorating the lapels.

"I believe inland voyaging agrees with you," Abner said, as he doffed his hat and held out his hand to China. "How well you look."

"And who have we here?" Elizabeth asked, glancing at Adeline.

"This is my daughter, Adeline Miles," China said. "Adeline, I'd like you to meet Mr. And Mrs. Giddings."

Adeline bobbed a little curtsy and murmured, "Pleased to meet you."

"You have already met my son, Clint Remick," China said.

Clint held out his hand, first to Elizabeth, then to Abner. "Nice to see you both again," he said.

China felt her heart swell with pride. Her children had remembered their manners.

Neither Abner nor Elizabeth betrayed any surprise to learn that China Havener now had two children, instead of one, in her care—quite the contrary, though they did wonder why they had not heard of it through their family connections. They glanced at one another, their look saying this was a story they wanted to hear.

"We want you to stay the night with us, of course," Elizabeth said. "Abner hired a wagon for your bags. It's just out on the street."

"Yes, young Master Clint," Abner said. "Let's heave to on this cargo and sail along toward Summer Street."

Clint grinned, grabbed China's camera, hoisted it to his shoulder, and headed for the door.

"Come, China. We will walk to Summer Street; as you know, it's not far, and the exercise will do us good," Elizabeth said. She took China's arm, slipped her hand into Adeline's, and steered them outside into the street. They breathed in the scent of the river, of mud, the ebbing tide, pine sap, and the presence of fall, an odor so familiar and dear it brought tears to China's eyes. Yes, it was good to be home.

Abner and Clint walked ahead of them, trailed by the wagon bearing their bags.

Evening was beginning to fall, and the first stars were just emerging in the darkening sky.

"Mum, it's like a fairy story," Adeline whispered. "All the big houses and the ships, and the pretty ladies in pretty dresses."

China and Elizabeth smiled at one another over Adeline's head.

After they had eaten supper, they sat in the parlor to talk.

Clint and Adeline went to a table to play checkers. Elizabeth also set out some puzzles she thought they might enjoy. The children's laughter punctuated the grown-ups' conversation.

"All is well at Fort Point," Elizabeth said. "Everything is as it should be."

"And what do you hear of India and Persia?" China asked.

"We saw them several weeks ago and they are well," Abner said. "Very busy."

"I bought some wool yarn from Persia. Her spinning is lovely, and everyone down that way, even across the bay, has heard of her and sends to her for yarn. She has more orders than she can keep up with."

"I spent an afternoon with India a month or so ago, singing a few sea chanteys she had never heard. I believe she said she has collected more than a hundred, though some are different versions of the same song," Abner said.

When the fire died, they went upstairs to bed, Adeline and China in the big four-poster, and Clint in a trundle bed nearby.

"We should photograph this house, inside and out," Clint whispered to China just before he drifted off to sleep.

China smiled in the dark, wondering how she had ever done without Clint and Adeline. Because of them her life was filled with a deeper richness; like a freshening breeze, they had blown out all the staleness that had infested her heart at the start of her inland journey, opening possibilities she had never known existed.

49.

For Clint and Adeline the steamboat trip down the Penobscot River to Fort Point was an adventure beyond anything they had ever imagined. China urged them to enjoy the scenery, even as she cautioned them not to make nuisances of themselves, and to stand by the rail, out of the way. However, when Clint begged to go aft to observe the workings of the great paddle wheel, China let him go. Adeline was content to admire the dresses of the lady passengers and chatter about the new song, *She'll Be Coming 'Round the Mountain*, she was looking forward to learning. Reverend and Mrs. Stearns had given her a copy of the song as a parting gift.

It was a clear, sunny morning, and the foliage along the riverbanks glowed red and gold beneath a nearly cloud-free sky. China acted as tour guide for Clint and Adeline, pointing out the tower of Hampden Academy, the steeple of the Winterport Congregational church, Waldo Mountain, Fort Knox in Prospect across the river from Bucksport, and Verona Island, Sandy Point, and the shores of the town of Penobscot across the bay.

"There it is," China said, pointing as the steamboat left the tip of Verona Island behind. "The Fort Point lighthouse. We're almost home now."

It pleased her to say those words to Clint and Adeline, knowing the children, especially Clint, had been without a true home for far too long.

"It's not very tall," Clint said. "I thought lighthouses were tall and round, with stripes painted on them."

"This lighthouse is on high ground, so it doesn't need to be any taller than it is," China replied. She and the children were the only passengers intending to get off the steamboat at Fort Point. As they approached the wharf, they gathered up bags, boxes, and the camera, and moved toward the rail where the gangway would soon be put down.

Even though China had asked India and Persia not to make a fuss about her arrival, she could not help searching the shore, hoping to see them waiting there. The wharf, however, was empty.

"I told you you'd be sorry if you didn't tell them to meet us," Clint said, noting how intently China was staring in the direction of the boat landing.

"I just didn't want a lot of fuss," China said. "I thought it would be easier on you and Adeline if you weren't caught up in a whirl of confusion, if you had time to get your bearings . . . "

Adeline slipped her hand into China's. "This is a pretty place," she said in a low voice. "It smells . . . Watery."

Even though Adeline appeared calm, China saw a shadow of apprehension flit across the child's face.

"It's a combination of the river and the ocean you smell . . . And mud and seaweed and wet rocks."

"And fir and pine," Clint said. "And a lot of wet rope."

"Look," China said, "over there in that tall tree . . . it's an osprey. Hear it?"

"Yes, yes! I see it, I see it!" Adeline exclaimed.

"What about bald eagles?" Clint asked. "Any around here?"

"Yes, we see bald eagles quite often, but apparently not today."

"Look over there, Adeline," Clint said, pointing toward the water. "It's a loon."

Soon, China and the children stood on the wharf with their baggage scattered around them. The steamboat pulled away to continue its journey to Belfast.

"We seem to be in the middle of nowhere," Clint remarked. "Now what?"

"It's a short walk to Abbott's Reach, the boardinghouse I've told you about. We'll leave our baggage here and go up there to make it known we've arrived. Ellis Harding has a rig that can carry us home."

"Will they like me?" Adeline asked softly. "Your sisters?"

"They will love you as much as I do," China whispered in Adeline's ear.

Adeline's smile encompassed her entire body.

Before they started up the narrow track, they heard the unmistakable jingle of harness and the happy chatter of more than a few voices.

"Must be a party of people on a picnic outing," China remarked. "It's a nice enough day for it, even though it's late in the season."

A horse-drawn cart and a buggy came into view, and the vehicles' occupants called and waved. Others walked beside and behind the conveyances.

"Who are those people?" Clint asked.

"Do we know them?" Adeline asked, breathlessly.

"Oh, my!" China said. "It's them! Fanny and Ellis Harding. Sam and Maude Webber. M and Madras Mitchell and their brood. And my sisters, India and Persia." Tears of happiness pricked her eyes. How could she have thought it would be better all around if no one came to meet them? Well, it only went to show how sometimes one's thinking could be out of kilter.

"Those are all your people?" Clint asked, a note of awe in his voice.

"They are," China said.

"There's a little girl! And boys! I can play with them!" Adeline exclaimed. She dropped China's hand and ran toward the oncoming

parade of people, drawn to their merriment, the bright flutter of the
ladies' skirts, and the children prancing about.

China slipped her hand through Clint's elbow. "Well, sir, shall we
go to meet them?"

Clint grinned. "I never met a clan before. This ought to be a caution."

"Better get used to it, Clint. Soon enough you will be one of
them. They won't have it any other way."

As China steered Clint forward, they caught up with Adeline and
herded her in the direction of the buggy containing Sam and Maude
Webber, and India and Persia, who walked beside it.

India and Persia opened their arms to China.

"Sister, home at last," India said.

"And about time, too," Persia said. "Things just weren't the same
without you."

"I am very glad to be home again," China said, knowing those
were precisely the words India and Persia wanted to hear. She drew
Clint and Adeline forward.

"India, Persia, you will remember my son, Clint Remick, whom
you already met some weeks back in Bangor. And my daughter, Adeline Miles, whom I wrote you about. I signed papers to adopt them
several days ago. They are part of our family now."

There was a moment of silence between India and Persia, as if
they didn't know what to say.

Clint glanced at China, then back at India and Persia, surprised
all over again at how much the sisters resembled one another.

Adeline, too, seemed a bit stunned. She recovered her composure
and said into the silence that had fallen around them, "Clint, when
you told me I'd find another mother, you never said anything about
finding three, just exactly alike!"

Her comment sent a wave of laughter echoing into the day. Everyone began to chatter all at once. Somehow, in the flurry of talk, Ellis

Harding and Madras Mitchell fell into step beside Clint. Together, they went down to the wharf to retrieve the bags.

India and Persia walked beside China, allowing the rest of the party to go on ahead. "Really, China—you might have told us," India said quietly, indicating Adeline.

"Why didn't you say anything about the adoption?" Persia inquired, with a note of annoyance in her voice.

"Because the formalities didn't take place until the day before we left . . . And there was reason to doubt that the adoptions would happen at all . . . many reasons, actually."

"You could have telegraphed," India said.

"I'm sorry if you disapprove—"

"Disapprove? Of course we don't disapprove!" Persia said. "What concerns us is that you seemed to forget you have two sisters who love you and care about you—that what you do affects us."

"Yes," India said. "You might have thought of that."

"I did think of that, but nothing was certain until the very last moment . . . Someone might have come forward to take Adeline, Clint could have easily changed his mind at the eleventh hour—"

"Well, be that as it may . . . if we had known, we could have made arrangements, sorted out what rooms to give the children, and made inquiries about sending Adeline to the village school, and Clint to the high school in Searsport. We could have cooked a bigger a chicken, made another pie or two . . . "

"I appreciate your wanting to help with all those things, but since I am now the mother of the children, I will want to do those things myself," China said gently.

India and Persia exchanged a glance that said, Oh dear, it's worse than we thought.

"And you needn't look at one another like that," China said, a bit crisply. "I have much to tell you, and I have been longing for your company in order to do just that."

India linked her arm through China's, and Persia, walking on the opposite side of China, did the same—gestures of understanding and forgiveness.

"In spite of scolding you, we are so very glad to see you," Persia said. "We have much to tell you, too. But let's agree to wait until tomorrow when we are all together under our own roof, and rested, with things sorted out."

At Abbott's Reach, Fanny, M, and Maude put together a buffet of sandwiches, cold sliced chicken, and pies spread out on a table on the piazza.

Blythe, who was ten, M's daughter and Fanny's great-granddaughter, immediately claimed Adeline for a friend, and soon the two girls were engaged in putting together a wooden puzzle as they sat at a table in a corner of the room, discussing the merits of their dolls.

"My doll is so old, she has wooden joints," Adeline declared.

"My doll has a china head and blue eyes made of glass," Blythe boasted. "It came all the way from Germany . . . That's a country in Europe, in case you didn't know."

"No, I didn't know," Adeline replied. "After all, I'm only six, and I haven't been to school much."

"I see," Blythe said. She fetched an atlas, and soon the two girls were poring over the maps, with Blythe filling in some of the gaps in Adeline's education.

Gordon Mitchell, between steamship commands and home for a visit, claimed Clint's attention with a pointed question. "My brother, Madras—that's M's husband, the one over there talking to Ellis Harding—said you'd been up to Greenville and had quite an adventure in a canoe. Is that right?"

"Yes, sir, that's right," Clint said, making no attempt to evade the question. He told his story, leaving out only the details of how he had tried to outrun the notion of being adopted, how it had caused him to do something foolish. He had a lot to say about Louis and Joseph Tomah, their canoe, and how a steamboat had played a part in searching for him.

"Some people have all the luck. I've never been in a canoe in all my life."

"Well, I've never been in a sailboat in all my life," Clint said.

"Come spring, Clint, when I'm likely to be between ships again, I'll remedy that. And what's more, I'll teach you to sail the *Zephyr*, M's little sailboat."

"Well, if we can find a canoe and a lake, I'll show you how to paddle one," Clint said, taking an instant liking to Gordon. "I'm not very good at it yet, but Miss Fannie Hardy, the girl who taught me, said all I needed was practice."

"Clint," China said, "Dr. Webber wants you to sit with him for a few minutes so he can get to know you a little."

Clint nodded, and followed China to the sofa where Sam Webber held court. The others in the room rearranged themselves so that Clint and Sam could talk alone.

"I don't suppose you have any opinion when it comes to politics?" Sam asked, though it was more of a statement than a question.

"No, sir," Clint said, a bit awed as he took in Sam's white hair and his lively dark blue eyes, his navy blue jacket, and the old-fashioned cravat arranged in neat folds around his neck.

"Well, I'm glad to hear that, because now we can talk about anything we want."

Clint laughed. "Thank you for your letters, sir," he said.

"My pleasure, young sir. I enjoyed hearing from you, too. Now, you being an inland boy, how do you rate your chances of living beside salt water?"

"I don't know, sir, but I liked the trip downriver on the steamboat. And Gordon told me that next spring he'll teach me to sail the . . . the *Zephyr*."

"Ah, the *Zephyr*. Let me tell you about her . . . "

And Sam launched into the story of how years ago, M had kept trying to run away to sea, and that led to the story of how M's sister had been lost at sea, which led to so many other seafaring stories, Clint was fairly dazzled by it all. He thought of the stories Plato Robinson had told him about the Kennebec River and ferrying upon it, the tales Louis and Joseph Tomah and their mother had told him about Moosehead Lake, and stories Fannie Hardy had told about canoe trips on the upper reaches of the Penobscot River with her father. Even in Patten he had heard stories about bodies of water, having to do with catching big fish, drownings, and strange occurrences on lakes and ponds at midnight on misty evenings. Now he was hearing stories about the ocean, and they were all about people and how they lived upon the water, lived beside the water, or used the water.

Thoughts of water as it related to his own life came to him. He had learned to propel a ferryboat across a river, to paddle a canoe on the vastness of a lake, and now, it seemed, he would, come summer, learn how to sail across a bay. Already, he had seen and done much more than either of his parents ever had. It seemed as if they were smiling down at him, nodding their heads in agreement that he should learn as much as he could as he was borne along in the current that was now his life, even though it did not, could not, include them, alive and real, in it.

When the clock struck the half-hour, Maude Webber made her way to the sofa.

"Sam, my dear, you've bent this boy's ear long enough. Come, Clint, a rugged boy like you needs a hearty plate of food. This won't be the last you'll hear from my talkative husband."

"Yes, ma'am," Clint said obediently, though he wanted to listen to Dr. Webber's stories until the cows came home.

"I suspect, just looking at you, that you have some stories of your own that would bear telling," Maude remarked after she had handed Clint a plate piled with sandwiches, pickles, and slices of apple.

"Yes, ma'am, I believe I do."

"Then I shall look forward to hearing those stories one day come winter when I will need to hear a new one."

Clint grinned and found himself forming sentences in his head—a story he would tell Mrs. Webber when the time came. "Did I ever tell you about the time I learned how to ferry folks across the Kennebec?" he would say.

But now was not the time. Now was the time to look around, get his bearings, find out more about what the days ahead might hold. Perhaps, he thought, I'll write down my story about the ferry to make sure I don't forget anything.

Blythe and Adeline, hand in hand, went to Fanny and sat down on the sofa beside her. "Adeline wants to sing for us," Blythe whispered to her great-grandmother. "But she needs someone to play music for her."

"Well, then, go and ask Ellis if he'd play us a tune on his fiddle," Fanny said.

Blythe skipped across the room to whisper in Ellis's ear.

A few minutes later, Adeline took her place in the center of the room and sang *Greensleeves*, while Ellis played the tune with great feeling. Everyone listened appreciatively, even M's lively little boys. One song led to another, and Gordon and Ellis joined Adeline in the chorus of one selection. Before long, everyone was singing, even Clint, despite the fact that his voice was changing, and he had to guard against making a squawk.

China, India, and Persia added their voices, until the room was filled with such lovely song, China thought her heart would burst with joy.

This was the gift Adeline brought to everyone gathered in the room, she thought—a gift they never would have enjoyed had China not decided to take up photography and strike out on her own for a while. She glanced at Clint, and it was as if there had never been a time when he had not been her son. She gave thanks for his parents, for Adeline's parents, who had brought these children into the world, had left it too soon, but had bestowed on her the privilege of giving them a home, the gift of putting on the sacred mantle of motherhood.

50.

As China, Clint, and Adeline settled in with India and Persia, things for the most part fell into place, though there were times when disharmony ruled. Sometimes Clint was restless, once stomping out of the house and not coming back for hours, causing China a great deal of worry. But she bided her time and stayed calm. When he returned just after dark, she asked where he had been.

"Watching the moon rise and thinking," he replied.

She couldn't argue with that, for she knew only too well the value of escaping to a quiet place to think things over.

Adeline was sometimes fretful because she couldn't spend every minute of every day with Blythe. Once, she threw a tantrum that included throwing a hairbrush out the window, which fortunately was not closed at the time.

Instead of inflicting punishment on both the children for their behavior, China required Clint to tell her where he was going and when he would be back, and stood by while Adeline searched for the brush in the tall, itchy grass where it had landed. For the most part, the household ran as smoothly as it had before Clint and Adeline had joined it.

China arranged for Adeline to attend school in Stockton Springs village, where she quickly made friends and became a favorite with her teacher. This ensured she would see Blythe frequently, and have new friends to visit, as well. She was a bit behind the others in her studies, but caught up quickly.

Clint, pointing out that he, too, was far behind in his schooling, still balked at the idea of boarding in Searsport in order to attend high school there. China agreed that he should stay at home, where he could read and work from the textbooks from which China and her sisters had done their lessons many, many years ago. China, India, and Persia took turns serving as his teacher.

Clint liked the arrangement very much. The sisters were impressed with how quickly Clint made progress in his studies. He was, they discovered, especially good at writing essays. He learned quickly and retained what he was taught. He liked learning new things, and had a healthy curiosity, asking questions when he encountered topics he found challenging.

When he was not studying, Clint made himself useful around the place, helping Persia with the sheep, and assisting India in making copies of her manuscript pages. He wrote a fair hand, and he enjoyed the work. As his voice settled into its mature octaves, he began humming the sea chanteys India taught him, harmonizing with Sam Webber when he came to visit. India began to teach him to play the piano, much to Adeline's delight.

"Who would have thought it," Clint remarked one snowy winter afternoon, when he discovered he could sight-read simple musical notation.

India and China glanced at one another over Clint's head. Who, indeed, would have thought?

China's worry that she might not fit as easily into the daily life from which she had fled all those months ago proved unfounded. She soon discovered that she and the children fit in perfectly well. The daily routine had not changed much. As before, she, India, and Persia shared housekeeping duties; now, they also oversaw the care of Clint and Adeline, and the days still contained ample time for everyone's individual pursuits.

Each day, China retreated to a small ell attached to the summer kitchen in back of the house. She whitewashed the rough boards that served as the room's walls. Clint and Ellis Harding installed a small woodstove to keep the room warm enough in winter for the use of photo chemicals.

Clint took a great interest in learning the process of developing and printing the glass-plate negatives, reading instruction manuals, helping to mix the potions, and figuring out what went wrong when things didn't turn out quite right. It took him and China several weeks of trial and error to produce what they considered to be a proper print. By then it was the middle of November, but after that, the process of printing and developing the photographs went well, much to their delight.

There were nearly one hundred glass-plate negatives to process, and each time China and Clint developed a batch, they were amazed at what they saw. The interior views of Mrs. Pomroy's house in Bingham had turned out very nicely. The one of Adeline sitting in the sun, drawing a picture for Clint, was so perfect that China almost wept when she saw it.

There were a few duds, of course, but not nearly as many as China had feared. The ones they had tried to take during the thunderstorm were something of a jumble, but one showed a very distinct fork of lightning.

"Look!" Clint exclaimed one afternoon as a print came up in the developing fluid. "It's me and Miss Hardy. In the canoe. I never even knew you took that one." It was a lovely photograph, the canoe so white against the dark body of the lake, Clint and Fannie unaware of the camera as they dug the paddles into the water, the ripples circling away from the paddles. This was what China loved about photography—the surprise, the not knowing what the camera had seen, what her eye had seen, what the light had or had not revealed. That delight repeated itself with every photograph she developed, and she never grew tired of it.

They made several prints of the photo of Fannie Hardy and Clint in the canoe—one to send to Miss Hardy, now a student at Smith College, one to send to her aunt, Mrs. Wheeler, and one for Clint, for the photo album he was compiling of his travels with China. The album of photographs also served as a tool for Clint's education. Each week China asked him to write an essay based on a photograph of his choice.

Another day, when Clint had gone to Abbott's Reach to spend the afternoon with Sam Webber, China found Plato Robinson's face looking up at her from the developing pan. He stood beside the ferry, looking directly at the camera—looking at her. He smiled in the tender way she recalled so well. Clint was in the frame, off to the side, busy with the ferry rope. The Kennebec River lay behind, the riverbank on the Concord side filigreed with new leaves. China could almost feel the breeze of early summer on her skin, almost hear the eternal murmur of the Kennebec as it flowed past on its way to the Atlantic.

China had received only one letter from Plato since her return to Fort Point. It had been brief—just a few lines saying he was glad to hear she had recovered from the accident, that he was well, and asking her to remember him to Clint. Once again, the letter left her disappointed, with a sense of having missed a boat she should have been on, but had never figured out how to get aboard.

There were many days when she wanted to write Plato a long letter telling him what it was like to be home again, describing how Clint and Adeline were adapting and adjusting, how the children called India and Persia "aunt," and how they all spent their days. But each time she took up her pen, something in her froze and she could not write; rather than simply telling him news of her family and friends, she wanted to tell him what was in her heart, even though she did not know precisely what that was. She knew that he was the only man she had ever met whose spirit spoke to hers in a way that went beyond anything she had ever experienced. But somehow, she could not write those words.

True, Plato certainly had indicated that he favored her and liked being in her company, but he had never spoken of affection or love. He was a riverman; she was a seafarer. He was an inlander; she was of the coast. It seemed impossible to bridge such distance, such disparity, with paper and postage stamps.

After China had printed the photograph of Plato to her satisfaction, she showed it to Clint for his approval. Then she wrapped it, along with other photographs she had taken in Bingham, including the ones of the Pomroys, Mrs. Chase, and various street scenes. She enclosed a short note, asking Plato to see that Mrs. Pomroy and Mrs. Chase got the prints intended for them. She took the package to the post office one day when Ellis Harding, in a pung pulled by a black horse, stopped to inquire if there were errands he might do for them in the village. China put on her heavy coat, hat, scarf, and mittens Persia had knit for her, and asked if she might go along.

When she returned, Clint was coming out of the darkroom. His mood was not light, and China knew at once that something was amiss.

"What is it, Clint?" China asked as she hung her outer garments on a hook in the front hallway. "Are you ill?"

Clint shook his head and went upstairs. China heard the door to his room close softly.

Persia was in the kitchen making a stew for supper. India was at the table rolling out pie dough. Adeline, a long white apron tied over her dress, a new one Elizabeth Giddings had made and sent her, was helping.

China leaned down to give Adeline a kiss on the cheek. "Good day at school?" she asked.

"Yes. I have lots of friends now, and I'm getting much better at spelling," Adeline confided. "Thanks to Aunt India." She turned back to a bit of pie dough she was fashioning into tarts.

"Clint seems out of sorts," China remarked.

"Perhaps he saw something in the darkroom that upset him," India said. Something in her voice was a bit off.

"And what might you mean by that?" China asked, trying to keep her tone neutral, fully aware that her own mood, because she had been thinking about Plato Robinson, had not been entirely even for the past several days.

"She doesn't mean anything, China," Persia said, trying to be the peacemaker. "Why don't you go and see what he has been doing out there all afternoon?"

"I'm sorry, India. I didn't mean to be sharp with you," China said.

"Forgiveness happily given," India replied.

It didn't take long for China to understand what had clouded Clint's mood when she went out to the darkroom. He had developed the photographs she had taken in Cambridge—the one of his camp, one of him in the yard of the old house where he had been born, where his parents had died, the house taken for unpaid taxes and sold to a new family, and several others he had not been aware she had taken. The dirty, ragged boy portrayed in the photographs was a far cry from the boy he had become.

The contrast was startling. There was no doubt in her mind that the photographs had stirred painful memories for him.

China went upstairs and knocked on Clint's door. When he did not respond, she turned the knob and stepped into the room.

Clint sat on the bed, gazing out the window at the snowy field behind the house.

"The Cambridge pictures look better than I thought they might. They were the first I took, and I had no idea what I was doing. You did a good job developing and printing them," China said quietly.

She sat down on the bed beside him and saw tear stains on his cheeks. She put her arm around his shoulders in a gesture of comfort, but he slid away from her touch.

Clint took a deep breath. "I'm not a little kid anymore," he said, with a harsh edge in his voice. "I'm not a baby like Adeline."

"No, indeed, you are not, Clint. You are a young man. But it's only natural you'd feel out of sorts when you saw those photographs," China said. "Cambridge is a part of your history, Clint. If you did not feel sad about it, you would not be true to yourself, or to your parents who loved you."

"But I don't want to feel sad. I'm tired of feeling sad."

"But you must. Until you don't need to feel sad anymore."

"When will that be?"

"There's no way to know, Clint. But it occurred to me that the more you look at the Cambridge photographs, the more it will help to ease your sadness. And if you write stories about them and what they mean to you, it will help to clear things, help you gain perspective and self-understanding."

China hesitated, gauging his reaction to her words before she went on. Clint's face was like stone. She took a deep breath and went on. "I would like to see you make some friends your own age, Clint. You have spent, and still do spend, far too much time with grown-ups, or children far younger than you are. You need to be a boy, Clint, while there is still time to do that. You will be a grown-up man soon enough, and for the rest of your life."

Clint nodded, as if he understood and agreed, which surprised China. She had expected resistance.

"Mrs. Webber is fond of saying that spring is the time for new beginnings. Let's talk more about it then. Meanwhile, supper is probably on the table by now. Adeline has made jam tarts especially for you. I'll tell Aunt India and Aunt Persia you'll be down in a few minutes," China said as she opened the door and stepped out into the hallway.

She leaned against the closed door for a moment, shutting her eyes. She understood completely why the Cambridge photographs had made Clint feel out of sorts. It was precisely what looking at the Bingham photographs did to her—to such a degree that she had not yet shown them to India and Persia. In fact, she had shown only a few of her photographs to them. She kept putting them off, telling them she wanted to print them all, then arrange them around the front parlor so they could look at them all at once. She would not include the portraits of Plato Robinson. Indeed, she had even thought of marring the prints in some way so she would have a legitimate excuse for not sharing them. But leaving them out would never do; it would be dishonest. Besides, Clint had already seen the photographs of Plato, and would ask why they were missing from the rest. As she descended the stairs, she said under her breath, "China Havener, get ahold of yourself. You are a mother now, and far too old for such conniving nonsense over a mere man and the ridiculous complications that goes along with it. Plato Robinson does not want you. Accept that fact and be done with it!"

51.

In spite of Clint's dark moods and China's fretting over Plato, the winter passed with only a few incidents of anyone being out of temper. Clint applied himself to his studies and made such progress that China knew he was ready for high school. Adeline was happy and content, singing her way, quite literally, through the days.

They often socialized with the Abbott's Reach crew, enjoying evenings when they sat around and sang, danced, or made fudge and taffy. On sunny, cold afternoons, they sometimes went sleighing or sledding, Sam and Maude staying behind to keep the fires burning so that when everyone returned they had mugs of hot cider and plates of warm doughnuts for refreshment.

India made a great deal of progress on her book, and was certain she would finish it by the time spring arrived.

Persia spun yarn at a furious rate, intent on having many skeins to sell when summer came. She looked forward to an early spring when the ice would disappear from the bay and the boats would run again, so she could to go to Castine to conduct her business of mittens and yarn.

Letters arrived every week—from Patten, Bingham, and Cambridge for China; from Castine, Belfast, and Bangor for Persia; from Searsport, Boston, and New York for India; from Smith College, Greenville, and Patten for Clint; and letters from Patten and Lincoln for Adeline. But in all those letters, the one China looked for did not arrive.

Clint noticed, for he, too, hoped for a letter from Plato Robinson. One day toward the end of March, he said, "Maybe when warm weather comes, Mr. Robinson will write and tell us how the ferry is going. I wish I knew why we haven't heard from him. Do you suppose he's sick? I'd like to visit him this summer."

"We'll see, Clint. Remember, Mr. Harding, Mr. Mitchell, and Dr. Webber will keep you very busy with your studies and other things this summer. You still have a bit of catching up to do in mathematics and science. Not to mention the work Persia will have for you in the garden, and helping with the sheep."

During the summer, Clint would continue studying at home and go several times each week to discuss books he had read with Sam Webber. They were looking forward to reading David Copperfield together.

"I know," he said. "I like helping Aunt Persia, I like the work, and I know I'm a good farmer because my father taught me how to do things right." And for the first time, at the mention of his father, China saw pride in Clint's eyes, not sorrow.

"Yes," she replied, "your father taught you well. I am sure he was very proud of you."

"He was," Clint said. "Just like Mr. Robinson." He paused. "Maybe you and I could go to Bingham for a week. Who knows—you might need to talk Mrs. Chase's parrot out of a tree again, or Mr. Robinson might need a rope spliced."

He grinned, and they both laughed at the memory of the day of their arrival in Bingham. Those days seemed dreamlike, as if that time had happened to someone else.

After that small exchange, China began to feel an easing of the pain at not hearing from Plato that had nipped at her heart all winter. She also observed that Clint seemed more at ease with himself, to such a degree that he asked Madras Mitchell to tell him about going to high school in Searsport in the fall. Madras suggested that Clint board at his house during the week; he had a large house, M and the children would like having him around, and they knew people with boys Clint's age he could chum around with. They had wanted to make the suggestion last fall, but knew he needed time to get his bearings before he undertook yet another change in his life.

By the time spring came to Fort Point, it was settled. Clint would board with M and Madras in Searsport and go to high school in the fall. He would come home to China, India, Persia, and Adeline each weekend.

During the winter, China learned much in the darkroom about the chemistry of turning negatives into photographs. That was the easy part. Learning how to look at her photographs to determine what made them compelling images was quite something else. She often asked Clint for his opinion, which he gave thoughtfully. But for the most part, it was a task she did alone in her room with the photographs tacked to the wall. She was drawn to the images of the landscapes—the layers of hills she had photographed in Bingham, and the ones of Mount Katahdin.

She also was pleased with the images of buildings. It had to do with how she had placed a structure in the frame; she supposed the word she was searching for was composition, but that wasn't quite it. It had more to do with instinct, of knowing when the light was right, how it created an odd shadow, seeing an architectural detail in a new way, or simply the way a man leaned against a wagon or how a woman glanced up just as the lens cap was removed from the camera. How much of that was simply luck and what the camera saw as opposed to what her eye saw, she did not know. It was one more layer of the mystery of photography that kept her interest engaged.

She noted, too, that Clint's photographs, especially the ones he had taken in Patten while she was recovering from her injury, had a depth of beauty that drew her eye again and again. He stood more closely to his subjects than she ever had, catching details that became integral elements in the composition and design of the photograph.

When at last she showed some of her photographs to India and Persia, they gave freely of their praise.

"I know this is an I-told-you-so comment," India said, "but when people see these portraits you made in Patten, they will want you to make a portrait of them. You will be in high demand."

Persia agreed.

One morning in early May, with a stack of what she considered to be the best of the photographs wrapped in brown paper and tucked into a large basket, China boarded the steamboat bound for Belfast.

"I wish you'd let me go with you," Clint complained as he stood at the wharf down the hill from Abbott's Reach. "Adeline doesn't need me to look after her—she's spending the day with Blythe—and I'm all caught up with my schoolwork."

"I will tell you all about it when I return, Clint," China said. "This is something I need to do by myself."

Clint sighed to indicate his displeasure, but said nothing more.

China stood at the rail and waved to Clint as the steamboat slid out into the bay. He waved back, but not for long.

What China had not told Clint was that she was on her way to show the photographs to a man whose postcard company purchased negatives. She wanted to be alone to take the rejection she fully expected to receive. Nor did she want Clint to know that she had included more than a dozen photographs he had taken. She believed Clint's point of view was unique: Not only did he get closer to his subjects than China did, but he also had a distinctive way of arranging people and things in his photographs. He made sure the camera saw details that were important and interesting to him, and at the same time, spoke volumes about the subject. For example, he portrayed Mr. Peavey at his forge in Patten, hammer and tongs in hand, in the act of hammering a horseshoe, sparks of glowing metal flying around it. In a photograph of Mrs. True, Clint had waited until the light illuminated a cameo brooch she wore at the neckline of her dress, choosing the moment she turned her head slightly to look away from the camera to remove the lens cap and capture her image, making it a record of his thinking as well as a portrait of Mrs. True.

China did not want to harbor in herself false expectations of what she might earn by means of her camera, but she still wanted to try. She held on to the idea of photographs for use as postcards because it meant a reason for travel, a way to visit other towns and villages. However, she had decided that if postcard photography was not possible, she would, indeed, set up a studio and take portraits. Perhaps she would do that in the winter months.

When the reply to her letter had come from the postcard company, asking her to bring some of her photographs for review, she was both startled and delighted. But then a measure of self-doubt set in. Surely, since she was still an amateur, her work would not yet pass muster for commercial purposes. Instead of giving her thoughts over to defeat, she had thought of India and Persia, and what they had accomplished in less than year. India now corresponded with several academics who had an interest in sea chanteys, including one from Harvard and one from Bowdoin. Those men were impressed with India's work. The Bowdoin man had offered to write an introduction for her book, which India had, at last, titled *Blow the Man Down: Songs from the Sea.*

As for Persia, she recently had hired a woman to knit mittens to keep up with the demand. She was planning a trip inland to Harmony to tour Bartlett's mill, to purchase roving for spinning, and finished yarn for making mittens. She continued to learn more about the business of sheep farming, seeking out others with small flocks for advice. She was thinking about expanding her garden in order to sell more produce. This, China suspected, had something to do with the fact that Mr. Beaumont was the person she consulted on business matters—just as India relied on the advice of Mr. Quinn when it came to the business of compiling her book and getting it published.

It occurred to China, more than once, that India and Persia might marry before too many more months had elapsed. Then, the shoe would be on the other foot. They would go off into lives of their own, leaving her behind. Dear me, she thought, I would not like that at all—just as they didn't like it when I went a-journeying with camera in hand.

Life had a way of doing the most unexpected things at the most inconvenient of times.

When China arrived at the steamboat wharf at the foot of Belfast's main street, she walked along, looking in shop windows, nodding to passersby, until she found the address she was looking for. Harboring no preconceived notions, yet full of hope, she climbed the stairs to the second-floor office. She was there to inquire, nothing more.

She opened the door to find a man of generous girth seated behind a large oak desk. The entire office was littered with stacks of photographs. The man held a photograph in one hand and a magnifying glass in the other as he puffed leisurely on a cigar clamped between his teeth. He glanced up when China arrived, wisps of blue smoke drifting around his head.

"And who might you be?" he asked gruffly, putting the photograph and magnifying glass down and staring up at her.

"I am Miss China Havener, Mr. Corbett . . . if, indeed, that is who you are. We corresponded, and you said I might stop by today to show you my photographs . . . "

He sat back in his chair and gazed at her as if he didn't like what he saw.

"All my photographers are men," he said gruffly.

His remark sent a dart of resentment through China, and she felt herself assuming her "captain" stance.

"Which, sir, you might have informed me before you invited me to show you my work. But since I have made this trip at my own expense, I trust you will give me a few minutes of your time to look at my photographs and tell me whether or not they might be of use to your company."

The unmistakable tone of command in her voice was so like her father's, she almost laughed out loud.

Mr. Corbett took the cigar out of his mouth, squashed it in an ashtray, and stared at China. Clearly, he was not used to being spoken to in that way by a mere woman.

"Somehow, I had it in my head you were a man," he said. He rummaged through some papers, selected a page, and glanced at it.

"C. Havener. That's how your letter is signed. Which led me to assume you were of the male gender . . . Charles, or Caleb."

"Well, as you can see, I am neither a Charles, nor a Caleb, nor a Calvin. Nor can I understand what possible difference it makes whether a man or a woman removes a lens cap to expose a negative," China said.

Mr. Corbett made a grumbling noise in his throat, indicating, China believed, that such a question had never been put to him before. He took a breath, leaned back in his chair, and regarded her with a jaundiced eye.

"What have you got there, lady?" he asked reluctantly, not in the least polite.

China unwrapped her photographs and put them on the desk.

Mr. Corbett picked up the magnifying glass and scanned each one carefully.

"Who did the developing? It's all right, but it needs some work."

"I did, but my son helped me."

"You took these pictures, you say?"

"Yes, except for the ones I have clearly marked on the back with my son's name."

Mr. Corbett scanned the photographs more closely, taking his time. He looked up, saying, "These aren't bad. Where did you take them?"

"Cambridge, Solon, and Bingham in Somerset County; Greenville in Piscataquis County; and Patten in northern Penobscot County."

Mr. Corbett's lack of interest vanished, replaced by something akin to guarded curiosity.

"Hmmm . . . I don't have any pictures taken in those counties, and I've been wanting someone who could do work over that way. I take it you know what my business is all about?"

"Yes. You make postcards of scenes around Maine."

"That's right. I hire photographers—men—to go out and take the pictures. But sometimes, I buy negatives from amateur photographers such as yourself. Then, I make prints in quantity to sell in stores, hotels, restaurants, and anyplace that will give them room."

"I see. Thank you."

China rose to take her leave. As she reached for her photographs, Mr. Corbett stayed her hand. He sighed.

"I suppose you're one of those down-and-out ladies who has to earn a living."

"I am not down-and-out, Mr. Corbett, but it is necessary for me to earn something to contribute to the expenses of my household," China said coldly.

Mr. Corbett glanced at her photographs again, pulled out a few.

"Tell you what I'll do. These pictures of buildings . . . Cambridge, Solon, Bingham, Greenville, and Patten. I'll buy the negatives from you for the going rate—a dollar apiece. That's more than fair, since we don't know what the market for these scenes will be," he said. "Might be that no one up that way can afford two cents for a postcard and another cent for the stamp to send it with. Might be not a one would sell at all. It's a gamble, you see."

"Yes, I do see. You will own my negatives and will make as many prints from them as you see fit, and all those pennies will find their way to your pocket, not mine. Very well, Mr. Corbett; I will accept your terms for now, for a limited number of my negatives. But if there is a market for such photographs, and I believe there is, I would like the opportunity to become an employee of your company from spring through late summer, to travel back to those towns and to others in those counties, and elsewhere, at my leisure, with a small allowance for travel expenses, so I can make more photographs," China said.

Mr. Corbett leaned back in his chair, his gaze leveled at China. He was all hardheaded businessman, weighing the risks, the advantages. He looked at her photographs again. She could tell he saw something in them to admire.

"You drive a hard bargain, Miss Havener," he said. "But your terms are no different than what I already do for several photographers who travel this part of the state, taking pictures of the various towns. Only difference is, they are men, and have a lot more experience than you do."

"But I must point out again, Mr. Corbett: No one can determine, just by looking at a photograph, whether or not it was made by a man or a woman. Not to mention the fact that once you hire me in an official capacity, you can boast to all and sundry that I am the first woman to become an employee of your company."

"Quite right," Mr. Corbett said, a reluctant grin breaking out under his mustache. He stood and extended his hand to China. She took it and they shook to seal the deal.

"I did not bring negatives with me, Mr. Corbett. Write me a list of the photographs you wish to have, and I will make arrangements to send the negatives to you."

"That will be fine, Miss Havener. Say, I've heard that name before. Something to do with the ship, the *Empress*." Corbett's eyes held a question.

"Yes, that ship belonged to my father."

"Then you know your way around the docks, and the ins and outs of ships."

"That I do, Mr. Corbett."

"People like pictures of sailing ships and steamboats. Think you could do anything like that?"

"Indeed, I could, Mr. Corbett."

"Well, take some pictures of ships and let me see them."

"Indeed, I shall."

The idea of photographing ships and other watercraft that plied the Penobscot excited China. Why had she never thought of that before?

She could plan day trips to various towns on the river and Penobscot Bay, and Clint and Adeline could go with her if they wished. She could take them to Castine to show them where she, India, and Persia had lived before they had moved to Fort Point. The coastal towns Down East had many a fine sea captain's mansion that would make for a wonderful photograph.

She left the office feeling much more confident, looking forward to telling Clint, Adeline, India, and Persia what had transpired.

52.

When China returned home late that afternoon, no one was around. She roamed through the downstairs rooms, calling to India and Persia, Clint and Adeline. No one answered. The house was deserted. A book had been left open on the sofa, as if its reader had been called away in haste. A glass half-full of water had been abandoned on the kitchen table, as if someone had been interrupted in mid-sip.

China took off her hat and returned the basket containing her photographs to her workroom in the ell.

As she passed the back door in the kitchen, she heard voices coming from the direction of the barn. Perhaps one of Persia's sheep had escaped and everyone had gone to round it up, or perhaps the pig had given birth that day.

Adeline burst through the door, greatly excited.

"Mum, Mum, you're home, you're home!" she exclaimed. "Clint says come outside, right now."

"How many piglets did the sow have?" China asked, convinced that was the news she was about to hear.

"Piglets? What piglets? Just come with me right now, please. Clint said so."

The tone in Adeline's voice was urgent, and China's heart lurched. Had Clint fallen from the haymow? Had the ram butted Persia a good one, leaving her badly bruised? Before she could ask, Adeline took her hand and pulled her out the door and into the barnyard.

A knot of people—India and Persia, Fanny and Ellis Harding, Clint and another man, whose back was to China, stood together talking. Clearly, no one had been injured. But who was that stranger, the man in the wide-brimmed straw hat that hid his face?

"Clint, here she is, here's Mum," Adeline called. At the sound of Adeline's voice, the man turned, removed his hat in a gesture of courtesy and greeting, and said, "Pleased to see you again."

China stopped in her tracks. Adeline let go of her hand.

"Clint said you'd be surprised," Adeline said, giggling and clapping her hands, pleased that she had kept the secret of the surprise so well.

"Mr. Robinson," China said, almost stuttering with discomposure.

She recovered her poise quickly, though she felt her cheeks flame with a joy she hoped the others did not detect.

"What brings you here?"

Even as she uttered the question, it struck her as inane—not at all what she might have said had she not been so astonished to see him, though she supposed it served as well as anything else.

"Well, all this winter I got to wondering if the ferry could do without me for a week or so," Plato said. "So I dickered with Edwin Beane until he said he'd take it on for two weeks. Then I went to the town office to look at a map of the state of Maine, to see how to get here; thought I might like to see what the Penobscot River looked like.

"And since I was in the vicinity, I stopped at Abbott's Reach . . . You'd told me a lot about it. Mr. And Mrs. Harding said they had a vacant room, and that I ought to stay a night or two, and we got to talking about one thing and another. They thought I ought to call on you since I was in the neighborhood."

He did not take his eyes from China's, and she read in them something beyond a simple desire to view the river, pay her a call, and be on his way.

"Well, it's good to have you in the neighborhood, Mr. Robinson. I see you've met my daughter, Adeline," China said.

"That I have; a fine young lady she is. And Clint has grown two inches taller since last June."

Plato, China surmised, had much more to say, things that were difficult to say in the present company—why he had stopped writing to her, for one thing.

"Well, since you are all here," Persia said, "why don't we make a supper party of it? Ellis, perhaps you and Clint could go back to get Maude and Sam." She smiled broadly at China, as if it were a signal of something.

"Bring that cold chicken and the rhubarb pie I was planning on for supper, and whatever else Maude thinks would be good to add to the fare," Fanny said.

"Adeline, why don't you come with Mr. Harding and me," Clint said.

Adeline ran to the Hardings' buggy and climbed into the backseat.

Fanny, India, and Persia glanced at one another in a meaningful way. No eyebrows were visibly raised, but China knew what they were thinking, and she felt her cheeks grow warm with embarrassment. Well, they were wrong—woefully wrong!

"Fanny, why don't you and India come along inside so we can decide what we need to do to get supper on the table," Persia said. "China, perhaps Mr. Robinson would like to see your darkroom and some of the photographs you have been printing."

Thus, China found herself alone with Plato in her darkroom.

"There's really not much to see," she said. "Just chemicals and pans and a little line with clips where I hang the prints to dry."

As it happened, several of the photographs she had taken in Bingham hung from the line. One was of the ferry, with Plato and Clint aboard, departing from the Bingham side of the Kennebec. Light played off the surface of the river, and the steep sides of Old Bluff on the Concord side added mystery to the ferry's destination. In the photograph, Clint's figure faced forward, as if looking toward the landing ahead; the figure that was Plato gazed back at the receding Bingham shore, as if he were reluctant to leave and looking forward to the return trip. It had not been among the photographs she had sent to Bingham.

"I found the negative for this one just this week," China said. "Otherwise, I would have sent it to you along with the others."

"Very nice, Miss Havener . . . China," Plato said, his voice wrapping around her name in a warm and intimate way. "Mrs. Chase told me to tell you that if any of your photographs end up on postcards, she'll carry them at the hotel. She thinks they'll be in as much demand as her jars of blueberry jam. And that's saying something."

China laughed. "If Mrs. Chase has that much faith in me, how can I possibly go wrong?"

"I thank you for sending those photographs, China. I should have written . . . Many times I started a letter, but I could never finish it; I could never get it to the point where I could put it in an envelope and mail it."

"So did I," China confessed, "not to mention all the letters I wrote to you in my head."

Plato grinned. "I did the same."

An awkward silence settled between them. China didn't know what else to say, nor, apparently, did Plato.

"Let me show you the rest of the place. Let's walk down the lane along the stone wall to the shore. That way you will be close to the water . . . perhaps that will keep you from feeling homesick for the Kennebec," she said.

"As it turns out, China, the minute I saw you again, any thought of being homesick for anything left me."

"Oh, my dear," she said, emotion welling within her. "Keep walking, Plato. I can tell you right now that there is at least one face, probably India's, in the window, watching us."

Indeed, eyes were watching, but it was Fanny Abbott Harding who peered out the window.

"Dear me, how it all comes back. I walked down that very lane toward my fate many years ago. And Elizabeth did the same not so many years after that," Fanny said to India. "There is no doubt in my mind that China, too, is walking a path toward what will become of the rest of her life."

"Fanny, come away from the window," India whispered, as if China and Plato might hear. She had been standing just behind Fanny, gazing just as intently at the receding pair.

"Well, then," Plato said, "let's give her something to talk about."

He reached for China's hand and tucked it into his elbow. She looked at him and smiled, her fondness for him written large in her face and eyes. She leaned softly against his arm, solid with the muscle earned from years of pulling the ferry ropes to get from one side of the river to the other. She felt pleasure grow within her with such power, she knew it would last her a lifetime.

Plato adjusted his stride to hers. A bond was forming between them, and she knew he felt it, too.

"The tide is on the way in," China said when they stood at the water's edge. "I'm very happy you are here, Plato. When I didn't hear from you . . . I wanted to . . . I thought . . . "

"Well, you were right in thinking it. I thought so, too. Didn't think I could leave the ferry, when it came right down to it, and that didn't seem fair to you, seeing as how this is where your people are and what you know. Didn't think I could put my feet on an unfamiliar road.

"Then one day, in the middle of winter, when we all thought spring would never get here, for no reason at all, Mrs. Chase allowed as since I hadn't ever been away from the ferry, how was I to know what it would be like. She talked a lot about what a nice woman you are, and how you and I seemed to get on so well and enjoy one another's company. I knew what she was getting at, and I knew she was right, so I talked to Edwin Beane. The closer it got to the time I'd leave Bingham and come here, the more I wanted to go. Darnedest thing I ever thought to know about myself.

"So here I am. I hope this won't come as too much of a shock to you . . . What I want to know is, will you do me the honor of becoming my wife?"

"Plato, I'm not going to pretend I have to think twice, or resort to maidenly reserve or a fainting fit. In spite of all my attempts to talk myself out of it, I know what I want," China said. She took Plato's face in her hands and gazed deeply into his eyes. "With all my heart, yes."

She touched her lips to his. He responded by drawing her fully into his strong arms and kissing her back so long and so ardently, it took her breath away.

"Let's marry soon," Plato said.

"Yes; we are far too old for long engagements."

Their laughter rang out over the water, a sound they knew would carry them into the future, whatever it might hold.

Later, they would talk long and seriously about everything—about what they were getting themselves into, Clint and Adeline, India and Persia, the Abbott's Reach people, the Kennebec, the ferry, China's photography. In time, they came to the conclusion they could have the best of both worlds. When summer came, they would live in Plato's house on the Kennebec and he would tend the ferry. China could wander where she wished to take photographs. At the end of summer, China, Clint, and Adeline would come home to Fort Point to school. When the Kennebec froze, Plato would come to Fort Point to live; he would find ways to make himself useful.

What they did not know, and could not foresee on that afternoon, was that Persia would marry her Mr. Beaumont and go to live with him in Castine; that India would marry her Mr. Quinn and set up housekeeping in Stockton Springs village; that China and Plato would have the house at Fort Point for their own during the winter months.

They could not know that Clint would study English and literature at Bowdoin College and become a journalist, capable of taking his own photographs to illustrate the stories he wrote about elderly people who once had sailed the world, or ridden long logs down the Penobscot and the Kennebec, or the blood charmers of Bingham; that he would interview Fannie Hardy Eckstorm, author of books on Maine Indians, Maine birds, and her canoe trips with her father, and that his stories would help to make her famous; that he would marry a girl from Cambridge, and they and their children would live in Bangor, where he would work for a newspaper; that he would write novels about homeless boys, their adventures, and the kind people they met along the way.

They did not know that Adeline would, indeed, become a singer of note, singing in concert halls throughout the world; that one day she would share billing with the famous Madame Nordica, who had grown up in Farmington, and that they would sing a duet in homage to the great state of Maine, where they had been born and their vocal gifts nurtured; that Adeline would marry into the minor nobility of England, giving birth to a son and a daughter, both of whom would be musically gifted; that she would visit her family in Maine every summer, bringing along her British relatives and friends from the world of music she inhabited. Many of them would stay at Abbott's Reach, now run by Madras and M's youngest son.

They did not know that India's book would find a wide audience and become a source for future musicology scholars to consult. They did not know that Persia would establish a carding mill in Belfast, and that she and her husband would become wealthy and give generously to libraries, opera houses, and a retirement home for aged seamen.

They did not know that China's photographs would, indeed, become much-sought-after picture postcards, which would provide her with a dependable income; that she would travel to photograph remote towns—often with Plato accompanying her—as far away as the Canadian border, inspiring a new generation of women to take up the challenge of the camera; that some of the portraits she made would find their way into museums in future years.

There was much China and Plato did not know then, but they did know they loved one another. They had faith in their ability to work things out, and they were willing to cross many bodies of water to stand beside one another and those they loved.

For in the end, as in all things, they knew that love, in its many mysterious, multifaceted incarnations, illuminated their path.

Ardeana Hamlin